JUDITH MERRIL, *a writer herself,*
is a noted anthologist whose collections sparkle
with the finest that science-fiction and fantasy
can offer. The four previous volumes in
this annual Dell series were widely
acclaimed by the critics:

"Best value for the money ever offered in
the field."
—*Chicago Sun-Times*

". . . another triumph for that peerless anthologist."
—*The New York Times*

"Science fiction fans have a treat in store."
—*Hartford Courant*

"The definitive 'Best' . . . modern s.f. at
its most widely appealing."
—*New York Herald Tribune*

The Year's Best

SF

5th Annual Edition

Edited by JUDITH MERRIL

A DELL BOOK

Published by
DELL PUBLISHING CO., INC.
750 Third Avenue
New York 17, N.Y.

Reprinted by arrangement with
Simon and Schuster, Inc.
New York, N.Y.

Designed and produced by
Western Printing and Lithographing Company

First Dell printing—January, 1961

Printed in U.S.A.

ACKNOWLEDGMENTS

"The Handler" by Damon Knight, reprinted from *Rogue* by permission. Copyright © 1960 by the Greenleaf Publishing Company.

"The Other Wife" by Jack Finney, reprinted from *The Saturday Evening Post* by permission. Copyright © 1960 by The Curtis Publishing Company.

"No Fire Burns" by Avram Davidson, reprinted by permission from *Playboy*. Copyright © 1959 by HMH Publishing Company, Inc.

"No, No, Not Rogov!" by Cordwainer Smith, reprinted by permission from *If*. Copyright © 1958 by Quinn Publishing Company, Inc.

"Shoreline at Sunset" by Ray Bradbury, reprinted by permission from *Medicine for Melancholy* by Ray Bradbury (Doubleday, 1959). Copyright © 1959 by Doubleday and Co., Inc.

"The Dreamsman" by Gordon R. Dickson, reprinted by permission from *Star Science Fiction Stories, Number Six* by Gordon R. Dickson (Ballantine, 1959). Copyright © 1959 by Ballantine Books, Inc.

"Multum in Parvo" by Jack Sharkey, reprinted by permission from *Gent*. Copyright © 1959 by Excellent Publications, Inc.

"Flowers for Algernon" by Daniel Keyes, reprinted by permission from *The Best from Fantasy and Science Fiction: Ninth Series* (Doubleday, 1960). Copyright © 1959 by Mercury Press, Inc.

" 'What Do You Mean . . . Human?' " by John W. Campbell, Jr., reprinted by permission from *Astounding Science Fiction*. Copyright © 1959 by Street & Smith Publications, Inc.

"Sierra Sam" by Ralph Dighton, reprinted by permission of M. J. Wing for Associated Press from *The New York Times*. Copyright © 1960 by Associated Press.

"A Death in the House" by Clifford Simak, reprinted by permission from *Galaxy Science Fiction*. Copyright © 1959 by Galaxy Publishing Corp.

"Mariana" by Fritz Leiber, reprinted by permission from *Fantastic Science Fiction*. Copyright © 1960 by Ziff-Davis Publishing Company.

"An Inquiry Concerning the Curvature of the Earth's Surface and Divers Investigations of a Metaphysical Nature" by Roger Price, reprinted by permission from *Monocle*. Copyright © 1958 by Monocle Magazine.

"Day at the Beach" by Carol Emshwiller, reprinted by permission from *Fantasy and Science Fiction*. Copyright © 1959 by Carol Emshwiller.

"Hot Argument" by Randall Garrett, reprinted by permission from *Fantasy and Science Fiction*. Copyright © 1959 by Mercury Press, Inc.

"What the Left Hand Was Doing" by Darrel T. Langart, reprinted by permission of the author and the author's agents, Scott Meredith Literary Agency, Inc., from *Analog Science Fact and Fiction*. Copyright © 1960 by Street & Smith Publications, Inc.

"The Sound Sweep" by J. G. Ballard, reprinted by permission from *Science Fantasy*. Copyright © 1960 by Nova Publications, Ltd., London.

"Plenitude" by Will Worthington, reprinted by permission from *Fantasy and Science Fiction*. Copyright © 1959 by Will Worthington.

"The Man Who Lost the Sea" by Theodore Sturgeon, reprinted by permission from *The Best from Fantasy and Science Fiction: Ninth Series* (Doubleday, 1960). Copyright © 1959 by Theodore Sturgeon.

"Make a Prison" by Lawrence Block, reprinted by permission of the author and the author's agents, Scott Meredith Literary Agency, Inc., from *Original Science Fiction Stories*. Copyright © 1958 by Columbia Publications, Inc.

"What Now, Little Man?" by Mark Clifton, reprinted by permission from *Fantasy and Science Fiction*. Copyright © 1959 by Mercury Press, Inc.

"Me" by Hilbert Schenck, Jr., reprinted by permission from *The Best from Fantasy and Science Fiction: Ninth Series* (Doubleday, 1960). Copyright © 1959 by Mercury Press, Inc.

Quotations appearing on pages 14, 30, 123 and 313 are from *New Maps of Hell* by Kingsley Amis and are reprinted by permission of Harcourt, Brace and Company, Inc. Copyright © 1960 by Kingsley Amis.

Introduction

In the beginning there was Wonder. Early Man lived in a world of alternating light and dark, where wind faded to calm and sun succeeded storm, all without cause—where summer heat and winter's ice were equally marvelous—where the fruit of the soil or the prize of the hunt might, unpredictably, either fill or kill a man.

Ancient Man learned about cause and effect. He sowed, and reaped; trapped the lightning for winter warmth; caught rain in pools against summer's drought. He flew an arrow with the feathers of a bird; smelted ore for a sharper stone to tip the arrow; modeled a wheel from a rolling stone. The natural miracles he could control ceased to astonish him; those outside his grasp were, perhaps, *super*-natural? He wondered—about giants, gods, and demons.

Historic Man, guided by the recorded increment of wonders noted (resolved or unsolved), harnessed the energies of wind and water, grouped with his kin to raise up walls of stone, to stop the enemy before the battle; lived longer and more leisurely; learned to think in abstractions; devised mental tools—logic, morality, philosophy; made new tools with which to peer through at the macro- and micro-cosmic realms of the gods and devils. He saw the magnificent orderliness of the universe; banished wonder and base superstition together; rejoiced, and proclaimed the Age of Reason.

Rational Man inhabited a law-abiding world controlled absolutely by Cold Facts and Logic, Physical Laws and Mechanical Principles. He himself was the inevitable sum of Mendelian Laws, Chemistry, Conditioning, and Reflexes. A minimum of marveling was contained in a Rational Deity—a Great Architect who had (with compass, protractor, and Euclid's Axioms) laid out the universe. The new verities were classified, catalogued, and cross-indexed for eternity. The new technique of observing, testing, and labeling, was called *the scientific method.*

Modern Man used the new tool of experimentation, and learned: to *un*leash the lightning; make water from air, cloth from coal, food from metals; to create whirlwinds and earthquakes, brew storms and dispel them; defy distance and gravity; outstrip his own noise; cause a sunburst on Earth; and (now, newly) to animate matter.

Wonder—informed, thoughtful, purposeful wonder—is loose on the Earth again. And this is what "SF" means, what "science fiction" is: not gimmicks and gadgets, monsters and supermen, but *trained wonderment*—educated and disciplined imagination—a marvelous mirror for Modern Man and the world he is only beginning to make.

J.M., Milford, May, 1960

THE HANDLER

by Damon Knight

from *Rogue*

In one of the two very small towns where both he and I live
—Milford, Pa., a river valley resort on the edge of the Po-
conos—Damon Knight is known as, "*You know, the one who
always walks down Broad Street reading!*"

Milford, with more than a thousand year-round regular
residents can, and does, offer a sort of pleased, affectionate,
perhaps slightly proud, understanding to its reckless-reader
street-crosser. The other (and much smaller) town we both
live in—the curiously close-knit community of "science-fictionists"—is less indulgent by far: not that anyone minds
how much *reading* he does; it's what he says *afterward* that
hurts.

When Anthony Boucher retired as reviewer for *Fantasy
and Science Fiction*, the only logical successor to the post
was Damon Knight, then already firmly established as "*the
other critic*" in science fantasy. (I do mean "critic." Damon
has been known to like a book—but rarely to *say* so. All in
all, he has probably poured more vinegar on troubled authors than any other monthly columnist ever thought to keep
in stock.)

It is a double pleasure then, to an author-editor like myself, to see him turn his acerbity, auctorially, on a field once-
removed from publishing—the world of entertainment.

When the big man came in, there was a movement in the
room like a lot of bird dogs pointing. Piano player quits
pounding, the two singing drunks shut up, all the beautiful
people with cocktails in their hands stop talking and laughing.

"Pete!" the nearest women shrilled, and he walked
straight into the room, arms around two girls, hugging them
tight. "How's my sweetheart? Susy, you look good enough

to eat, but I had it for lunch. George, you pirate"—he let go both girls, grabbed a bald blushing little man and thumped him on the arm— "you were great, sweetheart, I mean it, really great. Now HEAR THIS!" he shouted, over all the voices that were clamoring Pete this, Pete that.

Somebody put a martini in his hand and he stood holding it, bronzed and tall in his dinner jacket, teeth gleaming white as his shirt cuffs. "We had a show!" he told them.

A shriek of agreement went up, a babble of did we have a *show* my God Pete listen a *show*—

He held up his hand. "It was a good show!"

Another shriek and babble.

"The sponsor kinda liked it—he just signed for another one in the fall!"

A shriek, a roar, people clapping, jumping up and down. The big man tried to say something else, but gave up, grinning, while men and woman crowded up to him. They were all trying to shake his hand, talk in his ear, put their arms around him.

"I love ya *all!*" he shouted. "Now what do you say, let's live a little!"

The murmuring started again as people sorted themselves out. There was a clinking from the bar. "Jesus, Pete," a skinny pop-eyed little guy was saying, crouching in adoration, "when you dropped that fishbowl I thought I'd pee myself, honest to God—"

The big man let out a bark of happy laughter. "Yeah, I can still see the look on your face. And the fish, flopping all over the stage. So what can I *do,* I get down there on my knees—" The big man did so, bending over and staring at imaginary fish on the floor. "And I say, 'Well, fellows, back to the drawing board!'"

Screams of laughter as the big man stood up. The party was arranging itself around him in arcs of concentric circles, with people in the back standing on sofas and the piano bench so they could see. Somebody yelled, "Sing the goldfish song, Pete!"

Shouts of approval, please-do-Pete, the goldfish song.

"Okay, okay." Grinning, the big man sat on the arm of a chair and raised his glass. "And a vun, and a doo—vere's de moosic?" A scuffle at the piano bench. Somebody banged out a few chords. The big man made a comic face and sang, "Ohhh . . . how I wish . . . I was a little fish . . . and when I want some quail . . . I'd flap my little tail."

Laughter, the girls laughing louder than anybody and their red mouths farther open. One flushed blonde had her hand on the big man's knee, and another was sitting close behind him.

"But seriously—" the big man shouted. More laughter.

"No, seriously," he said in a vibrant voice as the room quieted, "I want to tell you in all seriousness I couldn't have done it alone. And incidentally I see we have some foreigners, litvaks and other members of the press here to-night, so I want to introduce all the important people. First of all, George here, the three-fingered band leader—and there isn't a guy in the world could have done what he did this afternoon—George, I love ya." He hugged the blushing little bald man.

"Next my real sweetheart, Ruthie, where are ya. Honey, you were the greatest, really perfect—I mean it, baby—" He kissed a dark girl in a red dress who cried a little and hid her face on his broad shoulder. "And Frank—" He reached down and grabbed the skinny pop-eyed guy by the sleeve. "What can I tell you? A sweetheart?" The skinny guy was blinking, all choked up; the big man thumped him on the back. "Sol and Ernie and Mack, my writers, Shakespeare should have been so lucky—" One by one, they came up to shake the big man's hand as he called their names; the women kissed him and cried. "My stand-in," the big man was calling out, and "my caddy," and "now," he said, as the room quieted a little, people flushed and sore-throated with enthusiasm, "I want you to meet my handler."

The room fell silent. The big man looked thoughtful and startled, as if he had had a sudden pain. Then he stopped moving. He sat without breathing or blinking his eyes. After a moment there was a jerky motion behind him. The girl who was sitting on the arm of the chair got up and moved away. The big man's dinner jacket split open in the back, and a little man climbed out. He had a perspiring

brown face under a shock of black hair. He was a very
small man, almost a dwarf, stoop-shouldered and round-
backed in a sweaty brown singlet and shorts. He climbed
out of the cavity in the big man's body, and closed the dinner jacket carefully. The big man sat motionless and his
face was doughy.

The little man got down, wetting his lips nervously.
Hello, Fred, a few people said. "Hello," Fred called, waving
his hand. He was about forty, with a big nose and big soft
brown eyes. His voice was cracked and uncertain. "Well,
we sure put on a show, didn't we?"

Sure did, Fred, they said politely. He wiped his brow
with the back of his hand. "Hot in there," he explained,
with an apologetic grin. Yes, I guess it must be Fred, they
said. People around the outskirts of the crowd were beginning to turn away, form conversational groups; the hum
of talk rose higher. "Say, Tim, I wonder if I could have
something to drink," the little man said. "I don't like to
leave him—you know—" He gestured toward the silent big
man.

"Sure, Fred, what'll it be?"

"Oh—you know—a glass of beer?"

Tim brought him a beer in a pilsener glass and he drank
it thirstily, his brown eyes darting nervously from side to
side. A lot of people were sitting down now; one or two
were at the door leaving.

"Well," the little man said to a passing girl, "Ruthie, that
was quite a moment there, when the fishbowl busted, wasn't
it?"

"Huh? Excuse me, honey. I didn't hear you." She bent
nearer.

"Oh—well, it don't matter. Nothing."

She patted him on the shoulder once, and took her hand
away. "Well, excuse me, sweetie, I have to catch Robbins
before he leaves." She went on toward the door.

The little man put his beer glass down and sat, twisting
his knobby hands together. The bald man and the pop-
eyed man were the only ones still sitting near him. An anxious smile flickered on his lips; he glanced at one face, then
another. "Well," he began, "that's one show under our

belts, huh, fellows, but I guess we got to start, you know, thinking about—"

"Listen, Fred," said the bald man seriously, leaning forward to touch him on the wrist, "why don't you get back inside?"

The little man looked at him for a moment with sad hound-dog eyes, then ducked his head, embarrassed. He stood up uncertainly, swallowed and said, "Well—" He climbed up on the chair behind the big man, opened the back of the dinner jacket and put his legs in one at a time. A few people were watching him, unsmiling. "Thought I'd take it easy a while," he said weakly, "but I guess—" He reached in and gripped something with both hands, then swung himself inside. His brown, uncertain face disappeared.

The big man blinked suddenly and stood up. "Well, *hey* there," he called, "what's a matter with this party anyway? Let's see some life, some action—" Faces were lighting up around him. People began to move in closer. "What I mean, let me hear that beat!"

The big man began clapping his hands rhythmically. The piano took it up. Other people began to clap. "What I mean, are we alive here or just waiting for the wagon to pick us up? How's that again, can't *hear* you!" A roar of pleasure as he cupped his hand to his ear. "Well, come on, let me hear it!" A louder roar. Pete, Pete; a gabble of voices. "I got nothing against Fred," said the bald man earnestly in the middle of the noise. "I mean for a square he's a nice guy." "Know what you mean," said the pop-eyed man, "I mean like he doesn't *mean* it." "Sure," said the bald man, "but, Jesus, that sweaty undershirt and all ..." Then they both burst out laughing as the big man made a comic face, tongue lolling, eyes crossed. Pete, Pete, Pete; the room was really jumping; it was a great party, and everything was all right far into the night.

THE OTHER WIFE

by Jack Finney

from *The Saturday Evening Post*

In a recent volume of considerable arrogance, ill-considered opinion, and unconsidering slovenliness of research, a British humorist with pretensions to critical judgment of science fantasy, one Kingsley Amis, refers to the (unnamed) writer of a story entitled "Of Missing Persons" as "an author who has yet to make his name."

" 'Of Missing Persons,' " says Mr. Amis, "is one of those things that offer themselves for analysis with an almost suspicious readiness." I was not able to determine, in the three pages of quotes and comments that followed, just what analysis was being made, or whose readiness for what was under suspicion—but I may have been prejudiced by having read the story, several times, with great enjoyment, when it was included in the first annual volume of *SF*.

For the benefit of any readers who, like Mr. Amis, are unfamiliar with the author's work—the name is Finney. Jack Finney. And it has been a familiar one in science-fantasy since Robert Heinlein's 1951 anthology, "Tomorrow the Stars," first offered it to the specialty field.

Mr. Finney's most recent books include *The Third Level* (Rinehart and Dell Book) and *The Body Snatchers* (Dell First Editions).

". . . Will let me know the number of the pattern," my wife was saying, following me down the hall toward our bedroom, "and I can knit it myself if I get the blocking done."

I think she said blocking, anyway—whatever that means. And I nodded, unbuttoning my shirt as I walked; it had been hot out today, and I was eager to get out of my office clothes. I began thinking about a dark-green eight-thousand-dollar sports car I'd seen during noon hour in that big showroom on Park Avenue.

". . . kind of a ribbed pattern with a matching freggel-heggis," my wife seemed to be saying as I stopped at my dresser. I tossed my shirt on the bed and turned to the mirror, arching my chest.

". . . middy collar, batten-barton sleeves with sixteen rows of smeddlycup balderdashes. . . ." Pretty good chest and shoulders, I thought, staring in the mirror; I'm twenty-six years old, kind of thin faced, not bad-looking, not good-looking.

". . . dropped hem, doppelganger waist, maroon-green, and a sort of frimble-framble daisystitch. . . ." Probably want two or three thousand bucks down on a car like that, I thought; the payments'd be more than the rent on this whole apartment. I began emptying the change out of my pants pockets, glancing at each of the coins. When I was a kid there used to be an ad in a boys' magazine; "Coin collecting can be PROFITABLE," it read, "and FUN too! Why don't you start TODAY!" It explained that a 1913 Liberty-head nickel—"and many others!"—was worth thousands, and I guess I'm still looking for one.

"So what do you think?" Marion was saying. "You think they'd go well together?"

"Sure." I nodded at her reflection in my dresser mirror; she stood leaning in the bedroom doorway, arms folded, staring at the back of my head. "They'd look fine." I brought a dime up to my eyes for a closer look; it was minted in 1958 and had a profile of Woodrow Wilson, and I turned to Marion. "Hey, look," I said, "here's a new kind of dime—Woodrow Wilson." But she wouldn't look at my hand. She just stood there with her arms folded, glaring at me; and I said, "Now what? What have I done wrong now?" Marion wouldn't answer, and I walked to my closet and began looking for some wash pants. After a moment I said coaxingly, "Come on, Sweetfeet, what'd I do wrong?"

"Oh, Al!" she wailed. "You don't listen to me; you really don't! Half the time you don't hear a word I say!"

"Why, sure I do, honey." I was rattling the hangers, hunting for my pants. "You were talking about knitting."

"An orange sweater, I said, Al—orange. I *knew* you

weren't listening and asked you how an orange sweater would go with— Close your eyes."

"What?"

"No, don't turn around! And close your eyes." I closed them, and Marion said, "Now, without any peeking, because I'll see you, tell me what I'm wearing right now."

It was ridiculous. In the last five minutes, since I'd come home from the office, I must have glanced at Marion maybe two or three times. I'd kissed her when I walked into the apartment, or I was pretty sure I had. Yet standing at my closet now, eyes closed, I couldn't for the life of me say what she was wearing. I worked at it; I could actually hear the sound of her breathing just behind me and could picture her standing there, a small girl five feet three inches tall, weighing just over a hundred pounds, twenty-four years old, nice complexion, pretty face, honey-blond hair, and wearing—wearing—

"Well, am I wearing a dress, slacks, medieval armor, or standing here stark naked?"

"A dress."

"What color?"

"Ah—dark green?"

"Am I wearing stockings?"

"Yes."

"Is my hair done up, shaved off or in a pony tail?"

"Done up."

"O.K., you can look now."

Of course the instant I turned around to look, I remembered. There she stood, eyes blazing, her bare foot angrily tapping the floor, and she was wearing sky-blue wash slacks and a white cotton blouse. As she swung away to walk out of the room and down the hall, her pony tail was bobbing furiously.

Well, brother—and you, too, sister—unless the rice is still in your hair, you know what came next: the hurt, indignant silence. I got into slacks, short-sleeved shirt and huarachos, strolled into the living room, and there on the davenport sat Madame Defarge grimly studying the list, disguised as a magazine, of next day's guillotine victims. I knew whose name headed the list; and I walked straight to the kitchen, mixed up some booze in tall glasses and found a screw driver in a kitchen drawer.

In the living room, coldly ignored by what had once been my radiant, laughing bride, I set the drinks on the coffee table, reached behind Marion's magazine and gripped her chin between thumb and forefinger. The magazine dropped, and I instantly inserted the tip of the screw driver between her front teeth, pried open her mouth, picked up a glass and tried to pour in some booze. She started to laugh, spilling some down her front, and I grinned, handing her the glass, and picked up mine. Sitting down beside her, I saluted Marion with my glass, then took a delightful sip; and as it hurried to my sluggish blood stream, I could feel the happy corpuscles dive in, laughing and shouting, and felt able to cope with the next item on the agenda, which followed immediately.

"You don't love me any more," said Marion.

"Oh, yes, I do." I leaned over to kiss her neck, glancing around the room over her shoulder.

"Oh, no, you don't; not really."

"Oh, yes, I do; really. Honey, where's that book I was reading last night?"

"There! You see! All you want to do is read all the time! You never want to go out! The honeymoon's certainly over around here, all right!"

"No, it isn't, Sweetknees; not at all. I feel exactly the way I did the day I proposed to you; I honestly do. Was there any mail?"

"Just some ads and a bill. You used to listen to every word I said before we were married and you always noticed what I wore and you complimented me and you sent me flowers and you brought me little surprises and"—suddenly she sat bolt upright—"remember those cute little notes you used to send me! I'd find them all the time," she said sadly, staring past my shoulder, her eyes widening wistfully. "Tucked in my purse maybe"—she smiled mournfully—"or in a glove. Or they'd come to the office on post cards, even in telegrams a couple times. All the other girls used to say they were just darling." She swung to face me. "Honey, why don't you ever—"

"Help!" I said. "Help, help!"

"What do you mean?" Marion demanded coolly, and I tried to explain.

"Look, honey," I said briskly, putting an arm companionably around her shoulders, "we've been married four years. Of course the honeymoon's over! What kind of imbeciles," I asked with complete reasonableness, "would we be if it weren't? I love you, sure," I assured her, shrugging a shoulder. "Of course. You bet. Always glad to see you; any wife of old Al Pullen is a wife of mine! But after four years I walk up the stairs when I come home; I no longer run up three at a time. That's life," I said, clapping her cheerfully on the back. "Even four-alarm fires eventually die down, you know." I smiled at her fondly. "And as for cute little notes tucked in your purse—help, help!" I should have known better, I guess; there are certain things you just can't seem to explain to a woman.

I had trouble getting to sleep that night—the davenport is much too short for me—and it was around two forty-five before I finally sank into a kind of exhausted and broken-backed coma. Breakfast next morning, you can believe me, was a glum affair at the town home of Mr. and Mrs. Alfred E. Pullen, devoted couple.

Who can say whether the events of the night before affected those which now followed? I certainly couldn't; I was too tired, dragging home from the office along Third Avenue, heading uptown from Thirty-fourth Street about five-thirty the next evening. I was tired, depressed, irritated and in no hurry at all to get home. It was hot and muggy outside, and I was certain Marion would give me cold cuts for supper—and all evening long, for that matter. My tie was pulled down, my collar open, hat shoved back, coat slung over one shoulder, and trudging along the sidewalk there I got to wishing things were different.

I didn't care how, exactly—just different. For example, how would things be right now, it occurred to me, if I'd majored in creative botany at college instead of physical ed? Or what would I be doing at this very moment if I'd the job with Enterprises, Incorporated, instead of Servgone to Siam with Tom Biehler that time? Or if I'd got

Eez? Or if I hadn't broken off with what's-her-name, that big, black-haired girl who could sing "Japanese Sandman" through her nose?

At Thirty-sixth Street I stopped at the corner newsstand, planking my dime down on the counter before the man who ran it; we knew each other long since, though I don't think we've ever actually spoken. Glancing at me, he scooped up my dime, grabbed a paper from one of the stacks and folded it as he handed it to me; and I nodded my thanks, tucking it under my arm, and walked on. And that's when it happened; I glanced up at a brick building kitty-corner across the street, and there on a blank side wall three or four stories up was a painted advertisement—a narrow-waisted bottle filled with a reddish-brown beverage and lying half buried in a bed of blue-white ice. Painted just over the bottle in a familiar script were the words, "Drink Coco-Coola."

Do you see? It didn't say "Coca-Cola"; not quite. And staring up at that painted sign, I knew it was no sign painters' mistake. They don't make mistakes like that; not on great big outdoor signs that take a couple of men several days to paint. I knew it couldn't possibly be a rival soft drink either; the spelling and entire appearance of this ad were too close to those of Coca-Cola. No, I knew that sign was meant to read "Coco-Coola," and turning to walk on finally—well, it may strike you as insane what I felt certain I knew from just the sight of that painted sign high above a New York street.

But within two steps that feeling was confirmed. I glanced out at the street beside me; it was rush hour and the cars streamed past, clean cars and dirty ones, old and new. But every one of them was painted a single color only, mostly black, and there wasn't a tail fin or strip of chromium in sight. These were modern, fast, good-looking cars, you understand, but utterly different in design from any I'd ever before seen. The traffic lights on Third Avenue clicked to red, the cars slowed and stopped, and now as I walked along past them I was able to read some of their names. There were a Ford, a Buick, two Wintons, a Stutz, a Cadillac, a Dort, a Kissel, an Oldsmobile and at least four or five small Pierce-Arrows. Then, glancing down Thirty-seventh Street as I passed it, I saw a billboard advertising Picayune Cigarettes; "America's Largest-Selling Brand." And now a Third Avenue bus dragged past me, crammed with people as usual this time of day, but it was shaped a little differently and it was painted blue and white.

I spun suddenly around on the walk, looking frantically for the Empire State Building. But it was there, all right, just where it was supposed to be; and I actually sighed with relief. It was shorter, though—by a good ten stories at least. When had all this happened? I wondered dazedly and opened my paper, but there was nothing unusual in it—till I noticed the name at the top of the page. *New York Sun,* it said, and I stood on the sidewalk gaping at it; because the *Sun* hasn't been published in New York for years.

Do you understand now? I did, finally, but of course I like to read—when I get the chance, that is—and I'm extremely well grounded in science from all the science-fiction I've read. So I was certain, presently, that I knew what had happened; maybe you've figured it out too.

Years ago someone had to decide on a name for a new soft drink and finally picked "Coca-Cola." But certainly he considered other possible alternatives; and if the truth could be known, I'll bet one of them was "Coco-Coola." It's not a bad name—sounds cool and refreshing—and he may have come very close to deciding on it.

And how come Ford, Buick, Chevrolet and Oldsmobile survived while the Moon, Willys-Knight, Hupmobile and Kissel didn't? Well, at some point or other maybe a decision was made by the men who ran the Kissel Company, for example, which might just as easily have been made another way. If it had, maybe Kissel would have survived and be a familiar sight today.

Instead of Lucky Strikes, Camels and Chesterfields, we might be buying chiefly Picayunes, Sweet Caporals and Piedmonts. We might not have the Japanese beetle or the atom bomb. While the biggest newspaper in New York could be the *Sun,* and George Coopernagel might be President. If—what would the world be like right now, what would you or I be doing?—if only things in the past had happened just a tiny bit differently. There are thousands of possibilities, of course; there are millions and trillions. There is every conceivable kind of world, in fact; and a theory of considerable scientific standing—Einstein believed it—is that these other possible worlds actually exist; all of them, side by side and simultaneously with the one we happen to be familiar with.

I believed it too now, naturally; I knew what had happened, all right. Walking along Third Avenue through the late afternoon on my way home from the office, I had come to one of the tiny points where two of these alternate worlds intersected somehow. And I had walked off out of one into another slightly altered, somewhat different world of "If" that was every bit as real, and which existed quite as much, as the one I'd just left.

For maybe a block I walked on, stunned, but with a growing curiosity and excitement—because it had occurred to me to wonder where I was going. I was walking on with a definite purpose and destination, I realized; and when a traffic light beside me clicked to green, I took the opportunity to cross La Guardia Avenue, as it was labeled now, and then continue west along Thirty-ninth Street. I was going somewhere, no doubt about that; and in the instant of wondering where, I felt a chill along my spine. Because suddenly I knew.

All the memories of my life in another world, you understand, still existed in my mind; from distant past to the present. But beginning with the moment that I had turned from the newsstand to glance up at that painted sign, another set of memories—an alternate set of memories of my other life in this alternate world—began stirring to life underneath the first. But they were dim and faint yet, out of focus. I knew where I was going—vaguely; and I no more had to think how to get there than any other man on his way home from work. My legs simply moved in an old familiar pattern, carrying me up to the double glass doors of a big apartment building, and the doorman said, "Evening, Mr. Pullen. Hot today."

"You said it, Charley," I answered and walked on into the lobby; and then my legs were carrying me up the stairs to the second floor, then down a corridor to an apartment door which stood open. And just as I did every night, I realized, I walked into the living room, tossing my copy of the *Sun* to the davenport. I was wearing a suit I'd never seen before, I noticed, but it fitted me perfectly, of course, and was a little worn.

"Hi, I'm home," I heard my voice call out as always; and at one and the same time I knew, with complete and time-dulled familiarity—and also wondered with intense and fascinated curiosity—who in the world was going to answer; who in *this* world?

An oven door slammed in the kitchen as I turned to hang up my suit coat in the hall closet as always, then footsteps sounded on the wood floor between the kitchen and the living room. And as she said, "Hi, darling," I turned to see my wife walking toward me.

I had to admire my taste in this world. She was a big girl, tall and not quite slim; black-haired and with a very fair complexion; quite a pretty face with a single vertical frown line between her brows; and she had an absolutely gorgeous figure with long handsome legs. "Why, hel-lo," I said slowly. "What a preposterously good-looking female you are!"

Her jaw dropped in simple astonishment, her blue eyes narrowing suspiciously. I held my arms wide then, walking toward her delightedly, and while she accepted my embrace, she drew back to sniff my breath. She couldn't draw back very far, though, because my embrace—I simply couldn't help this—was tight and close; this fine-looking girl was a spectacular armful. "Now I know why I go to the office every day," I was saying as I nuzzled her lovely white neck, an extremely agreeable sensation. "There had to be a reason, and now I know what it is. It's so I can come home to this."

"Al, what in the world is the matter with you!" she said. Her voice was still astonished, but she'd quit trying to draw back.

"Nothing you can't remedy," I said, "in a variety of delightful ways," and I kissed her again.

"Honey," she murmured after a considerable time, "I

have to fix supper," and she made a little token effort to get away.

"Supper can wait," I answered, and my voice was a full octave deeper, "but I can't." Again I kissed her, hard and eagerly, full on the lips. Her great big beautiful blue eyes widened in amazement—then they slowly closed and she smiled langorously.

Marion's face abruptly rose up in my mind. There in the forefront of my consciousness and conscience, suddenly, was her betrayed and indignant face, every bit as vivid as though she'd actually walked in through the door to discover this sultry brunette in my arms; and I could feel my face flame with guilt. Because I couldn't kid myself, I couldn't possibly deny the intensity of the pleasure I'd felt at this girl in my arms. I knew how very close I'd come to betraying Marion, and I felt terribly ashamed, and stood wondering—this long length of glorious girlhood still in my arms—how to end the situation, and with charm and grace. Now a moment later, her eyes opened, and she looked up at me questioningly, those full ripe moist lips slightly apart. "Hate to say this," I said then, sniffing the air thoughtfully, "but seems to me I smell something burning—besides me."

"Oh!"—she let out a little shriek, and as she ran to the kitchen I actually closed my eyes and sighed with a terrible relief. I didn't know how I'd walked into this other alternate world, or how I could leave it; but Marion was alive in my mind, while the world around me seemed unreal. In the kitchen I heard the oven door open, heard water run in the sink, then the momentary sizzle of cooking meat; and I walked quickly to the davenport and snatched up my copy of the *Sun*.

As I raised it to my face, the tap of high heels sounded on the wood floor just outside the kitchen door. There was silence as they crossed the rug toward me, then the davenport cushion beside me sank; I felt a deliciously warm breath on my cheek, and I had to lower my trembling, rattling newspaper, turn and manage to smile into the sloe eyes of the creature beside me.

Once again—my head slowly shaking in involuntary approval—I had to admire my own good taste; this was not a homely woman. "I turned the oven down," she murmured. "It might be better to have dinner a little later. When it gets cooler," she added softly.

I nodded quickly. "Good idea. Paper says it's the hottest day in five hundred years," I babbled. "Doctors advise complete immobility."

But the long-legged beauty beside me wasn't listening. "So I'm the reason you like to come home, am I?" she breathed into my ear. "It's been a long time, darling, since you said anything like that."

"H'm'm," I murmured and nodded frantically at the paper in my hands. "I see they're going to tear down City Hall," I muttered wildly, but she was blowing gently in my ear now; then she pulled the *Sun* from my paralyzed fingers, tossed it over her shoulder and leaned toward me. *Marion!* I was shrieking silently. *Help!* Then the raven-haired girl beside me had her arms around my neck, and I simply did not know what to do; I thought of pretending to faint, claiming sunstroke.

Then with the blinding force of a revelation it came to me. Through no fault of my own, I was in another world, another life. The girl in my arms—somehow that's where she was now—was singing softly, almost inaudibly. It took me a moment to recognize the tune; then finally I knew, finally I recognized this magnificent girl. "Just a Japanese Sand—man," she was singing softly through her lovely nose, and now I remembered fully everything about the alternate world I was in. I hadn't broken off with this girl at all—not in this particular world! Matter of fact, I suddenly realized, I'd never even met Marion in this world. It was even possible, it occurred to me now, that she'd never been born. In any case, this was the girl I'd married in this world. No denying it, this was my wife here beside me with her arms around my neck; we'd been married three years, in fact. And now I knew what to do—perfectly well.

Oh, boy! What a wonderful time Vera and I had in the months that followed. My work at the office was easy—no strain at all. I seemed to have an aptitude for it and, just as I'd always suspected, I made rather more money at Enterprises, Incorporated, than that Serv-Eez outfit ever paid in their lives. More than once, too, I left the office early, since no one seemed to mind, just to hurry back home —leaping up the stairs three at a time—to that lovely big old Vera again. And at least once every week I'd bring home a load of books under my arm, because she loved to read, just like me; and I'd made a wonderful discovery about this alternate world.

Life, you understand, was different in its details. The San Francisco Giants had won the 'Fifty-eight Series, for example; the Second Avenue El was still up; Yucatan gum was the big favorite; television was good; and several extremely prominent people whose names would astound you were in jail. But basically the two worlds were much the same. Drugstores, for example, looked and smelled just about the same; and one night on the way home from work I stopped in at a big drugstore to look over the racks of paper-back books and made a marvelous discovery.

There on the revolving metal racks were the familiar rows of glossy little books, every one of which, judging from the covers, seemed to be about an abnormally well-developed girl. Turning the rack slowly I saw books by William Faulkner, Bernard Glemser, Agatha Christie, and Charles Einstein, which I'd read and liked. Then, down near the bottom of the rack my eye was caught by the words, "By Mark Twain." The cover showed an old side-wheeler steamboat, and the title was *South From Cairo*. A reprint fitted out with a new title, I thought, feeling annoyed; and I picked up the book to see just which of Mark Twain's it really was. I've read every book he wrote— *Huckleberry Finn* at least a dozen times since I discovered it when I was eleven years old.

But the text of this book was new to me. It seemed to be an account, told in the first person by a young man of twenty, of his application for a job on a Mississippi steamboat. And then, from the bottom of a page, a name leaped out at me. " 'Finn, sir,' I answered the captain," the text read, " 'but mostly they call me Huckleberry.' "

For a moment I just stood there in the drugstore with my mouth hanging open; then I turned the little book in my hands. On the back cover was a photograph of Mark

Twain; the familiar shock of white hair, the mustache, that wise old face. But underneath this the brief familiar account of his life ended with saying that he had died in 1918 in Mill Valley, California. Mark Twain had lived eight years longer in this alternate world, and had written—well, I didn't yet know how many more books he had written in this wonderful world, but I knew I was going to find out. And my hand was trembling as I walked up to the cashier and gave her two bits for my priceless copy of *South From Cairo*.

I love reading in bed, and that night I read a good half of my new Mark Twain in bed with Vera, and then afterward—well, afterward she fixed me a nice cool Tom Collins. And oh, boy, this was the life all right.

In the weeks that followed—that lanky length of violet-eyed womanhood cuddled up beside me, singing softly through her nose—I read a new novel by Ernest Hemingway; the best yet, I think. I read a serious, wonderfully good novel by James Thurber, and something else I'd been hoping to find for years—the sequel to a marvelous book called *Delilah*, by Marcus Goodrich. In fact, I read some of the best reading since Gutenberg kicked things off—a good deal of it aloud to Vera, who enjoyed it as much as I did. I read *Mistress Murder*, a hilarious detective story by George S. Kaufman; *The Queen Is Dead*, by George Bernard Shaw; *The Third Level*, a collection of short stories by someone or other I never heard of, but not too bad; a wonderful novel by Allen Marple; a group of fine stories about the advertising business by Alfred Eichler; a terrific play by Orson Welles; and a whole new volume of Sherlock Holmes stories by A. Conan Doyle.

For four or five months, as Vera rather aptly remarked, I thought, it was like a second honeymoon. I did all the wonderful little things, she said, that I used to do on our honeymoon and before we were married; I even thought up some new ones. And then—all of a sudden one night—I wanted to go to a night club.

All of a sudden I wanted to get out of the house in the evening, and do something else for a change. Vera was astonished—wanted to know what was the matter with me, which is typical of a woman. If you don't react precisely the same way day after day after endless day, they think something must be wrong with you. They'll even insist on it. I didn't want any black-cherry ice cream for desert, I told Vera one night at dinner. Why not, she wanted to know—which is idiotic if you stop to think about it. I didn't want any because I didn't want any, that's all! But being a woman she had to have a reason; so I said, "Because I don't like it."

"But of course you like it," she said. "You always used to like it!"

You see what I mean? Anyway, we did go to this night club, but it wasn't much fun. Vera got sleepy, and we left, and were home before twelve. Then she wasn't sleepy, but I was. Couple nights later I came home from the office and was changing my clothes; she said something or other, and I didn't hear her and didn't answer, and we actually had a little argument. She wanted to know why I always looked at every coin in my pocket, like an idiot, every time I changed clothes. I explained quietly enough; told her about the ad I used to read as a kid and how I was still looking for a 1913 Liberty-head nickel worth thousands of dollars, which was the truth.

But it wasn't the whole truth. As I looked through the coins I'd collected in my pocket during the day—the Woodrow Wilson dimes, the Grover Cleveland pennies, the nickels with George Coopernagel's profile, and all the other familiar coins of the world I now lived in—I understood something that had puzzled me once.

These other alternate worlds in which we also live intersect here and there—at a corner newsstand, for example, on Third Avenue in New York and at many another place, too, no doubt. And from these intersecting places every once in a while something from one of these worlds—a Woodrow Wilson dime, for example—will stray into another one. I'd found such a dime and when I happened to plank it down on the counter of that little newsstand, there at an intersection of the two alternate worlds, that dime bought a newspaper in the world it belonged in. And I walked off into that world with the *New York Sun* under my arm. I knew this now, and I'd known it long since. I understood it finally, but I didn't tell Vera. I simply told her I was looking for a 1913 Liberty-head nickel. I didn't tell her I was also looking for a Roosevelt dime.

I found one too. One night, finally, sure enough, there it lay in my palm; a dime with the profile of Franklin D. Roosevelt on its face. And when I slapped it down on the counter of the little newsstand next evening, there at the intersection of two alternate worlds, I was trembling. The man snatched up a paper, folding it as he handed it to me, and I tucked it under my arm and walked on for three or four steps, hardly daring to breathe. Then I opened the paper and looked at it. *New York World-Telegram*, the masthead read, and I began to run—all the way to Forty-fourth Street, then east to First Avenue and then up three flights of stairs.

I could hardly talk I was so out of breath when I burst into the apartment, but I managed to gasp out the only word that mattered. "Marion!" I said and grabbed her to me, almost choking her, because my arms hit the back of her head about where Vera's shoulders would have been. But she managed to talk, struggling to break loose, her voice sort of muffled against my coat.

"Al!" she said. "What in the world is the matter with you?"

For her, of course, I'd been here last night and every night for the months and years past. And of course, back in this world, I remembered it, too, but dimly, mistily. I stepped back now and looked down at the marvelous tiny size of Marion, at that wonderful, petite figure, at her exquisite and fragile blond beauty. "Nothing's the matter with me," I said, grinning down at her. "It's just that I've got a beautiful wife and was in a hurry to get home to her. Anything wrong with that?"

There wasn't; not a thing, and—well, it's been wonderful, my life with Marion, ever since. It's an exciting life; we're out three and four nights a week, I guess—dancing, the theater, visiting friends, going to night clubs, having dinner out, even bowling. It's the way things used to be, as Marion has aptly said. In fact, she remarked recently, it's like a second honeymoon, and she's wonderfully happy these days and so am I.

Oh, sometimes I'm a little tired at night lately. There are times after a tough day at Serv-Eez when I'd almost rather stay home and read a good book; it's been quite a while since I did. But I don't worry about that. Because the other night, about two-thirty in the morning, just back from The Mirimba, standing at my dresser looking through the coins in my pocket, I found it—another Woodrow Wilson dime. You come across them every once in a while, I've noticed, if you just keep your eyes open; Wilson dimes, Ulysses Grant quarters, Coopernagel nickels. And I've got my Wilson dime safely tucked away, and—well, I'm sure Vera, that lithe-limbed creature, will be mighty glad to see her husband suddenly acting his old self once again. I imagine it'll be like a third honeymoon. Just as—in time—it will be for Marion.

So there you are, brother, coin collecting can be profitable. And fun too! Why don't you start—tonight!

NO FIRE BURNS

by Avram Davidson
from *Playboy*

The same Mr. Amis who was so "suspiciously ready" to attempt to analyze a nameless Jack Finney, says in the introductory chapter of his book that "*science fiction*" is hardly an appropriate name for the field any longer. Regretfully, I must agree with Mr. A. on this one point (without seeing the need for the emphasis on the first word). And I leap to agree, again, with his next statement:

"... the plea that politics and economics and psychology and anthropology and even ethics are really or nearly as much sciences as atomic physics, is chiefly valuable as an indication of a state of mind. ..."

Frankly, I am not certain our agreement on this is fundamental; I don't know what Mr. Amis *meant*, but what he *said* is very true. The fields of psychology, anthropology, sociology—yes, even ethics, hopefully—are now just at that burgeoning "state of mind" atomic physics was still passing through when science-fictionists began exploring its potential thirty years ago. As fine an example of the new "science fiction" as I know is this featured story from *Playboy*.

Doctor Colles was a thin, pale man with receding hair. Mr. Melchior's chauffeured car had picked him up at his stuffy little office, crowded with papers. He had begun to talk almost at once, and he was still at it now. While waiting for the traffic light to change and listening to Doctor Colles's conversation, Mr. Melchior took a long green cigar from his case and lit it.

"A breakdown of function and structure," said Colles. "An absolute lack of communication. Isn't it so?" Mr. Taylor, a trim, blond young man, who looked like an ad for expensive shirts, listened carefully, said nothing. Melchior looked impressed—and uncomprehending. Colles took his arm just above the elbow, pressed it. "Look at that fellow over there," he said. "The one in the brown suit—see? Now: can I communicate with him? Or can you? On any save the most primitive level? No. Impossible, I assure you. I've only to look at him to know." The crowd flowed across the street. The men in the car watched the vanishing brown suit.

"We think of, let us say, world problems. *He* thinks of bowling. We discuss art and letters. He watches the dog acts on TV. We are concerned with our vanishing natural resources. He wonders if he can put a dollar-fifty cab bill on his swindle sheet. Am I correct?" The car moved forward. "What do *you* think?"

Mr. Melchior thought he agreed one hundred per cent. Taylor smiled faintly. "Just the same," Melchior said, "there has to be some way of reaching these type people, getting inside of them."

Dr. Colles cleared his throat. "Psychology," he began.

"Good!" said Melchior. "Good. Go ahead— Oh. Here we are. You'll have to explain this to me when we're inside, Doctor."

They went up the steps of what appeared to be a small parochial school, but which was, in fact, a club—and not the sort at which members were fined for not using first names in addressing one another. The guests' dining room was small and dark. "A brandy to begin with, Doctor?"

"I hold with the ancient grammarian," Dr. Colles said, suddenly jovial. "It is better to decline six nouns than one drink. Ha, ha!"

Melchior rolled his eyes toward Taylor, who nodded. It was so ordered. "Would you believe it, Doctor," said Melchior, after the second sip, "I never tasted brandy till I was twenty-five years old? Times change . . . Ah. Good. Here's the menu. Anything you especially like?"

The food came. They ate slowly, with grave pleasure appropriate. "Times change," Melchior repeated presently. "Take, for example, business: When my business began to get too big for me to handle the paper work myself, I hired my brother-in-law's cousin to keep the books. But that family-style operation is outmoded. So now I have my personnel manager, Mr. Taylor here, he's a college man himself, help me select the top men from the accountants' college for Melchior Enterprises. Taylor knows what the score is."

Dr. Colles inquired the precise nature of these enterprises. His host said that they included importing, manufacturing and distributing.

"Well, that covers just about the whole range of commerce, doesn't it? Except for credit."

"We do that, too."

Colles chuckled, but seeing his host react with faint surprise, coughed. "Now, about these tests," he said. And he proceeded to talk about the tests with young Mr. Taylor, while Mr. Melchior listened, nodding. After a while the personnel manager said, "Well, that seems to be all right, then, about the standard tests. Now, Mr. Melchior would like to discuss with you the possibility of setting up another test, one which would have to be personally constructed."

"Oh?" Dr. Colles raised his eyebrows. "A *special* test. *Well.*"

Melchior rubbed his thin lips with his napkin. "We got —" He paused. "We have certain problems concerned with personnel procurement—maybe *dis*procurement is the right word, huh, Taylor? And we think you might be just the man to deal with them."

"Well, that's very flattering. 'Disprocurement'? Ha, ha. And challenging, too. Go on, go on."

Joe Clock looked up from his lathe. It was that pest, Aberdeen, again. "Whaddaya want, Ab?" he asked. *"Come on, come on—"*

Ab smiled ingratiatingly. "Whaddaya *want*, for crysake?" Joe demanded.

The man looked around, nervously. "Uh. Look, Joe, when you told me you needed that money couple weeks ago, you said you needed it so bad, I told you that I, uh, I, uh, could let you have it, sure, I mean, glad to help, I, uh—"

"Will ya quit needling me, for crysake? I told you I'd pay it back."

Ab smirked, weakly. "Yeah, but, uh, Joe, I told you then it was the, uh, *rent* money, so I'd, uh, I'd need it back in a week. And that was the truth; I mean . . . well, Joe, the, uh, the rent, I mean it was due a, a week ago, and I got to have it Joe. So—"

Joe turned back to his lathe. "You'll get it. Tell ya landlord to keep his pants on, because I don't have it now. So quit needling me."

Ab started to protest, explain, plead, but Joe wasn't paying any attention to him. Finally, with a helpless shrug he moved off, looking back over his shoulder with a puzzled expression, at the oblivious Joe Clock, who—after the other man was well out of sight—took a stroll down to the drinking fountain.

He was greeted there by a man with a wart between his eyes. "You get them new power tools for your cellar yet, that you were talking about?" the man asked.

Joe wiped his dripping mouth. "Yeah. Ordered 'em two weeks ago and they finally came couple a days ago," he said. "Beautiful stuff. Come on down and have a look some Sundy."

The man with the wart between his eyes said, thanks, he might do that. "What was Aberdeen doing over at your machine just now?" he asked. "He look like he was gonna bust out crying."

Joe frowned. "Who? Oh, Aberdeen. Aah, *I* dunno what he wanted." He nodded, moved off. In the corner of his mind was a faint recollection of what Aberdeen wanted, but it was too much trouble to remember. Hell with 'm.

"Did you read in the papers, last month," Mr. Melchior asked, over the fresh fruit cup, "about a fellow who worked for Atlantic Coast Canning—"

Dr. Colles said that he believed he did. "Shot the foreman and—"

"Not the foreman, no, but that's the case. They were both in line to become foreman, but only one could get the job, so this man, Grubacher, he invited Kelly—that was his competitor—to take a ride back from work in his car; then he killed him. Might've gotten away with it, too, only they traced the gun."

Atlantic Coast Canning, it seemed, was an affiliate of Melchior Enterprises, and the incident had disturbed Mr. Melchior a good deal. Dr. Colles was a psychologist; did he understand what would make a man, who had seemed perfectly normal—a good employee—a good husband—do something like that? There had to be something wrong with him, didn't there? ("Obviously," said Dr. C.) Well, they didn't want a repetition of the Grubacher case. They wanted Dr. Colles to help them weed out people like that beforehand.

The psychologist smiled. Society as a whole, and not just Mr. Melchior, he pointed out, would be glad to find a way to do that. But his host waved his hand and shook his head, respectfully impatient.

"No, no, Doctor. Don't be modest," he said. "These tests which you and Mr. Taylor are going to set up for our personnel department—you said before that what's wrong with our society is 'lack of communication,' yes? Well, these *tests* communicate, don't they? They help weed out all kinds of unfit people, don't they? *But they don't go far enough!* A man who thinks he hears voices and tells people that spies from outer space are after him, well, you can tell right away there's something wrong with him, and we tell him that we'll keep his name on file; don't call us, we'll call you . . ."

But Grubacher hadn't been that type. He didn't have hallucinations, he didn't mutter. In no way, either from his work record or his family life or from his friends, could the ordinary lay person have foreseen that he would kill a man in cold blood. When he was caught and his alibi broken down and—confronted with the ballistics test results—he confessed, he was asked (oh, most vain of all questions!) if he wasn't sorry. Grubacher seemed a little surprised. He was sorry he was *caught*, sure. But for the act itself? A bit surprised, answering what he obviously considered a foolish question, the killer said, no . . . what was there to

NO FIRE BURNS 35

be sorry about? It was the only thing to do: Kelly stood in his way.

Dr. Colles tapped his glasses on the tablecloth. He nodded rapidly. "This fellow would seem to be obviously a psychopath," he said. "An individual with an underdeveloped superego. They don't go around muttering or bubbling their lips, they don't often run amuck; generally speaking, they are calm—cool—and collected. They simply lack what we are accustomed to call conscience. To your man, his fellow-worker wasn't a being with equal rights, he was simply an obstacle. The sensible thing was to remove him."

A cigar came out of Mr. Melchior's case. He flicked his gold cigarette lighter. "All right," he said. "Now that we know what they *are*—how do we find them out in time?"

With a smile, "The FBI would like to know too, Mr. Melchior."

"Yes, but the FBI isn't asking you. Anthony Melchior is asking you. I have been very impressed with everything you've told us, and I feel quite confident you can do it."

"Well, thank you very much. But . . . let me ask you . . . why are you interested in weeding out only *psychopaths*? Why not people with other defects—paranoiacs, let's say?"

His employer seeming somewhat at a loss to answer this, Edward Taylor stepped almost instantly into the breach. "Mr. Melchior feels that men who suffer from more obvious defects are much more likely to be noticed. It is the man who *appears* to be all right, who *seems* to function normally, who is actually more in need of being detected. Once found out, our task would naturally be to see that this man is given the proper help. We see it as a three-fold program: discover him—remove him—help him." He smiled; his smile was rather charming, but it came and went too quickly.

Melchior nodded vigorously; Colles, more slowly. Was it a matter of time? he was asked. A matter of money? Neither factor should dissuade him: Melchior Enterprises would assist him one hundred per cent. Dr. Colles smiled, pursed his lips, shook his head. Then he frowned. He rubbed his eyes with his fingers.

"It would be an interesting project," he said, "it might

be a very fruitful one. I could try . . . I would promise you nothing in the way of results. But I could try—if I were to take on fewer projects with other corporations, perhaps . . ."

His host's thin lips stretched in a brief smile. "Good. Very good. And so now, just for a start—" He took out a gold fountain pen and a checkbook. Dr. Colles looked at the moving hand until the last letter of the signature was done; then—missing Mr. Melchior's upturned glance by a shaved second—he fixed his look on the wall. The check changed hands.

Dr. Colles told his assistant not to make any more appointments for him until further notice. "I'm going to be working on a private research project which will be taking up a great deal of my time," he explained. "You'll have to do some legwork for me . . . I'll have a list of books for you to get, and quite a number of articles published in professional journals. Then, too, these men are to be phoned— you see: Dr. Sherwind, of the Department of Correction, and so on—and you ask them if you can drop by and pick up case histories for me, as noted here."

The assistant was an unmarried and intelligent young woman, who had been (and had looked) a good bit younger when she first came to work for Dr. Colles. He had talked at one time about marriage—not during the past few years, however. Why buy milk if you're friendly with the cow?

" 'The Psychopathic Personality Among Prisoners . . .' " she read aloud from the list, pinching her lip: two unlovely habits she'd developed. It occurred to her employer that it would probably be easier (and wiser) to break himself of the habit of her, than to try to break her of any of her own habits.

He hummed a bit when she had gone. After all, the world was *full* of cows— He took out his bank book and regarded with favor both the latest entry and the considerable amount in cash folded neatly inside the little book. He had stopped off at the bank directly after leaving Mr. Melchior. The business baron had seemed quite in earnest, but, still, one never knew. . . .

Dr. Colles was a prudent man.

The test had been going on for most of the day. First one section went down to take it, then another. There had been some apprehension at first, but this vanished, by lunch time, in a rumble of laughter which ran through the whole plant: "So he hands back the papers when he's finished, and he says to the guy from Personnel, 'Hey, Mac, how come they wanna know is my sex-life satisfactory: they plannin' t' use me f' stud purposes?'"

When Joe Clock finally reached the head of the line, the girl there gave him a sheaf of papers and a pencil. "Take any seat at one of the tables and fill these out, please," she said.

Joe's eyes traveled from her to the papers and back again. Her hair, it was obvious, was not naturally red, and her expression was discontented. But she was young, and her figure— "If I had a nickel for every one of these I filled out, I'd be rich," he said.

For a moment their eyes met. "And if I had a nickel for every guy who said that, I'd be rich, too." Not too bad a beginning. He rapidly calculated his finances, took a breath, and was about to ask her what she was doing that night. But her eyes went past him, she picked up a sheaf of papers and a pencil, handed them to the man behind him. "Take any seat—" she began.

Joe Clock sighed, sat down at the table and took up the pencil. If they wanted to pay him to play school for an hour instead of running the lathe, it was all right with him. And it was easier on the feet. So now let's see . . . *I like mechanics magazines. Yes. No.* What a question to ask a machinist! Sure he liked them. You knew where you were with a mechanics magazine. It showed you what to do and how to do it. No dopey stories to figure out, why the guy acts so dopey trying to get the girl. There's an obstruction in the pipe, ream it out. Another guy steps out with the girl, kick him in the crotch. Joe circled the *Yes.* Next. *I have a good appetite.* Hell, yes. Then a real stupid one: *I would rather collect stamps than go fishing.* Joe put a heavy circle around the *No.* He relaxed. Collect *stamps,* for crysake! This was going to be easy. *Eskimos live in Europe.* Joe almost had to laugh at that one, another *No;* good thing he didn't have to say where they *did* live: Aleutia, or some place like that. Well . . .

A sensible man takes what he can get in this world. Isn't that the truth, though! Every damn time, and all you can get, too. Hell, yes. *Canada belongs to England.* That was right. The damn Canadian money has the King of England's face on it and you got to be careful because once Joe had got stuck with some of that English money from Canada, only he passed it on damn quick, too. *It is important to help a friend.* What do they mean, "a friend"? He paused, peered at the next one. *It is not so important to help a stranger.* He hesitantly put *Yes* for the first, *No* for the second. *It makes good sense to worry about a stranger.* He snorted. The hell it does. Catch a stranger worrying about *you!* A guy that you, like, want to borrow his car, now—but a *stranger?*

Henry Ford played a major role in developing . . . Molasses is made from . . . A sensible man does what he is paid to do. Of course he does. *Yes.*

I sleep well and wake up fresh and rested. Sure. *Yes.* A *stranger will risk his life to help you.* What a laugh. A guy'd have to be crazy! *No!*

There are lots worse crimes than murder. Probably . . . Sure. Lots worse. *The average person will do anything for money.* Absolutely right they would. Why not, if you can get away with it? Sure. And the same way, that's why you got to watch out for yourself.

There are worse things than losing your home. What? Catching leprosy?

And then the way to answer the question changed. Now you had to pick out an answer. Like, *Most people who hit someone with their car at night would (a) report to the police first (b) give first aid (c) make a getaway if possible.* Well, any damn fool would know it was the last. In fact, anyone but a damn fool would do just that. That's what *he* did that time. *(c)*

Now, a dope like Aberdeen: he'd probably stop *his* car. Stick his nose in someone else's tough luck. Anybody stupid enough to lend his rent money—

If you saw a man about to jump in the river, would you (a) move his clothes so he wouldn't trip on them (b) call your friends to watch (c) get something to eat afterward (d) none of these things.

The important thing with women is (a) have a knife in your pocket (b) make sure your hair is combed (c) drive a red car (d) something else.

Bright lights are a sign of (a) rain (b) foreign domination (c) poisoned drinking water (d) none of these things.

National security means (a) warmer weather than we used to have (b) television programs (c) political influence (d) something else.

The main point in criminal activity is (a) dressing real warm if it's cold (b) not to get caught (c) keep in your own lane on the highway (d) avoid such activity.

Test was kind of interesting, Joe thought, as he handed in the papers. And now—back to the lathe. Go around the long way, avoid Aberdeen's machine. Gahdamn pest.

Dr. Colles took a good look around his office. It had never seemed so cramped and grubby before. Once again he found himself wondering if he ought not to get out of test construction and evaluation—way out—into some more lucrative field of psychology. Not many clients paid so well as Melchior Enterprises; in plain fact, none of them had. Not by a long shot. And his work for them was about over now, anyway. A competent personnel man like Taylor could carry on the tests without the constructionist. There was something about Taylor . . . smooth, knowing . . . without too much eagerness, he considered asking the young man to send him follow-up reports on how the psychopaths turned up by the special test were responding to treatment. Of course, some of them were bound to reject treatment. And they couldn't be obliged to accept, either, worse luck. Well, that wasn't his responsibility. He didn't even know who was doing the therapy.

Except that they would get the credit. But that was how it went. Therapy, therapy, that was all the public thought about. How many articles in general publications did you ever see about test constructionists? Let alone movies or TV. "I do the work, others get the credit," Dr. Colles thought with some bitterness.

Feeling the inevitable postproject letdown, Colles's eyes wandered over the top of his desk. Mail . . . He'd checked through the mail: nothing of interest. Idly, he picked up a brochure-like thing on glossy paper. It had failed to attract his preoccupied attention earlier.

Ease-A-Just News Jottings. Published by and for the employees of Ease-A-Just Gear and Tool (a Melchior Enterprise). Oh, yes, he recalled talking to Taylor's assistant concerning a short piece about the test, for the house organs. He started to lay it aside, then opened it. Might be something about the test in there. Of course, the real reason hadn't been explained to the employees.

"Old friends of Mabel Quinn (formerly Stoltzfus), of the cafeteria staff, will be glad to learn that she and Patrolman Quinn are now the proud parents of twin boys. Congratulations, Mabel, we knew you had it in you!" Dr. Colles winced, turned a page. "Maintenance Wins Softball Tiff"— well, good for Maintenance . . . No, nothing here. He started to toss it away once more, but something caught his eye and was gone before he could fix what it had been. This was annoying. With a sigh, he opened the paper again, began a systematic search. He had to find it, or it would haunt him. There: a name.

The box score:

Maintenance				Machine shop			
	AB	R	H		AB	R	H
Smead cf	1	0	0	Guthrie 2b	2	0	1
Clock rf	2	0	0	Brandt ss	3	0	0
Dupont 1b	2	0	0	Rayan 1b	3	1	2

And the name was Clock. Frowning slightly, Dr. Colles repeated it. He muttered it again, as he took several files from the cabinet and leafed through the contents. *Clock!*

Dr. Colles whistled. Then, being a systematic man, he wrote down all the names in the *Ease-A-Just News Jottings*, rewrote them in alphabetical order; then began to compare them with the names in his files. He whistled again.

The door opened. His assistant said, "If you want me, Doctor, please call me by name. I'm not your dog; don't whistle."

For several seconds he stared at her, expressionless. Then he said, "My apologies, Miss Blick. It won't happen again. But, since you are here— Don't we subscribe to a clipping service on the various corporations which— We do. Thank you. Then, if you will be kind enough to bring me the clippings relating to Melchior Enterprises . . . *Thank you, Miss Blick.*"

Most of the clippings were from the financial and industrial pages of the papers and did not long engage Dr. Colles's attention. Several, however, were from the news sections, and these he proceeded to read. Once or twice he pursed his lips as if to whistle, but each time he glanced at the door and restrained himself. Instead, he said, "Well, well . . ."

Industrialist Linked to Forced Sales of beer. "Well!" *Murdered Man Revealed as Former Melchior Employee.* "Well, well!" *Grand Jury Probes Alleged Tie-in of Melchior with Local* . . . "Well, well, well!"

Dr. Colles was coming out of the Personnel Office when he met Edward Taylor coming in. "Your assistant told me you wouldn't be in today," Colles said.

"I didn't expect to be in . . . This is a rather large outfit, you know—not that it couldn't be larger if—yes, I've been occupied at another office. Can I help you?" He looked at Colles with cool gray eyes.

"No, I don't think so, but thank you. Your assistant was very helpful."

With smile swift as always, though perhaps a trifle less

charming, Edward Taylor said he was glad of it. "Where are you heading for now? To see Mr. Melchior? Ah, yes. A. M. thinks a lot of you. As do I." His manner, as they parted, seemed rather thoughtful.

Doctor Colles, crossing the large expanse of floor between the door and Mr. Melchior's desk, had ample time to note and admire the quality of the thick rug and massive furniture. "You do me an honor," said the businessman, shaking hands. "If you'd told me you were coming, I'd've sent my car."

The psychiatrist waved his hand. "I found myself with no appointments today," he said. "So I decided to catch up on things I'd been putting off. I discharged my assistant. And I came out here." Melchior said, Oh? He inquired if the assistant hadn't given satisfaction. "Not for a long time," said Dr. Colles. "Anyway. Yes, I wanted to ask you—how are those tests working, which I devised for you? Are *they* giving satisfaction?"

"Perfectly, Doctor."

"I'm naturally gratified to hear that. I was wondering how the idea was working out. I was wondering, too, if you'd tell me the names of the gentlemen who are working on the rehabilitation end of the scheme. The ones who are treating the people whom my special test has turned up."

He looked expectantly at Mr. Melchior. The latter said, after a moment, "Well, I wouldn't know about those details, Doctor. Edward Taylor, being in charge of personnel, would be in a better position to know. He knows the men, and they know him. But I kind of have an idea that the other part of the plan is still in its planning stage. But you could write to Edward and I'm sure he'll be happy to give you the details."

Dr. Colles nodded. "Odd sort of notion came to me this morning," he said. "Shall I tell you about it?"

Mr. Melchior, no longer quite so cordial, looked at his watch. "All right, if you want to," he said.

"You know, I was wondering how the whole idea was working out. So I called up your assistant personnel manager and asked to see the records. He told me to come over and help myself."

There was a pause. "He shouldn't have done that, Doctor," Mr. Melchior said. "Not without consulting me first. Those records are confidential."

Colles said he could understand that. He apologized, hoped it would not make any trouble for the assistant personnel manager. "I have a feeling, Mr. M.," he said, "that he was not fully aware of the implications of the testing scheme, anyway. May I elaborate? Thank you ... I do appreciate your not reminding me that you are a very busy man. Well." He cleared his throat. He waited, but as nothing else was offered, he continued, "Now, in regard to my own especially constructed test: Only certain particular questions were used in the marking, as you know, the others being either window-dressing, or designed to lull the testee into a state of unawareness, so that the chances of getting true answers to the others were increased. What were the results? Thirty-three individuals scored above the ninetieth percentile, showing marked psychopathic tendencies. Of these, eleven were women, and I rather imagine that they were sent packing pretty damned quick—though I hope in such a manner as not to hurt their feelings. The Mad Bomber and all that, eh, Mr. Melchior? Now, of the remaining twenty-two—a check of the records is in your personnel office, Mr. Taylor being fortuitously absent—*twenty are still employed*. What happened to the other two?" he shot the question.

"Quit," said Mr. Melchior. "We're planning to get rid of the others as soon as we can manage for them to get the treatment."

"Oh, I don't think you are," Colles said. There was a pause.

"No? Well ... what *do* you think, Doc?"

"What do I think?" Dr. Colles asked. "I combined the information I've just mentioned with certain intelligence gleaned from the newspapers, and I think that you, Mr. Melchior, are an Emperor of Crime—if I may wax a trifle purple in my prose—and that your purpose is not to weed the psychopaths *out*, but to weed them *in*."

The tycoon smiled a thin, cold smile. "Doc, you speak the most beautiful English I ever heard. But you flatter me. I'll level with you. An emperor? Not even a king. Maybe," he shrugged modestly, "a grand duke, let's say."

The doctor slowly let out his breath with a sound like that which Yoga calls *Sitali,* or serpent-hiss. He looked the other in the eyes. "But you will rise," he said. "You are bound to."

The grand duke said calmly that he hoped so. "Believe me, Doc, it isn't easy though. I got rivals. People with other territories would like to have mine. People who work for me would also like to have mine. But I figure I'll be OK. I move with the times. My father rode a mule. I ride a Cadillac." And he proceeded to explain.

Melchior Enterprises (he said) might be compared to an iceberg of which the greater mass is submerged. There were many similar icebergs in the country, some smaller, some bigger. They generally avoided coming in collision with others, but ships were not always so fortunate. In the crime business, of course, disputes could not be settled by an industry-wide arbitrator. In which case . . .

"I'm not the only one who has personnel trouble, Doc," Melchior explained. "Lots of times the others get in touch with me: 'Anthony, I need somebody. Send somebody good.' Well, one hand washes the other, I like to help out. But it's *hard,* you know, Doc, to *get* somebody really good."

Dr. Colles said he could appreciate that.

It used to be, Melchior went on, that the syndicates got the tough boys from the slums. But they did not really suit the tempo of the times. They were not so dependable. They were conspicuous. They got into fights over matters which had nothing to do with business. Right after the war there had been a supply of combat veterans available, they had been generally satisfactory, but there weren't many around any more. The turnover was rather high.

"You know what I want, Doc?" he said. "Or, better, what I don't want? I don't want guys who're outstanding. Guys with criminal records. Guys who kill for the fun of it, or to pay off grudges or they have no control of their tempers, and another acrobat grabs their girl in the wrong place. *Not* them.

"What I want are steady fellows. Dull types who live in tract houses and have small families. I don't care what their religion is, but only *small* families. Shows what I call prudence. Or maybe they live with a mother, or with a brother or sister who has the family. Now, people like this are working for me right along, on the legitimate. Or applying for jobs with me. But how do you know who's suitable? How? You can't just ask a guy right out."

Colles said, "And so you came to me to help you find them. Exactly as you go to business school to find accountants. And I know just the type you mean." He nodded, smiled faintly.

"I pay a flat salary," Melchior said. "Plus a bonus in negotiable bonds. That's good for everybody, nothing shows on the books for taxes. But nothing spectacular. These men I want, they're not for the spectacular and it isn't for them."

"How right you are," Doctor Colles said.

The type Melchior wanted (Colles went on) was the distillation of the average man, except, of course, that he was killer-prone. *Why* will he kill? Why will he kill perfect strangers? "We were speaking, at our first meeting," he said, "of 'lack of communication.' We might add, 'lack of religion'—'lack of love'—of the capacity to really love. These men are the men who lack. There is something dead in them. They don't kill because a fire burns in them, but because *no* fire burns in them. The potential was always there —men like your Grubacher, who shot his rival for the foreman's place—but it took my test to discover it, to channel it." He paused. *"My* test," he said.

"Oh, yes, I know the type. Men who will calmly and coolly kill to get another twenty dollars a week. Who'll kill rather than cut down on their American Standard of Living, rather than change their way of life. Why, yes—I imagine that my twenty little discoveries were quite willing to go forth and slay, once it was shown how safe and profitable it was. . . . Yes, I imagine they perform their missions with dispatch, with no more excitement and as much efficiency as they would in repossessing a car, reading a gas meter, or serving a summons—and then try to cheat a little on their expense account—but just a little."

"So what now, Doc?"

"So what now? Melchior, when I'd calculated all this, and your role in it, I decided that you were by way of being one of those men-who-lack, yourself."

"Yeah?"

"And then, do you know what?"

"What?"

"Then I came to the conclusion that I was by way of being one of them, too."

The grand duke raised not only his eyebrows, but his eyelids. He made a little noise resembling a giggle. And again he asked, "So now what, Doc?"

"Why—" The psychologist considered. "Now I suggest that we discuss how I may be of further use to you. I rather think I will enjoy the Professor Moriarty bit. Is Taylor privy to— He is? Yes, I see it now, never mind, he's young, and lacks what I— But before that, my dear Anthony: shall we discuss that bonus, payable in negotiable bonds? In advance, of course: you are certain to attain kingly rank, perhaps even imperial, but—the hazards of the chase, you know—so: in advance."

Toward the close of that year, at late of night, two men came down the steps of Mr. Melchior's club. It was cold, and there was a noisy wind.

"Where is your car?" Dr. Colles asked, gazing up and down the empty street.

"I told him to be here at eleven-thirty," said Mr. Melchior. "He ought to be here any minute now. You want to go back in—?" But Colles suggested a walk around the block.

As they rounded the corner and turned up their coat collars, two men turned to them, one of whom said, "Excuse me, Mac: This the way to the Terminal?"

"Oh, no," said Dr. Colles, gesturing. "You go—" One of the men took a revolver from inside his brown suit and shot Dr. Colles in the head. He fell without further words.

"Has Taylor gone crazy?" hissed Melchior, aghast. "Not here, you fool! Not now!"

"Here *and* now," the man said, stepping to one side as his companion moved forward.

"Do you know who I am?" Melchior cried.

"It don't matter," said the second man. The wind tore away the sound of the second shot and the noise Melchior made when he went down. The two walked a few blocks to a more traveled street, hailed a cab.

"What is this, about an eighty-cent fare?" the man in the brown suit asked his companion, who had a wart between his eyes, as he peered at the passing street signs.

"About eighty, yeah. What do you think, Joe? Taylor won't check—we could make it, say, three dollars on the swindle sheet?" Joe said he thought they could get away with three.

"You going fishing Sundy?" his companion asked.

But Joe Clock shook his head. "Sattady night is the bowling turnamint," he pointed out. "So that means I be out too late to get up early enough for fishing. You know what a late night can do if you don't get your sleep: it takes all the strenth out of you."

The other man nodded his agreement. "Well, so Sundy you can do some work on them power-tools you got in your cellar. A quiet weekend at home is a good thing in lotsa ways."

And they gazed out of the windows of the cab with no great interest and they chewed their gum as if they tasted in it the mild, approaching flavor of the quiet weekend at home.

NO, NO, NOT ROGOV!

by Cordwainer Smith
from *If*

Cordwainer Smith is the pseudonym of a gentleman who is undoubtedly the farthest-out Professor of Sociology ever to hide his dignity behind a fantasy-barrel. I have yet to see two stories alike from "Mr. Smith"—or one that did not somehow fascinate me.

That golden shape on the golden steps shook and fluttered like a bird gone mad—like a bird imbued with an intellect and a soul, and, nevertheless, driven mad by ecstasies and terrors beyond human understanding. A thousand worlds watched.

Had the ancient calendar continued, this would have been A.D. 13,582. After defeat, after disappointment, after ruin and reconstruction, mankind had leaped among the stars.

Out of the shock of meeting inhuman art, of confronting nonhuman dances, mankind had made a superb esthetic effort and had leaped upon the stage of all the worlds.

The golden steps reeled. Some eyes that watched had retinas. Some had crystalline cones. Yet all eyes were fixed upon the golden shape which interpreted "The Glory and Affirmation of Man" in the Inter-World Dance Festival of what might have been A.D. 13,582.

Once again mankind was winning the contest. Music and dance were hypnotic beyond the limits of systems, compelling, shocking to human and inhuman eyes. The dance was a triumph of shock—the shock of dynamic beauty.

The golden shape on the golden steps executed shimmering intricacies of meaning. The body was gold and still human. The body was a woman, but more than a woman.

On the golden steps, in golden light, she trembled and fluttered like a bird gone mad.

The ministry of State Security had been positively shocked when they found that a Nazi agent, more heroic than prudent, had almost reached N. Rogov.

Rogov was worth more to the Soviet armed forces than any two air armies, more than three motorized divisions. His brain was a weapon, a weapon for the Soviet power.

Since the brain was a weapon, Rogov was a prisoner.

He didn't mind.

Rogov was a pure Russian type, broad-faced, sandy-haired, blue-eyed, with whimsy in his smile and amusement in the wrinkles at the tops of his cheeks.

"Of course I'm a prisoner," Rogov used to say. "I am a prisoner of State service to the Soviet peoples. But the workers and peasants are good to me. I am an academician of the All Union Academy of Sciences, a major general in the Red Air Force, a professor in the University of Kharkov, a deputy works manager of the Red Flag Combat Aircraft Production Trust. From each of these I draw a salary."

Sometimes he would narrow his eyes at his Russian scientific colleagues and ask them in dead earnest, "Would I serve capitalists?"

The affrighted colleagues would try to stammer their way out of the embarrassment, protesting their common loyalty to Stalin or Beria, or Zhukov, or Molotov, or Bulganin, as the case may have been.

Rogov would look very Russian: calm, mocking, amused. He would let them stammer.

Then he'd laugh.

Solemnity transformed into hilarity, he would explode into bubbling, effervescent, good-humored laughter: "Of course I could not serve the capitalists. My little Anastasia would not let me."

The colleagues would smile uncomfortably and would wish that Rogov did not talk so wildly, or so comically, or so freely.

Rogov was afraid of nothing. Most of his colleagues were

afraid of each other, of the Soviet system, of the world, of life, and of death.

Perhaps Rogov had once been ordinary and mortal like other people, and full of fears.

But he had become the lover, the colleague, the husband of Anastasia Fyodorovna Cherpas.

Comrade Cherpas had been his rival, his antagonist, his competitor, in the struggle for scientific eminence in the frontiers of Russian science. Russian science could never overtake the inhuman perfection of German method, the rigid intellectual and moral discipline of German team-work, but the Russians could and did get ahead of the Germans by giving vent to their bold, fantastic imaginations. Rogov had pioneered the first rocket launchers of 1939. Cherpas had finished the job by making the best of the rockets radio-directed.

Rogov in 1942 had developed a whole new system of photo-mapping. Comrade Cherpas had applied it to color film. Rogov, sandy-haired, blue-eyed, and smiling, had recorded his criticisms of Comrade Cherpas's naïveté and theoretical unsoundness at the top-secret meetings of Russian scientists during the black winter nights of 1943. Comrade Cherpas, her butter-yellow hair flowing down like living water to her shoulders, her unpainted face gleaming with fanaticism, intelligence, and dedication, would snarl her own defiance at him, deriding his Communist theory, pinching at his pride, hitting his hypotheses where they were weakest.

By 1944 a Rogov-Cherpas quarrel had become something worth traveling to see.

In 1945 they were married.

Their courtship was secret, their wedding a surprise, their partnership a miracle in the upper ranks of Russian science.

The *émigré* press had reported that the great scientist, Peter Kapitza, once remarked, "Rogov and Cherpas, there is a team. They're Communists, good Communists; but they're better than that! They're *Russian,* Russian enough to beat the world. Look at them. That's the future, our Russian future!" Perhaps the quotation was an exaggeration, but it did show the enormous respect in which both Rogov and Cherpas were held by their colleagues in Soviet science.

Shortly after their marriage strange things happened to them.

Rogov remained happy. Cherpas was radiant.

Nevertheless, the two of them began to have haunted expressions, as though they had seen things which words could not express, as though they had stumbled upon secrets too important to be whispered even to the most secure agents of the Soviet State Police.

In 1947 Rogov had an interview with Stalin. As he left Stalin's office in the Kremlin, the great leader himself came to the door, his forehead wrinkled in thought, nodding, "Da, da, da."

Even his own personal staff did not know why Stalin was saying "Yes, yes, yes," but they did see the orders that went forth marked ONLY BY SAFE HAND, and TO BE READ AND RETURNED, NOT RETAINED, and furthermore stamped FOR AUTHORIZED EYES ONLY AND UNDER NO CIRCUMSTANCES TO BE COPIED.

Into the true and secret Soviet budget that year by the direct personal orders of a noncommittal Stalin, an item was added for "Project Telescope." Stalin tolerated no inquiry, brooked no comment.

A village which had had a name became nameless.

A forest which had been opened to the workers and peasants became military territory.

Into the central post office in Kharkov there went a new box number for the *village of Ya. Ch.*

Rogov and Cherpas, comrades and lovers, scientists both and Russians both, disappeared from the everyday lives of their colleagues. Their faces were no longer seen at scientific meetings. Only rarely did they emerge.

On the few occasions they were seen, usually going to and from Moscow at the time the All Union budget was made up each year, they seemed smiling and happy. But they did not make jokes.

What the outside world did not know was that Stalin in giving them their own project, granting them a paradise restricted to themselves, had seen to it that a snake went with them in the paradise. The snake this time was not one, but two personalities—Gausgofer and Gauck.

Stalin died.

Beria died too—less willingly.

The world went on.

Everything went into the forgotten village of Ya. Ch. and nothing came out.

It was rumored that Khrushchev himself visited Rogov and Cherpas. It was even whispered that Khrushchev said as he went to the Kharkov airport to fly back to Moscow, "It's big, big, big. There'll be no cold war if they do it. There won't be any war of any kind. We'll finish capitalism before the capitalists can ever begin to fight. If they do it. If they do it." Khrushchev was reported to have shaken his head slowly in perplexity and to have said nothing more but to have put his initials on the unmodified budget of Project Telescope when a trusted messenger next brought him an envelope from Rogov.

Anastasia Cherpas became a mother. Their first boy looked like the father. He was followed by a little girl. Then another little boy. The children didn't stop Cherpas's work. The family had a large *dacha* and trained nursemaids took over the household.

Every night the four of them dined together.

Rogov, Russian, humorous, courageous, amused.

Cherpas, older, more mature, more beautiful than ever, but just as biting, just as cheerful, just as sharp as she had ever been.

But then the other two, two who sat with them across the years of all their days, the two colleagues who had been visited upon them by the all-powerful word of Stalin himself.

Gausgofer was a female: bloodless, narrow-faced, with a voice like a horse's whinny. She was a scientist and a policewoman, and competent at both jobs. In 1920 she had reported her own mother's whereabouts to the Bolshevik Terror Committee. In 1924 she had commanded her father's execution. He was a Russian German of the old Baltic nobility and he had tried to adjust his mind to the new system, but he had failed. In 1930 she had let her lover trust her a little too much. He was a Rumanian Communist, very high in the Party, but he had a sneaking sympathy for Trotsky. When he whispered into her ear in the privacy of their bedroom, whispered with the tears pouring down his face, she had listened affectionately and quietly and had delivered his words to the police the next morning.

With that she came to Stalin's attention.

Stalin had been tough. He addressed her brutally, "Comrade, you have some brains. I can see you know what Communism is all about. You understand loyalty. You're going to get ahead and serve the Party and the working class, but is that all you want?" He had spat the question at her.

She was so astonished that she gaped.

The old man had changed his expression, favoring her with leering benevolence. He had put his forefinger on her chest, "Study science, Comrade. Study science. Communism plus science equals victory. You're too clever to stay in police work."

Gausgofer fell in love with Rogov the moment she saw him.

Gausgofer fell in hate—and hate can be as spontaneous and miraculous as love—with Cherpas the moment she saw *her.*

But Stalin had guessed that too.

With the bloodless, fanatic Gausgofer he had sent a man named B. Gauck.

Gauck was solid, impassive, blank-faced. In body he was about the same height as Rogov. Where Rogov was muscular, Gauck was flabby. Where Rogov's skin was fair and shot through with the pink and health of exercise, Gauck's skin was like stale lard, greasy, gray-green, sickly even on the best of days.

Gauck's eyes were black and small. His glance was as cold and sharp as death. Gauck had no friends, no enemies, no beliefs, no enthusiasms.

Gauck never drank, never went out, never received mail, never sent mail, never spoke a spontaneous word. He was rude, never kind, never friendly, never really withdrawn:

He couldn't withdraw any more than the constant withdrawal of all his life.

Rogov had turned to his wife in the secrecy of their bedroom soon after Gausgofer and Gauck came and had said, "Anastasia, is that man sane?"

Cherpas intertwined the fingers of her beautiful, expressive hands. She who had been the wit of a thousand scientific meetings was now at a loss for words. She looked up at her husband with a troubled expression. "I don't know, comrade . . . I just don't know."

Rogov smiled his amused Slavic smile. "At the least then I don't think Gausgofer knows either."

Cherpas snorted with laughter and picked up her hairbrush. "That she doesn't. She really doesn't know, does she? I'll wager she doesn't even know to whom he reports."

That conversation had reached into the past. Gauck, Gausgofer, bloodless eyes and the black eyes—they remained.

Every dinner the four sat down together.

Every morning the four met in the laboratory.

Rogov's great courage, high sanity, and keen humor kept the work going.

Cherpas's flashing genius fueled him whenever the routine overloaded his magnificent intellect.

Gausgofer spied and watched and smiled her bloodless smiles; sometimes, curiously enough, Gausgofer made genuinely constructive suggestions. She never understood the whole frame of reference of their work, but she knew enough of the mechanical and engineering details to be very useful on occasion.

Gauck came in, sat down quietly, said nothing, did nothing. He did not even smoke. He never fidgeted. He never went to sleep. He just watched.

The laboratory grew and with it there grew the immense configuration of the espionage machine.

In theory what Rogov had proposed and Cherpas seconded was imaginable. It consisted of an attempt to work out an integrated theory for all the electrical and radiation phenomena accompanying consciousness, and to duplicate the electrical functions of mind without the use of animal material.

The range of potential products was immense.

The first product Stalin had asked for was a receiver, if possible, one capable of tuning in the thoughts of a human mind and of translating those thoughts either into a punch tape machine, an adapted German Hellschreiber machine, or phonetic speech. If the grids could be turned around, the brain-equivalent machine as a transmitter might be able to send out stunning forces which would paralyze or kill the process of thought.

At its best, Rogov's machine was designed to confuse human thought over great distances, to select human targets to be confused, and to maintain an electronic jamming system which would jam straight into the human mind without the requirements of tubes or receivers.

He had succeeded—in part. He had given himself a violent headache in the first year of work.

In the third year he had killed mice at a distance of ten kilometers. In the seventh year he had brought on mass hallucinations and a wave of suicides in a neighboring village. It was this which impressed Khrushchev.

Rogov was now working on the receiver end. No one had ever explored the infinitely narrow, infinitely subtle bands of radiation which distinguished one human mind from another, but Rogov was trying, as it were, to tune in on minds far away.

He had tried to develop a telepathic helmet of some kind, but it did not work. He had then turned away from the reception of pure thought to the reception of visual and auditory images. Where the nerve-ends reached the brain itself, he had managed over the years to distinguish whole packets of microphenomena, and on some of these he had managed to get a fix.

With infinitely delicate tuning he had succeeded one day in picking up the eyesight of their second chauffeur, and had managed, thanks to a needle thrust in just below his own right eyelid, to "see" through the other man's eyes as the other man, all unaware, washed their Zis limousine sixteen hundred meters away.

Cherpas had surpassed his feat later that winter, and had managed to bring in an entire family having dinner over in a near-by city. She had invited B. Gauck to have a needle inserted into his cheekbone so that he could see with the eyes of an unsuspecting spied-on stranger. Gauck had refused any kind of needles, but Gausgofer had joined in the experiment and had expressed her satisfaction with the work.

The espionage machine was beginning to take form.

Two more steps remained. The first step consisted of tuning in on some remote target, such as the White House in Washington or the NATO Headquarters outside Paris.

The second problem consisted of finding a method of jamming those minds at a distance, stunning them so that the subject personnel fell into tears, confusion, or insanity.

Rogov had tried, but he had never gotten more than thirty kilometers from the nameless village of Ya. Ch.

One November there had been seventy cases of hysteria, most of them ending in suicide, down in the city of Kharkov several hundred kilometers away, but Rogov was not sure that his own machine was doing it.

Comrade Gausgofer dared to stroke his sleeve. Her white lips smiled and her watery eyes grew happy as she said in her high, cruel voice, *"You* can do it, comrade. You can do it."

Cherpas looked on with contempt. Gauck said nothing.

The female agent Gausgofer saw Cherpas's eyes upon her, and for a moment an arc of living hatred leaped between the two women.

The three of them went back to work on the machine.

Gauck sat on his stool and watched them.

It was the year in which Eristratov died that the machine made a breakthrough. Eristratov died after the Soviet and People's democracies had tried to end the cold war with the Americans.

It was May. Outside the laboratory the squirrels ran among the trees. The leftovers from the night's rain dripped on the ground and kept the earth moist. It was comfortable to leave a few windows open and to let the smell of the forest into the workshop.

The smell of their oil-burning heaters, the stale smell of insulation, of ozone, and of the heated electronic gear was something with which all of them were much too familiar.

Rogov had found that his eyesight was beginning to suffer because he had to get the receiver needle somewhere near his optic nerve in order to obtain visual impressions from the machine. After months of experimentation with both animal and human subjects he had decided to copy one of their last experiments, successfully performed on a prisoner boy fifteen years of age, by having the needle slipped directly through the skull, up and behind the eye. Rogov had disliked using prisoners, because Gauck, speaking on behalf of security, always insisted that a prisoner used in experiments be destroyed in not less than five days from the beginning of the experiment. Rogov had satisfied himself that the skull-and-needle technique was safe, but he was very tired of trying to get frightened, unscientific people to carry the load of intense, scientific attentiveness required by the machine.

Somewhat ill-humored, he shouted at Gauck, "Have you ever known what this is all about? You've been here years. Do you know what we're trying to do? Don't you ever want to take part in the experiments yourself? Do you realize how many years of mathematics have gone into the making of these grids and the calculation of these wave patterns? Are you good for anything?"

Gauck had said, tonelessly and without anger, "Comrade professor, I am obeying orders. You are obeying orders too. I've never impeded you."

Rogov raved, "I know you never got in my way. We're all good servants of the Soviet State. It's not a question of loyalty. It's a question of enthusiasm. Don't you ever want to glimpse the science we're making? We are a hundred years or a thousand years ahead of the capitalist Americans. Doesn't that excite you? Aren't you a human being? Why don't you take part? How will you understand me when I explain it?"

Gauck said nothing; he looked at Rogov with his beady

eyes. His dirty-gray face did not change expression. Cherpas said, "Go ahead, Nikolai. The comrade can follow if he wants to."

Gausgofer looked enviously at Cherpas. She seemed inclined to keep quiet, but then had to speak. She said, "Do go ahead, comrade professor."

Said Rogov, "*Kharosho,* I'll do what I can. The machine is now ready to receive minds over immense distances." He wrinkled his lip in amused scorn. "We may even spy into the brain of the chief rascal himself and find out what Eisenhower is planning to do today against the Soviet people. Wouldn't it be wonderful if our machine could stun him and leave him sitting addled at his desk?"

Gauck commented, "Don't try it. Not without orders."

Rogov ignored the interruption and went on. "First I receive. I don't know what I will get, who I will get, or where they will be. All I know is that this machine will reach out across all the minds of men and beasts now living and it will bring the eyes and ears of a single mind directly into mine. With the new needle going directly into the brain it will be possible for me to get a very sharp fixation of position. The trouble with that boy last week was that even though we knew he was seeing something outside this room, he appeared to be getting sounds in a foreign language and did not know enough English or German to realize where or what the machine had taken him to see."

Cherpas laughed. "I'm not worried. I saw then it was safe. You go first, my husband. If our comrades don't mind—?"

Gauck nodded.

Gausgofer lifted her bony hand breathlessly to her skinny throat and said, "Of course, Comrade Rogov, of course. You did *all* the work. You *must* be the first."

Rogov sat down.

A white-smocked technician brought the machine over to him. It was mounted on three rubber-tired wheels and it resembled the small X-ray units used by dentists. In place of the cone at the head of the X-ray machine there was a long, incredibly tough needle. It had been made for them by the best surgical steel craftsmen in Prague.

Another technician came up with a shaving bowl, a brush, and a straight razor. Under the gaze of Gauck's deadly eyes he shaved an area of four square centimeters on the top of Rogov's head.

Cherpas herself then took over. She set her husband's head in the clamp and used a micrometer to get the skull-fittings so tight and so accurate that the needle would push through the dura mater at exactly the right point.

All this work she did deftly with kind, very strong fingers. She was gentle, but she was firm. She was his wife, but she was also his fellow scientist and his colleague in the Soviet State.

She stepped back and looked at her work. She gave him one of their own very special smiles, the secret gay smiles which they usually exchanged with each other only when they were alone. "You won't want to do this every day. We're going to have to find some way of getting into the brain without using this needle. But it won't hurt you."

"Does it matter if it does hurt?" said Rogov. "This is the triumph of all our work. *Bring it down.*"

Cherpas, her eyes gleaming with attention, reached over and pulled down the handle which brought the tough needle to within a tenth of a millimeter of the right place.

Rogov spoke very carefully: "All I felt was a little sting. You can turn the power on now."

Gausgofer could not contain herself. Timidly she addressed Cherpas, "*May* I turn on the power?"

Cherpas nodded. Gauck watched. Rogov waited. Gausgofer pulled down the bayonet switch.

The power went on.

With an impatient twist of her hand, Anastasia Cherpas ordered the laboratory attendants to the other end of the room. Two or three of them had stopped working and were staring at Rogov, staring like dull sheep. They looked embarrassed and then they huddled in a white-smocked herd at the other end of the laboratory.

The wet May wind blew in on all of them. The scent of forest and leaves was about them.

The three watched Rogov.

Rogov's complexion began to change. His face became

flushed. His breathing was so loud and heavy they could hear it several meters away. Cherpas fell on her knees in front of him, eyebrows lifted in mute inquiry.

Rogov did not dare nod, not with a needle on his brain. He spoke through flushed lips, speaking thickly and heavily, "Do—not—stop—now."

Rogov himself did not know what was happening. He had thought he might see an American room, or a Russian room, or a tropical colony. He might see palm trees, or forests, or desks. He might see guns or buildings, washrooms or beds, hospitals, homes, churches. He might see with the eyes of a child, a woman, a man, a soldier, a philosopher, a slave, a worker, a savage, a religious, a Communist, a reactionary, a governor, a policeman. He might hear voices; he might hear English, or French, or Russian, Swahili, Hindi, Malay, Chinese, Ukrainian, Armenian, Turkish, Greek. He did not know.

None of these things had happened.

It seemed to him that he had left the world, that he had left time. The hours and the centuries shrank up like the meters, and the machine, unchecked, reached out for the most powerful signal which any human mind had transmitted. Rogov did not know it, but the machine had conquered time.

The machine had reached the dance, the human challenger and the dance festival of the year that might have been A.D. 13,582.

Before Rogov's eyes the golden shape and the golden steps shook and fluttered in a ritual a thousand times more compelling than hypnotism. The rhythms meant nothing and everything to him. This was Russia, this was Communism. This was his life—indeed it was his soul acted out before his very eyes.

For a second, the last second of his ordinary life, he looked through flesh and blood eyes and saw the shabby woman whom he had once thought beautiful. He saw Anastasia Cherpas, and he did not care.

His vision concentrated once again on the dancing image, this woman, those postures, that dance!

Then the sound came in—music that would have made a Tschaikovsky weep, orchestras which would have silenced Shostakovich or Khachaturian forever.

The people-who-were-not-people between the stars had taught mankind many arts. Rogov's mind was the best of its time, but his time was far, far behind the time of the great dance. With that one vision Rogov went firmly and completely mad.

He became blind to the sight of Cherpas, Gausgofer, and Gauck. He forgot the village of Ya. Ch. He forgot himself. He was like a fish, bred in stale fresh water, which is thrown for the first time into a living stream. He was like an insect emerging from the chrysalis. His twentieth-century mind could not hold the imagery and the impact of the music and the dance.

But the needle was there and the needle transmitted into his mind more than his mind could stand.

The synapses of his brain flicked like switches. The future flooded into him.

He fainted.

Cherpas leaped forward and lifted the needle. Rogov fell out of the chair.

It was Gauck who got the doctors. By nightfall they had Rogov resting comfortably and under heavy sedation. There were two doctors, both from the military headquarters. Gauck had obtained authorization for their services by a direct telephone call to Moscow.

Both the doctors were annoyed. The senior one never stopped grumbling at Cherpas.

"You should not have done it, Comrade Cherpas. Comrade Rogov should not have done it either. You can't go around sticking things into brains. That's a medical problem. None of you people are doctors of medicine. It's all right for you to contrive devices with the prisoners, but you can't inflict things like this on Soviet scientific personnel. I'm going to get blamed because I can't bring Rogov back. You heard what he was saying. All he did was mutter, 'That golden shape on the golden steps, that music, that me is a true me, that golden shape, that golden shape, I want to be with that golden shape,' and rubbish like that. Maybe you've ruined a first-class brain forever—" He stopped short as though he had said too much. After all, the problem was a security problem and apparently both Gauck and Gausgofer represented the security agencies.

Gausgofer turned her watery eyes on the doctor and said in a low, even, unbelievably poisonous voice, "Could *she* have done it, comrade doctor?"

The doctor looked at Cherpas, answering Gausgofer, "How? You were there. I wasn't. *How* could she have done it? *Why* should she do it? You were there."

Cherpas said nothing. Her lips were compressed tight with grief. Her yellow hair gleamed, but her hair was all that remained, at that moment, of her beauty. She was frightened and she was getting ready to be sad. She had no time to hate foolish women or to worry about security; she was concerned with her colleague, her lover, her husband Rogov.

There was nothing much for them to do except to wait. They went into a large room and waited.

The servants had laid out immense dishes of cold sliced meat, pots of caviar, and an assortment of sliced breads, pure butter, genuine coffee, and liquors.

None of them ate much. At 9:15 the sound of rotors beat against the house. The big helicopter had arrived from Moscow.

Higher authorities took over.

The higher authority was a deputy minister, a man named V. Karper.

Karper was accompanied by two or three uniformed colonels, by an engineer civilian, by a man from the headquarters of the Communist Party of the Soviet Union, and by two doctors.

They dispensed with the courtesies. Karper merely said, "You are Cherpas. I have met you. You are Gausgofer. I have seen your reports. You are Gauck."

The delegation went into Rogov's bedroom. Karper snapped, "Wake him."

The military doctor who had given him sedatives said, "Comrade, you mustn't—"

Karper cut him off. "Shut up." He turned to his own physician, pointed at Rogov. "Wake him up."

The doctor from Moscow talked briefly with the senior military doctor. He too began shaking his head. He gave Karper a disturbed look. Karper guessed what he might hear. He said, "Go ahead. I know there is some danger to the patient, but I've got to get back to Moscow with a report."

The two doctors worked over Rogov. One of them gave Rogov an injection. Then all of them stood back from the bed.

Rogov writhed in his bed. He squirmed. His eyes opened, but he did not see the people. With childishly clear and simple words Rogov began to talk, ". . . that golden shape, the golden stairs, the music, take me back to the music, I want to be with the music, I really am the music . . ." and so on in an endless monotone.

Cherpas leaned over him so that her face was directly in his line of vision. "My darling! My darling, wake up. This is serious."

It was evident to all of them that Rogov did not hear her.

For the first time in many years Gauck took the initiative. He spoke directly to the man from Moscow. "Comrade, may I make a suggestion?"

Karper looked at him. Gauck nodded at Gausgofer. "We were both sent here by orders of Comrade Stalin. She is senior. She bears the responsibility. All I do is double check."

The deputy minister turned to Gausgofer. Gausgofer had been staring at Rogov on the bed; her blue, watery eyes were tearless and her face was drawn into an expression of extreme tension.

Karper ignored that and said to her firmly, clearly, commandingly, "What do you recommend?"

Gausgofer looked at him very directly and said in a measured voice, "I do not think that the case is one of brain damage. I believe that he has obtained a communication which he must share with another human being and that unless one of us follows him there may be no answer."

Karper barked, "Very well. But what do we do?"

"Let *me* follow—into the machine."

Anastasia Cherpas began to laugh slyly and frantically. She seized Karper's arm and pointed her finger at Gausgofer. Karper stared at her.

Cherpas restrained her laughter and shouted at Karper, "The woman's mad. She has loved my husband for many years. She has hated my presense, and now she thinks that she can save him. She thinks that she can follow. She thinks that he wants to communicate with her. That's ridiculous. I will go myself!"

Karper looked about. He selected two of his staff and stepped over into a corner of the room. They could hear him talking, but they could not distinguish the words. After a conference of six or seven minutes he returned.

"You people have been making serious security charges against each other. I find that one of our finest weapons, the mind of Rogov, is damaged. Rogov's not just a man. He is a Soviet project." Scorn entered his voice. "I find that the senior security officer, a policewoman with a notable record, is charged by another Soviet scientist with a silly infatuation. I disregard such charges. The development of the Soviet State and the work of Soviet science cannot be impeded by personalities. Comrade Gausgofer will follow. I am acting tonight because my own staff physician says that Rogov may not live and it is very important for us to find out just what has happened to him and why."

He turned his baleful gaze on Cherpas. "You will not protest, comrade. Your mind is the property of the Russian State. Your life and your education have been paid for by the workers. You cannot throw these things away because of personal sentiment. If there is anything to be found, Comrade Gausgofer will find it for both of us."

The whole group of them went back into the laboratory. The frightened technicians were brought over from the barracks. The lights were turned on and the windows were closed. The May wind had become chilly.

The needle was sterilized. The electronic grids were warmed up.

Gausgofer's face was an impassive mask of triumph as she sat in the receiving chair. She smiled at Gauck as an attendant brought the soap and the razor to shave clean a patch on her scalp.

Gauck did not smile back. His black eyes stared at her. He said nothing. He did nothing. He watched.

Karper walked to and fro, glancing from time to time at the hasty but orderly preparation of the experiment.

Anastasia Cherpas sat down at a laboratory table about five meters away from the group. She watched the back of Gausgofer's head as the needle was lowered. She buried her face in her hands. Some of the others thought they heard her weeping, but no one heeded Cherpas very much. They were too intent on watching Gausgofer.

Gausgofer's face became red. Perspiration poured down the flabby cheeks. Her fingers tightened on the arm of her chair. Suddenly she shouted at them, *"That golden shape on the golden steps."*

She leaped to her feet, dragging the apparatus with her. No one had expected this. The chair fell to the floor. The needle holder, lifted from the floor, swung its weight sidewise. The needle twisted like a scythe in Gausgofer's brain.

The body of Gausgofer lay on the floor, surrounded by excited officials.

Karper was acute enough to look around at Cherpas.

She stood up from the laboratory table and walked toward him. A thin line of blood flowed down from her cheekbone. Another line of blood dripped down from a position on her cheek, one and a half centimeters forward of the opening of her left ear.

With tremendous composure, her face as white as fresh snow, she smiled at him. "I eavesdropped."

Karper said, "What?"

"I eavesdropped, eavesdropped," repeated Anastasia Cherpas. "I found out where my husband has gone. It is not somewhere in this world. It is something hypnotic beyond all the limitations of our science. We have made a great gun, but the gun has fired upon us before we could fire it.

"Project Telescope is finished. You may try to get someone else to finish it, but you will not."

Karper stared at her and then turned aside.

Gauck stood in his way.

"What do you want?"

"To tell you," said Gauck very softly, "to tell you, comrade deputy minister, that Rogov is gone as she says he is gone, that she is finished if she says she is finished, that all this is true. I know."

Karper glared at him. "How do you know?"

Gauck remained utterly impassive. With superhuman assurance and calm he said to Karper, "Comrade, I do not dispute the matter. I know these people, though I do not know their science. Rogov is done for."

At last Karper believed him.

They all looked at Anastasia Cherpas, at her beautiful hair, her determined blue eyes, and the two thin lines of blood.

Karper turned to her. "What do we do now?"

For an answer she dropped to her knees and began sobbing. "No, no, not Rogov! No, no, not Rogov!"

And that was all that they could get out of her. Gauck looked on.

On the golden steps in the golden light, a golden shape danced a dream beyond the limits of all imagination, danced and drew the music to herself until a sigh of yearning, yearning which became a hope and a torment, went through the hearts of living things on a thousand worlds.

Edges of the golden scene faded raggedly and unevenly into black. The golden dimmed down to a pale gold-silver sheen and then to silver, last of all to white. The dancer who had been golden was now a forlorn white-pink figure standing, quiet and fatigued, on the immense white steps. The applause of a thousand worlds roared in upon her.

She looked blindly at them. The dance had overwhelmed her, too. Their applause could mean nothing. The dance was an end in itself. She would have to live, somehow, until she danced again.

THE SHORELINE AT SUNSET

by Ray Bradbury

from *A Medicine for Melancholy* (Doubleday, 1959)

By definition, the only "formula" for science fantasy is no-formula; a genre of speculation and extrapolation can exist only in a state of flux. But even flux, over a period of time, trends to a preferred shape. Against a background of the inevitable ninety per cent of inept or hackster trash, the better stories, as they emerge each year, always show some very definite—and different from the year before—emphasis on one area of speculation or another.

This time the focus is summed up in the title of the editorial reprinted some pages farther on from John W. Campbell Jr.'s erstwhile *Astounding*, now—take a deep breath—retitled *Analog Science Fact and Fiction:* "What Do You Mean ... Human?"

In a rather different sense, this is of course the query underlying all fiction, and all art. But the stories in this book, almost all, treat the question also in the special science-fiction sense as well—exploring with postulated answers and *what if*'s the boundaries of distinction by which we define ourselves.

Ray Bradbury, who needs no introduction in or out of the science-fiction field (even Mr. Amis knows *his* name!) selects a delicate and haunting legendary boundary to explore.

Tom, kneedeep in the waves, a piece of driftwood in his hand, listened.

The house, up toward the coast highway in the late afternoon, was silent. The sounds of closets being rummaged, suitcase locks snapping, vases being smashed, and of a final door crashing shut, all had faded away.

Chico, standing on the pale sand, flourished his wire-strainer to shake out a harvest of lost coins. After a moment, without glancing at Tom, he said, "Let her go."

So it was every year. For a week, or a month, their house would have music swelling from the windows, there would be new geraniums potted on the porch-rail, new paint on the doors and steps. The clothes on the wire-line changed from harlequin pants to sheath-dresses to hand-made Mexican frocks like white waves breaking behind the house. Inside, the paintings on the walls shifted from imitation Matisse to pseudo-Italian Renaissance. Sometimes, looking up, he would see a woman drying her hair like a bright yellow flag on the wind. Sometimes the flag was black or red. Sometimes the woman was tall, sometimes short, against the sky. But there was never more than one woman at a time. And, at last, a day like today came. . . .

Tom placed his driftwood on the growing pile near where Chico sifted the billion footprints left by people long vanished from their holidays.

"Chico. What are we doing here?"

"Living the life of Reilly, boy!"

"I don't feel like Reilly, Chico."

"Work at it, boy!"

Tom saw the house a month from now, the flowerpots blowing dust, the walls hung with empty squares, only sand carpeting the floors. The rooms would echo like shells in the wind. And all night every night, bedded in separate rooms, he and Chico would hear a tide falling away and away down a long shore, leaving no trace.

Tom nodded, imperceptibly. Once a year he himself brought a nice girl here knowing she was right at last and that in no time they would be married. But his women always stole silently away before dawn, feeling they had been mistaken for someone else, not being able to play the part. Chico's friends left like vacuum cleaners, with a terrific drag, roar, rush, leaving no lint unturned, no clam unprized of its pearl, taking their purses with them like toy dogs which Chico had petted as he opened their jaws to count their teeth.

"That's four women so far this year."

"Okay, referee." Chico grinned. "Show me the way to the showers."

"Chico—" Tom bit his lower lip, then went on. "I been thinking. Why don't we split up?"

Chico just looked at him.

"I mean," said Tom, quickly, "maybe we'd have better luck, alone."

"Well, I'll be god-damned," said Chico, slowly, gripping the strainer in his big fists before him. "Look here, boy, don't you know the facts? You and me, we'll be here come the year 2000. A couple of crazy dumb old gooney-birds drying their bones in the sun. Nothing's ever going to happen to us now, Tom, it's too late. Get that through your head and shut up."

Tom swallowed and looked steadily at the other man. "I'm thinking of leaving—next week."

"Shut up, shut up, and get to work!"

Chico gave the sand an angry showering rake that tilled him forty-three cents in dimes, pennies, and nickels. He stared blindly at the coins shimmering down the wires like a pinball game all afire.

Tom did not move, holding his breath.

They both seemed to be waiting for something.

The something happened.

"Hey . . . hey . . . oh, hey . . . !"

From a long way off down the coast a voice called.

The two men turned slowly.

"Hey . . . hey . . . oh, hey . . . !"

A boy was running, yelling, waving, along the shore two hundred yards away. There was something in his voice that made Tom feel suddenly cold. He held onto his own arms, waiting.

"Hey!"

The boy pulled up, gasping, pointing back along the shore.

"A woman, a funny woman, by the North Rock!"

"A woman!" The words exploded from Chico's mouth and he began to laugh. "Oh, no, no!"

"What you mean, a 'funny' woman?" asked Tom.

"I don't know," cried the boy, his eyes wide. "You got to come see! Awfully funny!"

"You mean drowned?"

"Maybe! She came out of the water, she's lying on the shore, you got to see, yourself . . . funny . . ." The boy's voice died. He gazed off north again. "She's got a fish's tail."

Chico laughed. "Not before supper, thanks."

"Please," cried the boy, dancing now. "No lie! Oh, hurry!"

He ran off, sensed he was not followed, and looked back in dismay.

Tom felt his lips move. "Boy wouldn't run this far for a joke, would he, Chico?"

"People have run further for less."

Tom started walking. "All right, son."

"Thanks, mister, oh, thanks!"

The boy ran. Twenty yards up the coast, Tom looked back. Behind him, Chico scowled, shrugged, dusted his hands wearily, and followed.

They moved north along the twilight beach, their skin weathered in tiny lizard folds about their burnt pale-water eyes, looking younger for their hair cut close to the skull so you could not see the gray. There was a fair wind and the ocean rose and fell with prolonged concussions.

"What," said Tom, "what if we get to North Rock and it's true? What if the ocean *has* washed some *thing* up?"

But before Chico could answer, Tom was gone, his mind racing down a coast littered with horseshoe crabs, sand-dollars, starfish, kelp, and stone. From all the times he'd talked on what lives in the sea, the names returned with the breathing fall of waves. Argonauts, they whispered, codlings, pollacks, houndfish, tautog, tench, sea-elephant, they whispered, gillings, flounders, and beluga the white whale and grampus the sea-dog . . . always you thought how these must look from their deep-sounding names. Perhaps you would never in your life see them rise from the salt meadows beyond the safe limits of the shore, but they were there, and their names, with a thousand others, made pic-

tures. And you looked and wished you were a frigate-bird
that might fly nine thousand miles around to return some
year with the full size of the ocean in your head.

"Oh, quick!" The boy had run back to peer in Tom's
face. "It might be gone!"

"Keep your shirt on, boy," said Chico.

They came around the North Rock. A second boy stood
there, looking down.

Perhaps from the corner of his eye, Tom saw something on the sand that made him hesitate to look straight
at it, but fix instead on the face of the boy standing there.
The boy was pale and he seemed not to breathe. On occasion he remembered to take a breath, his eyes focused, but
the more they saw there on the sand the more they took
time off from focusing and turned blank and looked
stunned. When the ocean came in over his tennis shoes, he
did not move or notice.

Tom glanced away from the boy to the sand.

And Tom's face, in th   ⁀ʰ moment, became the face of
the boy. His hands assu   ̣̣he same curl at his sides and
his mouth moved to open and stay half open and his eyes,
which were light in color, seemed to bleach still more with
so much looking.

The setting sun was ten minutes above the sea.

"A big wave came in and went out," said the first boy,
"and here she was."

They looked at the woman lying there.

Her hair was very long and it lay on the beach like the
threads of an immense harp. The water stroked along the
threads and floated them up and let them down, each time
in a different fan and silhouette. The hair must have been
five or six feet long and now it was strewn on the hard
wet sand and it was the color of limes.

Her face . . .

The men bent half down in wonder.

Her face was white sand sculpture, with a few water
drops shimmering on it like summer rain upon a cream-
colored rose. Her face was that moon which when seen
by day is pale and unbelievable in the blue sky. It was milk-
marble veined with faint violet in the temples. The eyelids,

closed down upon the eyes, were powdered with a faint water-color, as if the eyes beneath gazed through the fragile tissue of the lids and saw them standing there above her looking down and looking down. The mouth was a pale flushed sea-rose, full and closed upon itself. And her neck was slender and white and her breasts were small and white, now covered, uncovered, covered, uncovered in the flow of water, the ebb of water, the flow, the ebb, the flow. And the breasts were flushed at their tips, and her body was startlingly white, almost an illumination, a white-green lightning against the sand. And as the water shifted her, her skin glinted like the surface of a pearl.

The lower half of her body changed itself from white to very pale blue, from very pale blue to pale green, from pale green to emerald green, to moss and lime green, to scintillas and sequins all dark green, all flowing away in a fount, a curve, a rush of light and dark, to end in a lacy fan, a spread of foam and jewel on the sand. The two halves of this creature were so joined as to reveal no point of fusion where pearl woman, woman of a whiteness made of cream-water and clear sky, merged with that half which belonged to the amphibious slide and rush of current that came up on the shore and shelved down the shore, tugging its half toward its proper home. The woman was the sea, the sea was woman. There was no flaw or seam, no wrinkle or stitch; the illusion, if illusion it was, held perfectly together and the blood from one moved into and through and mingled with what must have been the ice-waters of the other.

"I wanted to run get help." The first boy seemed not to want to raise his voice. "But Skip said she was dead and there's no help for that. Is she?"

"She was never alive," said Chico. "Sure," he went on, feeling their eyes on him suddenly. "It's something left over from a movie studio. Liquid rubber skinned over a steel frame. A prop, a dummy."

"Oh, no, it's real!"

"We'll find a label somewhere," said Chico. "Here."

"Don't!" cried the first boy.

"Hell." Chico touched the body to turn it, and stopped. He knelt there, his face changing.

"What's the matter?" asked Tom.

Chico took his hand away and looked at it. "I was wrong." His voice faded.

Tom took the woman's wrist. "There's a pulse."

"You're feeling your own heartbeat."

"I just don't know . . . maybe . . . maybe . . ."

The woman was there and her upper body was all moon pearl and tidal cream and her lower body all slithering ancient green-black coins that slid upon themselves in the shift of wind and water.

"There's a trick somewhere!" cried Chico, suddenly.

"No. No!" Just as suddenly Tom burst out in laughter. "No trick! My God, my God, I feel great! I haven't felt so great since I was a kid!"

They walked slowly around her. A wave touched her white hand so the fingers faintly softly waved. The gesture was that of someone asking for another and another wave to come in and lift the fingers and then the wrist and then the arm and then head and finally the body and take all of them together back down out to sea.

"Tom." Chico's mouth opened and closed. "Why don't you go get our truck?"

Tom didn't move.

"You hear me?" said Chico.

"Yes, but—"

"But what? We could sell this somewhere, I don't know —the university, that aquarium at Seal Beach or . . . well, hell, why couldn't we just set up a place? Look." He shook Tom's arm. "Drive to the pier. Buy us three hundred pounds of chipped ice. When you take anything out of the water you *need* ice, don't you?"

"I never thought."

"Think about it! Get moving!"

"I don't know, Chico."

"What you mean? She's real, isn't she?" He turned to the boys. "*You* say she's real, don't you? Well, then, what are we waiting for?"

"Chico," said Tom. "You better go get the ice yourself."

"Someone's got to stay and make sure she don't go back out with the tide!"

"Chico," said Tom. "I don't know how to explain. I don't want to get that ice for you."

"I'll go myself, then. Look, boys, build the sand up here to keep the waves back. I'll give you five bucks apiece. Hop to it!"

The sides of the boys' faces were bronze-pink from the sun which was touching the horizon now. Their eyes were a bronze color looking at Chico.

"My God!" said Chico. "This is better than finding ambergris!" He ran to the top of the nearest dune, called, "Get to work!" and was gone.

Now Tom and the two boys were left with the lonely woman by the north rock and the sun was one-fourth of the way below the western horizon. The sand and the woman were pink-gold.

"Just a little line," whispered the second boy. He drew his fingernail along under his own chin, gently. He nodded to the woman. Tom bent again to see the faint line under either side of her firm white chin, the small almost invisible line where the gills were or had been and were now almost sealed shut, invisible.

He looked at the face and the great strands of hair spread out in a lyre on the shore.

"She's beautiful," he said.

The boys nodded without knowing it.

Behind them, a gull leaped up quickly from the dunes. The boys gasped and turned to stare.

Tom felt himself trembling. He saw the boys were trembling, too. A car horn hooted. Their eyes blinked, suddenly afraid. They looked up toward the highway.

A wave poured about the body, framing it in a clear white pool of water.

Tom nodded the boys to one side.

The wave moved the body an inch in and two inches out toward the sea.

The next wave came and moved the body two inches in and six inches out toward the sea.

"But—" said the first boy.

Tom shook his head.

The third wave lifted the body two feet down toward the sea. The wave after that drifted the body another foot down the shingles and the next three moved it six feet down.

The first boy cried out and ran after it.

Tom reached him and held his arm. The boy looked helpless and afraid and sad.

For a moment there were no more waves. Tom looked at the woman, thinking, she's true, she's real, she's mine . . . but . . . she's dead. Or will be if she stays here.

"We can't let her go," said the first boy. "We can't, we just can't!"

The other boy stepped between the woman and the sea. "What would we do with her," he wanted to know, looking at Tom, "if we kept her?"

The first boy tried to think. "We could—we could—" He stopped and shook his head. "Oh, my gosh."

The second boy stepped out of the way and left a path from the woman to the sea.

The next was a big one. It came in and went out and the sand was empty. The whiteness was gone and the black diamonds and the great threads of the harp.

They stood by the edge of the sea, looking out, the man and the two boys, until they heard the truck driving up on the dunes behind them.

The last of the sun was gone.

They heard footsteps running down the dunes and someone yelling.

They drove back down the darkening beach in the light truck with the big-treaded tires, in silence. The two boys sat in the rear on the bags of chipped ice. After a long while, Chico began to swear steadily, half to himself, spitting out the window.

"Three hundred pounds of ice. Three hundred *pounds* of ice! What do I do with it now? And I'm soaked to the skin, soaked! You didn't even move when I jumped in and swam out to look around! Idiot, idiot! You haven't changed! Like every other time, like always, you do nothing, nothing, just stand there, stand there, do nothing, nothing, just stare!"

"And what did you do, I ask, what?" said Tom, in a tired voice, looking ahead. "The same as you always did, just the same, no different at all. You should've seen yourself."

They dropped the boys off at their beach-house. The youngest spoke in a voice you could hardly hear against the wind.

"Gosh, nobody'll ever believe . . ."

The two men drove down the coast and parked.

Chico sat for two or three minutes waiting for his fists to relax on his lap, and then he snorted.

"Hell. I guess things turn out for the best." He took a deep breath. "It just came to me. Funny. Twenty, thirty years from now, middle of the night, our phone'll ring. It'll be one of those two boys, grown up, calling long-distance from a bar somewhere. Middle of the night, them calling to ask one question. It's *true*, isn't it? they'll say. It *did* happen, didn't it? Back in 1958, it really happened to *us?* And we'll sit there on the edge of the bed, middle of the night, saying, Sure, boy, sure, it really happened, to us, in 1958. And they'll say, Thanks, and we'll say, Don't mention it, any old time. And we'll all say good night. And maybe they won't call again for a couple of years."

The two men sat on their front-porch steps in the dark.

"Tom?"

"What?"

Chico waited a moment.

"You're not going away."

It was not a question but a quiet statement.

Tom thought about it, his cigarette dead in his fingers. And he knew he would never go away now. For tomorrow and the day after and the day after the day after that, he knew he would walk down and go swimming there in all the green lace and the white fires and the dark caverns in the hollows under the waves. Tomorrow and tomorrow and tomorrow.

"That's right, Chico. I'm staying here."

Now the silver looking-glasses advanced in a crumpling

line all along the coast from a thousand miles north to a thousand miles south. The mirrors did not reflect so much as one building or one tree or one highway or one car or even one man himself. The mirrors reflected only the quiet moon and then shattered into a billion bits of glass that spread out in a glaze on the shore. Then the sea was dark awhile, preparing another line of mirrors to rear up and surprise the two men who sat there for a long time, never once blinking their eyes, waiting.

THE DREAMSMAN

by Gordon R. Dickson

from *Star Science Fiction* #6 (Ballantine Books, 1959)

Every profession has its fringe benefits, and Gordy Dickson is one of science fiction's. A big rangy ex-Canadian from the tall beer country of Minnesota, he turns up, not quite often enough, at conventions and conferences with his guitar over one shoulder and a sort of shining shield of great good humor over the other. One of these days a bright song publisher will introduce nonconvention-goers to the Dickson-Cogswell-Anderson science-fantasy ballads and blues. Meantime, novels like his explosive *Dorsai!* in ASF last year, and short stories like this one fill the gap moderately well.

Mr. Willer is shaving. He uses an old-fashioned straight-edged razor and the mirror above his bathroom washbasin reflects a morning face that not even the fluffy icing of the lather can make very palatable. Above the lather his skin is dark and wrinkled. His eyes are somewhat yellow where they ought to show white and his sloping forehead is embarrassingly short of hair. No matter. Mr. Willer poises the razor for its first stroke—and instantly freezes in position. For a second he stands immobile. Then his false teeth clack once and he starts to pivot slowly toward the northwest, razor still in hand, quivering like a directional antenna seeking its exact target. This is as it should be. Mr. Willer, wrinkles, false teeth and all, *is* a directional antenna.

Mr. Willer turns back to the mirror and goes ahead with his shaving. He shaves skilfully and rapidly, beaming up at a sign over the mirror which proclaims that a stitch in time saves nine. Four minutes later, stitchless and in need of none, he moves out of the bathroom, into his bedroom. Here he dresses rapidly and efficiently, at the last adjusting his four-in-hand before a dresser mirror which has inlaid about its frame the message *Handsome is as handsome does.* Fully dressed, Mr. Willer selects a shiny malacca cane from the collection in his hall closet and goes out behind his little house to the garage.

His car, a 1937 model sedan painted a sensible gray, is waiting for him. Mr. Willer gets in, starts the motor and carefully warms it up for two minutes. He then backs out into the May sunshine. He points the hood ornament of the sedan toward Buena Vista and drives off.

Two hours later he can be seen approaching a small yellow-and-white rambler in Buena Vista's new development section, at a considerate speed two miles under the local limit. It is 10:30 in the morning. He pulls up in front of the house, sets the handbrake, locks his car and goes up to ring the doorbell beside the yellow front door.

The door opens and a face looks out. It is a very pretty face with blue eyes and marigold-yellow hair above a blue apron not quite the same shade as the eyes. The young lady to which it belongs cannot be much more than in her very early twenties.

"Yes?" says the young lady.

"Mr. Willer, Mrs. Conalt," says Mr. Willer, raising his hat and producing a card. "The Liberty Mutual Insurance agent, to see your husband."

"Oh!" says the pretty face, somewhat flustered, opening the door and stepping back. "Please come in." Mr. Willer enters. Still holding the card, Mrs. Conalt turns and calls across the untenanted small living room toward the bedroom section at the rear of the house, "Hank!"

"Coming!" replies a young baritone. Seconds later a tall, quite thin man about the same age as his wife, with a cheerfully unhandsome face, emerges rapidly into the living room.

"The insurance man, honey," says the young lady, who has whisked off her apron while Mr. Willer was turned to face the entrance through which the young man has come. She hands her husband the card.

"Insurance?" says young Mr. Conalt frowning, reading

the card. "What insurance? Liberty Mutual? But I don't—we don't have any policies with Liberty Mutual. If you're selling—"

"Not at the moment," says Mr. Willer, beaming at them as well as the looseness of his false teeth will permit. "I actually *am* an insurance agent, but that hasn't anything to do with this. I only wanted to see you first."

"First before what?" demands Mr. Conalt, staring hard at him.

"Before revealing myself," says Mr. Willer. "You are the two young people who have been broadcasting a call to any other psi-sensitives within range, aren't you?"

"Oh, Hank!" gasps Mrs. Conalt; but Conalt does not unbend.

"What are you talking about?" he demands.

"Come, come," replies Mr. Willer deprecatingly.

"But, Hank—" begins Mrs. Conalt.

"Hush, Edie. I think this guy—"

"Oh, wad the power the Giftie gie us, to see oorselves as ithers see us—more or less, if you young people will pardon the accent."

"What's that? That's Robert Burns, isn't it," says Hank. "It goes—*it would frae mony an error free us.*" He hesitates.

"And foolish notion. Yes," says Mr. Willer. "And now that the sign and counter-sign have been given, let us get down to facts. You were broadcasting, both of you, were you not?"

"Were you receiving?" demands Hank.

"Of course," says Mr. Willer unperturbed. "How else would I know what quotation to use for a password?" He beams at them again. "May I sit down?"

"Oh, of course!" says Edie hastily. They all sit down. Edie bounces up again. "Would you like some coffee, Mr. —er—" she glances over at the card, still in Hank's hands —"Willer?"

"Thank you, no," replies Mr. Willer, clacking his teeth. "I have one cup of coffee a day, after dinner. I believe in moderation of diet. But to the point. You are the people I heard."

"Say we were," says Hank finally. "You claim to be psi-sensitive yourself, huh?"

"Claim? No doubt about it, my boy. Ash tray?" He lifts his hand. An ash tray on an end table across the room comes sailing on the air like a miniature ceramic UFO to light gently upon his upturned palm. Mr. Willer sets it down and closes his eyes.

"You have seven dollars in your wallet, Hank. One five-dollar bill and two singles. At this moment you are interrupting your main line of thought to wonder worriedly what happened to the third one-dollar bill, as you had eight dollars in the wallet earlier this morning. Rest easy. You were stopped by the newspaper delivery boy shortly after ten this morning while you were mowing the lawn and paid him eighty cents. The two dimes change are in your right-hand pants pocket."

He opens his eyes. "Well?"

"All right," says Hank with a heavy sigh. "You sold me. We can't do anything like that, Edie and I. We can just read each other's minds—and other people's if they're thinking straight at us." He stares a little at Mr. Willer. "You're pretty good."

"Tut," says Mr. Willer. "Experience, nothing else. I will be a hundred and eighty-four next July 12th. One learns things."

"A hundred and eighty-four!" gasps Edie.

"And some months, ma'am," says Mr. Willer, giving her a little half-bow from his chair. "Sensible living, no extravagances and peace of mind—the three keys to longevity. But to return to the subject, what caused you young people to send out a call?"

"Well, we—" began Edie.

"What we thought," says Hank, "is that if there were any more like us, we ought to get together and decide what to do about it. Edie and I talked it all over. Until we met each other we never thought there could be anybody else like ourselves in the world. But if there were two of us, then it stood to reason there must be more. And then Edie pointed out that maybe if a bunch of us could get together we could do a lot for people. It was sort of a duty, to see what we could do for the rest of the world."

"Very commendable," says Mr. Willer.

"I mean, we could read the minds of kids that fall in a well and get trapped—and send emergency messages maybe. All sorts of things. There must be a lot more we haven't thought of."

"No doubt there are," says Mr. Willer.

"Then you're with us?" says Hank. "Together, I'll bet we can darn near start a new era in the world."

"Well, yes," replies Mr. Willer. "And no. A hundred and eighty-four years have taught me caution. Moreover, there is more to the story than you young people think." He clacks his teeth. "Did you think you were the first?"

"The first?" echoes Hank.

"The first to discover you possess unusual abilities. I see by the expression on your faces you have taken just that for granted. I must, I'm afraid, correct that notion. You are not the first any more than I was. There have been many."

"Many?" asked Edie faintly.

"A great number within my experience," says Mr. Willer, rubbing his leathery old hands together.

"But what happened to them?" asked Edie.

"Many things," replies Mr. Willer. "Some were burned as witches, some were put in insane asylums. Fifteen years ago one was lynched in a small town called Pashville. Yes, indeed. Many things happen."

The two others stare at him.

"Yeah?" says Hank. "How come you're in such good shape, then?"

"Ah, that's the thing. Look before you leap. I always have. It pays."

"What—what do you mean?" asks Edie.

"I mean it's fortunate I was around to hear you when you broadcast." Mr. Willer turns to her. "Lucky for you I reached you before you went ahead trying to put this help-the-world plan of yours into effect."

"I still think it's a good notion!" says Hank almost fiercely.

"Because you're young," replies Mr. Willer with a slight quaver in his voice. "And idealistic. You wouldn't want to expose your wife to the sort of thing I've mentioned, eh?"

"Anything Hank decides!" says Edie stoutly.

"Well, well," says Mr. Willer, shaking his head. "Well, well, well!"

"Look here!" says Hank. "You can't tell me there's no way of putting what we've got to good use."

"Well . . ." says Mr. Willer.

"Look. If you want out," says Hank, "you just get in your car—"

Mr. Willer shakes his head.

"No," he says. And suddenly his face lights up with a smile. He beams at them. "You'd really let me go?"

"Shove off," says Hank.

"Good!" cried Mr. Willer. He does not move. "Congratulations, both of you. Forgive me for putting you both to the test this way but for the sake of everybody else in the Colony, I had to make sure you were ready to go through with it before I told you anything."

"Colony?" says Edie.

"Anything?" says Hank.

Nine hours later, just at dusk, a small, gray 1937 sedan in good repair is to be seen approaching the gate of a certain military installation in New Mexico. It stops at the wide gate and two MPs in white helmets approach it. There is a short conversation between them and the driver, and then they march rather stiffly and woodenly back to their small, glassed-in gatehouse. The sedan proceeds on into the interior of the installation.

A little under an hour later, after several more like conversations, the sedan parks. Its three occupants leave it for another gate, another guard, another compound within another area, and finally find themselves standing at the foot of an enormous tall, tapering metallic creation.

There are some half-dozen guards around this creation, but after a short conversation with the oldest of the party they have all stretched out beside their weapons and gone to sleep.

"Here we are," says the oldest of the party, who is, of course, Mr. Willer.

The other two are speechless and stare at the enormous ship beside them. They seem rather impressed.

"Will it—" falters Edie, and then her voice fails her.

"Will it take the two of you to Venus? Absolutely," says Mr. Willer, fondling the smooth head curve of his malacca walking stick. "I had a long talk with one of the chief men who designed it, just a week ago. You just follow these instructions—" He reaches for an inside pocket of his coat and withdraws a typewritten sheet of paper, which he hands to Hank. "Just run down the list on this, doing everything in order, and off you go."

Hank takes the paper rather gingerly. "Seems like stealing," he mumbles.

"Not when you stop to think," says Mr. Willer. "It's for the Colony, for the ultimate good of humanity." He puts a wrinkled hand confidentially on Hank's arm. "My boy, this has come so suddenly to both of you as to be quite a severe shock, but you will adjust to it in time. Fate has selected you two young people to be of that dedicated band of psychical pioneers who will one day lift humanity from this slough of fear and pain and uncertainty in which it has wallowed ever since the first man lifted his face to the skies in wonder. Have faith in your own destiny."

"Yeah," says Hank, still doubtful. But Edie is gazing with shining eyes at Mr. Willer.

"Oh!" she says. "Isn't it wonderful, Hank?"

"Yeah," says Hank.

"Well, then," says Mr. Willer, patting them both on the arm and pushing them gently to the metal ladder of a framework tower that stretches up alongside the ship. "Up you go. Don't worry about the controls. This is built on a new, secret principle. It's as easy to drive as a car."

"Just a minute!" cries a sudden, ringing voice. They all hesitate and turn away from the ship. Approaching rapidly through the air from the northwest is something that can only be described as a scintillant cloud of glory. It swoops in for a landing before them and thins away to reveal a tall, handsome man in a tight sort of coverall of silver mesh.

"Up to your old tricks, again, Wilo, aren't you?" he barks at Mr. Willer. "Can't keep your hands off? Want everything your own way, don't you?"

"Fools rush in," says Mr. Willer, "where angels fear to tread."

"What?" demands Hank, looking from one to the other. "What's all this about? Who're you?"

"You wouldn't understand if I told you," says the tall man. "The point is, having psi-talents puts you under my protection. Half a dozen people a year I have to come chasing in and rescue. And all on account of him!" He glares at Mr. Willer.

"I still don't—" Hank begins.

"Of course not. How could you? If Wilo here had started leaving things alone as little as a hundred years ago, you humans would have developed into probationary members of Galactic Society by this time. Natural evolution. More psi-talents in every generation. Recognition of such. Alteration of local society. But no, not Wilo. The minute he discovers anyone with psi-talent he points them toward destruction. I have to save them. The only safe way to save them with Wilo around is to take them off the planet. Wilo knows this. So—no progress for humanity."

Hank blinks a couple of times.

"But how come?" he cries, staring at Mr. Willer. "He's one himself! I mean, he can do all sorts of things Edie and I can't do—"

"Nonsense!" says the tall man. "He's just sensitive. An antenna, you might say. He can feel when real ones are sending."

"But—the ash tray . . ." falters Edie.

"There, there, I scan you perfectly," soothes the tall man. "Illusion. Nothing more. Even an *ordinary* intelligence can learn something in a hundred and eighty-four years and some months, after all. Wilo, Master Hypnotist.

That's the way he used to bill himself back in his days on the stage. He hypnotized you, just as he hypnotized these soldiers."

"With a glance," mutters Mr. Willer darkly.

"Unfortunately very true," says the tall man. He glares at Mr. Willer again. "If it wasn't for the fact that we truly advanced civilization members can't harm anyone—!"

He turns back to Hank and Edie.

"Well," he sighs heavily, "come along. This world will have to stay stuck in its present stage of development until something happens to Wilo, or he changes his mind."

Edie stares at the old man.

"Oh, Mr. Willer!" she says. "Why can't you let people just go ahead and develop like Hank and I did?"

"Bah!" says Willer. "Humbug!"

"But the world would be a much better place!"

"Young lady!" snaps Mr. Willer. "I like it the way it is!" He turns his back on them.

"Come on," says the tall man.

They take off. Mr. Willer turns back to look at them as they ascend into the new rays of the just-risen moon and the New Mexico night sky, trailing clouds of glory as they go.

The clouds of glory light up the landscape.

"Bah!" says Mr. Willer again. With a snap of his fingers he produces some flash paper which, at the touch of flame from a palmed match, flares brightly for a moment. It's one tiny recalcitrant beacon of stability and permanence in the whole of the madly whirling, wild and evolving universe.

MULTUM IN PARVO

by Jack Sharkey
from *Gent*

Once upon a time, little children used to frighten naughty parents at bedtime with a radio program known as "The Shadow." And out of those dim and dear days comes Bruce Elliott, who used to write the show—before he turned to comic books, mysteries, science fiction, magic, and heaven-knows-how-much-else, only to wind up respectably editing a happily not-too-respectable magazine duo.

For satire, fantasy, wit with spice, and all around fun, *Gent* and *The Dude* are giving some stiff competition these days to a magazine which will not be referred to here as *Playboy*. These excerpts from a still running series of histori-cal frictions (*Return of Parvo, Parvo Rides Again*, etc.) by Jack Sharkey have been selected as those most appropriate to a family science-fantasy anthology.

ROBOTS

The first robot was constructed by Max Roe and Harold Bott, in the year 1653, for exhibition at the World's Fair at Istanbul (not Constantinople). It was a rather rough con-struction, consisting mainly of a tin hand to hold cards and a glass eye for viewing them. It had one function: to play poker. Max and Harold taught it everything they knew, taking great pains to root out a distressing habit it had of trying to fill inside straights, and soon it was a better player than either of them. It had a painted mouth which never changed expression, which came in handy when it was only bluffing.

Anyhow, they lugged it down to Istanbul (not Constan-tinople) for the Fair, and proceeded to set it up in the tent near the center of the exposition. After completing the job, they stepped around the corner to the brewer's exhibit to sample the wares on display there, and to clean out the little reed pipe which they used to signal the robot to begin its play (alcohol was the perfect cleanser for it).*

While they were gone, however, the paraphernalia of the next tent (that of Omar, the Trussmocker), was delivered to theirs by mistake, and when they returned they were horrified to discover that their robot was laden with barbells and other weights of enormous tonnage.

"Max!" gasped Harold, "we can't lift up the lid to get at the starting switch!"

"Heavens," Max groaned, "you're right!"

"Say," said a man in the crowd which had come to see the robot, "ain't that thing gonna play poker for us?"

"I'm afraid not," said Max, indicating the weighted-down lid. "We can't get at the starting switch."

"Can't you do it by strength alone?" asked the man.

"Nope," said Harold, sadly. "It's going to take jacks or better to open."

AIRCRAFT

As most people know, the first man to fly was called Icarus, who should have had more sense. He and his father escaped from jail on an island (men of Alcatraz take note) by the expedient of attaching feathers to their arms with beeswax (it sounds reckless, I know, but this was before cellophane tape), and flapped away into the skies.

Well, everything was going fine till Icarus, who was a little dopey, decided to take a look at the sun, up close. Naturally, the beeswax began to melt and dribble away, and he began to lose his feathers.

"Say, son," his father observed, flapping down where it was cooler, "your topside is dripping. You'd better flip over on your back and come lower, so's the wax'll get hard again."

But Icarus said no, and flew still higher, till the wax began running like water, the feathers fluttered away and

---

* Hence the phrase, "To wet one's whistle."

Icarus plunged down toward the ocean, his right "wing" completely gone.

"Son," said his father, "are you falling?"

Icarus replied, "It's a matter of a pinion, Dad."

"If I've told you once, I've told you a thousand times, son," said his father as Icarus vanished into the sea, *"Loop before you leak!"*

Moral: He who levitates is washed.

VAMPIRISM

This habit was begun in 1357 by a group of five men who felt that they weren't getting enough out of their diet, which consisted mainly of turnips.

"Say, men," said the eldest, named George, "we're just *missing* something in our nutrition. How about we go and terrorize the countryside and maybe get us something we can really sink our teeth into?"

The others thought this a fine idea, and soon the near-by villages were getting it in the neck.

"My people," said the Mayor of the largest village, "it's about time we stop this leeching. That gang's been putting the bite on us long enough."

"So okay, so what do we do?" asked the villagers.

"We go out to the mausoleum where they sleep all day, and we try and touch their hearts by pointing out what we have at stake," he said.

"We'll hammer the point home," the villagers agreed.

So they took five sharpened sticks and went out to where the five men were sleeping. Gus, the blacksmith, had brought his hammer and proceeded to open the first of the five coffins and nailed the vampire before he could fly.

"Hurry, Gus," said the Mayor, "the other four are going batty."

But Gus came up to him empty-handed. "I'm sorry, Your Honor," he said, "but I got carried away and used up all five stakes on that first guy."

"Idiot," said the Mayor, "look what you've done! The other four have flipped their lids and flown the crypt!"

"It's all my fault," said Gus, "for putting all my pegs in one casket."

ATOMIC FISSION

This was discovered in 1944 by two scientists who were working in their lab on something else entirely. Sam, the younger man, came up to Ted, the older man, and said, "Say, Ted, how you getting on with that circular radio-wave of yours?"

"Not so good, Sam," said Ted, showing him a diagram. "I've devised this thing to carry a magnetic current in a circle, but that's all the farther I am. I call it a cyclotron."

"What?" said Sam, abused. "Ten years we've been working on this project, and all you have is this diagram? Why, it's nothing but a circle, a plain old cipher."

"I never took up drafting," Ted admitted sadly. "Anyhow, that's the shape it should be."

"Years of work, and you draw a cipher," Sam muttered. "I'll show you what *I* think of this diagram!"

And with that, he rolled the blueprint into a cylinder and ran it through the pencil-sharpener, leaving the scraps on the floor.

Immediately an angry crowd of janitors gathered, all of them telling the two scientists what they thought of that litter.

Instantly the building vanished in a white-hot blast, followed by a mushroom-shaped cloud.

And to this day, that's what happens when you get a critical mass at a ground zero.

For the last item, I was going to give the history of *Fallout*. I had to save it for last because— Well, look for yourself. . .

FALLOUT

That covers *everything*, doesn't it?

FLOWERS FOR ALGERNON

by Daniel Keyes
from *Fantasy and Science Fiction*

Daniel Keyes is a reformed science-fiction editor (Marvel, some few years ago) turned high-school English teacher. Either of these dubious professions should be enough to keep a sensible man on the spectator's side of a byline. If he didn't write the stuff when he could buy it from himself, one might think the rigors of New York City's blackboard jungle would prevent him from beginning now.

One way and another, it is difficult to believe that this is Keyes' second published story—much more difficult after reading it than before.

progris riport 1—march 5 1965

Dr Strauss says I shud rite down what I think and evrey thing that happins to me from now on. I dont know why but he says its importint so they will see if they will use me. I hope they use me. Miss Kinnian says maybe they can make me smart. I want to be smart. My name is Charlie Gordon. I am 37 years old and 2 weeks ago was my brithday. I have nuthing more to rite now so I will close for to-day.

progris riport 2—martch 6

I had a test today. I think I faled it. and I think that maybe now they wont use me. What happind is a nice young man was in the room and he had some white cards with ink spillled all over them. He sed Charlie what do you see on this card. I was very skared even tho I had my rabits foot in my pockit because when I was a kid I always faled tests in school and I spillled ink to.

I told him I saw a inkblot. He said yes and it made me feel good. I thot that was all but when I got up to go he stopped me. He said now sit down Charlie we are not thru yet. Then I dont remember so good but he wantid me to say what was in the ink. I dint see nuthing in the ink but he said there was picturs there other pepul saw some picturs. I coudnt see any picturs. I reely tryed to see. I held the card close up and then far away. Then I said if I had my glases I coud see better I usally only ware my glases in the movies or TV but I said they are in the closit in the hall. I got them. Then I said let me see that card agen I bet Ill find it now.

I tryed hard but I still coudnt find the picturs I only saw the ink. I told him maybe I need new glases. He rote something down on a paper and I got skared of faling the test. I told him it was a very nice inkblot with littel points all around the eges. He looked very sad so that wasnt it. I said please let me try agen. Ill get it in a few minits becaus Im not so fast somtimes. Im a slow reeder too in Miss Kinnians class for slow adults but I'm trying very hard.

He gave me a chance with another card that had 2 kinds of ink spillled on it red and blue.

He was very nice and talked slow like Miss Kinnian does and he explaned it to me that it was a *raw shok*. He said pepul see things in the ink. I said show me where. He said think. I told him I think a inkblot but that wasnt rite eather. He said what does it remind you—pretend somthing. I closd my eyes for a long time to pretend. I told him I pretend a fowntan pen with ink leeking all over a table cloth. Then he got up and went out.

I dont think I passd the *raw shok* test.

progris report 3—martch 7

Dr Strauss and Dr Nemur say it dont matter about the inkblots. I told them I dint spill the ink on the cards and I coudnt see anything in the ink. They said that maybe they will still use me. I said Miss Kinnian never gave me tests like that one only spelling and reading. They said Miss Kinnian told that I was her bestist pupil in the adult nite scool becaus I tryed the hardist and I reely wantid to lern. They said how come you went to the adult nite scool all by yourself Charlie. How did you find it. I said I askd pepul and sumbody told me where I shud go to lern to read and spell good. They said why did you want to. I told them becaus all my life I wantid to be smart and not dumb. But its very hard to be smart. They said you know it will probly be tempirery. I said yes. Miss Kinnian told me. I dont care if it herts.

Later I had more crazy tests today. The nice lady who gave it me told me the name and I asked her how do you spellit so I can rite it in my progris riport. THEMATIC APPERCEPTION TEST. I dont know the frist 2 words but I know what *test* means. You got to pass it or you get bad marks. This test lookd easy becaus I coud see the picturs. Only this time she dint want me to tell her the picturs. That mixd me up. I said the man yesterday said I shoud tell him what I saw in the ink she said that dont make no difrence. She said make up storys about the pepul in the picturs.

I told her how can you tell storys about pepul you never met. I said why shud I make up lies. I never tell lies any more becaus I always get caut.

She told me this test and the other one the raw-shok was for getting personalty. I laffed so hard. I said how can you get that thing from inkblots and fotos. She got sore and put her picturs away. I dont care. It was sily. I gess I faled that test too.

Later some men in white coats took me to a difernt part of the hospitil and gave me a game to play. It was like a race with a white mouse. They called the mouse Algernon. Algernon was in a box with a lot of twists and turns like all kinds of walls and they gave me a pencil and a paper with lines and lots of boxes. On one side it said START and on the other end it said FINISH. They said it was *amazed* and that Algernon and me had the same *amazed* to do. I dint see how we could have the same *amazed* if Algernon had a box and I had a paper but I dint say nothing. Anyway there wasnt time because the race started.

One of the men had a watch he was trying to hide so I woudnt see it so I tryed not to look and that made me nervus.

Anyway that test made me feel worser than all the others because they did it over 10 times with difernt *amazeds* and Algernon won every time. I dint know that mice were so smart. Maybe thats because Algernon is a white mouse. Maybe white mice are smarter then other mice.

progris riport 4—Mar 8

Their going to use me! Im so exited I can hardly write. Dr Nemur and Dr Strauss had a argament about it first. Dr Nemur was in the office when Dr Strauss brot me in. Dr Nemur was worried about using me but Dr Strauss told him Miss Kinnian rekemmended me the best from all the people who she was teaching. I like Miss Kinnian becaus shes a very smart teacher. And she said Charlie your going to have a second chance. If you volenteer for this experament you mite get smart. They dont know if it will be perminint but theirs a chance. Thats why I said ok even when I was scared because she said it was an operashun. She said dont be scared Charlie you done so much with so little I think you deserv it most of all.

So I got scaird when Dr Nemur and Dr Strauss argud about it. Dr Strauss said I had something that was very good. He said I had a good *motor-vation*. I never even knew I had that. I felt proud when he said that not every body with an eye-q of 68 had that thing. I dont know what it is or where I got it but he said Algernon had it too. Algernons *motor-vation* is the cheese they put in his box. But it cant be that because I didnt eat any cheese this week.

Then he told Dr Nemur something I dint understand so while they were talking I wrote down some of the words.

He said Dr Nemur I know Charlie is not what you had in mind as the first of your new brede of intelek* * (coudnt get the word) superman. But most people of his low ment** are host** and uncoop** they are usualy dull apath** and hard to reach. He has a good natcher hes intristed and eager to please.

Dr Nemur said remember he will be the first human

beeng ever to have his intelijence trippled by surgicle meens.

Dr Strauss said exakly. Look at how well hes lerned to read and write for his low mentel age its as grate an acheve** as you and I lerning einstines therey of **vity without help. That shows the intenss motor-vation. Its comparat** a tremen** achev** I say we use Charlie.

I dint get all the words and they were talking to fast but it sounded like Dr Strauss was on my side and like the other one wasnt.

Then Dr Nemur nodded he said all right maybe your right. We will use Charlie. When he said that I got so exited I jumped up and shook his hand for being so good to me. I told him thank you doc you wont be sorry for giving me a second chance. And I mean it like I told him. After the operashun Im gonna try to be smart. Im gonna try awful hard.

progris ript 5—Mar 10

Im skared. Lots of people who work here and the nurses and the people who gave me the tests came to bring me candy and wish me luck. I hope I have luck. I got my rabits foot and my lucky penny and my horse shoe. Only a black cat crossed me when I was comming to the hospitil. Dr Strauss says dont be supersitis Charlie this is sience. Anyway Im keeping my rabits foot with me.

I asked Dr Strauss if Ill beat Algernon in the race after the operashun and he said maybe. If the operashun works Ill show that mouse I can be as smart as he is. Maybe smarter. Then Ill be abel to read better and spell the words good and know lots of things and be like other people. I want to be smart like other people. If it works perminint they will make everybody smart all over the wurld.

They dint give me anything to eat this morning. I dont know what that eating has to do with getting smart. Im very hungry and Dr Nemur took away my box of candy. That Dr Nemur is a grouch. Dr Strauss says I can have it back after the operashun. You cant eat befor a operashun. . . .

Progress Report 6—Mar 15

The operashun dint hurt. He did it while I was sleeping. They took off the bandijis from my eyes and my head today so I can make a PROGRESS REPORT. Dr. Nemur who looked at some of my other ones says I spell PROGRESS wrong and he told me how to spell it and REPORT too. I got to try and remember that.

I have a very bad memary for spelling. Dr Strauss says its ok to tell about all the things that happin to me but he says I shoud tell more about what I feel and what I think. When I told him I dont know how to think he said try. All the time when the bandijis were on my eyes I tryed to think. Nothing happened. I dont know what to think about. Maybe if I ask him he will tell me how I can think now that Im suppose to get smart. What do smart people think about. Fancy things I suppose. I wish I knew some fancy things alredy.

Progress Report 7—mar 19

Nothing is happining. I had lots of tests and different kinds of races with Algernon. I hate that mouse. He always beats me. Dr Strauss said I got to play those games. And he said some time I got to take those tests over again. Thse inkblots are stupid. And those pictures are stupid too. I like to draw a picture of a man and a woman but I wont make up lies about people.

I got a headache from trying to think so much. I thot Dr Strauss was my frend but he dont help me. He dont tell me what to think or when Ill get smart. Miss Kinnian dint come to see me. I think writing these progress reports are stupid too.

Progress Report 8—Mar 23

Im going back to work at the factery. They said it was better I shud go back to work but I cant tell anyone what the operashun was for and I have to come to the hospitil for an hour evry night after work. They are gonna pay me mony every month for lerning to be smart.

Im glad Im going back to work because I miss my job and all my frends and all the fun we have there.

Dr Strauss says I shud keep writing things down but I dont have to do it every day just when I think of something or something speshul happins. He says dont get discoridged because it takes time and it happins slow. He says it took a long time with Algernon before he got 3 times smarter than he was before. Thats why Algernon beats me all the time because he had that operashun too. That makes me feel better. I coud probly do that *amazed* faster than a reglar mouse. Maybe some day Ill beat Algernon. Boy that would be something. So far Algernon looks like he mite be smart perminent.

Mar 25 (I dont have to write PROGRESS REPORT on top any more just when I hand it in once a week for Dr Nemur to read. I just have to put the date on. That saves time)

We had a lot of fun at the factery today. Joe Carp said hey look where Charlie had his operashun what did they do Charlie put some brains in. I was going to tell him but I remembered Dr Strauss said no. Then Frank Reilly said what did you do Charlie forget your key and open your door the hard way. That made me laff. Their really my friends and they like me.

Sometimes somebody will say hey look at Joe or Frank or George he really pulled a Charlie Gordon. I dont know why they say that but they always laff. This morning Amos Borg who is the 4 man at Donnegans used my name when he shouted at Ernie the office boy. Ernie lost a packige. He said Ernie for godsake what are you trying to be a Charlie Gordon. I dont understand why he said that. I never lost any packiges.

Mar 28 Dr Strauss came to my room tonight to see why I dint come in like I was suppose to. I told him I dont like to race with Algernon any more. He said I dont have to for a while but I shud come in. He had a present for me only it wasnt a present but just for lend. I thot it was a little television but it wasnt. He said I got to turn it on when I go to sleep. I said your kidding why shud I turn it on when Im going to sleep. Who ever herd of a thing like that. But he said if I want to get smart I got to do what he says. I told him I dint think I was going to get smart and he put his hand on my sholder and said Charlie you dont know it yet but your getting smarter all the time. You wont notice for a while. I think he was just being nice to make me feel good because I dont look any smarter.

Oh yes I almost forgot. I asked him when I can go back to the class at Miss Kinnians school. He said I wont go their. He said that soon Miss Kinnian will come to the hospitil to start and teach me speshul. I was mad at her for not comming to see me when I got the operashun but I like her so maybe we will be frends again.

Mar 29 That crazy TV kept me up all night. How can I sleep with something yelling crazy things all night in my ears. And the nutty pictures. Wow. I dont know what it says when Im up so how am I going to know when Im sleeping.

Dr Strauss says its ok. He says my brains are lerning when I sleep and that will help me when Miss Kinnian starts my lessons in the hospitl (only I found out it isnt a hospitil its a labatory). I think its all crazy. If you can get smart when your sleeping why do people go to school. That thing I dont think will work. I use to watch the late show and the late late show on TV all the time and it never made me smart. Maybe you have to sleep while you watch it.

PROGRESS REPORT 9—April 3

Dr Strauss showed me how to keep the TV turned low so now I can sleep. I don't hear a thing. And I still dont understand what it says. A few times I play it over in the morning to find out what I lerned when I was sleeping and I dont think so. Miss Kinnian says Maybe its another langwidge or something. But most times it sounds american. It talks so fast faster then even Miss Gold who was my teacher in 6 grade and I remember she talked so fast I coudnt understand her.

I told Dr Strauss what good is it to get smart in my sleep. I want to be smart when Im awake. He says its the same thing and I have two minds. Theres the *subconscious* and the *conscious* (thats how you spell it). And one dont tell the other one what its doing. They dont even talk to each other. Thats why I dream. And boy have I been having crazy dreams. Wow. Ever since that night TV. The late late late late late show.

I forgot to ask him if it was only me or if everybody had those two minds.

(I just looked up the word in the dictionary Dr Strauss gave me. The word is *subconscious. adj. Of the nature of mental operations yet not present in consciousness; as, sub-conscious conflict of desires.*) There's more but I still dont know what it means. This isnt a very good dictionary for dumb people like me.

Anyway the headache is from the party. My frends from the factery Joe Carp and Frank Reilly invited me to go with them to Muggsys Saloon for some drinks. I dont like to drink but they said we will have lots of fun. I had a good time.

Joe Carp said I shoud show the girls how I mop out the toilet in the factory and he got me a mop. I showed them and everyone laffed when I told that Mr Donnegan said I was the best janiter he ever had because I like my job and do it good and never come late or miss a day except for my operashun.

I said Miss Kinnian always said Charlie be proud of your job because you do it good.

Everybody laffed and we had a good time and they gave me lots of drinks and Joe said Charlie is a card when hes potted. I dont know what that means but everybody likes me and we have fun. I cant wait to be smart like my best frends Joe Carp and Frank Reilly.

I dont remember how the party was over but I think I went out to buy a newspaper and coffe for Joe and Frank and when I came back there was no one their. I looked for them all over till late. Then I dont remember so good but

I think I got sleepy or sick. A nice cop brot me back home. Thats what my landlady Mrs Flynn says.

But I got a headache and a big lump on my head and black and blue all over. I think maybe I fell but Joe Carp says it was the cop they beat up drunks some times. I dont think so. Miss Kinnian says cops are to help people. Anyway I got a bad headache and Im sick and hurt all over. I dont think Ill drink anymore.

April 6 I beat Algernon! I dint even know I beat him until Burt the tester told me. Then the second time I lost because I got so exited I fell off the chair before I finished. But after that I beat him 8 more times. I must be getting smart to beat a smart mouse like Algernon. But I dont *feel* smarter.

I wanted to race Algernon some more but Burt said thats enough for one day. They let me hold him for a minit. Hes not so bad. Hes soft like a ball of cotton. He blinks and when he opens his eyes their black and pink on the eges.

I said can I feed him because I felt bad to beat him and I wanted to be nice and make frends. Burt said no Algernon is a very specshul mouse with an operashun like mine, and he was the first of all the animals to stay smart so long. He told me Algernon is so smart that every day he has to solve a test to get his food. Its a thing like a lock on a door that changes every time Algernon goes in to eat so he has to lern something new to get his food. That made me sad because if he coudnt lern he woud be hungry.

I dont think its right to make you pass a test to eat. How woud Dr Nemur like it to have to pass a test every time he wants to eat. I think Ill be frends with Algernon.

April 9 Tonight after work Miss Kinnian was at the laboratory. She looked like she was glad to see me but scared. I told her dont worry Miss Kinnian Im not smart yet and she laffed. She said I have confidence in you Charlie the way you struggled so hard to read and right better than all the others. At werst you will have it for a littel wile and your doing somthing for sience.

We are reading a very hard book. I never read such a hard book before. Its called *Robinson Crusoe* about a man who gets merooned on a dessert Iland. Hes smart and figers out all kinds of things so he can have a house and food and hes a good swimmer. Only I feel sorry because hes all alone and has no frends. But I think their must be somebody else on the iland because theres a picture with his funny umbrella looking at footprints. I hope he gets a frend and not be lonly.

April 10   Miss Kinnian teaches me to spell better. She says look at a word and close your eyes and say it over and over until you remember. I have lots of truble with *through* that you say *threw* and *enough* and *tough* that you dont say *enew* and *tew*. You got to say *enuff* and *tuff*. Thats how I use to write it before I started to get smart. Im confused but Miss Kinnian says theres no reason in spelling.

Apr 14   Finished *Robinson Crusoe*. I want to find out more about what happens to him but Miss Kinnian says thats all there is. *Why*

Apr 15   Miss Kinnian says Im lerning fast. She read some of the Progress Reports and she looked at me kind of funny. She says Im a fine person and Ill show them all. I asked her why. She said never mind but I shoudnt feel bad if I find out that everybody isnt nice like I think. She said for a person who god gave so little to you done more then a lot of people with brains they never even used. I said all my frends are smart people but there good. They like me and they never did anything that wasnt nice. Then she got something in her eye and she had to run out to the ladys room.

Apr 16   Today, I lerned the *comma,* this is a comma (,) a period, with a tail, Miss Kinnian, says its importent, because, it makes writing, better, she said, somebody, coud lose, a lot of money, if a comma, isnt, in the, right place, I dont have, any money, and I dont see, how a comma, keeps you, from losing it,

But she says, everybody, uses commas, so Ill use, them too,

Apr 17 I used the comma wrong. Its punctuation. Miss Kinnian told me to look up long words in the dictionary to lern to spell them. I said whats the difference if you can read it anyway. She said its part of your education so now on Ill look up all the words Im not sure how to spell. It takes a long time to write that way but I think Im remembering. I only have to look up once and after that I get it right. Anyway thats how come I got the word *punctuation* right. (Its that way in the dictionary.) Miss Kinnian says a period is punctuation too, and there are lots of other marks to lern. I told her I thot all the periods had to have tails but she said no.

You got to mix them up, she showed? me" how. to mix! them(up,. and now; I can! mix up all kinds" of punctuation, in! my writing? There, are lots! of rules? to lern; but Im gettin'g them in my head.

One thing I? like about, Dear Miss Kinnian: (thats the way it goes in a business letter if I ever go into business) is she, always gives me' a reason" when—I ask. She's a gen'ius! I wish! I cou'd be smart" like, her;

(Punctuation, is; fun!)

Apr 18 What a dope I am! I didn't even understand what she was talking about. I read the grammar book last night and it explanes the whole thing. Then I saw it was the same way as Miss Kinnian was trying to tell me, but I didn't get it. I got up in the middle of the night, and the whole thing straightened out in my mind.

Miss Kinnian said that the TV working in my sleep helped out. She said I reached a plateau. Thats like the flat top of a hill.

After I figgered out how punctuation worked, I read over all my old Progress Reports from the beginning. Boy, did I have crazy spelling and punctuation! I told Miss Kinnian I ought to go over the pages and fix all the mistakes but she said, "No, Charlie, Dr. Nemur wants them just as they are. That's why he let you keep them after they were photostated, to see your own progress. You're coming along fast, Charlie."

That made me feel good. After the lesson I went down and played with Algernon. We don't race any more.

April 20   I feel sick inside. Not sick like for a doctor, but inside my chest it feels empty like getting punched and a heartburn at the same time.

I wasn't going to write about it, but I guess I got to, because its important. Today was the first time I ever stayed home from work.

Last night Joe Carp and Frank Reilly invited me to a party. There were lots of girls and some men from the factory. I remembered how sick I got last time I drank too much, so I told Joe I didn't want anything to drink. He gave me a plain coke instead. It tasted funny, but I thought it was just a bad taste in my mouth.

We had a lot of fun for a while. Joe said I should dance with Ellen and she would teach me the steps. I fell a few times and I couldn't understand why because no one else was dancing besides Ellen and me. And all the time I was tripping because somebody's foot was always sticking out.

Then when I got up I saw the look on Joe's face and it gave me a funny feeling in my stomack. "He's a scream," one of the girls said. Everybody was laughing.

Frank said, "I ain't laughed so much since we sent him off for the newspaper that night at Muggsy's and ditched him."

"Look at him. His face is red."

"He's blushing. Charlie is blushing."

"Hey, Ellen, what'd you do to Charlie? I never saw him act like that before."

I didn't know what to do or where to turn. Everyone was looking at me and laughing and I felt naked. I wanted to hide myself. I ran out into the street and I threw up. Then I walked home. It's a funny thing I never knew that Joe and Frank and the others liked to have me around all the time to make fun of me. Now I know what it means when they say "to pull a Charlie Gordon."

I'm ashamed.

PROGRESS REPORT 11

April 21   Still didn't go into the factory. I told Mrs. Flynn my landlady to call and tell Mr. Donnegan I was sick. Mrs. Flynn looks at me very funny lately like she's scared of me.

I think it's a good thing about finding out how everybody laughs at me. I thought about it a lot. It's because I'm so dumb and I don't even know when I'm doing something dumb. People think it's funny when a dumb person can't do things the same way they can.

Anyway, now I know I'm getting smarter every day. I know punctuation and I can spell good. I like to look up all the hard words in the dictionary and I remember them. I'm reading a lot now, and Miss Kinnian says I read very fast. Sometimes I even understand what I'm reading about, and it stays in my mind. There are times when I can close my eyes and think of a page and it all comes back like a picture.

Besides history, geography and arithmetic, Miss Kinnian said I should start to learn a few foreign languages. Dr. Strauss gave me some more tapes to play while I sleep. I still don't understand how that conscious and unconscious mind works, but Dr. Strauss says not to worry yet. He asked me to promise that when I start learning college subjects next week I wouldn't read any books on psychology—that is, until he gives me permission.

I feel a lot better today, but I guess I'm still a little angry that all the time people were laughing and making fun of me because I wasn't so smart. When I become intelligent like Dr. Strauss says, with three times my I.Q. of 68, then maybe I'll be like everyone else and people will like me and be friendly.

I'm not sure what an *I.Q.* is. Dr. Nemur said it was something that measured how intelligent you were—like a scale in the drugstore weighs pounds. But Dr. Strauss had a big arguement with him and said an I.Q. didn't weigh intelligence at all. He said an I.Q. showed how much intelligence you could get, like the numbers on the outside of a measuring cup. You still had to fill the cup up with stuff.

Then when I asked Burt, who gives me my intelligence tests and works with Algernon, he said that both of them were wrong (only I had to promise not to tell them he said so). Burt says that the I.Q. measures a lot of different things including some of the things you learned already, and it really isn't any good at all.

So I still don't know what I.Q. is except that mine is going to be over 200 soon. I didn't want to say anything, but I don't see how if they don't know *what* it is, or *where* it is—I don't see how they know *how much* of it you've got.

Dr. Nemur says I have to take a *Rorshach Test* tomorrow. I wonder what *that* is.

April 22   I found out what a *Rorshach* is. It's the test I took before the operation—the one with the inkblots on the pieces of cardboard. The man who gave me the test was the same one.

I was scared to death of those inkblots. I knew he was going to ask me to find the pictures and I knew I wouldn't be able to. I was thinking to myself, if only there was some way of knowing what kind of pictures were hidden there. Maybe there weren't any pictures at all. Maybe it was just a trick to see if I was dumb enough too look for something that wasn't there. Just thinking about that made me sore at him.

"All right, Charlie," he said, "you've seen these cards before, remember?"

"Of course I remember."

The way I said it, he knew I was angry, and he looked surprised. "Yes, of course. Now I want you to look at this one. What might this be? What do you see on this card? People see all sorts of things in these inkblots. Tell me what it might be for you—what it makes you think of."

I was shocked. That wasn't what I had expected him to say at all. "You mean there are no pictures hidden in those inkblots?"

He frowned and took off his glasses. "What?"

"Pictures. Hidden in the inkblots. Last time you told me

that everyone could see them and you wanted me to find them too."

He explained to me that the last time he had used almost the exact same words he was using now. I didn't believe it, and I still have the suspicion that he misled me at the time just for the fun of it. Unless—I don't know any more—could I have been *that* feeble-minded?

We went through the cards slowly. One of them looked like a pair of bats tugging at something. Another one looked like two men fencing with swords. I imagined all sorts of things. I guess I got carried away. But I didn't trust him any more, and I kept turning them around and even looking on the back to see if there was anything there I was supposed to catch. While he was making his notes, I peeked out of the corner of my eye to read it. But it was all in code that looked like this:

WF+A   DdF-Ad orig.   WF-A   SF+obj ·

The test still doesn't make sense to me. It seems to me that anyone could make up lies about things that they didn't really see. How could he know I wasn't making a fool of him by mentioning things that I didn't really imagine? Maybe I'll understand it when Dr. Strauss lets me read up on psychology.

April 25   I figured out a new way to line up the machines in the factory, and Mr. Donnegan says it will save him ten thousand dollars a year in labor and increased production. He gave me a $25 bonus.

I wanted to take Joe Carp and Frank Reilly out to lunch to celebrate, but Joe said he had to buy some things for his wife, and Frank said he was meeting his cousin for lunch. I guess it'll take a little time for them to get used to the changes in me. Everybody seems to be frightened of me. When I went over to Amos Borg and tapped him on the shoulder, he jumped up in the air.

People don't talk to me much any more or kid around the way they used to. It makes the job kind of lonely.

April 27   I got up the nerve today to ask Miss Kinnian to have dinner with me tomorrow night to celebrate my bonus.

At first she wasn't sure it was right, but I asked Dr. Strauss and he said it was okay. Dr. Strauss and Dr. Nemur don't seem to be getting along so well. They're arguing all the time. This evening when I came in to ask Dr. Strauss about having dinner with Miss Kinnian, I heard them shouting. Dr. Nemur was saying that it was *his* experiment and *his* research, and Dr. Strauss was shouting back that he contributed just as much, because he found me through Miss Kinnian and he performed the operation. Dr. Strauss said that someday thousands of neuro-surgeons might be using his technique all over the world.

Dr. Nemur wanted to publish the results of the experiment at the end of this month. Dr. Strauss wanted to wait a while longer to be sure. Dr. Strauss said that Dr. Nemur was more interested in the Chair of Psychology at Princeton than he was in the experiment. Dr. Nemur said that Dr. Strauss was nothing but an opportunist who was trying to ride to glory on *his* coattails.

When I left afterward, I found myself trembling. I don't know why for sure, but it was as if I'd seen both men clearly for the first time. I remember hearing Burt say that Dr. Nemur had a shrew of a wife who was pushing him all the time to get things published so that he could become famous. Burt said that the dream of her life was to have a big shot husband.

Was Dr. Strauss really trying to ride on his coattails?

April 28 I don't understand why I never noticed how beautiful Miss Kinnian really is. She has brown eyes and feathery brown hair that comes to the top of her neck. She's only thirty-four! I think from the beginning I had the feeling that she was an unreachable genius—and very, very old. Now, every time I see her she grows younger and more lovely.

We had dinner and a long talk. When she said that I was coming along so fast that soon I'd be leaving her behind, I laughed.

"It's true, Charlie. You're already a better reader than I am. You can read a whole page at a glance while I can take in only a few lines at a time. And you remember every single thing you read. I'm lucky if I can recall the main thoughts and the general meaning."

"I don't feel intelligent. There are so many things I don't understand."

She took out a cigarette and I lit it for her. "You've got to be a *little* patient. You're accomplishing in days and weeks what it takes normal people to do in half a lifetime. That's what makes it so amazing. You're like a giant sponge now, soaking things in. Facts, figures, general knowledge. And soon you'll begin to connect them, too. You'll see how the different branches of learning are related. There are many levels, Charlie, like steps on a giant ladder that take you up higher and higher to see more and more of the world around you.

"I can see only a little bit of that, Charlie, and I won't go much higher than I am now, but you'll keep climbing up and up, and see more and more, and each step will open new worlds that you never even knew existed." She frowned. "I hope . . . I just hope to God—"

"What?"

"Never mind, Charles. I just hope I wasn't wrong to advise you to go into this in the first place."

I laughed. "How could that be? It worked, didn't it? Even Algernon is still smart."

We sat there silently for a while and I knew what she was thinking about as she watched me toying with the chain of my rabbit's foot and my keys. I didn't want to think of that possibility any more than elderly people want to think of death. I *knew* that this was only the beginning. I knew what she meant about levels because I'd seen some of them already. The thought of leaving her behind made me sad.

I'm in love with Miss Kinnian.

PROGRESS REPORT 12

April 30 I've quit my job with Donnegan's Plastic Box Company. Mr. Donnegan insisted that it would be better for all concerned if I left. What did I do to make them hate me so?

The first I knew of it was when Mr. Donnegan showed me the petition. Eight hundred and forty names, everyone connected with the factory, except Fanny Girden. Scanning the list quickly, I saw at once that hers was the only missing name. All the rest demanded that I be fired.

Joe Carp and Frank Reilly wouldn't talk to me about it. No one else would either, except Fanny. She was one of the few people I'd known who set her mind to something and believed it no matter what the rest of the world proved, said or did—and Fanny did not believe that I should have been fired. She had been against the petition on principle and despite the pressure and threats she'd held out.

"Which don't mean to say," she remarked, "that I don't think there's something mighty strange about you, Charlie. Them changes. I don't know. You used to be a good, dependable, ordinary man—not too bright maybe, but honest. Who knows what you done to yourself to get so smart all of a sudden. Like everybody around here's been saying, Charlie, it's not right."

"But how can you say that, Fanny? What's wrong with a man becoming intelligent and wanting to acquire knowledge and understanding of the world around him?"

She stared down at her work and I turned to leave. Without looking at me, she said: "It was evil when Eve listened to the snake and ate from the tree of knowledge. It was evil when she saw that she was naked. If not for that none of us would ever have to grow old and sick, and die."

Once again now I have the feeling of shame burning inside me. This intelligence has driven a wedge between me and all the people I once knew and loved. Before, they laughed at me and despised me for my ignorance and dullness; now, they hate me for my knowledge and understanding. What in God's name do they want of me?

They've driven me out of the factory. Now I'm more alone than ever before. . . .

May 15 Dr. Strauss is very angry at me for not having

written any progress reports in two weeks. He's justified because the lab is now paying me a regular salary. I told him I was too busy thinking and reading. When I pointed out that writing was such a slow process that it made me impatient with my poor handwriting, he suggested that I learn to type. It's much easier to write now because I can type nearly seventy-five words a minute. Dr. Strauss continually reminds me of the need to speak and write simply so that people will be able to understand me.

I'll try to review all the things that happened to me during the last two weeks. Algernon and I were presented to the *American Psychological Association* sitting in convention with the *World Psychological Association* last Tuesday. We created quite a sensation. Dr. Nemur and Dr. Strauss were proud of us.

I suspect that Dr. Nemur, who is sixty—ten years older than Dr. Strauss—finds it necessary to see tangible results of his work. Undoubtedly the result of pressure by Mrs. Nemur.

Contrary to my earlier impressions of him, I realize that Dr. Nemur is not at all a genius. He has a very good mind, but it struggles under the specter of self-doubt. He wants people to take him for a genius. Therefore, it is important for him to feel that his work is accepted by the world. I believe that Dr. Nemur was afraid of further delay because he worried that someone else might make a discovery along these lines and take the credit from him.

Dr. Strauss on the other hand might be called a genius, although I feel that his areas of knowledge are too limited. He was educated in the tradition of narrow specialization; the broader aspects of background were neglected far more than necessary—even for a neuro-surgeon.

I was shocked to learn that the only ancient languages he could read were Latin, Greek and Hebrew, and that he knows almost nothing of mathematics beyond the elementary levels of the calculus of variations. When he admitted this to me, I found myself almost annoyed. It was as if he'd hidden this part of himself in order to deceive me, pretending—as do many people I've discovered—to be what he is not. No one I've ever known is what he appears to be on the surface.

Dr. Nemur appears to be uncomfortable around me. Sometimes when I try to talk to him, he just looks at me strangely and turns away. I was angry at first when Dr. Strauss told me I was giving Dr. Nemur an inferiority complex. I thought he was mocking me and I'm oversensitive at being made fun of.

How was I to know that a highly respected psycho-experimentalist like Nemur was unacquainted with Hindustani and Chinese? It's absurd when you consider the work that is being done in India and China today in the very field of his study.

I asked Dr. Strauss how Nemur could refute Rahajamati's attack on his method and results if Nemur couldn't even read them in the first place. That strange look on Dr. Strauss' face can mean only one of two things. Either he doesn't want to tell Nemur what they're saying in India, or else—and this worries me—Dr. Strauss doesn't know either. I must be careful to speak and write clearly and simply so that people won't laugh.

May 18 I am very disturbed. I saw Miss Kinnian last night for the first time in over a week. I tried to avoid all discussions of intellectual concepts and to keep the conversation on a simple, everyday level, but she just stared at me blankly and asked me what I meant about the mathematical variance equivalent in Dorbermann's *Fifth Concerto*.

When I tried to explain she stopped me and laughed. I guess I got angry, but I suspect I'm approaching her on the wrong level. No matter what I try to discuss with her, I am unable to communicate. I must review Vrostadt's equations on *Levels of Semantic Progression*. I find that I don't communicate with people much any more. Thank God for books and music and things I can think about. I am alone in my apartment at Mrs. Flynn's boarding house most of the time and seldom speak to anyone.

May 20 I would not have noticed the new dishwasher, a

boy of about sixteen, at the corner diner where I take my evening meals if not for the incident of the broken dishes.

They crashed to the floor, shattering and sending bits of white china under the tables. The boy stood there, dazed and frightened, holding the empty tray in his hand. The whistles and catcalls from the customers (the cries of "hey, there go the profits!" ... *"Mazeltov!"* ... and "well, *he* didn't work here very long ..." which invariably seems to follow the breaking of glass or dishware in a public restaurant) all seemed to confuse him.

When the owner came to see what the excitement was about, the boy cowered as if he expected to be struck and threw up his arms as if to ward off the blow.

"All right! All right, you dope," shouted the owner, "don't just stand there! Get the broom and sweep that mess up. A broom ... a broom, you idiot! It's in the kitchen. Sweep up all the pieces."

The boy saw that he was not going to be punished. His frightened expression disappeared and he smiled and hummed as he came back with the broom to sweep the floor. A few of the rowdier customers kept up the remarks, amusing themselves at his expense.

"Here, sonny, over here there's a nice piece behind you...."

"C'mon, do it again...."

"He's not so dumb. It's easier to break 'em than to wash 'em...."

As his vacant eyes moved across the crowd of amused onlookers, he slowly mirrored their smiles and finally broke into an uncertain grin at the joke which he obviously did not understand.

I felt sick inside as I looked at his dull, vacuous smile, the wide, bright eyes of a child, uncertain but eager to please. They were laughing at him because he was mentally retarded.

And I had been laughing at him too.

Suddenly, I was furious at myself and all those who were smirking at him. I jumped up and shouted, "Shut up! Leave him alone! It's not his fault he can't understand! He can't help what he is! But for God's sake . . . he's still a human being!"

The room grew silent. I cursed myself for losing control and creating a scene. I tried not to look at the boy as I paid my check and walked out without touching my food. I felt ashamed for both of us.

How strange it is that people of honest feelings and sensibility, who would not take advantage of a man born without arms or legs or eyes—how such people think nothing of abusing a man born with low intelligence. It infuriated me to think that not too long ago I, like this boy, had foolishly played the clown. And I had almost forgotten.

I'd hidden the picture of the old Charlie Gordon from myself because now that I was intelligent it was something that had to be pushed out of my mind. But today in looking at that boy, for the first time I saw what I had been. *I was just like him!*

Only a short time ago, I learned that people laughed at me. Now I can see that unknowingly I joined with them in laughing at myself. That hurts most of all.

I have often reread my progress reports and seen the illiteracy, the childish naïveté, the mind of low intelligence peering from a dark room, through the keyhole, at the dazzling light outside. I see that even in my dullness I knew that I was inferior, and that other people had something I lacked—something denied me. In my mental blindness, I thought that it was somehow connected with the ability to read and write, and I was sure that if I could get those skills I would automatically have intelligence too.

Even a feeble-minded man wants to be like other men.

A child may not know how to feed itself, or what to eat, yet it knows of hunger.

This then is what I was like. I never knew. Even with my gift of intellectual awareness, I never really knew.

This day was good for me. Seeing the past more clearly, I have decided to use my knowledge and skills to work in the field of increasing human intelligence levels. Who is better equipped for this work? Who else has lived in both worlds? These are my people. Let me use my gift to do something for them.

Tomorrow, I will discuss with Dr. Strauss the manner in which I can work in this area. I may be able to help him work out the problems of widespread use of the technique which was used on me. I have several good ideas of my own.

There is so much that might be done with this technique. If I could be made into a genius, what about thousands of others like myself? What fantastic levels might be achieved by using this technique on normal people? On *geniuses*?

There are so many doors to open. I am impatient to begin.

PROGRESS REPORT 13

May 23   It happened today. Algernon bit me. I visited the lab to see him as I do occasionally, and when I took him out of his cage, he snapped at my hand. I put him back and watched him for a while. He was unusually disturbed and vicious.

May 24   Burt, who is in charge of the experimental animals, tells me that Algernon is changing. He is less cooperative; he refuses to run the maze any more; general motivation has decreased. And he hasn't been eating. Everyone is upset about what this may mean.

May 25   They've been feeding Algernon, who now refuses to work the shifting-lock problem. Everyone identifies me with Algernon. In a way we're both the first of our kind. They're all pretending that Algernon's behavior is not necessarily significant for me. But it's hard to hide the fact that some of the other animals who were used in this experiment are showing strange behavior.

Dr. Strauss and Dr. Nemur have asked me not to come to the lab any more. I know what they're thinking but I can't accept it. I am going ahead with my plans to carry their research forward. With all due respect to both of these fine scientists, I am well aware of their limitations. If there is an answer, I'll have to find it out for myself. Suddenly, time has become very important to me.

May 29 I have been given a lab of my own and permission to go ahead with the research. I'm on to something. Working day and night. I've had a cot moved into the lab. Most of my writing time is spent on the notes which I keep in a separate folder, but from time to time I feel it necessary to put down my moods and my thoughts out of sheer habit.

I find the *calculus of intelligence* to be a fascinating study. Here is the place for the application of all the knowledge I have acquired. In a sense it's the problem I've been concerned with all my life.

May 31 Dr. Strauss thinks I'm working too hard. Dr. Nemur says I'm trying to cram a lifetime of research and thought into a few weeks. I know I should rest, but I'm driven on by something inside that won't let me stop. I've got to find the reason for the sharp regression in Algernon. I've got to know *if* and *when* it will happen to me.

June 4
LETTER TO DR. STRAUSS (copy)
Dear Dr. Strauss:

Under separate cover I am sending you a copy of my report entitled, "The Algernon-Gordon Effect: A study of Structure and Function of Increased Intelligence," which I would like to have you read and have published.

As you see, my experiments are completed. I have included in my report all of my formulae, as well as mathematical analysis in the appendix. Of course, these should be verified.

Because of its importance to both you and Dr. Nemur (and need I say to myself, too?) I have checked and rechecked my results a dozen times in the hope of finding an error. I am sorry to say the results must stand. Yet for the sake of science, I am grateful for the little bit that I here add to the knowledge of the function of the human mind and of the laws governing the artificial increase of human intelligence.

I recall your once saying to me that an experimental *failure* or the *disproving* of a theory was as important to the advancement of learning as a success would be. I know now that this is true. I am sorry, however, that my own contribution to the field must rest upon the ashes of the work of two men I regard so highly.

> Yours truly,
> Charles Gordon

encl.: rept.

June 5 I must not become emotional. The facts and the results of my experiments are clear, and the more sensational aspects of my own rapid climb cannot obscure the fact that the tripling of intelligence by the surgical technique developed by Drs. Strauss and Nemur must be viewed as having little or no practical applicability (at the present time) to the increase of human intelligence.

As I review the records and data on Algernon, I see that although he is still in his physical infancy, he has regressed mentally. Motor activity is impaired; there is a general reduction of glandular activity; there is an accelerated loss of co-ordination.

There are also strong indications of progressive amnesia.

As will be seen by my report, these and other physical and mental deterioration syndromes can be predicted with statistically significant results by the application of my formula.

The surgical stimulus to which we were both subjected has resulted in an intensification and acceleration of all mental processes. The unforeseen development, which I have taken the liberty of calling the *Algernon-Gordon Effect,* is the logical extension of the entire intelligence speed-up. The hypothesis here proven may be described simply in the following terms: Artificially increased intelligence deteriorates at a rate of time directly proportional to the quantity of the increase.

I feel that this, in itself, is an important discovery.

As long as I am able to write, I will continue to record my thoughts in these progress reports. It is one of my few pleasures. However, by all indications, my own mental deterioration will be very rapid.

I have already begun to notice signs of emotional instability and forgetfulness, the first symptoms of the burn-out.

June 10 Deterioration progressing. I have become absent-minded. Algernon died two days ago. Dissection shows my predictions were right. His brain had decreased in weight and there was a general smoothing out of cerebral convolutions as well as a deepening and broadening of brain fissures.

I guess the same thing is or will soon be happening to me. Now that it's definite, I don't want it to happen.

I put Algernon's body in a cheese box and buried him in the back yard. I cried.

June 15 Dr. Strauss came to see me again. I wouldn't open the door and I told him to go away. I want to be left to myself. I have become touchy and irritable. I feel the darkness closing in. It's hard to throw off thoughts of suicide. I keep telling myself how important this introspective journal will be.

It's a strange sensation to pick up a book that you've read and enjoyed just a few months ago and discover that you don't remember it. I remembered how great I thought John Milton was, but when I picked up *Paradise Lost* I couldn't understand it at all. I got so angry I threw the book across the room.

I've got to try to hold on to some of it. Some of the things I've learned. Oh, God, please don't take it all away.

June 19 Sometimes, at night, I go out for a walk. Last night I couldn't remember where I lived. A policeman took me home. I have the strange feeling that this has all happened to me before—a long time ago. I keep telling myself I'm the only person in the world who can describe what's happening to me.

June 21 Why can't I remember? I've got to fight. I lie in bed for days and I don't know who or where I am. Then it all comes back to me in a flash. Fugues of amnesia. Symptoms of senility—second childhood. I can watch them coming on. It's so cruelly logical. I learned so much and so fast. Now my mind is deteriorating rapidly. I won't let it happen. I'll fight it. I can't help thinking of the boy in the restaurant, the blank expression, the silly smile, the people laughing at him. No—please—not that again ...

June 22—I'm forgetting things that I learned recently. It seems to be following the classic pattern—the last things learned are the first things forgotten. Or is that the pattern? I'd better look it up again. . . .

I reread my paper on the *Algernon-Gordon Effect* and I get the strange feeling that it was written by someone else. There are parts I don't even understand.

Motor activity impaired. I keep tripping over things, and it becomes increasingly difficult to type.

June 23 I've given up using the typewriter completely. My co-ordination is bad. I feel that I'm moving slower and slower. Had a terrible shock today. I picked up a copy of an article I used in my research, Krueger's *Uber psychische Ganzheit*, to see if it would help me understand what I had done. First I thought there was something wrong with my eyes. Then I realized I could no longer read German. I tested myself in other languages. All gone.

June 30 A week since I dared to write again. It's slipping away like sand through my fingers. Most of the books I have are too hard for me now. I get angry with them because I know that I read and understood them just a few weeks ago.

I keep telling myself I must keep writing these reports so that somebody will know what is happening to me. But it gets harder to form the words and remember spellings. I have to look up even simple words in the dictionary now and it makes me impatient with myself.

Dr. Strauss comes around almost every day, but I told him I wouldn't see or speak to anybody. He feels guilty. They all do. But I don't blame anyone. I knew what might happen. But how it hurts.

July 7 I don't know where the week went. Todays Sunday I know because I can see through my window people going to church. I think I stayed in bed all week but I remember Mrs. Flynn bringing food to me a few times. I keep saying over and over Ive got to do something but then I forget or maybe its just easier not to do what I say Im going to do.

I think of my mother and father a lot these days. I found a picture of them with me taken at a beach. My father has a big ball under his arm and my mother is holding me by the hand. I dont remember them the way they are in the picture. All I remember is my father drunk most of the time and arguing with mom about money.

He never shaved much and he used to scratch my face when he hugged me. My mother said he died but Cousin Miltie said he heard his mom and dad say that my father ran away with another woman. When I asked my mother she slapped my face and said my father was dead. I dont think I ever found out which was true but I dont care much. (He said he was going to take me to see cows on a farm once but he never did. He never kept his promises. . . .)

July 10 My landlady Mrs Flynn is very worried about me. She says the way I lay around all day and dont do anything I remind her of her son before she threw him out of the house. She said she doesnt like loafers. If Im sick its one thing, but if Im a loafer thats another thing and she wont have it. I told her I think Im sick.

I try to read a little bit every day, mostly stories, but sometimes I have to read the same thing over and over again because I dont know what it means. And its hard to write. I know I should look up all the words in the dictionary but its so hard and Im so tired all the time.

Then I got the idea that I would only use the easy words instead of the long hard ones. That saves time. I put flowers on Algernons grave about once a week. Mrs Flynn thinks Im crazy to put flowers on a mouses grave but I told her that Algernon was special.

July 14 Its Sunday again. I dont have anything to do to

keep me busy now because my television set is broke and I dont have any money to get it fixed. (I think I lost this months check from the lab. I dont remember)

I get awful headaches and asperin doesnt help me much. Mrs Flynn knows Im really sick and she feels very sorry for me. Shes a wonderful woman whenever someone is sick.

July 22 Mrs Flynn called a strange doctor to see me. She was afraid I was going to die. I told the doctor I wasnt too sick and that I only forget sometimes. He asked me did I have any friends or relatives and I said no I dont have any. I told him I had a friend called Algernon once but he was a mouse and we used to run races together. He looked at me kind of funny like he thought I was crazy.

He smiled when I told him I used to be a genius. He talked to me like I was a baby and he winked at Mrs Flynn. I got mad and chased him out because he was making fun of me the way they all used to.

July 24 I have no more money and Mrs Flynn says I got to go to work somewhere and pay the rent because I havent paid for over two months. I dont know any work but the job I used to have at Donnegans Plastic Box Company. I dont want to go back there because they all knew me when I was smart and maybe they'll laugh at me. But I dont know what else to do to get money.

July 25 I was looking at some of my old progress reports and its very funny but I cant read what I wrote. I can make out some of the words but they dont make sense.

Miss Kinnian came to the door but I said go away I dont want to see you. She cried and I cried too but I wouldnt let her in because I didnt want her to laugh at me. I told her I didn't like her any more. I told her I didn't want to be smart any more. Thats not true. I still love her and I still want to be smart but I had to say that so shed go away. She gave Mrs. Flynn money to pay the rent. I dont want that. I got to get a job.

Please ... please let me not forget how to read and write. ...

July 27   Mr. Donnegan was very nice when I came back and asked him for my old job of janitor. First he was very suspicious but I told him what happened to me then he looked very sad and put his hand on my shoulder and said Charlie Gordon you got guts.

Everybody looked at me when I came downstairs and started working in the toilet sweeping it out like I used to. I told myself Charlie if they make fun of you dont get sore because you remember their not so smart as you once thot they were. And besides they were once your friends and if they laughed at you that doesnt mean anything because they liked you too.

One of the new men who came to work there after I went away made a nasty crack he said hey Charlie I hear your a very smart fella a real quiz kid. Say something intelligent. I felt bad but Joe Carp came over and grabbed him by the shirt and said leave him alone you lousy cracker or Ill break your neck. I didnt expect Joe to take my part so I guess hes really my friend.

Later Frank Reilly came over and said Charlie if anybody bothers you or trys to take advantage you call me or Joe and we will set em straight. I said thanks Frank and I got choked up so I had to turn around and go into the supply room so he wouldnt see me cry. Its good to have friends.

July 28   I did a dumb thing today I forgot I wasnt in Miss Kinnians class at the adult center any more like I use to be. I went in and sat down in my old seat in the back of the room and she looked at me funny and she said Charles. I dint remember she ever called me that before only Charlie so I said hello Miss Kinnian Im redy for my lesin today only I lost my reader that we was using. She startid to cry and run out of the room and everybody looked at me and I saw they wasnt the same pepul who use to be in my class.

Then all of a suddin I rememberd some things about

the operashun and me getting smart and I said holy smoke I reely pulled a Charlie Gordon that time. I went away before she come back to the room.

Thats why Im going away from New York for good. I dont want to do nothing like that agen. I dont want Miss Kinnian to feel sorry for me. Evry body feels sorry at the factery and I dont want that eather so Im going someplace where nobody knows that Charlie Gordon was once a genius and now he cant even reed a book or rite good.

Im taking a cuple of books along and even if I cant reed them Ill practise hard and maybe I wont forget every thing I lerned. If I try reel hard maybe Ill be a littel bit smarter then I was before the operashun. I got my rabits foot and my luky penny and maybe they will help me.

If you ever reed this Miss Kinnian dont be sorry for me Im glad I got a second chanse to be smart becaus I lerned a lot of things that I never even new were in this world and Im grateful that I saw it all for a littel bit. I dont know why Im dumb agen or what I did wrong maybe its becaus I dint try hard enuff. But if I try and practis very hard maybe Ill get a littl smarter and know what all the words are. I remember a littel bit how nice I had a feeling with the blue book that has the torn cover when I red it. Thats why Im gonna keep trying to get smart so I can have that feeling agen. Its a good feeling to know things and be smart. I wish I had it rite now if I did I woud sit down and reed all the time. Anyway I bet Im the first dumb person in the world who ever found out somthing importent for sience. I remember I did somthing but I dont remember what. So I gess its like I did it for all the dumb pepul like me.

Good-by Miss Kinnian and Dr. Strauss and evreybody. And P.S. please tell Dr Nemur not to be such a grouch when pepul laff at him and he woud have more frends. Its easy to make frends if you let pepul laff at you. Im going to have lots of frends where I go.

P.P.S. Please if you get a chanse put some flowrs on Algernons grave in the bak yard. . . .

"WHAT DO YOU MEAN . . . HUMAN?"

by John W. Campbell, Jr.
from *Astounding Science Fiction*

The incredible Mr. Amis singles out John Campbell several times for special notice. This is not unusual; almost anyone writing about modern American science fiction finds himself paying respects to the man under whose sometimes daft but always deft—and vigorous and enthusiastic—guidance, *ASF* (which you can take as *Astounding Science Fiction* or the new title, *Analog Science Fact and*—gasp—*Fiction*) has been the consistent leader in the field—both as to sales and influence. Mr. A., however, limits his comments about Campbell's influence to a snidish remark about cranks whose rapid departure would benefit the whole field and a description of the editor as "a deviant figure of marked ferocity."

I am here to say that I have talked with Campbell, literally and actually—and lived to go back for more. (I don't want to give the impression that talking *with* John is *easy*. But listening is lots of fun too, you know.) But we had lunch together, and both ate spaghetti, and there were no fangs, claws, or horns in evidence.

The following selection is a Campbell editorial from *ASF*. And now that I think of it, I suppose it is rather ferociously deviant of Mr. Campbell to want to "play robot."

There are some questions that only small children and very great philosophers are supposed to ask—questions like "What is Death?" and "Where is God?"

And then there are some questions that, apparently, no one is supposed to ask at all; largely, I think, because people have gotten so many wrong answers down through the centuries, that it's been agreed-by-default not to ask the questions at all.

Science fiction, however, by its very existence, has been asking one question that belongs in the "Let's agree not to discuss it at all" category—of course, simply by implication, but nevertheless very persistently. To wit: "What do you mean by the term 'human being'?"

It asks the question in a number of ways; the question of "What is a superman?" requires that we first define the limits of "normal man." The problem of "What's a robot?" asks the question in another way.

Some years ago now, Dr. Asimov introduced the Three Laws of Robotics into science fiction:

1. A robot cannot harm, nor allow harm to come to, a human being.

2. A robot must obey the orders of human beings.

3. A robot must, within those limits, protect itself against damage.

The crucial one is, of course, the First Law. The point that science fiction has elided very deftly is . . . how do you tell a robot what a human being is?

Look . . . I'll play robot; you tell me what you mean by "human being." What is this entity-type that I'm required to leave immune, and defend? How am I, Robot, to distinguish between the following entities: 1. A human idiot. 2. Another robot. 3. A baby. 4. A chimpanzee.

We might, quite legitimately, include a humanoid alien —or even Tregonsee, E. E. Smith's Rigellian Lensman, and Worsel, the Velantian—which we, as science-fictioneers, have agreed fulfill what we *really* mean by "human"! But let's not make the problem that tough just yet.

We do, however, have to consider the brilliant question Dr. W. Ross Ashby raised: If a mechanic with an artificial arm is working on an engine, is the mechanical arm part of the organism struggling with the environment, or part of the environment the organism is struggling with? If I, Robot, am to be instructed properly, we must consider human beings with prosthetic attachments. And, if I am a really functional robot, then that implies a level of technology that could turn up some very fancy prosthetic devices. Henry Kuttner some years back had a story about a man who had, through an accident, been reduced to a brain in a box; the box, however, had plug-in connections whereby it could be coupled to allow the brain in the box to "be" a whole spaceship, or a power-excavator, or any other appropriate machine.

Is this to be regarded as "a robot" or "a human being"? Intuitively we feel that, no matter how many prosthetic devices may be installed as replacements, the human being remains.

The theologians used to have a very handy answer to most of those questions; a human being, unlike animals or machines, has a soul. If that is to be included in the discussion, however, we must also include the associated problems of distinguishing between human beings and incubi, succubi, demons and angels. The problem then takes on certain other aspects . . . but the problem remains. History indicates that it was just as difficult to distinguish between humans and demons as it is, currently, to distinguish between humans and robots.

Let's try a little "truth-table" of the order that logicians sometimes use, and that advertisers are becoming fond of. We can try various suggested tests, and check off how the various entities we're trying to distinguish compare.

You can, of course, continue to extend this, with all the tests you care to think of. I believe you'll find that you can find no test within the entire scope of permissible-in-our-society-evaluations that will permit a clear distinction between the five entities in the table.

Note, too, that that robot you want to follow the Three Laws is to modify the Second Law—obedience—rather extensively with respect to children and idiots, after you've told it how to distinguish between humanoids and chimpanzees.

There have been a good many wars fought over the question "What do you mean . . . human?" To the Greeks, the peoples of other lands didn't really speak languages—which meant Greek—but made mumbling noises that sounded like *bar-bar-bar*, which proved they were *barbarians*, and not really human.

The law should treat all human beings alike; that's been held as a concept for a long, long time. The Athenians subscribed to that concept. Of course, barbarians weren't really human, so the Law didn't apply to them, and slaves weren't; in fact only Athenian citizens were.

The easy way to make the law apply equally to all men is to so define "men" that the thing actually works. "Equal Justice for All! (All who are equal, of course.)"

Test	Idiot	Robot	Baby	Chimp.	Man with Prosthetic aids
1. Capable of logical thought.	No	Yes	No	No	Yes.
2. "Do I not bleed?" (Merchant of Venice test.)	Yes	No	Yes	Yes	Depends.
3. Capable of speech.	Yes	Yes	No	No	Yes.
4. "Rational animal"; this must be divided into a. Rational b. Animal	No Yes	Yes No	No Yes	No Yes	Yes. Partly.
5. Humanoid form & size.	Yes	Yes	No	Yes	Maybe.
6. Lack of fur or hair.	*	Yes	Yes	Yes	Maybe partly.
7. A living being.	Yes	No	Yes	No	Depends on what test you use for "living."

*A visit to a beach in summer will convince you that some adult male humans have a thicker pelt than some gorillas.

This problem of defining what you mean by "human being" appears to be at least as prolific a source of conflict as religion—and may, in fact, be why religion, that being the relationship between Man and God, has been so violent a ferment.

The law never has and never will apply equally to all; there are inferiors and superiors, whether we like it or not, and Justice does not stem from applying the same laws equally to different levels of beings. Before blowing your stack on that one, look again and notice that every human culture has recognized that you could *not* have the same set of laws for children and adults—not since the saurians lost dominance on the planet has that concept been workable. (Reptilian forms are hatched from the egg with all the wisdom they're ever going to have; among reptiles of one species, there is only a difference of size and physical strength.)

Not only is there difference on a vertical scale, but there's displacement horizontally—i.e., different-but-equal, also exists. A woman may be equal to a man, but she's not the same as a man.

This, also, makes for complications when trying to decide "what is a human being"; there have been many cultures in history that definitely held that women weren't human.

I have a slight suspicion that the basic difficulty is that we can't get anything even approximating a workable concept of Justice so long as we consider equality a necessary, inherent part of it. The Law of Gravity applies equally to all bodies in the Universe—but that doesn't mean that the *force* of gravity is the same for all! Gravity—the universal law—is the same on Mars and a white dwarf star as it is on Earth. That doesn't mean that the *force* of gravity is the same.

But it takes considerable genius to come up with a Universal Law of Gravity for sheer, inanimate mass. What it takes to discover the equivalent for intelligent entities . . . the human race hasn't achieved as yet! Not even once has an individual reached that level!

This makes defining "human" a somewhat explosive subject.

Now the essence of humanity most commonly discussed by philosophers has been Man, the Rational Animal. The ability to think logically; to have ideas, and be conscious of having those ideas. The implied intent in "defining humanness" is to define the unique, highest-level attribute that sets man apart from all other entities.

That "rational animal" gimmick worked pretty well for a long time; the development of electronic computers, and the clear implication of robots calls it into question. That, plus the fact that psychological experiments have shown that logical thought isn't quite so unique-to-Man as philosophers thought.

The thing that is unique to human beings is something the philosophers have sputtered at, rejected, damned, and loudly forsworn throughout history. Man is the only known entity that laughs, weeps, grieves, and yearns. There's been considerable effort made to prove that those are the result of simple biochemical changes of endocrine balance. That is, that you feel angry because there is adrenalin in the bloodstream, released from the suprarenal glands. Yes, and the horse moves because the cart keeps pushing him. Why did the gland start secreting that extra charge of adrenalin?

The essence of our actual definition of humanness is "I am human; any entity that *feels* as I feel is human also. But any entity that merely thinks, and *feels* differently is not human."

The "inhuman scientist" is so called because he doesn't appear to *feel* as the speaker does. While we were discussing possible theological ramifications of the humanness question, we might have included the zombie. Why isn't a zombie "human" any longer? Because he has become the logical philosopher's ideal; a purely rational, nonemotional entity.

Why aren't Tregonsee, the Rigellian, and Worsel, the Velantian, to be compared with animals and/or robots?

Because, as defined in E. E. Smith's stories, they *feel* as we do.

Now it's long since been observed that an individual will find his logical thinking subtly biased in the direction of his emotional feelings. His actions will be controlled not by his logic and reason but, in the end, by his emotional pulls. If a man is my loyal friend— i.e., if he *feels* favorable-to-me —then whatever powers of physical force or mental brilliance he may have are no menace to me, but are a menace to my enemies. If he *feels* about things as I do, I need not concern myself with how he *thinks* about them, or what he does. He is "human"—my kind of human.

But . . . if he can *choose* his feelings, if his emotions are subject to his conscious, judicious, volitional choice . . . ? What then? If his emotional biases are not as rigidly unalterable as his bones? If he can exercise judgment and vary his feelings, can I trust him to remain "human"?

Could an entity who felt differently about things—whose emotions were different—be "human"?

That question may be somewhat important to us. Someone, sooner or later, is going to meet an alien, a really *alien* alien, not just a member of Homo sapiens from a divergent breed and culture.

Now it's true that all things are relative. Einstein proved the relativity of even the purely physical level of reality. But be it noted that Einstein proved that *Law* of Relativity; things aren't "purely relative" in the sense that's usually used—"I can take any system of relationships I choose!" There are laws of relativity.

The emotional biases a culture induces in its citizens vary widely. Mores is a matter of cultural relativity.

That doesn't mean that ethics is; there are laws of relativity, and it's not true that any arbitrary system of relationships is just as good as any other.

Can we humans-who-define-humanness-in-emotional-terms—despite what we theoretically say!—meet an equally wise race with different emotions—and know them for fellow humans?

A man who thinks differently we can tolerate and understand, but our history shows we don't know how to understand a man who feels differently.

The most frightening thing about a man who feels differently is this; his feelings might be contagious. We might learn to feel *his* way—and then, of course, we wouldn't be human any more.

The wiser and sounder his different feelings are, the greater the awful danger of learning to feel that way. And that would make us inhuman, of course.

How do you suppose an Athenian Greek of Pericles's

time would have felt if threatened with a change of feelings such that he would not feel disturbed if someone denied the reality of the Gods, or suggested that the Latins had a sounder culture? Why—only a nonhuman barbarian could feel that way!

The interesting thing is that the implication of "inhuman" is invariably *sub*human.

I suspect one of the most repugnant aspects of Darwin's concept of evolution was—not that we descended from monkeys—but its implication that something was apt to descend from us! Something that wasn't human . . . *and wasn't subhuman.*

The only perfect correlation is auto-correlation; "I am exactly what I am." Any difference whatever makes the correlation less perfect.

Then if what I feel is human—anything different is less perfectly correlated with humanness. Hence any entity not identical is more or less subhuman; there can't possibly be something more like me than I am.

Anybody want to try for a workable definition of "human"? One warning before you get started too openly; logical discussion doesn't lead to violence—until it enters the area of emotion.

As of now, we'd have to tell that robot "A human being is an entity having an emotional structure, as well as a physical and mental structure. Never mind what kind of emotional structure—good, indifferent, or insane. It's the fact of its existence that distinguishes the human."

Of course, that does lead to the problem of giving the robot emotion-perceptors so he can detect the existence of an emotion-structure.

And that, of course, gets almost as tough as the problem of distinguishing a masquerading demon from a man. You know . . . maybe they are the same problem?

It's always puzzled me that in the old days they detected so many demons, and so few angels, too. It always looked as though the Legions of Hell greatly outnumbered the Host of Heaven, or else were far more diligent on Earth.

But then . . . the subhuman is so much more acceptable than the superhuman.

SIERRA SAM

by Ralph Dighton
from Associated Press

Some years back I got tired of that aching feeling in my head, and resolved never again to pit an opinion of mine against one of John Campbell's—his are so much *stronger*.

By now, the habit of responding to Campbellian emphasis only with a) questions, or b) facts, is so ingrained that, lacking a really good question-story...

MAN-LIKE DEVICES USED IN U. S. TESTS

THEY FEEL HEAT AND COLD, SENSE SHOCK AND EVEN BREATHE AND BLEED

LOS ANGELES, Jan. 9 (AP)—The age of the robot is closer than you think.

Synthetic men that can feel heat and cold, sense shock in a way that is equivalent to pain, even bleed and breathe, are in use every day as stand-ins for humans in dangerous experiments.

They are anthropomorphic; that is, they have the shape of men. They are anthropometric, or weighted like men, with a man's center of gravity.

And they can be made to talk and walk like men whenever the need arises.

They can be bought for $1,500 up, depending on instrumentation.

The $1,500 model can't do much. He's the rugged, stupid type that gets thrown out of airplanes to test parachutes.

Headlines from *The New York Times*, Jan. 10, 1960.

TESTS GRAVITY

A $5,000 model rides on rocket sleds and centrifuges, pre-testing the forces of gravity and velocity that man will meet in space travel.

What would a walkie-talkie model cost?

"That's hard to say. We haven't made one yet," says Harry Daulton, President of Sierra Engineering Company in suburban Sierra Madre, the country's largest manufacturer of the robots.

"But I know we could make one," he says. "Two producers have asked us about them for science-fiction movies and our engineers said it could be done."

Daulton's top seller is Sierra Sam, a six-foot, 200-pounder made of vinyl-dipped foam Latex, with bones and joints of steel and aluminum.

Sam's midwife and physician is John Meyers, a former truck driver. "He can take 100 G's," Mr. Meyers said with pride.

That's 100 times the force of gravity, or five times as much as a strong man can take.

Mr. Meyers has made more than 200 Sams, and repaired most of them. Some have come back six or seven times from Air Force tests with their heads torn off, their backs and limbs broken, their bodies slashed, smashed, burnt and bent.

Mr. Meyers simply whips up a batch of foam Latex, pours it from mixer into mold and cures it in an electric oven. After dipping in vinyl, the new torso, head or limb is bolted into place.

The Air Force recently ordered a five-foot-six-inch dummy that may take a ride into space in a Project Mercury capsule one day.

The first Sam was built in 1949. As a maker of prosthetic devices—artificial arms and legs—Sierra Engineering saw the need for an instrumented human-like shape for rocket-sled speed tests.

The company fabricated a dummy and sold it to the Air Force, where it was promptly dubbed "Sierra Sam," a name that the company has copyrighted.

Since then Sams have parachuted from planes, tested ejection seats, whirled in centrifuges and crashed in hundreds of cars. They have figuratively saved thousands of lives by improving the safety design of vehicles that man rides in.

Now Sam has been instrumented with electronic devices that sense heat, cold, gravity forces, shock and wind velocity. Other devices closely duplicate human breathing apparatus for determination of what would happen to a man under such stresses.

A DEATH IN THE HOUSE

by Clifford D. Simak
from Galaxy

My first conscious acquaintance with Cliff Simak was in the body of a Jovian "Loper"—a lizard-sort-of-thing through whose keen senses we—Simak and I, along with the hero of the story, and his dog—were able to perceive for the first time the true grandeur of the giant planet's beauty.

If this sounds like a travelogue, it's just because it is. I doubt that anyone who read "Desertion" when it was first published in Astounding, or later as part of the prize-winning book, City, has ever quite forgotten the fresh tingling scent of that ammonia storm. . . .

Well, that was way back; and that was when I started looking for the Simak label on story titles. Exactly what sort of awareness Mr. Simak has that enables him to understand with a unique clarity the nature of strange beasts, I do not know; nor what specialized talent it is that contrives to communicate this empathy so sharply even to such a human-jingoist as me (as cool a clam as ever you've come across when it comes to cats and dogs and canaries, yet, let alone alien entities). All I know is that he is a newspaperman in Milwaukee, which is almost far enough away from Milford, Pa., for me to believe—most anything.

Old Mose Abrams was out hunting cows when he found the alien. He didn't know it was an alien, but it was alive and it was in a lot of trouble and Old Mose, despite everything the neighbors said about him, was not the kind of man who could bear to leave a sick thing out there in the woods.

It was a horrid-looking thing, green and shiny, with some purple spots on it, and it was repulsive even twenty feet away. And it stank.

It had crawled, or tried to crawl, into a clump of hazel

brush, but hadn't made it. The head part was in the brush and the rest lay out there naked in the open. Every now and then the parts that seemed to be arms and hands clawed feebly at the ground, trying to force itself deeper in the brush, but it was too weak; it never moved an inch.

It was groaning, too, but not too loud—just the kind of keening sound a lonesome wind might make around a wide, deep eave. But there was more in it than just the sound of winter wind; there was a frightened, desperate note that made the hair stand up on Old Mose's nape.

Old Mose stood there for quite a spell, making up his mind what he ought to do about it, and a while longer after that working up his courage, although most folks offhand would have said that he had plenty. But this was the sort of situation that took more than just ordinary screwed-up courage. It took a lot of foolhardiness.

But this was a wild, hurt thing and he couldn't leave it there, so he walked up to it and knelt down, and it was pretty hard to look at, though there was a sort of fascination in its repulsiveness that was hard to figure out—as if it were so horrible that it dragged one to it. And it stank in a way that no one had ever smelled before.

Mose, however, was not finicky. In the neighborhood, he was not well known for fastidity. Ever since his wife had died almost ten years before, he had lived alone on his untidy farm and the housekeeping that he did was the scandal of all the neighbor women. Once a year, if he got around to it, he sort of shoveled out the house, but the rest of the year he just let things accumulate.

So he wasn't as upset as some might have been with the way the creature smelled. But the sight of it upset him, and it took him quite a while before he could bring himself to touch it, and when he finally did, he was considerably surprised. He had been prepared for it to be either cold or slimy, or maybe even both. But it was neither. It was warm and hard and it had a clean feel to it, and he was reminded of the way a green corn stalk would feel.

He slid his hand beneath the hurt thing and pulled it gently from the clump of hazel brush and turned it over so he could see its face. It hadn't any face. It had an enlargement at the top of it, like a flower on top of a stalk, although its body wasn't any stalk, and there was a fringe around this enlargement that wiggled like a can of worms, and it was then that Mose almost turned around and ran.

But he stuck it out.

He squatted there, staring at the no-face with the fringe of worms, and he got cold all over and his stomach doubled up on him and he was stiff with fright—and the fright got worse when it seemed to him that the keening of the thing was coming from the worms.

Mose was a stubborn man. One had to be stubborn to run a runty farm like this. Stubborn and insensitive in a lot of ways. But not insensitive, of course, to a thing in pain.

Finally he was able to pick it up and hold it in his arms and there was nothing to it, for it didn't weigh much. Less than a half-grown shoat, he figured.

He went up the woods path with it, heading back for home, and it seemed to him the smell of it was less. He was hardly scared at all and he was warm again and not cold all over.

For the thing was quieter now and keening just a little. And although he could not be sure of it, there were times when it seemed as if the thing were snuggling up to him, the way a scared and hungry baby will snuggle to any grown person that comes and picks it up.

Old Mose reached the buildings and he stood out in the yard a minute, wondering whether he should take it to the barn or house. The barn, of course, was the natural place for it, for it wasn't human—it wasn't even as close to human as a dog or cat or sick lamb would be.

He didn't hesitate too long, however. He took it into the house and laid it on what he called a bed, next to the kitchen stove. He got it straightened out all neat and orderly and pulled a dirty blanket over it, and then went to the stove and stirred up the fire until there was some flame.

Then he pulled up a chair beside the bed and had a good, hard, wondering look at this thing he had brought home. It had quieted down a lot and seemed more comfortable than it had out in the woods. He tucked the blanket snug around it with a tenderness that surprised himself. He wondered what he had that it might eat, and even if he knew, how he'd manage feeding it, for it seemed to have no mouth.

"But you don't need to worry none," he told it. "Now that I got you under a roof, you'll be all right. I don't know too much about it, but I'll take care of you the best I can."

By now it was getting on toward evening, and he looked out the window and saw that the cows he had been hunting had come home by themselves.

"I got to go get the milking done and the other chores," he told the thing lying on the bed, "but it won't take me long. I'll be right back."

Old Mose loaded up the stove so the kitchen would stay warm and he tucked the thing in once again, then got his milk pails and went down to the barn.

He fed the sheep and pigs and horses and he milked the cows. He hunted eggs and shut the chicken house. He pumped a tank of water.

Then he went back to the house.

It was dark now and he lit the oil lamp on the table, for he was against electricity. He'd refused to sign up when REA had run out the line and a lot of the neighbors had gotten sore at him for being unco-operative. Not that he cared, of course.

He had a look at the thing upon the bed. It didn't seem to be any better, or any worse, for that matter. If it had been a sick lamb or an ailing calf, he could have known right off how it was getting on, but this thing was different. There was no way to tell.

He fixed himself some supper and ate it and wished he knew how to feed the thing. And he wished, too, that he knew how to help it. He'd got it under shelter and he had it warm, but was that right or wrong for something like this? He had no idea.

He wondered if he should try to get some help, then felt squeamish about asking help when he couldn't say exactly what had to be helped. But then he wondered how he would feel himself if he were in a far, strange country, all played out and sick, and no one to get him any help because they didn't know exactly what he was.

That made up his mind for him and he walked over to the phone. But should he call a doctor or a veterinarian? He decided to call the doctor because the thing was in the house. If it had been in the barn, he would have called the veterinarian.

He was on a rural line and the hearing wasn't good and he was halfway deaf, so he didn't use the phone too often. He had told himself at times it was nothing but another aggravation and there had been a dozen times he had threatened to have it taken out. But now he was glad he hadn't.

The operator got old Doctor Benson and they couldn't hear one another too well, but Mose finally made the doctor understand who was calling and that he needed him and the doctor said he'd come.

With some relief, Mose hung up the phone and was just standing there, not doing anything, when he was struck by the thought that there might be others of these things down there in the woods. He had no idea what they were or what they might be doing or where they might be going, but it was pretty evident that the one upon the bed was some sort of stranger from a very distant place. It stood to reason that there might be more than one of them, for far traveling was a lonely business and anyone—or anything—would like to have some company along.

He got the lantern down off the peg and lit it and went stumping out the door. The night was as black as a stack of cats and the lantern light was feeble, but that made not a bit of difference, for Mose knew this farm of his like the back of his hand.

He went down the path into the woods. It was a spooky place, but it took more than woods at night to spook Old Mose. At the place where he had found the thing, he looked around, pushing through the brush and holding the lantern high so he could see a bigger area, but he didn't find another one of them.

He did find something else, though—a sort of outsize birdcage made of metal lattice work that had wrapped itself around an eight-inch hickory tree. He tried to pull it loose, but it was jammed so tight that he couldn't budge it.

He sighted back the way it must have come. He could see where it had plowed its way through the upper branches of the trees, and out beyond were stars, shining bleakly with the look of far away.

Mose had no doubt that the thing lying on his bed beside the kitchen stove had come in this birdcage contraption. He marveled some at that, but he didn't fret himself too much, for the whole thing was so unearthly that he knew he had little chance of pondering it out.

He walked back to the house and he scarcely had the lantern blown out and hung back on its peg than he heard a car drive up.

The doctor, when he came up to the door, became a little grumpy at seeing Old Mose standing there.

"You don't look sick to me," the doctor said. "Not sick enough to drag me clear out here at night."

"I ain't sick," said Mose.

"Well, then," said the doctor, more grumpily than ever, "what did you mean by phoning me?"

"I got someone who is sick," said Mose. "I hope you can help him. I would have tried myself, but I don't know how to go about it."

The doctor came inside and Mose shut the door behind him.

"You got something rotten in here?" asked the doctor.

"No, it's just the way he smells. It was pretty bad at first, but I'm getting used to it by now."

The doctor saw the thing lying on the bed and went over to it. Old Mose heard him sort of gasp and could see him standing there, very stiff and straight. Then he bent down and had a good look at the critter on the bed.

When he straightened up and turned around to Mose, the only thing that kept him from being downright angry was that he was so flabbergasted.

"Mose," he yelled, "what *is* this?"

"I don't know," said Mose. "I found it in the woods and it was hurt and wailing and I couldn't leave it there."

"You think it's sick?"

"I know it is," said Mose. "It needs help awful bad. I'm afraid it's dying."

The doctor turned back to the bed again and pulled the blanket down, then went and got the lamp so that he could see. He looked the critter up and down, and he prodded it with a skittish finger, and he made the kind of mysterious clucking sound that only doctors make.

Then he pulled the blanket back over it again and took the lamp back to the table.

"Mose," he said, "I can't do a thing for it."

"But you're a doctor!"

"A human doctor, Mose. I don't know what this thing is, but it isn't human. I couldn't even guess what is wrong with it, if anything. And I wouldn't know what could be safely done for it even if I could diagnose its illness. I'm not even sure its an animal. There are a lot of things about it that argue it's a plant."

Then the doctor asked Mose straight out how he came to find it and Mose told him exactly how it happened. But he didn't tell him anything about the birdcage, for when he thought about it, it sounded so fantastic that he couldn't bring himself to tell it. Just finding the critter and having it here was bad enough, without throwing in the birdcage.

"I tell you what," the doctor said. "You got something here that's outside all human knowledge. I doubt there's ever been a thing like this seen on Earth before. I have no idea what it is and I wouldn't try to guess. If I were you, I'd get in touch with the university up at Madison. There might be someone there who could get it figured out. Even if they couldn't they'd be interested. They'd want to study it."

Mose went to the cupboard and got the cigar box almost full of silver dollars and paid the doctor. The doctor put the dollars in his pocket, joshing Mose about his eccentricity.

But Mose was stubborn about his silver dollars. "Paper money don't seem legal, somehow," he declared. "I like the feel of silver and the way it clinks. It's got authority."

The doctor left and he didn't seem as upset as Mose had

been afraid he might be. As soon as he was gone, Mose pulled up a chair and sat down beside the bed.

It wasn't right, he thought, that the thing should be so sick and no one to help—no one who knew any way to help it.

He sat in the chair and listened to the ticking of the clock, loud in the kitchen silence, and the crackling of the wood burning in the stove.

Looking at the thing lying on the bed, he had an almost fierce hope that it could get well again and stay with him. Now that its birdcage was all banged up, maybe there'd be nothing it could do but stay. And he hoped it would, for already the house felt less lonely.

Sitting in the chair between the stove and bed, Mose realized how lonely it had been. It had not been quite so bad until Towser died. He had tried to bring himself to get another dog, but he never had been able to. For there was no dog that would take the place of Towser and it had seemed unfaithful to even try. He could have gotten a cat, of course, but that would remind him too much of Molly; she had been very fond of cats, and until the time she died, there had always been two or three of them underfoot around the place.

But now he was alone. Alone with his farm and his stubbornness and his silver dollars. The doctor thought, like all the rest of them, that the only silver Mose had was in the cigar box in the cupboard. There wasn't one of them who knew about the old iron kettle piled plumb full of them, hidden underneath the floor boards of the living room. He chuckled at the thought of how he had them fooled. He'd give a lot to see his neighbors' faces if they could only know. But he was not the one to tell them. If they were to find it out, they'd have to find it out themselves.

He nodded in the chair and finally he slept, sitting upright, with his chin resting on his chest and his crossed arms wrapped around himself as if to keep him warm.

When he woke, in the dark before the dawn, with the lamp flickering on the table and the fire in the stove burned low, the alien had died.

There was no doubt of death. The thing was cold and

rigid and the husk that was its body was rough and drying out—as a corn stalk in the field dries out, whipping in the wind once the growing had been ended.

Mose pulled the blanket up to cover it, and although this was early to do the chores, he went out by lantern light and got them done.

After breakfast, he heated water and washed his face and shaved, and it was the first time in years he'd shaved any day but Sunday. Then he put on his one good suit and slicked down his hair and got the old jalopy out of the machine shed and drove into town.

He hunted up Eb Dennison, the town clerk, who also was the secretary of the cemetery association.

"Eb," he said, "I want to buy a lot."

"But you've got a lot," protested Eb.

"That plot," said Mose, "is a family plot. There's just room for me and Molly."

"Well, then," asked Eb, "why another one? You have no other members of the family."

"I found someone in the woods," said Mose. "I took him home and he died last night. I plan to bury him."

"If you found a dead man in the woods," Eb warned him, "you better notify the coroner and sheriff."

"In time I may," said Mose, not intending to. "Now how about that plot?"

Washing his hands of the affair entirely, Eb sold him the plot.

Having bought his plot, Mose went to the undertaking establishment run by Albert Jones.

"Al," he said, "there's been a death out at the house. A stranger I found out in the woods. He doesn't seem to have anyone and I aim to take care of it."

"You got a death certificate?" asked Al, who subscribed to none of the niceties affected by most funeral parlor operators.

"Well, no, I haven't."

"Was there a doctor in attendance?"

"Doc Benson came out last night."

"He should have made you out one. I'll give him a ring."

He phoned Doctor Benson and talked with him a while

and got red around the gills. He finally slammed down the phone and turned on Mose.

"I don't know what you're trying to pull off," he fumed, "but Doc tells me this thing of yours isn't even human. I don't take care of dogs or cats or—"

"This ain't no dog or cat."

"I don't care what it is. It's got to be human for me to handle it. And don't go trying to bury it in the cemetery, because it's against the law."

Considerably discouraged, Mose left the undertaking parlor and trudged slowly up the hill toward the town's one and only church.

He found the minister in his study working on a sermon. Mose sat down in a chair and fumbled his battered hat around and around in his work-scarred hands.

"Parson," he said, "I'll tell you the story from first to last," and he did. He added, "I don't know what it is. I guess no one else does, either. But it's dead and in need of decent burial and that's the least that I can do. I can't bury it in the cemetery, so I suppose I'll have to find a place for it on the farm. I wonder if you could bring yourself to come out and say a word or two."

The minister gave the matter some deep consideration.

"I'm sorry, Mose," he said at last. "I don't believe I can. I am not sure at all the church would approve of it."

"This thing may not be human," said Old Mose, "but it is one of God's critters."

The minister thought some more, and did some wondering out loud, but made up his mind finally that he couldn't do it.

So Mose went down the street to where his car was waiting and drove home, thinking about what heels some humans are.

Back at the farm again, he got a pick and shovel and went into the garden, and there, in one corner of it, he dug a grave. He went out to the machine shed to hunt up some boards to make the thing a casket, but it turned out that he had used the last of the lumber to patch up the hog pen.

Mose went to the house and dug around in a chest in one of the back rooms which had not been used for years, hunting for a sheet to use as a winding shroud, since there would be no casket. He couldn't find a sheet, but he did unearth an old white linen table cloth. He figured that would do, so he took it to the kitchen.

He pulled back the blanket and looked at the critter lying there in death and a sort of lump came into his throat at the thought of it—how it had died so lonely and so far from home without a creature of its own to spend its final hours with. And naked, too, without a stitch of clothing and with no possession, with not a thing to leave behind as a remembrance of itself.

He spread the table cloth out on the floor beside the bed and lifted the thing and laid it on the table cloth. As he laid it down, he saw the pocket in it—if it was a pocket—a sort of slitted flap in the center of what could be its chest. He ran his hand across the pocket area. There was a lump inside it. He crouched for a long moment beside the body, wondering what to do.

Finally he reached his fingers into the flap and took out the thing that bulged. It was a ball, a little bigger than a tennis ball, made of cloudy glass—or, at least, it looked like glass. He squatted there, staring at it, then took it to the window for a better look.

There was nothing strange at all about the ball. It was just a cloudy ball of glass and it had a rough, dead feel about it, just as the body had.

He shook his head and took it back and put it where he'd found it and wrapped the body securely in the cloth. He carried it to the garden and put it in the grave. Standing solemnly at the head of the grave, he said a few short words and then shoveled in the dirt.

He had meant to make a mound above the grave and he had intended to put up a cross, but at the last he didn't do either one of these. There would be snoopers. The word would get around and they'd be coming out and hunting for the spot where he had buried this thing he had found out in the woods. So there must be no mound to mark the place and no cross as well. Perhaps it was for the best, he told himself, for what could he have carved or written on the cross?

By this time it was well past noon and he was getting hungry, but he didn't stop to eat, because there were other things to do. He went out into the pasture and caught up Bess and hitched her to the stoneboat and went down into the woods.

He hitched her to the birdcage that was wrapped around the tree and she pulled it loose as pretty as you please. Then he loaded it on the stoneboat and hauled it up the hill and stowed it in the back of the machine shed, in the far corner by the forge.

After that, he hitched Bess to the garden plow and gave the garden a cultivating that it didn't need so it would be fresh dirt all over and no one could locate where he'd dug the grave.

He was just finishing the plowing when Sheriff Doyle drove up and got out of the car. The sheriff was a soft-spoken man, but he was no dawdler. He got right to the point.

"I hear," he said, "you found something in the woods."

"That I did," said Mose.

"I hear it died on you."

"Sheriff, you heard right."

"I'd like to see it, Mose."

"Can't. I buried it. And I ain't telling where."

"Mose," the sheriff said, "I don't want to make you trouble, but you did an illegal thing. You can't go finding people in the woods and just bury them when they up and die on you."

"You talk to Doc Benson?"

The sheriff nodded. "He said it wasn't any kind of thing he'd ever seen before. He said it wasn't human."

"Well, then," said Mose, "I guess that lets you out. If it wasn't human, there could be no crime against a person. And if it wasn't owned, there ain't any crime against property. There's been no one around to claim they owned the thing, is there?"

The sheriff rubbed his chin. "No, there hasn't. Maybe you're right. Where did you study law?"

"I never studied law. I never studied nothing. I just use common sense."

"Doc said something about the folks up at the university might want a look at it."

"I tell you, Sheriff," said Mose. "This thing came here from somewhere and it died. I don't know where it came from and I don't know what it was and I don't hanker none to know. To me it was just a living thing that needed help real bad. It was alive and it had its dignity and in death it commanded some respect. When the rest of you refused it decent burial, I did the best I could. And that is all there is to it."

"All right, Mose," the sheriff said, "if that's how you want it."

He turned around and stalked back to the car. Mose stood beside old Bess hitched to her plow and watched him drive away. He drove fast and reckless as if he might be angry.

Mose put the plow away and turned the horse back to the pasture and by now it was time to do chores again.

He got the chores all finished and made himself some supper and after supper sat beside the stove, listening to the ticking of the clock, loud in the silent house, and the crackle of the fire.

All night long the house was lonely.

The next afternoon, as he was plowing corn, a reporter came and walked up the row with him and talked with him when he came to the end of the row. Mose didn't like this reporter much. He was too flip and he asked some funny questions, so Mose clammed up and didn't tell him much.

A few days later, a man showed up from the university and showed him the story the reporter had gone back and written. The story made fun of Mose.

"I'm sorry," the professor said. "These newspapermen are unaccountable. I wouldn't worry too much about anything they write."

"I don't," Mose told him.

The man from the university asked a lot of questions and made quite a point about how important it was that he should see the body.

But Mose only shook his head. "It's at peace," he said. "I aim to leave it that way."

The man went away disgusted, but still quite dignified.

For several days there were people driving by and dropping in, the idly curious, and there were some neighbors Mose hadn't seen for months. But he gave them all short shrift and in a little while they left him alone and he went on with his farming and the house stayed lonely.

He thought again that maybe he should get a dog, but he thought of Towser and he couldn't do it.

One day, working in the garden, he found the plant that grew out of the grave. It was a funny-looking plant and his first impulse was to root it out.

But he didn't do it, for the plant intrigued him. It was a kind he'd never seen before and he decided he would let it grow, for a while at least, to see what kind it was. It was a bulky, fleshy plant, with heavy, dark-green, curling leaves, and it reminded him in some ways of the skunk cabbage that burgeoned in the woods come spring.

There was another visitor, the queerest of the lot. He was a dark and intense man who said he was the president of a flying saucer club. He wanted to know if Mose had talked with the thing he'd found out in the woods and seemed terribly disappointed when Mose told him he hadn't. He wanted to know if Mose had found a vehicle the creature might have traveled in and Mose lied to him about it. He was afraid, the wild way the man was acting, that he might demand to search the place, and if he had, he'd likely have found the birdcage hidden in the machine shed back in the corner by the forge. But the man got to lecturing Mose about withholding vital information.

Finally Mose had taken all he could of it, so he stepped into the house and picked up the shotgun from behind the door. The president of the flying saucer club said good-by rather hastily and got out of there.

Farm life went on as usual, with the corn laid by and the haying started and out in the garden the strange plant kept on growing and now was taking shape. Old Mose couldn't believe his eyes when he saw the sort of shape it took and he spent long evening hours just standing in the garden, watching it and wondering if his loneliness were playing tricks on him.

The morning came when he found the plant standing at the door and waiting for him. He should have been surprised, of course, but he really wasn't, for he had lived with it, watching it of eventide, and although he had not dared admit it even to himself, he had known what it was.

For here was the creature he'd found in the woods, no longer sick and keening, no longer close to death, but full of life and youth.

It was not the same entirely, though. He stood and looked at it and could see the differences—the little differences that might have been those between youth and age, or between a father and a son, or again the differences expressed in an evolutionary pattern.

"Good morning," said Mose, not feeling strange at all to be talking to the thing. "It's good to have you back."

The thing standing in the yard did not answer him. But that was not important; he had not expected that it would. The one important point was that he had something he could talk to.

"I'm going out to do the chores," said Mose. "You want to tag along?"

It tagged along with him and it watched him as he did the chores and he talked to it, which was a vast improvement over talking to himself.

At breakfast, he laid an extra plate for it and pulled up an extra chair, but it turned out the critter was not equipped to use a chair, for it wasn't hinged to sit.

Nor did it eat. That bothered Mose at first, for he was hospitable, but he told himself that a big, strong, strapping youngster like this one knew enough to take care of itself, and he probably didn't need to worry too much about how it got along.

After breakfast, he went out to the garden, with the critter accompanying him, and sure enough, the plant was gone. There was a collapsed husk lying on the ground, the outer covering that had been the cradle of the creature at his side.

Then he went to the machine shed and the creature saw the birdcage and rushed over to it and looked it over minutely. Then it turned around to Mose and made a sort of pleading gesture.

Mose went over to it and laid his hands on one of the twisted bars and the critter stood beside him and laid its hands on, too, and they pulled together. It was no use. They could move the metal some, but not enough to pull it back in shape again.

They stood and looked at one another, although looking may not be the word, for the critter had no eyes to look with. It made some funny motions with its hands, but Mose couldn't understand. Then it lay down on the floor and showed him how the birdcage ribs were fastened to the base.

It took a while for Mose to understand how the fastening worked and he never did know exactly why it did. There wasn't, actually, any reason that it should work that way.

First you applied some pressure, just the right amount at the exact and correct angle, and the bar would move a little. Then you applied some more pressure, again the exact amount and at the proper angle, and the bar would move some more. You did this three times and the bar came loose, although there was, God knows, no reason why it should.

Mose started a fire in the forge and shoveled in some coal and worked the bellows while the critter watched. But when he picked up the bar to put it in the fire, the critter got between him and the forge and wouldn't let him near. Mose realized then he couldn't—or wasn't supposed to— heat the bar to straighten it and he never questioned the entire rightness of it. For, he told himself, this thing must surely know the proper way to do it.

So he took the bar over to the anvil and started hammering it back into shape again, cold, without the use of fire, while the critter tried to show him the shape that it should be. It took quite a while, but finally it was straightened out to the critter's satisfaction.

Mose figured they'd have themselves a time getting the bar back in place again, but it slipped on as slick as could be.

Then they took off another bar and this one went faster, now that Mose had the hang of it.

But it was hard and grueling labor. They worked all day and only straightened out five bars.

It took four solid days to get the bars on the birdcage hammered into shape and all the time the hay was waiting to be cut.

But it was all right with Mose. He had someone to talk to and the house had lost its loneliness.

When they got the bars back in place, the critter slipped into the cage and starting fooling with a dingus on the roof of it that looked like a complicated basket. Mose, watching, figured that the basket was some sort of control.

The critter was discouraged. It walked around the shed looking for something and seemed unable to find it. It came back to Mose and made its despairing, pleading gesture. Mose showed it iron and steel; he dug into a carton where he kept bolts and clamps and bushings and scraps of metal and other odds and ends, finding brass and copper and even some aluminum, but it wasn't any of these.

And Mose was glad—a bit ashamed for feeling glad, but glad all the same.

For it had been clear to him that when the birdcage was all ready, the critter would be leaving him. It had been impossible for Mose to stand in the way of the repair of the cage, or to refuse to help. But now that it apparently couldn't be, he found himself well pleased.

Now the critter would have to stay with him and he'd have someone to talk to and the house would not be lonely. It would be welcome, he told himself, to have folks again. The critter was almost as good a companion as Towser.

Next morning, while Mose was fixing breakfast, he reached up in the cupboard to get the box of oatmeal and his hand struck the cigar box and it came crashing to the floor. It fell over on its side and the lid came open and the dollars went free-wheeling all around the kitchen.

Out of the corner of his eye, Mose saw the critter leaping quickly in pursuit of one of them. It snatched it up and turned to Mose, with the coin held between its fingers, and a sort of thrumming noise was coming out of the nest of worms on top of it.

It bent and scooped up more of them and cuddled them and danced a sort of jig, and Mose knew, with a sinking heart, that it had been silver the critter had been hunting.

So Mose got down on his hands and knees and helped the critter gather up all the dollars. They put them back into the cigar box and Mose picked up the box and gave it to the critter.

The critter took it and hefted it and had a disappointed look. Taking the box over to the table, it took the dollars out and stacked them in neat piles and Mose could see it was very disappointed.

Perhaps, after all, Mose thought, it had not been silver the thing had been hunting for. Maybe it had made a mistake in thinking that the silver was some other kind of metal.

Mose got down the oatmeal and poured it into some water and put it on the stove. When it was cooked and the coffee was ready, he carried his breakfast to the table and sat down to eat.

The critter still was standing across the table from him, stacking and restacking the piles of silver dollars. And now it showed him with a hand held above the stacks, that it needed more of them. This many stacks, it showed him, and each stack so high.

Mose sat stricken, with a spoon full of oatmeal halfway to his mouth. He thought of all those other dollars, the iron kettle packed with them, underneath the floor boards in the living room. And he couldn't do it; they were the only thing he had—except the critter now. And he could not give them up so the critter could go and leave him too.

He ate his bowl of oatmeal without tasting it and drank two cups of coffee. And all the time the critter stood there and showed him how much more it needed.

"I can't do it for you," Old Mose said. "I've done all you can expect of any living being. I found you in the woods and I gave you warmth and shelter. I tried to help you, and when I couldn't, at least I gave you a place to die in. I buried you and protected you from all those other people and I did not pull you up when you started growing once again. Surely you can't expect me to keep on giving endlessly."

But it was no good. The critter could not hear him and he did not convince himself.

He got up from the table and walked into the living room with the critter trailing him. He loosened the floor boards and took out the kettle, and the critter, when it saw what was in the kettle, put its arms around itself and hugged in happiness.

They lugged the money out to the machine shed and Mose built a fire in the forge and put the kettle in the fire and started melting down that hard-saved money.

There were times he thought he couldn't finish the job, but he did.

The critter got the basket out of the birdcage and put it down beside the forge and dipped out the molten silver with an iron ladle and poured it here and there into the basket, shaping it in place with careful hammer taps.

It took a long time, for it was exacting work, but finally it was done and the silver almost gone. The critter lugged the basket back into the birdcage and fastened it in place.

It was almost evening now and Mose had to go and do the chores. He half expected the thing might haul out the birdcage and be gone when he came back to the house. And he tried to be sore at it for its selfishness—it had taken from him and had not tried to pay him back—it had not, so far as he could tell, even tried to thank him. But he made a poor job of being sore at it.

It was waiting for him when he came from the barn carrying two pails full of milk. It followed him inside the house and stood around and he tried to talk to it. But he didn't have the heart to do much talking. He could not forget that it would be leaving, and the pleasure of its present company was lost in his terror of the loneliness to come.

For now he didn't even have his money to help ward off the loneliness.

As he lay in bed that night, strange thoughts came creeping in upon him—the thought of an even greater loneliness than he had ever known upon this runty farm, the terrible, devastating loneliness of the empty wastes that lay between the stars, a driven loneliness while one hunted for a place or person that remained a misty thought one could not define, but which it was most important one should find.

It was a strange thing for him to be thinking, and quite suddenly he knew it was no thought of his, but of this other that was in the room with him.

He tried to raise himself, he fought to raise himself, but he couldn't do it. He held his head up a moment, then fell back upon the pillow and went sound asleep.

Next morning, after Mose had eaten breakfast, the two of them went to the machine shed and dragged the birdcage out. It stood there, a weird alien thing, in the chill brightness of the dawn.

The critter walked up to it and started to slide between two of the bars, but when it was halfway through, it stepped out again and moved over to confront Old Mose.

"Good-by, friend," said Mose. "I'll miss you."

There was a strange stinging in his eyes.

The other held out its hand in farewell, and Mose took it and there was something in the hand he grasped, something round and smooth that was transferred from its hand to his.

The thing took its hand away and stepped quickly to the birdcage and slid between the bars. The hands reached for the basket and there was a sudden flicker and the birdcage was no longer there.

Mose stood lonely in the barnyard, looking at the place where there was no birdcage and remembering what he had felt or thought—or been told?—the night before as he lay in bed.

Already the critter would be there, out between the stars, in that black and utter loneliness, hunting for a place or thing or person that no human mind could grasp.

Slowly Mose turned around to go back to the house, to get the pails and go down to the barn to get the milking done.

He remembered the object in his hand and lifted his still-clenched fist in front of him. He opened his fingers and the little crystal ball lay there in his palm—and it was exactly like the one he'd found in the slitted flap in the body he had buried in the garden. Except that one had been dead and cloudy and this one had the living glow of a distant-burning fire.

Looking at it, he had the strange feeling of a happiness and comfort such as he had seldom known before, as if there were many people with him and all of them were friends.

He closed his hand upon it and the happiness stayed on —and it was all wrong, for there was not a single reason that he should be happy. The critter finally had left him and his money was all gone and he had no friends, but still he kept on feeling good.

He put the ball into his pocket and stepped spryly for the house to get the milking pails. He pursed up his whiskered lips and began to whistle and it had been a long, long time since he had even thought to whistle.

Maybe he was happy, he told himself, because the critter had not left without stopping to take his hand and try to say good-by.

And a gift, no matter how worthless it might be, how cheap a trinket, still had a basic value in simple sentiment. It had been many years since anyone had bothered to give him a gift.

It was dark and lonely and unending in the depths of space with no Companion. It might be long before another was obtainable.

It perhaps was a foolish thing to do, but the old creature had been such a kind savage, so fumbling and so pitiful and eager to help. And one who travels far and fast must likewise travel light. There had been nothing else to give.

MARIANA

by Fritz Leiber

from *Fantastic*

The first *definite* and *absolutely unchangeable* selection I made for this edition of SF was Fritz Leiber's story, "The Silver Eggheads," from *Fantasy and Science Fiction.*

That was in January of '59. For some sixteen months since, *F&SF* has remained incurably readable. In the same period of time, Leiber has been turning out stories, and yet better stories, at such a rate that *Fantastic* broke every rule in the business and published one complete all-Leiber issue last November.

The arithmetic of anthology selection, in such a case, is evident, and so is the usual lady's prerogative. But I mourn for the "Eggheads," and urge you all to storm your back-number magazine stores for it.

And one more thing (that's the *other* prerogative, no?)—We're all going to have to stop saying scornfully, "I mean *good* science fiction—not that Buck Rogers stuff!" Leiber is writing the *Buck Rogers* comic strip now. . . .

Mariana had been living in the big villa and hating the tall pine trees around it for what seemed like an eternity when she found the secret panel in the master control panel of the house.

The secret panel was simply a narrow blank of aluminum—she'd thought of it as room for more switches if they ever needed any, perish the thought!—between the air-conditioning controls and the gravity controls. Above the switches for the three-dimensional TV but below those for the robot butler and maids.

Jonathan had told her not to fool with the master control panel while he was in the city, because she would wreck anything electrical, so when the secret panel came loose under her aimlessly questing fingers and fell to the solid rock floor of the patio with a musical *twing* her first reaction was fear.

Then she saw it was only a small blank oblong of sheet aluminum that had fallen and that in the space it had covered was a column of six little switches. Only the top one was identified. Tiny glowing letters beside it spelled TREES and it was on.

When Jonathan got home from the city that evening she gathered her courage and told him about it. He was neither particularly angry nor impressed.

"Of course there's a switch for the trees," he informed her deflatingly, motioning the robot butler to cut his steak. "Didn't you know they were radio trees? I didn't want to wait twenty-five years for them and they couldn't grow in this rock anyway. A station in the city broadcasts a master pine tree and sets like ours pick it up and project it around homes. It's vulgar but convenient."

After a bit she asked timidly, "Jonathan, are the radio pine trees ghostly as you drive through them?"

"Of course not! They're solid as this house and the rock under it—to the eye and to the touch too. A person could even climb them. If you ever stirred outside you'd know these things. The city station transmits pulses of alternating matter at sixty cycles a second. The science of it is over your head."

She ventured one more question: "Why did they have the tree switch covered up?"

"So you wouldn't monkey with it—same as the fine controls on the TV. And so you wouldn't get ideas and start changing the trees. It would unsettle *me*, let me tell you, to come home to oaks one day and birches the next. I like consistency and I like pines." He looked at them out of the dining-room picture window and grunted with satisfaction.

She had been meaning to tell him about hating the pines, but that discouraged her and she dropped the topic.

About noon the next day, however, she went to the secret panel and switched off the pine trees and quickly turned around to watch them.

At first nothing happened and she was beginning to think that Jonathan was wrong again, as he so often was though would never admit, but then they began to waver and specks of pale green light churned across them and then they faded and were gone, leaving behind only an intolerably bright single point of light—just as when the TV is switched off. The star hovered motionless for what seemed a long time, then backed away and raced off toward the horizon.

Now that the pine trees were out of the way Mariana could see the real landscape. It was flat gray rock, endless miles of it, exactly the same as the rock on which the house was set and which formed the floor of the patio. It was the same in every direction. One black two-lane road drove straight across it—nothing more.

She disliked the view almost at once—it was dreadfully lonely and depressing. She switched the gravity to moon-normal and danced about dreamily, floating over the middle-of-the-room bookshelves and the grand piano and even having the robot maids dance with her, but it did not cheer her. About two o'clock she went to switch on the pine trees again, as she had intended to do in any case before Jonathan came home and was furious.

However, she found there had been changes in the column of six little switches. The TREES switch no longer had its glowing name. She remembered that it had been the top one, but the top one would not turn on again. She tried to force it from "off" to "on" but it would not move.

All the rest of the afternoon she sat on the steps outside the front door watching the black two-lane road. Never a car or a person came into view until Jonathan's tan roadster appeared, seeming at first to hang motionless in the distance and then to move only like a microscopic snail although she knew he always drove at top speed—it was one of the reasons she would never get in the car with him.

Jonathan was not as furious as she had feared. "Your own damn fault for meddling with it," he said curtly. "Now we'll have to get a man out here. Dammit, I hate to eat supper looking at nothing but those rocks! Bad enough driving through them twice a day."

She asked him haltingly about the barrenness of the landscape and the absence of neighbors.

"Well, you wanted to live *way out*," he told her. "You wouldn't ever have known about it if you hadn't turned off the trees."

"There's one other thing I've got to bother you with, Jonathan," she said. "Now the second switch—the one next below—has got a name that glows. It just says HOUSE. It's turned on—I haven't touched it! Do you suppose . . ."

"I want to look at this," he said, bounding up from the couch and slamming his martini-on-the-rocks tumbler down on the tray of the robot maid so that she rattled. "I bought this house as solid, but there are swindles. Ordinarily I'd spot a broadcast style in a flash, but they just might have slipped me a job relayed from some other planet or solar system. Fine thing if me and fifty other multi-megabuck men were spotted around in identical houses, each thinking his was unique."

"But if the house is based on rock like it is . . ."

"That would just make it easier for them to pull the trick, you dumb bunny!"

They reached the master control panel. "There it is," she said helpfully, jabbing out a finger . . . and hit the HOUSE switch.

For a moment nothing happened, then a white churning ran across the ceiling, the walls and furniture started to swell and bubble like cold lava, and then they were alone on a rock table big as three tennis courts. Even the master control panel was gone. The only thing that was left was a slender rod coming out of the gray stone at their feet and bearing at the top, like some mechanistic fruit, a small block with the six switches—that and an intolerably bright star hanging in the air where the master bedroom had been.

Mariana pushed frantically at the HOUSE switch, but it was unlabeled now and locked in the "off" position, although she threw her weight at it stiff-armed.

The upstairs star sped off like an incendiary bullet, but

its last flashbulb glare showed her Jonathan's face set in lines of fury. He lifted his hands like talons.

"You little idiot!" he screamed, coming at her.

"No, Jonathan, no!" she wailed, backing off, but he kept coming.

She realized that the block of switches had broken off in her hands. The third switch had a glowing name now: JONATHAN. She flipped it.

As his fingers dug into her bare shoulders they seemed to turn to foam rubber, then to air. His face and gray flannel suit seethed iridescently, like a leprous ghost's, then melted and ran. His star, smaller than that of the house but much closer, seared her eyes. When she opened them again there was nothing at all left of the star or Jonathan but a dancing dark after-image like a black tennis ball.

She was alone on an infinite flat rock plain under the cloudless, star-specked sky.

The fourth switch had its glowing name now: STARS.

It was almost dawn by her radium-dialed wristwatch and she was thoroughly chilled, when she finally decided to switch off the stars. She did not want to do it—in their slow wheeling across the sky they were the last sign of orderly reality—but it seemed the only move she could make.

She wondered what the fifth switch would say. ROCKS? AIR? Or even . . . ?

She switched off the stars.

The Milky Way, arching in all its unalterable glory, began to churn, its component stars darting about like midges. Soon only one remained, brighter even than Sirius or Venus —until it jerked back, fading, and darted to infinity.

The fifth switch said DOCTOR and it was not on but off.

An inexplicable terror welled up in Mariana. She did not even want to touch the fifth switch. She set the block of switches down on the rock and backed away from it.

But she dared not go far in the starless dark. She huddled down and waited for dawn. From time to time she looked at her watch dial and at the night-light glow of the switch-label a dozen yards away.

It seemed to be growing much colder.

She read her watch dial. It was two hours past sunrise. She remembered they had taught her in third grade that the sun was just one more star.

She went back and sat down beside the block of switches and picked it up with a shudder and flipped the fifth switch.

The rock grew soft and crisply fragrant under her and lapped up over her legs and then slowly turned white.

She was sitting in a hospital bed in a small blue room with a white pin-stripe.

A sweet, mechanical voice came out of the wall, saying, "You have interrupted the wish-fulfillment therapy by your own decision. If you now recognize your sick depression and are willing to accept help, the doctor will come to you. If not, you are at liberty to return to the wish-fulfillment therapy and pursue it to its ultimate conclusion."

Mariana looked down. She still had the block of switches in her hands and the fifth switch still read DOCTOR.

The wall said, "I assume from your silence that you will accept treatment. The doctor will be with you immediately."

The inexplicable terror returned to Mariana with compulsive intensity.

She switched off the doctor.

She was back in the starless dark. The rocks had grown very much colder. She could feel icy feathers falling on her face—snow.

She lifted the block of switches and saw, to her unutterable relief, that the sixth and last switch now read, in tiny glowing letters: MARIANA.

AN INQUIRY CONCERNING THE CURVATURE OF THE EARTH'S SURFACE AND DIVERS INVESTIGATIONS OF A METAPHYSICAL NATURE

by Roger Price
from *Monocle*

This is *not* a droodle.
    Anyhow, I don't *think* it is...

In recent months I have grown increasingly concerned about the tendency on the part of Western Man[1] to make a cult of conservatism and orthodoxy. New Ideas, except in the field of tax-evasion, are viewed with suspicion and, in most instances, hostility. This is unhealthy. Science has taught us that we must constantly re-examine our basic premises and consider any innovation in the light of to-day's knowledge and accept or reject it on its own merits.

Fortunately Washington is not unaware of this situation and certain elements there are attempting to create a more favorable atmosphere for fresh, original thinking—in spite of the opposition of intrenched conservatives such as Admiral Rickover (who recently refused even to consider a revolutionary plan submitted by a high-ranking Pentagon official to install steam power in submarines).

These more progressive elements, represented mostly by alert southern and mid-western Congressmen, have just sponsored a New Movement which I have become interested in.

This Group call themselves the "Flat Earthers" and they don't believe in all those old-fashioned, 17th century theories about the earth being a round ball which spins around the sun at a speed of 19,000 miles per hour. You must admit

---

[1]Bret Maverick, to name but one.

they have a point there because if the Earth were spinning that fast we would feel a constant breeze. Also if the earth were globular it is difficult to understand—from a purely pragmatic point of view—why the oceans and lakes do not slop over and inundate the land masses located beneath them (i. e. Australia, Brazil, Illinois, etc).

This Movement may turn out to be idealistic and premature but nevertheless I believe it should have "its day in court." We must remember that people once laughed at men whose names are now household words as familiar to us as our own; men such as Oliver and Wilmer Write, Eli Fulton and Thomas Steamboat[2]. The Flat Earthers are quite progressive in all of their ideas and they plan to get national publicity for their Movement next New Year's Day by pushing a number of people off the edge. Their only difficulty so far has been in obtaining volunteers[3].

Of course, the Flat Earthers have run into a certain amount of opposition, mostly from a rival group composed of reactionaries, alleged scientists and people like that (you know the type) who call themselves the "Round Earthers" and still cling to the antique notion that the earth is spherical. These Round Earthers are ineffectual however because of internal bickering within their own membership. One extremist faction wants to do away with the Flat Earthers altogether by pushing *them* over the edge. But cooler heads have pointed out that this could be interpreted by some as positive evidence of Pro-Flatearthism. It presents an interesting problem.

[2]Inventor of the Steamboat.
[3]If you have anyone you would like to see used in this capacity don't write to me; I have my own list.

DAY AT THE BEACH

by Carol Emshwiller

from *Fantasy and Science Fiction*

The first Milford Science Fiction Writers' Conference was held in 1956. Among those invited were a number of artists, agents, editors, and publishers in the field. So artist Ed "Emsh" came up for the week—with his family.

Carol Emshwiller had then published two or three stories; but she didn't know she was a writer, and the bated-breath humility with which she asked if she *possibly might be allowed* to sit in on workshop meetings has come back to haunt us Older Hands each summer since. Each summer, I mean, when Carol pops out of the playpen-and-baby-bottle laden car, an infant (at least figuratively) under one arm, and her newest manuscript under the other. (Ed carries two kids and his brushes in his teeth—nothing to it when you get the knack.)

The first time I read *Day at the Beach* was in one of these workshop sessions. After that, I just waited for someone to print it first, so *I* could next. . . .

"It's Saturday," the absolutely hairless woman said, and she pulled at her frayed, green kerchief to make sure it covered her head. "I sometimes forget to keep track of the days, but I marked three more off on the calender because I think that's how many I forgot, so this *must* be Saturday."

Her name was Myra and she had neither eyebrows nor lashes nor even a faint, transparent down along her cheeks. Once she had had long, black hair, but now, looking at her pink, bare face, one would guess she had been a redhead.

Her equally hairless husband, Ben, sprawled at the kitchen table waiting for breakfast. He wore red plaid Bermuda shorts, rather faded, and a tee shirt with a large hole under the arm. His skull curved above his staring eyes more naked-seeming than hers because he wore no kerchief or hat.

"We used to always go out on Saturdays," she said, and she put a bowl of oatmeal at the side of the table in front of a youth chair.

Then she put the biggest bowl between her husband's elbows.

"I have to mow the lawn this morning," he said. "All the more so if it's Saturday."

She went on as if she hadn't heard. "A day like today we'd go to the beach. I forget a lot of things, but I remember that."

"If I were you, I just wouldn't think about it." Ben's empty eyes finally focused on the youth chair and he turned then to the open window behind him and yelled, "Littleboy, Littleboy," making the sound run together all L's and Y. "Hey, it's breakfast, Boy," and under his breath he said, "He won't come."

"But I *do* think about it. I remember hot dogs and clam chowder and how cool it was days like this. I don't suppose I even have a bathing suit around any more."

"It wouldn't be like it used to be."

"Oh, the sea's the same. That's one thing sure. I wonder if the boardwalk's still there."

"Hah," he said. "I don't have to see it to know it's all gone for firewood. It's been four winters now."

She sat down, put her elbows on the table and stared at her bowl. "Oatmeal," she said, putting in that one word everything she felt about the beach and wanting to go there.

"It's not that I don't want to do better for you," Ben said. He touched her arm with the tips of his fingers for just a moment. "I wish I could. And I wish I could have hung on to that corned beef hash last time, but it was heavy and I had to run and there was a fight on the train and I lost the sugar too. I wonder which bastard has it now."

"I know how hard you try, Ben. I do. It's just sometimes everything comes on you at once, especially when it's a Saturday like this. Having to get water way down the block and that only when there's electricity to run the pump, and this oatmeal; sometimes it's just once too often, and then, most of all, you commuting in all that danger to get food."

"I make out. I'm not the smallest one on that train."

"God, I think that everyday. Thank God, I say to myself, or where would we be now. Dead of starvation that's where."

She watched him leaning low over his bowl, pushing his lips out and making a sucking sound. Even now she was still surprised to see how long and naked his skull arched, and she had an impulse, seeing it there so bare and ugly and thinking of the commuting, to cover it gently with her two hands, to cup it and make her hands do for his hair; but she only smoothed at her kerchief again to make sure it covered her own baldness.

"Is it living, though? Is it living, staying home all the time, hiding like, in this house? Maybe it's the rest of them, the dead ones, that are lucky. It's pretty sad when a person can't even go to the beach on a Saturday."

She was thinking the one thing she didn't want to do most of all was to hurt him. No, she told herself inside, sternly. Stop it right now. Be silent for once and eat, and, like Ben says, don't think; but she was caught up in it somehow and she said, "You know, Littleboy never did go to the beach yet, not even once, and it's only nine miles down," and she knew it would hurt him.

"Where is Littleboy?" he said and yelled again out the window. "He just roams."

"It isn't as if there were cars to worry about any more, and have you seen how fast he is and how he climbs so good for three and a half? Besides, what can you do when he gets up so early."

He was finished eating now and he got up and dipped a cup of water from the large pan on the stove and drank it. "I'll take a look," he said. "He won't come when you call."

She began to eat finally, watching him out the kitchen window and listening to him calling. Seeing him hunched forward and squinting because he had worn glasses before and his last pair had been broken a year ago. Not in a fight, because he was careful not to wear them commuting even then, when it wasn't quite so bad. It was Littleboy who had done it, climbed up and got them himself from the very top drawer, and he was a whole year younger. Next thing she knew they were on the floor, broken.

Ben disappeared out of range of the window and Littleboy came darting in as though he had been huddling by the door behind the arbor vitae all the time.

He was the opposite of his big, pink and hairless parents, with thick and fine black hair growing low over his forehead and extending down the back of his neck so far that she always wondered if it ended where hair used to end before, or whether it grew too far down. He was thin and small for his age, but strong-looking and wiry with long arms and legs. He had a pale, olive skin, wide, blunt features and a wary stare, and he looked at her now, waiting to see what she would do.

She only sighed, lifted him and put him in his youth chair and kissed his firm, warm cheek, thinking, what beautiful hair, and wishing she knew how to cut it better so he would look neat.

"We don't have any more sugar," she said, "but I saved you some raisins," and she took down a box and sprinkled some on his cereal.

Then she went to the door and called, "He's here, Ben. He's here." And in a softer voice she said, "The pixy." She heard Ben answer with a whistle and she turned back to the kitchen to find Littleboy's oatmeal on the floor in a lopsided oval lump, and him, still looking at her with wise and wary brown eyes.

She knelt down first, and spooned most of it back into the bowl. Then she picked him up rather roughly, but there was gentleness to the roughness, too. She pulled at the elastic topped jeans and gave him two hard, satisfying slaps on bare buttocks. "It isn't as if we had food to waste," she said, noticing the down that grew along his backbone and wondering if that was the way the three year olds had been before.

He made an *Aaa, Aaa,* sound, but didn't cry, and after that she picked him up and held him so that he nuzzled into her neck in the way she liked. "Aaa," he said again, more softly, and bit her just above the collar bone.

She dropped him down, letting him kind of slide with her arms still around him. It hurt and she could see there was a shallow, half-inch piece bitten right out.

"He bit me again," she shouted, hearing Ben at the door. "He bit me. A real piece out even, and look, he has it in his mouth still."

"God, what a . . ."

"Don't hurt him. I already slapped him good for the floor and three is a hard age." She pulled at Ben's arm. "It says so in the books. Three is hard, it says." But she remembered it really said that three was a beginning to be co-operative age.

He let go and Littleboy ran out of the kitchen back toward the bedrooms.

She took a deep breath. "I've just got to get out of this house. I mean really away."

She sat down and let him wash the place and cross two bandaids over it. "Do you think we could go? Do you think we could go just one more time with a blanket and a picnic lunch? I've just got to do *something.*"

"All right. All right. You wear the wrench in your belt and I'll wear the hammer, and we'll risk taking the car."

She spent twenty minutes looking for bathing suits and not finding them, and then she stopped because she knew it didn't really matter, there probably wouldn't be anyone there.

The picnic was simple enough. She gathered it together in five minutes, a precious can of tuna fish and hard, home-made biscuits baked the evening before when the electricity had come on for a while, and shriveled, worm-eaten apples, picked from neighboring trees and hoarded all winter in another house that had a cellar.

She heard Ben banging about in the garage, measuring out gas from his cache of cans, ten miles' worth to put in the car and ten miles' worth in a can to carry along and hide someplace for the trip back.

Now that he had decided they would go, her mind began to be full of what-ifs. Still, she thought, she would *not* change her mind. Surely once in four years was not too often to risk going to the beach. She had thought about it all last year too, and now she was going and she would enjoy it.

She gave Littleboy an apple to keep him busy and she packed the lunch in the basket, all the time pressing her lips tight together, and she said to herself that she was *not* going to think of any more what-ifs, and she *was* going to have a good time.

Ben had switched after the war from the big-finned Dodge to a small and rattly European car. They fitted into it cozily, the lunch in back with the army blanket and a pail and shovel for playing in the sand, and Littleboy in front on her lap, his hair brushing her cheek as he turned, looking out.

They started out on the empty road. "Remember how it was before on a weekend?" she said, and laughed. "Bumper to bumper, they called it. We didn't like it then."

A little way down they passed an old person on a bicycle, in jeans and a bright shirt with the tail out. They couldn't tell if it was a man or a woman, but the person smiled and they waved and called, "Aaa."

The sun was hot, but as they neared the beach there began to be a breeze and she could smell the sea. She began to feel as she had the very first time she had seen it. She had been born in Ohio and she was twelve before she had taken a trip and come out on the wide, flat, sunny sands and smelled this smell.

She held Littleboy tight though it made him squirm, and she leaned against Ben's shoulder. "Oh, it's going to be fun!" she said. "Littleboy, you're going to see the sea. Look, darling, keep watching, and smell. It's delicious." And Littleboy squirmed until she let go again.

Then, at last, there was the sea, and it *was* exactly as it had always been, huge and sparkling and making a sound like . . . no, *drowning out* the noises of wars. Like the black sky with stars, or the cold and stolid moon, it dwarfed even what had happened.

They passed the long, brick bathhouses, looking about as they always had, but the boardwalks between were gone, as Ben had said, not a stick left of them.

"Let's stop at the main bathhouse."

"No," Ben said. "We better keep away from those places. You can't tell who's in there. I'm going way down beyond."

She was glad, really, especially because at the last bathhouse she thought she saw a dark figure duck behind the wall.

They went down another mile or so, then drove the car off behind some stunted trees and bushes.

"Nothing's going to spoil this Saturday," she said, pulling out the picnic things, "just nothing. Come, Littleboy." She kicked off her shoes and started running for the beach, the basket bouncing against her knee.

Littleboy slipped out of his roomy sneakers easily and scampered after her. "You can take your clothes off," she told him. "There's nobody here at all."

When Ben came, later, after hiding the gas, she was settled, flat on the blanket in old red shorts and a halter, and still the same green kerchief, and Littleboy, brown and naked, splashed with his pail in the shallow water, the wetness bringing out the hairs along his back.

"Look," she said, "nobody as far as you can see and you can see so far. It gives you a different feeling from home. You know there are people here and there in the houses, but here, it's like we were the only ones, and here it doesn't even matter. Like Adam and Eve, we are, just you and me and our baby."

He lay on his stomach next to her. "Nice breeze," he said.

Shoulder to shoulder they watched the waves and the gulls and Littleboy, and later they splashed in the surf and then ate the lunch and lay watching again, lazy, on their stomachs. And after a while she turned on her back to see his face. "With the sea it doesn't matter at all," she said and she put her arm across his shoulder. "And we're just part of everything, the wind and the earth and the sea too, my Adam."

"Eve," he said and smiled and kissed her and it was a longer kiss than they had meant. "Myra. Myra."

"There's nobody but us."

She sat up. "I don't even know a doctor since Press Smith was killed by those robbing kids and I'd be scared."

"We'll find one. Besides, you didn't have any trouble. It's been so damn long." She pulled away from his arm. "And I love you. And Littleboy, he'll be way over four by the time we'd have another one."

She stood up and stretched and then looked down the beach and Ben put a hand around her ankle. She looked down the other way. "Somebody's coming," she said, and then he got up too.

Far down, walking in a business-like way on the hard, damp part of the sand, three men were coming toward them.

"You got your wrench?" Ben asked. "Put it just under the blanket and sit down by it, but keep your knees under you."

He put his tee shirt back on, leaving it hanging out, and he hooked the hammer under his belt in back, the top covered by the shirt. Then he stood and waited for them to come.

They were all three bald and shirtless. Two wore jeans cut off at the knees and thick belts, and the other had checked shorts and a red leather cap and a pistol stuck in his belt in the middle of the front at the buckle. He was older. The others looked like kids and they held back as they neared and let the older one come up alone. He was a small man, but looked tough. "You got gas," he said, a flat-voiced statement of fact.

"Just enough to get home."

"I don't mean right here. You got gas at home is what I mean."

Myra sat stiffly, her hand on the blanket on top of where the wrench was. Ben was a little in front of her and she could see his curving, forward-sloping shoulders and the lump of the hammer-head at the small of his back. If he stood up straight, she thought, and held his shoulders like they ought to be, he would look broad and even taller and he would show that little man, but the other had the pistol. Her eyes kept coming back to its shining black.

Ben took a step forward. "Don't move," the little man said. He shifted his weight to one leg, looking relaxed, and put his hand on his hip near the pistol. "Where you got the gas to get you home? Maybe we'll come with you and you might lend us a little of that gas you got there at your house. Where'd you hide the stuff to get you back, or I'll let my boys play a bit with your little one and you might not like it."

Littleboy, she saw, had edged down, away from them, and he crouched now, watching with his wide-eyed stare. She could see the tense, stringy muscles along his arms and legs and he reminded her of gibbons she had seen at the zoo long ago. His poor little face looks old, she thought, too old for three years. Her fingers closed over the blanket-covered wrench. They'd better not hurt Littleboy.

She heard her husband say, "I don't know." "Oh, Ben," she said, "oh, Ben."

The man made a motion and the two youths started out, but Littleboy had started first, she saw. She pulled at her wrench and then had to stop and fumble with the blanket, and it took a long time because she kept her eyes on Littleboy and the two others chasing.

She heard a shout and a grunt beside her. "Oh, Ben," she said again, and turned, but it was Ben on top attacking the other, and the small man was trying to use his pistol as a club but he had hold of the wrong end for that, and Ben had the hammer and he was much bigger.

He was finished in a minute. She watched, empty-eyed, the whole of it, holding the wrench in a white-knuckled hand in case he needed her.

Afterward, he moved from the body into a crouching run, hammer in one hand and pistol, by the barrel, in the other. "You stay here," he shouted back.

She looked at the sea a few minutes, and listened to it, but her own feelings seemed more important than the stoic sea now. She turned and followed, walking along the marks where the feet had swept at the soft sand.

Where the bushes began she saw him loping back. "What happened?"

"They ran off when they saw me after them with the other guy's gun. No bullets though. You'll have to help look now."

"He's lost!"

"He won't come when you call. We'll just have to look. He could be way out. I'll try that and you stay close and look here. The gas is buried under that bush there, if you need it."

"We've got to find him, Ben. He doesn't know his way home from here."

He came to her and kissed her and held her firmly across the shoulders with one arm. She could feel his muscles bunch into her neck as hard almost as the head of his hammer that pressed against her arm. She remembered a time four years ago when his embrace had been soft and comfortable. He had had hair then, but he had been quite fat, and now he was hard and bald, having gained something and lost something.

He turned and started off, but looked back and she smiled and nodded to show him she felt better from his arm around her and the kiss.

I would die if anything happened and we would lose Littleboy, she thought, but mostly I would hate to lose Ben. Then the world would really be lost altogether, and everything would be ended.

She looked, calling in a whisper, knowing she had to peer under each bush and watch behind and ahead for scampering things. He's so small when he huddles into a ball and he can sit so still. Sometimes I wish there was another three-year-old around to judge him by. I forget so much about how it used to be, before. Sometimes I just wonder about him.

"Littleboy, Littleboy. Mommy wants you," she called softly. "Come. There's still time to play in the sand and there are apples left." She leaned forward, and her hand reached to touch the bushes.

Later the breeze began to cool and a few clouds gathered. She shivered in just her shorts and halter, but it was mostly an inner coldness. She felt she had circled, hunting, for well over an hour, but she had no watch, and at a time like this she wasn't sure of her judgment. Still, the sun seemed low. They should go home soon. She kept watching now, too, for silhouettes of people who might *not* be Ben or Littleboy, and she probed the bushes with her wrench with less care. Every now and then she went back to look at the blanket and the basket and the pail and shovel, lying alone and far from the water, and the body there, with the red leather cap beside it.

And then, when she came back another time to see if all the things were still there, undisturbed, she saw a tall, two-headed seeming monster walking briskly down the beach, and one head, bouncing directly over the other one, had hair and was Littleboy's.

The sunset was just beginning. The rosy glow deepened as they neared her and changed the colors of everything. The red plaid of Ben's shorts seemed more emphatic. The sand turned orangeish. She ran to meet them, laughing and splashing her feet in the shallow water, and she came up and held Ben tight around the waist and Littleboy said, "Aaa."

"We'll be home before dark," she said. "There's even time for one last splash."

They packed up finally while Littleboy circled the body by the blanket, touching it sometimes until Ben slapped him for it and he went off and sat down and made little cat sounds to himself.

He fell asleep in her lap on the way home, lying forward against her with his head at her neck the way she liked. The sunset was deep, with reds and purples.

She leaned against Ben. "The beach always makes you tired," she said. "I remember that from before too. I'll be able to sleep tonight."

They drove silently along the wide empty parkway. The car had no lights, but that didn't matter.

"We did have a good day after all," she said. "I feel renewed."

"Good," he said.

It was just dark as they drove up to the house. Ben stopped the car and they sat a moment and held hands before moving to get the things out.

"We had a good day," she said again. "And Littleboy saw the sea." She put her hand on the sleeping boy's hair, gently so as not to disturb him and then she yawned. "I wonder if it really *was* Saturday."

HOT ARGUMENT

by Randall Garrett
from *Fantasy and Science Fiction*

Willy and his girl-friend, Bea,
While working for the A.E.C.,
Got in a fight and failed to hear
The warning of a bomb test near.
Their friends were sad to hear, no doubt,
That they had had a falling-out.

WHAT THE LEFT HAND WAS DOING

by Darrel T. Langart

from *Astounding Science Fiction*

What *is* human? How different can it be, and still seem "one of us"? How much can one of *us* change, and not be one of *them*? (And who are they? Or are they *what*?)

Earlier selections here have approached the line of definition in a variety of ways. Mr. Langart, an author new to science fiction (so far as I have been able to determine from his tight-lipped agents), here presents an exceptionally thoughtful and convincing examination of one of the potentialities for human development.

The building itself was unprepossessive enough. It was an old-fashioned six-floor, brick structure that had, over the years, served first as a private home, then as an apartment building, and finally as the headquarters for the organization it presently housed.

It stood among others of its kind in a lower-middle-class district of Arlington, Virginia, within howitzer range of the Capitol of the United States, and even closer to the Pentagon. The main door was five steps up from the sidewalk, and the steps were flanked by curving balustrades of ornamental ironwork. The entrance itself was closed by a double door with glass panes, beyond which could be seen a small foyer. On both doors, an identical message was blocked out in neat gold letters: *The Society for Mystical and Metaphysical Research, Inc.*

It is possible that no more nearly perfect cover, no more misleading front for a secret organization ever existed in the history of man. It possessed two qualities which most other cover-up titles do not have. One, it was so obviously crackpot that no one paid any attention to it except crackpots, and, two, it was perfectly, literally true.

Spencer Candron had seen the building so often that the functional beauty of the whole setup no longer impressed him as it had several years before. Just as a professional actor is not impressed by being allowed backstage, or as a multimillionaire considers expensive luxuries as commonplace, so Spencer Candron thought of nothing more than his own personal work as he climbed the five steps and pushed open the glass-paned doors.

Perhaps, too, his matter-of-fact attitude was caused partially by the analogical resemblance between himself and the organization. Physically, Candron, too, was unprepossessing. He was a shade less than five-eight, and his weight fluctuated between a hundred and forty and a hundred and forty-five, depending on the season and his state of mind. His face consisted of a well-formed snub nose, a pair of introspective gray eyes, a rather wide, thin-lipped mouth that tended to smile even when relaxed, a high, smooth forehead, and a firm cleft chin, plus the rest of the normal equipment that normally goes to make up a face. The skin was slightly tanned, but it was the tan of a man who goes to the beach on summer weekends, not that of an outdoors man. His hands were strong and wide and rather large; the palms were uncalloused and the fingernails were clean and neatly trimmed. His hair was straight and light brown, with a pronounced widow's peak, and he wore it combed back and rather long to conceal the fact that a thin spot had appeared on the top rear of his scalp. His clothing was conservative and a little out of style, having been bought in 1981, and thus three years past being up-to-date.

Physically, then, Spencer Candron, was a fine analog of the Society. He looked unimportant. On the outside, he was just another average man whom no one would bother to look twice at.

The analogy between himself and the S.M.M.R. was completed by the fact that his interior resources were vastly greater than anything that showed on the outside.

The doors swung shut behind him, and he walked into the foyer, then turned left into the receptionist's office. The woman behind the desk smiled her eager smile and said, "Good morning, Mr. Candron!"

Candron smiled back. He liked the woman, in spite of her semifanatic overeagerness, which made her every declarative sentence seem to end with an exclamation point.

"Morning, Mrs. Jesser," he said, pausing at the desk for a moment. "How have things been?"

Mrs. Jesser was a stout matron in her early forties who would have been perfectly happy to work for the Society for nothing, as a hobby. That she was paid a reasonable salary made her job almost heaven for her.

"Oh, just *fine*, Mr. Candron!" she said. "Just *fine!*" Then her voice lowered, and her face took on a serious, half conspiratorial expression. "Do you know what?"

"No," said Candron, imitating her manner. "What?"

"We have a gentleman . . . he came in yesterday . . . a *very* nice man . . . and very intelligent, too. And, you know what?"

Candron shook his head. "No," he repeated. "What?"

Mrs. Jesser's face took on the self-pleased look of one who has important inside knowledge to impart. "He has actual photographs . . . three-D, full-color *pho*tographs . . . of the con*trol* room of a flying saucer! And one of the Saucerites, too!"

"Really?" Candron's expression was that of a man who was both impressed and interested. "What did Mr. Balfour say?"

"Well—" Mrs. Jesser looked rather miffed. "I don't really *know!* But the gentleman is supposed to be back to*mor*row! With some *more* pictures!"

"Well," said Candron. "Well. That's really fine. I hope he has something. Is Mr. Taggert in?"

"Oh, yes, Mr. Candron! He said you should go on up!" She waved a plump hand toward the stairway. It made Mrs. Jesser happy to think that she was the sole controller of the only way, except for the fire escape, that anyone could get to the upper floors of the building. And as long as she thought that, among other things, she was useful to the Society. Someone had to handle the crackpots and lunatic-fringe fanatics that came to the Society, and one of their own kind could do the job better than anyone else. As long as Mrs. Jesser and Mr. Balfour were on duty, the Society's camouflage would remain intact.

Spencer Candron gave Mrs. Jesser a friendly gesture with one hand and then headed up the stairs. He would rather not have bothered to take the stairway all the way up to the fifth floor, but Mrs. Jesser had sharp ears, and she might wonder why his footsteps were not heard all the way up. Nothing—but *nothing*—must ever be done to make Mrs. Jesser wonder about anything that went on here.

The door to Brian Taggert's office was open when Candron finally reached the fifth floor. Taggert, of course, was not only expecting him, but had long been aware of his approach.

Candron went in, closed the door, and said, "Hi, Brian," to the dark-haired, dark-eyed, hawk-nosed man who was sprawled on the couch that stood against one corner of the room. There was a desk at the other rear corner, but Brian Taggert wasn't a desk man. He looked like a heavyweight boxer, but he preferred relaxation to exercise.

But he did take his feet from the couch and lift himself to a sitting position as Candron entered. And, at the same time, the one resemblance between Taggert and Candron manifested itself—a warm, truly human smile.

"Spence," he said warmly, "you look as though you were bored. Want a job?"

"No," said Candron, "but I'll take it. Who do I kill?"

"Nobody, unless you absolutely have to," said Taggert.

Spencer Candron understood. The one thing that characterized the real members of The Society for Mystical and Metaphysical Research—not the "front" members, like Balfour and Mrs. Jesser, not the hundreds of "honorable" members who constituted the crackpot portion of the membership, but the real core of the group—the thing that characterized them could be summed up in one word: *understanding*. Without that one essential property, no human mind can be completely free. Unless a human mind is capable of understanding the only forces that can be pitted against it—the forces of other human minds—that mind cannot avail itself of the power that lies within it.

Of course, it is elementary that such understanding must also apply to oneself. Understanding of self must come before understanding of others. *Total* understanding is not necessary—indeed, utter totality is very likely impossible to any human mind. But the greater the understanding, the freer the mind, and, at a point which might be called the "critical point," certain abilities inherent in the individual human mind become controllable. A change, not only in quantity, but in quality, occurs.

A cube of ice in a glass of water at zero degrees Celsius exhibits certain properties and performs certain actions at its surface. Some of the molecules drift away, to become one with the liquid. Other molecules from the liquid become attached to the crystalline ice. But the ice cube remains essentially an entity. Over a period of time, it may change slowly, since dissolution takes place faster than crystallization at the corners of the cube. Eventually, the cube will become a sphere, or something very closely approximating it. But the change is slow, and, once it reaches that state, the situation becomes static.

But, if you add heat, more and more and more, the ice cube will change, not only its shape, but its state. What it was previously capable of doing only slightly and impermanently, it can now do completely. The critical point has been passed.

Roughly—for the analog itself is rough—the same thing occurs in the human mind. The psionic abilities of the human mind are, to a greater or lesser degree, there to begin with, just as an ice cube has the *ability* to melt if the proper conditions are met with.

The analogy hardly extends beyond that. Unlike an ice cube, the human mind is capable of changing the forces outside it—as if the ice could seek out its own heat in order to melt. And, too, human minds vary in their inherent ability to absorb understanding. Some do so easily, others do so only in spotty areas, still others cannot reach the critical point before they break. And still others can never really understand at all.

No one who had not reached his own critical point could become a "core" member of the S.M.M.R. It was not snobbery on their part; they understood other human beings too well to be snobbish. It was more as though a Society for Expert Mountain Climbers met each year on the peak of Mount Everest—anyone who can get up there to attend the meeting is automatically a member.

Spencer Candron sat down in a near-by chair. "All right, so I refrain from doing any more damage than I have to. What's the objective?"

Taggert put his palms on his muscular thighs and leaned forward. "James Ch'ien is still alive."

Candron had not been expecting the statement, but he felt no surprise. His mind merely adjusted to the new data. "He's still in China, then," he said. It was not a question, but a statement of a deduction. "The whole thing was a phony. The death, the body, the funeral. What about the executions?"

"They were real," Taggert said. "Here's what happened as closely as we can tell:

"Dr. Ch'ien was kidnaped on July 10th, the second day of the conference in Peiping, at some time between two and three in the morning. He was replaced by a double, whose name we don't know. It's unimportant, anyway. The double was as perfect as the Chinese surgeons could make him. He was probably not aware that he was slated to die; it is more likely that he was hypnotized and misled. At any rate, he took Ch'ien's place on the rostrum to speak that afternoon.

"The man who shot him, and the man who threw the flame bomb, were probably as equally deluded as to what they were doing as the double was. They did a perfect job, though. The impersonator was dead, and his skin was charred and blistered clear up to the chest—no fingerprints.

"The men were tried, convicted, and executed. The Chinese government sent us abject apologies. The double's body was shipped back to the United States with full honors, but by the time it reached here, the eye-cone patterns had deteriorated to the point where they couldn't be identified any more than the fingerprints could. And there were half a hundred reputable scientists of a dozen friendly nations who were eye-witnesses to the killing and who are all absolutely certain that it was James Ch'ien who died."

Candron nodded. "So, while the whole world was mourning the fact that one of Earth's greatest physicists had died, he was being held captive in the most secret and secure prison that the Red Chinese government could put him in."

Taggert nodded. "And your job will be to get him out," he said softly.

Candron said nothing for a moment, as he thought the problem out. Taggert said nothing to interrupt him.

Neither of them worried about being overheard or spied upon. Besides being equipped with hush devices and blanketing equipment, the building was guarded by Reeves and Donahue, whose combined senses of perception could pick up any activity for miles around which might be inimical to the Society.

"How much backing do we get from the Federal Government?" Candron asked at last.

"We can swing the cover-up afterward all the way," Taggert told him firmly. "We can arrange transportation back. That is, the Federal Government can. But getting over there and getting Ch'ien out of durance vile is strictly up to the Society. Senator Kerotski and Secretary Gonzales are giving us every opportunity they can, but there's no use approaching the President until after we've proven our case."

Candron gestured his understanding. The President of the United States was a shrewd, able, just, and ethical human being—but he was not yet a member of the Society, and perhaps would never be. As a consequence it was still impossible to convince him that the S.M.M.R. knew what it was talking about—and that applied to nearly ninety per cent of the Federal and State officials of the nation.

Only a very few knew that the Society was an *ex officio* branch of the government itself. Not until the rescue of James Ch'ien was an accomplished fact, not until there was physical, logical proof that the man was still alive would the government take official action.

"What's the outline?" Candron wanted to know.

Taggert outlined the proposed course of action rapidly. When he was finished, Spencer Candron simply said, "All right. I can take care of my end of it." He stood up. "I'll see you, Brian."

Brian Taggert lay back down on the couch, propped up his feet, and winked at Candron. "Watch and check, Spence."

Candron went back down the stairs. Mrs. Jesser smiled up at him as he entered the reception room. "Well! That didn't take long! Are you leaving, Mr. Candron?"

"Yes," he said, glancing at the wall clock. "Grab and run, you know. I'll see you soon, Mrs. Jesser. Be an angel."

He went out the door again and headed down the street. Mrs. Jesser had been right; it hadn't taken him long. He'd been in Taggert's office a little over one minute, and less than half a dozen actual words had been spoken. The rest of the conversation had been on a subtler level, one which was almost completely nonverbal. Not that Spencer Candron was a telepath; if he had been, it wouldn't have been necessary for him to come to the headquarters building. Candron's talents simply didn't lie along that line. His ability to probe the minds of normal human beings was spotty and unreliable at best. But when two human beings understand each other at the level that existed between members of the Society, there is no need for long-winded discourses.

The big stratoliner slowed rapidly as it approached the Peiping People's Airfield. The pilot, a big-boned Britisher who had two jobs to do at once, watched the airspeed indicator. As the needle dropped, he came in on a conventional landing lane, aiming for the huge field below. Then, as the needle reached a certain point, just above the landing minimum, he closed his eyes for a fraction of a second and thought, with all the mental power at his command: *NOW!*

For a large part of a second, nothing happened, but the pilot knew his message had been received.

Then a red gleam came into being on the control board.

"What the hell?" said the co-pilot.

The pilot swore. "I *told* 'em that door was weak! We've ripped the luggage door off her hinges. Feel her shake?"

The co-pilot looked grim. "Good thing it happened now instead of in mid-flight. At that speed, we'd been torn apart."

"*Blown* to bits, you mean," said the pilot. "Let's bring her in."

By that time, Spencer Candron was a long way below the ship, falling like a stone, a big suitcase clutched tightly in his arms. He knew that the Chinese radar was watching the jetliner, and that it had undoubtedly picked up two objects dropping from the craft—the door and one other. Candron had caught the pilot's mental signal—anything that powerful could hardly be missed—and had opened the door and leaped.

But those things didn't matter now. Without a parachute, he had flung himself from the plane toward the earth below, and his only thought was his loathing, his repugnance, for that too, too solid ground beneath.

He didn't hate it. That would be deadly, for hate implies as much attraction as love—the attraction of destruction. Fear, too, was out of the question; there must be no such relationship as that between the threatened and the threatener. Only loathing could save him. The earth beneath was utterly repulsive to him.

And he slowed.

His mind would not accept contact with the ground, and his body was forced to follow suit. He slowed.

Minutes later, he was drifting fifty feet above the surface, his altitude held steady by the emotional force of his mind. Not until then did he release the big suitcase he had been holding. He heard it thump as it hit, breaking open and scattering clothing around it.

In the distance, he could hear the faint moan of a siren. The Chinese radar had picked up two falling objects. And they would find two: one door and one suitcase, both of which could be accounted for by the "accident." They would know that no parachute had opened; hence, if they found no body, they would be certain that no human being could have dropped from the plane.

The only thing remaining now was to get into the city itself. In the darkness, it was a little difficult to tell exactly where he was, but the lights of Peiping weren't far away, and a breeze was carrying him toward it. He wanted to be in just the right place before he set foot on the ground.

By morning, he would be just another one of the city's millions.

Morning came three hours later. The sun came up quietly, as if its sole purpose in life were to make a liar out of Kipling. The venerable old Chinese gentleman who strolled quietly down Dragon Street looked as though he were merely out for a placid walk for his morning constitutional. His clothing was that of a middle-class office worker, but his dignified manner, his wrinkled brown face, his calm brown eyes, and his white hair brought respectful looks from the other passers-by on the Street of the Dragon. Not even the thirty-five years of Communism, which had transformed agrarian China into an industrial and technological nation that ranked with the best, had destroyed the ancient Chinese respect for age.

That respect was what Spencer Candron relied on to help him get his job done. Obvious wealth would have given him respect, too, as would the trappings of power; he could have posed as an Honorable Director or a People's Advocate. But that would have brought unwelcome attention as well as respect. His disguise would never stand up under careful examination, and trying to pass himself off as an important citizen might bring on just such an examination. But an old man had both respect and anonymity.

Candron had no difficulty in playing the part. He had known many elderly Chinese, and he understood them well. Even the emotional control of the Oriental was simple to simulate; Candron knew what "emotional control" *really* meant.

You don't control an automobile by throwing the transmission out of gear and letting the engine run wild. Suppressing an emotion is not controlling it, in the fullest sense. "Control" implies guidance and use.

Peiping contained nearly three million people in the city itself, and another three million in the suburbs; there was little chance that the People's Police would single out one venerable oldster to question, but Candron wanted an escape route just in case they did. He kept walking until he found the neighborhood he wanted, then he kept his eyes open for a small hotel. He didn't want one that was too expensive, but, on the other hand, he didn't want one so cheap that the help would be untrustworthy.

He found one that suited his purpose, but he didn't want to go in immediately. There was one more thing to do. He waited until the shops were open, and then went in search of second-hand luggage. He had enough money in his pockets to buy more brand-new expensive luggage than a man could carry, but he didn't want luggage that looked either expensive or new. When he finally found what he wanted, he went in search of clothing, buying a piece at a time, here and there, in widely scattered shops. Some of it was new, some of it was second-hand, all of it fit both the body and the personality of the old man he was supposed to be. Finally, he went to the hotel.

The clerk was a chubby, blandly happy, youngish man who bowed his head as Candron approached. There was still the flavor of the old politeness in his speech, although the flowery beauty of half a century before had disappeared.

"Good morning, venerable sir; may I be of some assistance?"

Candron kept the old usages. "This old one would be greatly honored if your excellent hostelry could find a small corner for the rest of his unworthy body," he said in excellent Cantonese.

"It is possible, aged one, that this miserable hovel may provide some space, unsuited though it may be to your honored presence," said the clerk, reverting as best he could to the language of a generation before. "For how many people would you require accommodations?"

"For my humble self only," Candron said.

"It can, I think, be done," said the clerk, giving him a pleasant smile. Then his face took on an expression of contrition. "I hope, venerable one, that you will not think this miserable creature too bold if he asks for your papers?"

"Not at all," said Candron, taking a billfold from his inside coat pocket. "Such is the law, and the law of the People of China is to be always respected."

He opened the billfold and spread the papers for the clerk's inspection. They were all there—identification, travel papers, everything. The clerk looked them over and jotted down the numbers in the register book on the desk, then turned the book around. "Your chop, venerable one."

The "chop" was a small stamp bearing the ideograph which indicated the name Candron was using. Illiteracy still ran high in China because of the difficulty in memorizing the tens of thousands of ideographs which made up the written language, so each man carried a chop to imprint his name. Officially, China used the alphabet, spelling out the Chinese words phonetically—and, significantly, they had chosen the Latin alphabet of the Western nations rather than the Cyrillic of the Soviets. But old usages die hard.

Candron imprinted the ideograph on the page, then, beside it, he wrote *Ying Lee* in Latin characters.

The clerk's respect for this old man went up a degree. He had expected to have to put down the Latin characters himself. "Our humble establishment is honored by your esteemed presence, Mr. Ying," he said. "For how long will it be your pleasure to bestow this honor upon us?"

"My poor business, unimportant though it is, will require at least one week; at the most, ten days," Candron said, knowing full well that twenty-four hours would be his maximum, if everything went well.

"It pains me to ask for money in advance from so honorable a gentleman as yourself," said the clerk, "but such are the rules. It will be seven and a half yuan per day, or fifty yuan per week."

Candron put five ten-yuan notes on the counter. Since the readjustment of the Chinese monetary system, the yuan had regained a great deal of its value.

A young man who doubled as bellhop and elevator operator took Candron up to the third floor. Candron tipped him generously, but not extravagantly, and then proceeded to unpack his suitcase. He hung the suits in the closet and put the shirts in the clothes chest. By the time he was through, it looked as though Ying Lee was prepared to stay for a considerable length of time.

Then he checked his escape routes, and found two that were satisfactory. Neither led downward to the ground floor, but upward, to the roof. The hotel was eight stories high, higher than any of the near-by buildings. No one would expect him to go up.

Then he gave his attention to the room itself. He went over it carefully, running his fingers gently over the walls and the furniture, noticing every detail with his eyes. He examined the chairs, the low bed, the floor—everything.

He was not searching for spy devices. He didn't care whether there were any there or not. He wanted to know that room. To know it, become familiar with it, make it a part of him.

Had there been any spy devices, they would have noticed nothing unusual. There was only an old man there, walking slowly around the room, muttering to himself as though he were thinking over something important or, perhaps, merely reminiscing on the past, mentally chewing over his memories.

He did not peer, or poke, or prod. He did not appear to be looking for anything. He picked up a small, cheap vase and looked at it as though it were an old friend; he rubbed his hand over the small writing desk as though he had written many things in that familiar place; he sat down in a chair and leaned back in it and caressed the armrests with his palms as though it were an honored seat in his own home. And, finally, he undressed, put on his nightclothes, and lay down on the bed, staring at the ceiling with a soft smile on his face. After ten minutes or so, his eyes closed and remained that way for three-quarters of an hour.

Unusual? No. An old man must have his rest. There is nothing unusual about an old man taking a short nap.

When he got up again, Spencer Candron was thoroughly familiar with the room. It was home, and he loved it.

Nightfall found the honorable Mr. Ying a long way from his hotel. He had, as his papers had said, gone to do business with a certain Mr. Yee, had haggled over the price of certain goods, and had been unsuccessful in establishing a mutual price. Mr. Yee was later to be able to prove to the People's Police that he had done no business whatever with Mr. Ying, and had had no notion whatever that Mr. Ying's business connections in Nanking were totally nonexistent.

But, on that afternoon, Mr. Ying had left Mr. Yee with

the impression that he would return the next day with, perhaps, a more amenable attitude toward Mr. Yee's prices. Then Mr. Ying Lee had gone to a restaurant for his evening meal.

He had eaten quietly by himself, reading the evening edition of the Peiping *Truth* as he ate his leisurely meal. Although many of the younger people had taken up the use of the knife and fork, the venerable Mr. Ying clung to the chopsticks of an earlier day, plied expertly between the thumb and forefinger of his right hand. He was not the only elderly man in the place who did so.

Having finished his meal and his newspaper in peace, Mr. Ying Lee strolled out into the gathering dusk. By the time utter darkness had come, and the widely spaced street lamps of the city had come alive, the elderly Mr. Ying Lee was within half a mile of the most important group of buildings in China.

The Peiping Explosion, back in the sixties, had almost started World War Three. An atomic blast had leveled a hundred square miles of the city and started fires that had taken weeks to extinguish. Soviet Russia had roared in its great bear voice that the Western Powers had attacked, and was apparently on the verge of coming to the defense of its Asian comrade when the Chinese Government had said irritatedly that there had been no attack, that traitorous and counterrevolutionary Chinese agents of Formosa had sabotaged an atomic plant, nothing more, and that the honorable comrades of Russia would be wise not to set off anything that would destroy civilization. The Russian Bear grumbled and sheathed its claws.

The vast intelligence system of the United States had reported that (A) the explosion had been caused by carelessness, not sabotage, but the Chinese had had to save face, and (B) the Soviet Union had no intention of actually starting an atomic war at that time. If she had, she would have shot first and made excuses afterwards. But she *had* hoped to make good propaganda usage of the blast.

The Peiping Explosion had caused widespread death and destruction, yes; but it had also ended up being the fastest slum-clearance project on record. The rebuilding had taken somewhat more time than the clearing had taken, but the results had been a new Peiping—a modern city in every respect. And nowhere else on Earth was there one hundred square miles of *completely* modern city. Alteration takes longer than starting from scratch if the techniques are available; there isn't so much dead wood to clear away.

In the middle of the city, the Chinese Government had built its equivalent of the Kremlin—nearly a third of a square mile of ultramodern buildings designed to house every function of the Communist Government of China. It had taken slave labor to do the job, but the job had been done.

A little more than half a mile on a side, the area was surrounded by a wall that had been designed after the Great Wall of China. It stood twenty-five feet high and looked very quaint and picturesque.

And somewhere inside it James Ch'ien, American-born physicist, was being held prisoner. Spencer Candron, alias Mr. Ying Lee, had to get him out.

Dr. Ch'ien was important. The Government of the United States knew he was important, but they did not yet know *how* important he was.

Man had already reached the Moon and returned. The Martian expedition had landed safely, but had not yet returned. No one had heard from the Venusian expedition, and it was presumed lost. But the Moon was being jointly claimed by Russian and American suits at the United Nations, while the United Nations itself was trying to establish a claim. The Martian expedition was American, but a Russian ship was due to land in two months. The lost Venusian expedition had been Russian, and the United States was ready to send a ship there.

After nearly forty years, the Cold War was still going on, but now the scale had expanded from the global to the interplanetary.

And now, up-and-coming China, defying the Western Powers and arrogantly ignoring her Soviet allies, had decided to get into the race late and win it if she could.

And she very likely could, if she could exploit the abili-

ties of James Ch'ien to the fullest. If Dr. Ch'ien could finish
his work, travel to the stars would no longer be a wild-
eyed idea; if he could finish, spatial velocities would no
longer be limited to the confines of the rocket, nor even to
the confines of the velocity of light. Man could go to the
stars.

The United States Federal Government knew—or, at
least, the most responsible officers of that government knew
—that Ch'ien's equations led to interstellar travel, just as
Einstein's equations had led to atomic energy. Normally, the
United States would never have allowed Dr. Ch'ien to attend the International Physicists Conference in Peiping. But
diplomacy has its rules, too.

Ch'ien had published his preliminary work—a series of
highly abstruse and very controversial equations—back in
'80. The paper had appeared in a journal that was circu-
lated only in the United States and was not read by the
majority of mathematical physicists. Like the work of Dr.
Fred Hoyle, thirty years before, it had been laughed at by
the majority of the men in the field. Unlike Hoyle's work,
it had never received any publicity. Ch'ien's paper had remained buried.

In '81, Ch'ien had realized the importance of his work,
having carried it further. He had reported his findings to the
proper authorities of the United States Government, and
had convinced that particular branch of the government that
his work had useful validity. But it was too late to cover up
the hints that he had already published.

Dr. James Ch'ien was a friendly, gregarious man. He
liked to go to conventions and discuss his work with his colleagues. He was, in addition, a man who would never let
anything go once he had got hold of it, unless he was convinced that he was up a blind alley. And, as far as Dr.
Ch'ien was concerned, that took a devil of a lot of convincing.

The United States Government was, therefore, faced with
a dilemma. If they let Ch'ien go to the International Conferences, there was the chance that he would be forced, in
some way, to divulge secrets that were vital to the national
defense of the United States. On the other hand, if they for-

bade him to go, the Communist governments would suspect that Ch'ien knew something important, and they would check back on his previous work and find his publications of 1980. If they did, and realized the importance of that paper, they might be able to solve the secret of the interstellar drive.

The United States Government had figuratively flipped a coin, and the result was that Ch'ien was allowed to come and go as he pleased, as though he were nothing more than just another government physicist.

And now he was in the hands of China.

How much did the Chinese know? Not much, evidently; otherwise they would never have bothered to go to the trouble of kidnaping Dr. James Ch'ien and covering the kidnaping so elaborately. They *suspected*, yes; but they couldn't *know*. They knew that the earlier papers meant something, but they didn't know what—so they had abducted Ch'ien in the hope that he would tell them.

James Ch'ien had been in their hands now for two months. How much information had they extracted by now? Personally, Spencer Candron felt that they had got nothing. You can force a man to work; you can force him to tell the truth. But you can *not* force a man to create against his will.

Still, even a man's will can be broken, given enough time. If Dr. Ch'ien weren't rescued soon . . .

Tonight, Candron thought with determination. *I'll get Ch'ien tonight.* That was what the S.M.M.R. had sent him to do. And that's what he would—*must*—do.

Ahead of him loomed the walls of the Palace of the Great Chinese People's Government. Getting past them and into the inner court was an act that was discouraged as much as possible by the special police guard which had charge of those walls. They were brilliantly lighted and heavily guarded. If Candron tried to levitate himself over, he'd most likely be shot down in midair. They might be baffled afterward, when they tried to figure out how he had come to be flying around up there, but that wouldn't help Candron any.

Candron had a better method.

When the automobile carrying the People's Minister of Finance, the Honorable Chou Lung, went through the Gate of the Dog to enter the inner court of the Palace, none of the four men inside it had any notion that they were carrying an unwanted guest. How could they? The car was a small one; its low, streamlined body carried only four people, and there was no luggage compartment, since the powerful little vehicle was designed only for maneuvering in a crowded city or for fast, short trips to near-by towns. There was simply no room for another passenger, and both the men in the car and the guards who passed it through were so well aware of that fact that they didn't even bother to think about it. It never occurred to them that a slight, elderly-looking gentleman might be hanging beneath the car, floating a few inches off the ground, holding on with his fingertips, and allowing the car to pull him along as it moved on into the Palace of the Great Chinese People's Government.

Getting into the subterranean cell where Dr. James Ch'ien was being held was a different kind of problem. Candron knew the interior of the Palace by map only, and the map he had studied had been admittedly inadequate. It took him nearly an hour to get to the right place. Twice, he avoided a patrolling guard by taking to the air and concealing himself in the darkness of an overhead balcony. Several other times, he met men in civilian clothing walking along the narrow walks, and he merely nodded at them. He looked too old and too well-dressed to be dangerous.

The principle that made it easy was the fact that no one expects a lone man to break into a heavily guarded prison.

After he had located the building where James Ch'ien was held, he went high-flying. The building itself was one which contained the living quarters of several high-ranking officers of the People's Government. Candron knew he would be conspicuous if he tried to climb up the side of the building from the outside, but he managed to get into the second floor without being observed. Then he headed for the elevator shafts.

It took him several minutes to jimmy open the elevator door. His mind was sensitive enough to sense the nearness of others, so there was no chance of his being caught red-handed. When he got the door open, he stepped into the shaft, brought his loathing for the bottom into the fore, and floated up to the top floor. From there it was a simple matter to get to the roof, drop down the side, and enter the open window of an officer's apartment.

He entered a lighted window rather than a darkened one. He wanted to know what he was getting into. He had his gun ready, just in case, but there was no sign of anyone in the room he entered. A quick search showed that the other two rooms were also empty. His mind had told him that there was no one awake in the apartment, but a sleeping man's mind, filled with dimmed, chaotic thoughts, blended into the background and might easily be missed.

Then Spencer Candron used the telephone, punching the first of the two code numbers he had been given. A connection was made to the room where a twenty-four-hour guard kept watch over James Ch'ien via television pickups hidden in the walls of his prison apartment in the basement.

Candron had listened to recordings of one man's voice for hours, getting the exact inflection, accent, and usage. Now, he made use of that practice.

"This is General Soong," he said sharply. "We are sending a Dr. Wan down to persuade the guest. We will want recordings of all that takes place."

"Yes, sir," said the voice at the other end.

"Dr. Wan will be there within ten minutes, so be alert."

"Yes, sir. All will be done to your satisfaction."

"Excellent," said Candron. He smiled as he hung up. Then he punched another secret number. This one connected him with the guards outside Ch'ien's apartment. As General Soong, he warned them of the coming of Dr. Wan. Then he went to the window, stepped out, and headed for the roof again.

There was no danger that the calls would be suspected. Those two phones could not be contacted except from inside the Palace, and not even then unless the number was known.

Again he dropped down Elevator Shaft Three. Only Number One was operating this late in the evening, so there was no fear of meeting it coming up. He dropped lightly to the roof of the car, where it stood empty in the basement, opened the escape hatch in the roof, dropped inside, opened the door, and emerged into the first basement. Then he started down the stairs to the subbasement.

The guards were not the least suspicious, apparently. Candron wished he were an honest-to-God telepath, so he could be absolutely sure. The officer at the end of the corridor that led to Ch'ien's apartment was a full captain, a tough-looking, swarthy Mongol with dark, hard eyes. "You are Dr. Wan?" he asked in a guttural baritone.

"I am," Candron said. This was no place for traditional politeness. "Did not General Soong call you?"

"He did, indeed, doctor. But I assumed you would be carrying—" He gestured, as though not quite sure what to say.

Candron smiled blandly. "Ah. You were expecting the little black bag, is it not so? No, my good captain; I am a psychologist, not a medical doctor."

The captain's face cleared. "So. The persuasion is to be of the more subtle type."

"Indeed. Only thus can we be assured of his co-operation. One cannot force the creative mind to create; it must be cajoled. Could one have forced the great K'ung Fu-tse to become a philosopher at the point of a sword?"

"It is so," said the captain. "Will you permit me to search you?"

The affable Dr. Wan emptied his pockets, then permitted the search. The captain casually looked at the identification in the wallet. It was, naturally, in perfect order for Dr. Wan. The identification of Ying Lee had been destroyed hours ago, since it was of no further value.

"These things must be left here until you come out, doctor," the captain said. "You may pick them up when you leave." He gestured at the pack of cigarettes. "You will be given cigarettes by the interior guard. Such are my orders."

"Very well," Candron said calmly. "And now, may I see the patient?" He had wanted to keep those cigarettes. Now he would have to find a substitute.

The captain unlocked the heavy door. At the far end, two

more guards sat, complacently playing cards, while a third stood at a door a few yards away. A television screen imbedded in the door was connected to an interior camera which showed the room within.

The corridor door was closed and locked behind Candron as he walked toward the three interior guards. They were three more big, tough Mongols, all wearing the insignia of lieutenants. This was not a prisoner who could be entrusted to the care of common soldiers; the secret was too important to allow *hoi polloi* in on it. They carried no weapons; the three of them could easily take care of Ch'ien if he tried anything foolish, and besides, it kept weapons out of Ch'ien's reach. There were other methods of taking care of the prisoner if the guards were inadequate.

The two officers who were playing cards looked up, acknowledged Dr. Wan's presence, and went back to their game. The third, after glancing at the screen, opened the door to James Ch'ien's apartment. Spencer Candron stepped inside.

It was because of those few seconds—the time during which that door was open—that Candron had called the monitors who watched Ch'ien's apartment. Otherwise, he wouldn't have bothered. He needed fifteen seconds in which to act, and he couldn't do it with that door open. If the monitors had given an alarm in these critical seconds . . .

But they hadn't, and they wouldn't. Not yet.

The man who was sitting in the easy-chair on the opposite side of the room looked up as Candron entered.

James Ch'ien (B.S., M.S., M.I.T.; Ph.D., U.C.L.A.) was a young man, barely past thirty. His tanned face no longer wore the affable smile that Candron had seen in photographs, and the jet-black eyes beneath the well-formed brows were cold instead of friendly, but the intelligence behind the face still came through.

As the door was relocked behind him, Candron said, in Cantonese: "This unworthy one hopes that the excellent doctor is well. Permit me to introduce my unworthy self: I am Dr. Wan Feng."

Dr. Ch'ien put the book he was reading in his lap. He looked at the ceiling in exasperation, then back at Candron.

"All right," he said in English, "so you don't believe me. But I'll repeat it again in the hope that I can get it through your skulls." It was obvious that he was addressing, not only his visitor, but anyone else who might be listening.

"I do not speak Chinese," he said, emphasizing each word separately. "I can say 'Good morning' and 'Good-by', and that's about it. I *do* wish I could say 'drop dead,' but that's a luxury I can't indulge. If you can speak English, then go ahead; if not, quit wasting my time and yours. Not," he added, "that it won't be a waste of time anyway, but at least it will relieve the monotony."

Candron knew that Ch'ien was only partially telling the truth. The physicist spoke the language badly, but he understood it fairly well.

"Sorry, doctor," Candron said in English, "I guess I forgot myself. I am Dr. Wan Feng."

Ch'ien's expression didn't change, but he waved to a near-by chair. "Sit down, Dr. Feng, and tell me what propaganda line you've come to deliver now."

Candron smiled and shook his head slowly. "That was unworthy of you, Dr. Ch'ien. Even though you have succumbed to the Western habit of putting the family name last, you are perfectly aware that 'Wan,' not 'Feng,' is my family name."

The physicist didn't turn a hair. "Force of habit, Dr. Wan. Or, rather, a little retaliation. I was called 'Dakta Chamis' for two days, and even those who could pronounce the name properly insisted on 'Dr. James.' But I forget myself. I am supposed to be the host here. Do sit down and tell me why I should give myself over to Communist China just because my grandfather was born here back in the days when China was a republic."

Spencer Candron knew that time was running out, but he had to force Ch'ien into the right position before he could act. He wished again that he had been able to keep the cigarettes. Ch'ien was a moderately heavy smoker, and one of those drugged cigarettes would have come in handy now. As it was, he had to handle it differently. And that meant a different approach.

"No, Dr. Ch'ien," he said, in a voice that was deliberately too smooth, "I will not sit down, thank you. I would prefer that you stand up."

The physicist's face became a frozen mask. "I see that the doctorate you claim is not for studies in the field of physics. You're not here to worm things out of me by discussing my work—talking shop. What is it, *Doctor* Wan?"

"I am a psychologist," Candron said. He knew that the monitors watching the screens and listening to the conversation were recording everything. He knew that they shouldn't be suspicious yet. But if the real General Soong should decide to check on what his important guest was doing—

"A psychologist," Ch'ien repeated in a monotone. "I see."

"Yes. Now, will you stand, or do I have to ask the guards to lift you to your feet?"

James Ch'ien recognized the inevitable, so he stood. But there was a wary expression in his black eyes. He was not a tall man; he stood nearly an inch shorter than Candron himself.

"You have nothing to fear, Dr. Ch'ien," Candron said smoothly. "I merely wish to test a few of your reactions. We do not wish to hurt you." He put his hands on the other man's shoulders, and positioned him. "There," he said. "Now. Look to the left."

"Hypnosis, eh?" Ch'ien said with a grim smile. "All right. Go ahead." He looked to his left.

"Not with your head," Candron said calmly. "Face me and look to the left with your eyes."

Ch'ien did so, saying, "I'm afraid you'll have to use drugs after all, Dr. Wan. I will not be hypnotized."

"I have no intention of hypnotizing you. Now look to the right."

Ch'ien obeyed.

Candron's right hand was at his side, and his left hand was toying with a button on his coat. "Now up," he said.

Dr. James Ch'ien rolled his eyeballs upward.

Candron had already taken a deep breath. Now he acted. His right hand balled into a fist and arced upwards in a crashing uppercut to Ch'ien's jaw. At almost the same time, he jerked the button off his coat, cracked it with his fingers along the special fissure line, and threw it to the floor.

As the little bomb spewed forth unbelievable amounts of ultra-finely divided carbon in a dense black cloud of smoke, Candron threw both arms around the collapsing physicist, ignoring the pain in the knuckles of his right hand. The smoke cloud billowed around them, darkening the room and obscuring the view from the monitor screens that were watching them. Candron knew that the guards were acting now; he knew that the big Mongols outside were already inserting the key in the door and inserting their nose plugs; he knew that the men in the monitor room had hit an alarm button and had already begun to flood the room with sleep gas. But he paid no attention to these things.

Instead, he became homesick.

Home. It was a little place he knew and loved. He could no longer stand the alien environment around him; it was repugnant, repelling. All he could think of was a little room, a familiar room, a beloved room. He knew the cracks in its ceiling, the feel of the varnish on the homely little desk, the touch of the worn carpet against his feet, the very smell of the air itself. And he loved them and longed for them with all the emotional power that was in him.

And suddenly the darkness of the smoke-filled prison apartment was gone.

Spencer Candron stood in the middle of the little hotel room he had rented early that morning. In his arms, he held the unconscious figure of Dr. James Ch'ien.

He gasped for breath, then, with an effort, he stooped, allowed the limp body of the physicist to collapse over his shoulder, and stood straight again, carrying the man like a sack of potatoes. He went to the door of the room and opened it carefully. The hall was empty. Quickly, he moved outside, closing the door behind him, and headed toward the stairs. This time, he dared not trust the elevator shaft. The hotel only boasted one elevator, and it might be used at any time. Instead, he allowed his dislike for the stair treads to adjust his weight to a few pounds, and then ran up them two at a time.

On the roof of the hotel, he adjusted his emotional state

once more, and he and his sleeping burden drifted off into the night, toward the sea.

No mind is infinitely flexible, infinitely malleable, infinitely capable of taking punishment, just as no material substance, however constructed, is capable of absorbing the energies brought to bear against it indefinitely.

A man can hate with a virulent hatred, but unless time is allowed to dull and soothe that hatred, the mind holding it will become corroded and cease to function properly, just as a machine of the finest steel will become corroded and begin to fail if it is drenched with acid or exposed to the violence of an oxidizing atmosphere.

The human mind can insulate itself, for a time, against the destructive effects of any emotion, be it hatred, greed, despondency, contentment, happiness, pleasure, anger, fear, lust, boredom, euphoria, determination, or any other of the myriads of "ills" that man's mind—and thus his flesh—is heir to. As long as a mind is capable of changing from one to another, to rotate its crops, so to speak, the insulation will remain effective, and the mind will remain undamaged. But any single emotional element, held for too long, will break down the resistance of the natural insulation and begin to damage the mind.

Even that least virulent of emotions, love, can destroy. The hot, passionate love between new lovers must be modified or it will kill. Only when its many facets can be shifted around, now one and now the other coming into play, can love be endured for any great length of time.

Possibly the greatest difference between the sane and the unsane is that the sane know when to release a destructive force before it does more than minimal damage; to modify or eliminate an emotional condition before it becomes a deadly compulsion; to replace one set of concepts with another when it becomes necessary to do so; to recognize that point when the mind must change its outlook or die. To stop the erosion, in other words, before it becomes so great that it cannot be repaired.

For the human mind cannot contain any emotion, no matter how weak or how fleeting, without change. And the point at which that change ceases to be *con*structive and becomes, instead, *de*structive—*that* is the ultimate point beyond which no human mind can go without forcing a change—*any* change—in itself.

Spencer Candron knew that. To overuse the psionic powers of the human mind is as dangerous as overusing morphine or alcohol. There are limits to mental powers, even as there are limits to physical powers.

Psychokinesis is defined as the ability of a human mind to move, no matter how slightly, a physical object by means of psionic application alone. In theory, then, one could move planets, stars, even whole galaxies by thought alone. But, in physical terms, the limit is easily seen. Physically, it would be theoretically possible to destroy the sun if one had enough atomic energy available, but that would require the energy of another sun—or more. And, at that point, the Law of Diminishing Returns comes into operation. If you don't want a bomb to explode, but the only way to destroy that bomb is by blowing it up with another bomb of equal power, where is the gain?

And if the total mental power required to move a planet is greater than any single human mind can endure—or even greater than the total mental endurance of a thousand planetsfull of minds, is there any gain?

There is not, and can never be, a system without limits, and the human mind is a system which obeys that law.

None the less, Spencer Candron kept his mind on flight, on repulsion, on movement, as long as he could. He was perfectly willing to destroy his own mind for a purpose, but he had no intention of destroying it uselessly. He didn't know how long he kept moving eastward; he had no way of knowing how much distance he had covered nor how long it had taken him. But, somewhere out over the smoothly undulating surface of the Pacific, he realized that he was approaching his limit. And, a few seconds later, he detected the presence of men beneath the sea.

He knew they were due to rise an hour before dawn, but he had no idea how long that would be. He had lost all track of time. He had been keeping his mind on controlling his altitude and motion, and, at the same time, been careful to see whether Dr. Ch'ien came out of his unconscious state. Twice more he had had to strike the physicist to keep him out cold, and he didn't want to do it again.

So, when he sensed the presence of the American submarine beneath the waves, he sank gratefully into the water, changing the erosive power of the emotion that had carried him so far, and relaxing into the simple physical routine of keeping both himself and Ch'ien afloat.

By the time the submarine surfaced a dozen yards away, Spencer Candron was both physically and mentally exhausted. He yelled at the top of his lungs, and then held on to consciousness just long enough to be rescued.

"The official story," said Senator Kerotski, "is that an impostor had taken Dr. Ch'ien's place before he ever left the United States—" He grinned. "At least, the substitution took place before the delegates reached China. So the 'assassination' was really no assassination at all. Ch'ien was kidnaped here, and a double put in his place in Peiping. That absolves both us and the Chinese Government of any complicity. We save face for them, and they save face for us. Since he turned up here, in the States, it's obvious that he couldn't have been in China." He chuckled, but there was no mirth in it. "So the cold war still continues. We know what they did, and—in a way—they know what we did. But not how we did it."

The senator looked at the other two men who were with him on the fifth floor office of the *Society for Mystical and Metaphysical Research*. Taggert was relaxing on his couch, and Spencer Candron, just out of the hospital, looked rather pale as he sat in the big, soft chair that Taggert had provided.

The senator looked at Candron. "The thing I don't understand is, why was it necessary to knock out Ch'ien? He'll have a sore jaw for weeks. Why didn't you just tell him who you were and what you were up to?"

Candron glanced at Taggert, but Taggert just grinned and nodded.

"We couldn't allow that," said Candron, looking at Senator Kerotski. "Dr. James Ch'ien has too much of a logical, scientific mind for that. We'd have ruined him if he'd seen me in action."

The senator looked a little surprised. "Why? We've convinced other scientists that they were mistaken in their observations. Why not Ch'ien?"

"Ch'ien is too good a scientist," Candron said. "He's not the type who would refuse to believe something he saw simply because it didn't agree with his theories. Ch'ien is one of those dangerous in-betweens. He's too brilliant to be allowed to go to waste, and, at the same time, too rigid to change his manner of thinking. If he had seen me teleport or levitate, he wouldn't reject it—he'd try to explain it. And that would have effectively ruined him."

"Ruined him?" The senator looked a little puzzled.

Taggert raised his heavy head from the couch. "Sure, Leo," he said to the senator. "Don't you see? We *need* Ch'ien on this interstellar project. He absolutely *must* dope out the answer somehow, and no one else can do it as quickly."

"With the previous information," the senator said, "we would have been able to continue."

"Yeah?" Taggert said, sitting up. "Has anyone been able to dope out Fermat's Last Theorem without Fermat? No. So why ruin Ch'ien?"

"It would ruin him," Candron broke in, before the senator could speak. "If he saw, beyond any shadow of a doubt, that levitation and teleportation were possible, he would have accepted his own senses as usable data on definite phenomena. But, limited as he is by his scientific outlook, he would have tried to evolve a scientific theory to explain what he saw. What else could a scientist *do?*"

Senator Kerotski nodded, and his nod said, "I see. He would have diverted his attention from the field of the interstellar drive to the field of psionics. And he would have wasted years trying to explain an inherently nonlogical area of knowledge by logical means."

"That's right," Candron said. "We would have set him off on a wild goose chase, trying to solve the problems of psionics by the scientific, the logical method. We would have presented him with an unsolvable problem."

Taggert patted his knees. "We would have given him a problem that he could not solve with the methodology at hand. It would be as though we had proved to an ancient Greek philosopher that the cube *could* be doubled, and then allowed him to waste his life trying to do it with a straight-edge and compass."

"We know Ch'ien's psychological pattern," Candron continued. "He's not capable of admitting that there is any other thought pattern than the logical. He would try to solve the problems of psionics by logical methods, and would waste the rest of his life trying to do the impossible."

The senator stroked his chin. "That's clear," he said at last. "Well, it was worth a cracked jaw to save him. We've given him a perfectly logical explanation of his rescue, and, simultaneously, we've put the Chinese Government into absolute confusion. They have no idea of how you got out of there, Candron."

"That's not as important as saving Ch'ien," Candron said.

"No," the senator said quickly, "of course not. After all, the Secretary of Research needs Dr. Ch'ien—the man's important."

Spencer Candron smiled. "I agree. He's practically indispensable—as much as a man can be."

"He's the Secretary's right-hand man," said Taggert firmly.

THE SOUND SWEEP

by J. G. Ballard

from *Science Fantasy*

It was Fletcher Pratt who first brought to my attention the use of fantasy, or more specifically of the fantastic or science-fictional environment, to spotlight or enlarge human reactions: "The intensification of emotion," he called it. Very often, this is the main function of a fantastic backdrop: to set the stage for a close-up view of an emotional interchange which, under "normal," "realistic" circumstances occurs at such low intensity as to be almost imperceptible; or to magnify a "normal" experience of the "real" world to, for example, Faustian proportion.

J. G. Ballard, one of the young British writers whose work has been much too little seen in this country, here provides an example of this sort of emotional intensification performed on a (literal) future stage-set of the past.

1

By midnight Madame Gioconda's headache had become intense. All day the derelict walls and ceiling of the sound stage had reverberated with the endless din of traffic accelerating across the mid-town flyover which arched fifty feet above the studio's roof, a frenzied hypomaniac babel of jostling horns, shrilling tires, plunging brakes and engines that hammered down the empty corridors and stairways to the sound stage on the second floor, making the faded air feel leaden and angry.

Exhausting but at least impersonal, these sounds Madame Gioconda could bear. At dusk, however, when the flyover quietened, they were overlaid by the mysterious clapping of her phantoms, the sourceless applause that rustled down onto the stage from the darkness around her, at first a few scattered ripples from the front rows that soon spread to the entire auditorium, mounting to a tumultuous ovation in which she suddenly detected a note of sarcasm, a single shout of derision that drove a spear of pain through her forehead, followed by an uproar of boos and catcalls that filled the tortured air, driving her away toward her couch where she lay gasping helplessly until Mangon arrived at midnight, hurrying onto the stage with his sonovac.

Understanding her, he first concentrated on sweeping the walls and ceiling clean, draining away the heavy depressing underlayer of traffic noises. Carefully he ran the long snout of the sonovac over the ancient scenic flats (relics of her previous roles at the Metropolitan Opera House) which screened-in Madame Gioconda's makeshift home—the great collapsing Byzantine bed (*Othello*) mounted against the microphone turret; the huge framed mirrors with their peeling silverscreen (*Orpheus*) stacked in one corner by the bandstand; the stove (*Trovatore*) set up on the program director's podium; the gilt-trimmed dressing table and wardrobe (*Figaro*) stuffed with newspaper and magazine cuttings. He swept them methodically, moving the sonovac's nozzle in long strokes, drawing out the dead residues of sound that had accumulated during the day.

By the time he finished the air was clear again, the atmosphere lightened, its overtones of fatigue and irritation dissipated. Gradually Madame Gioconda recovered. Sitting up weakly, she smiled wanly at Mangon. Mangon grinned back encouragingly, slipped the kettle onto the stove for Russian tea, sweetened by the usual phenobarbitone chaser, switched off the sonovac and indicated to her that he was going outside to empty it.

Down in the alley behind the studio he clipped the sonovac onto the intake manifold of the sound truck. The vacuum drained in a few seconds, but he waited a discretionary two or three minutes before returning, keeping up the pretense that Madame Gioconda's phantom audience was real. Of course the cylinder was always empty, containing only the usual daily detritus—the sounds of a door slam, a partition collapsing somewhere or the kettle whistling, a grunt or two, and later, when the headaches began, Madame Gioconda's pitiful moanings. The riotous applause, that would have lifted the roof off the Met, let alone a small radio station, the jeers and hoots of derision were, he knew, quite imaginary, figments of Madame Gioconda's world of fantasy, phantoms from the past of a once great prima donna who had been dropped by her public and had retreated in her imagination, each evening conjuring up a blissful dream of being once again applauded by a full house at the Metropolitan, a dream that guilt and resentment turned sour by midnight, inverting it into a nightmare of fiasco and failure.

Why she should torment herself was difficult to understand, but at least the nightmare kept Madame Gioconda just this side of sanity and Mangon, who revered and loved Madame Gioconda, would have been the last person in the world to disillusion her. Each evening, when he finished his calls for the day, he would drive his sound truck all the way over from the West Side to the abandoned radio station under the flyover at the deserted end of F Street, go through the pretense of sweeping Madame Gioconda's apartment on the stage of studio 2, charging no fee, make tea and listen to her reminiscences and plans for revenge, then see her asleep and tiptoe out, a wry but pleased smile on his youthful face.

He had been calling on Madame Gioconda for nearly a year, but what his precise role was in relation to her he had not yet decided. Oddly enough, although he was more or less indispensable now to the effective operation of her fantasy world, she showed little personal interest or affection for Mangon; but he assumed that this indifference was merely part of the autocratic personality of a world-famous prima donna, particularly one very conscious of the tradition, now alas meaningless, Melba—Callas—Gioconda. To serve at all was the privilege. In time, perhaps, Madame Gioconda might accord him some sign of favor.

Without him, certainly, her prognosis would have been poor. Lately the headaches had become more menacing, as she insisted that the applause was growing stormier, the boos and catcalls more vicious. Whatever the psychic mechanism generating the fantasy system, Mangon realized that ultimately she would need him at the studio all day,

holding back the enveloping tides of nightmare and insanity
with dummy passes of the sonovac. Then, perhaps, when
the dream crumbled, he would regret having helped her to
delude herself. With luck though she might achieve her ambition of making a comeback. She had told him something
of her scheme—a serpentine mixture of blackmail and
bribery—and privately Mangon hoped to launch a plot of
his own to return her to popularity. By now she had unfortunately reached the point where success alone could
save her from disaster.

She was sitting up when he returned, propped back on an
enormous gold lamé cushion, the single lamp at the foot of
the couch throwing a semicircle of light onto the great flats
which divided the sound stage from the auditorium. These
were all from her last operatic role—*The Medium*—and
represented a complete interior of the old spiritualist's
séance chamber, the one coherent feature in Madame Gioconda's present existence. Surrounded by fragments from a
dozen roles, even Madame Gioconda herself, Mangon reflected, seemed compounded of several separate identities.
A tall regal figure, with full shapely shoulders and massive
rib-cage, she had a large handsome face topped by a magnificent coiffure of rich blue-black hair—the exact proto-
type of the classical diva. She must have been almost fifty,
yet her soft creamy complexion and small features were
those of a child. The eyes, however, belied her. Large and
watchful, slashed with mascara, they regarded the world
around her balefully, narrowing even as Mangon approached. Her teeth too were bad, stained by tobacco and
cheap cocaine. When she was roused, and her full violet
lips curled with rage revealing the blackened hulks of her
dentures and the acid flickering tongue, her mouth looked
like a very vent of hell. Altogether she was a formidable
woman.

As Mangon brought her tea she heaved herself up and
made room for him by her feet among the debris of beads,
loose diary pages, horoscopes and jeweled address books
that littered the couch. Mangon sat down, surreptitiously
noting the time (his first calls were at 9:30 the next morn-

ing and loss of sleep deadened his acute hearing), and prepared himself to listen to her for half an hour.

Suddenly she flinched, shrank back into the cushion and gestured agitatedly in the direction of the darkened bandstand.

"They're still clapping!" she shrieked. "For God's sake sweep them away, they're driving me insane. Oooohh . . ." she rasped theatrically, "over there, quickly . . . !"

Mangon leapt to his feet. He hurried over to the bandstand and carefully focused his ears on the tiers of seats and plywood music stands. They were all immaculately clean, well below the threshold at which embedded sounds began to radiate detectable echoes. He turned to the corner walls and ceiling. Listening very carefully he could just hear seven muted pads, the dull echoes of his footsteps across the floor. They faded and vanished, followed by a low threshing noise like blurred radio static—in fact Madame Gioconda's present tantrum. Mangon could almost distinguish the individual words, but repetition muffled them.

Madame Gioconda was still writhing about on the couch, evidently not to be easily placated, so Mangon climbed down off the stage and made his way through the auditorium to where he had left his sonovac by the door. The power lead was outside in the truck but he was sure Madame Gioconda would fail to notice.

For five minutes he worked away industriously, pretending to sweep the bandstand again, then put down the sonovac and returned to the couch.

Madame Gioconda emerged from the cushion, sounded the air carefully with two or three slow turns of the head, and smiled at him.

"Thank you, Mangon," she said silkily, her eyes watching him thoughtfully. "You've saved me again from my assassins. They've become so cunning recently, they can even hide from you."

Mangon smiled ruefully to himself at this last remark. So he had been a little too perfunctory earlier on; Madame Gioconda was keeping him up to the mark.

However, she seemed genuinely grateful. "Mangon, my dear," she reflected as she remade her face in the mirror of

an enormous compact, painting on magnificent green eyes
like a cobra's, "what would I do without you? How can I
ever repay you for looking after me?"

The questions, whatever their sinister undertones (had he
detected them, Mangon would have been deeply shocked)
were purely rhetorical, and all their conversations for that
matter entirely one-sided. For Mangon was a mute. From
the age of three, when his mother had savagely punched
him in the throat to stop him crying, he had been stone
dumb, his vocal cords irreparably damaged. In all their endless exchanges of midnight confidences, Mangon had contributed not a single spoken word.

His muteness, naturally, was part of the attraction he felt
for Madame Gioconda. Both of them in a sense had lost
their voices, he to a cruel mother, she to a fickle and unfaithful public. This bound them together, gave them a
shared sense of life's injustice, though Mangon, like all
innocents, viewed his misfortune without rancor. Both, too,
were social outcasts. Rescued from his degenerate parents
when he was four, Mangon had been brought up in a suc-
cession of state institutions, a solitary wounded child. His
one talent had been his remarkable auditory powers, and
at fourteen he was apprenticed to the Metropolitan Sonic
Disposal Service. Regarded as little better than garbage
collectors, the sound-sweeps were an outcast group of illit-
erates, mutes (the city authorities preferred these—their
discretion could be relied upon) and social cripples who
lived in a chain of isolated shacks on the edge of an old explosives plant in the sand dunes to the north of the city
which served as the sonic dump.

Mangon had made no friends among the sound-sweeps,
and Madame Gioconda was the first person in his life with
whom he had been intimately involved. Apart from the
pleasure of being able to help her, a considerable factor in
Mangon's devotion was that until her decline she had represented (as to all mutes) the most painful possible reminder
of his own voiceless condition, and that now he could at
last come to terms with years of unconscious resentment.

This soon done, he devoted himself wholeheartedly to
serving Madame Gioconda.

Inhaling moodily on a black cigarette clamped into a long jade holder, she was outlining her plans for a comeback. These had been maturing for several months and involved nothing less than persuading Hector LeGrande, chairman-in-chief of Video City, the huge corporation that transmitted a dozen TV and radio channels, into providing her with a complete series of television spectaculars. Built around Madame Gioconda and lavishly dressed and orchestrated, they would spearhead the international revival of classical opera that was her unfading dream.

"La Scala, Covent Garden, the Met—what are they now?" she demanded angrily. "Bowling alleys! Can you believe, Mangon, that in those immortal theaters where I created my Tosca, my Butterfly, my Brünnhilde, they now have"—she spat out a gust of smoke—"beer and skittles!"

Mangon shook his head sympathetically. He pulled a pencil from his breast pocket and on the wrist-pad stitched to his left sleeve wrote: *Mr. LeGrande?*

Madame Gioconda read the note, let it fall to the floor.

"Hector? Those lawyers poison him. He's surrounded by them, I think they steal all my telegrams to him. Of course Hector had a complete breakdown on the spectaculars. Imagine, Mangon, what a scoop for him, a sensation! 'The great Gioconda will appear on television!' Not just some moronic bubblegum girl, but the Gioconda in person."

Exhausted by this vision Madame Gioconda sank back into her cushion, blowing smoke limply through the holder.

Mangon wrote: *Contract?*

Madame Gioconda frowned at the note, then pierced it with the glowing end of her cigarette.

"I am having a new contract drawn up. Not for the mere 300,000 I was prepared to take at first, not even 500,000. For each show I shall now demand precisely *one million* dollars. Nothing less! Hector will have to pay for ignoring me. Anyway, think of the publicity value of such a figure. Only a star could think of such vulgar extravagance. If he's short of cash he can sack all those lawyers. Or devalue the dollar, I don't mind."

Madame Gioconda hooted with pleasure at the prospect.

Mangon nodded, then scribbled another message: *Be practical*.

Madame Gioconda ground out her cigarette. "You think I'm raving, don't you, Mangon? 'Fantastic dreams, million-dollar contracts, poor old fool.' But let me assure you that Hector will be only too eager to sign the contract. And I don't intend to rely solely on his good judgment as an impresario." She smirked archly to herself.

What else?

Madame Gioconda peered round the darkened stage, then lowered her eyes.

"You see, Mangon, Hector and I are very old friends. You know what I mean, of course?" She waited for Mangon, who had swept out a thousand honeymoon hotel suites, to nod and then continued, "How well I remember that first season at Bayreuth, when Hector and I . . ."

Mangon stared unhappily at his feet as Madame Gioconda outlined this latest venture into blackmail. Certainly she and LeGrande had been intimate friends—the cuttings scattered around the stage testified frankly to this. In fact, were it not for the small monthly check which LeGrande sent Madame Gioconda she would long previously have disintegrated. To turn on him and threaten ancient scandal (LeGrande was shortly to enter politics) was not only grotesque but extremely dangerous, for LeGrande was ruthless and unsentimental. Years earlier he had used Madame Gioconda as a stepping stone, reaping all the publicity he could from their affair, then abruptly kicking her away.

Mangon fretted. A solution to her predicament was hard to find. Brought about through no fault of her own, Madame Gioconda's decline was all the harder to bear. Since the introduction a few years earlier of ultrasonic music, the human voice—indeed, audible music of any type—had gone completely out of fashion. Ultrasonic music, employing a vastly greater range of octaves, chords and chromatic scales than perceptible to the human ear, provided a direct neural link between the sound stream and the auditory lobes, generating an apparently sourceless sensation of harmony, rhythm, cadence and melody uncontaminated by the noise and vibration of audible music. The rescoring of the classical repertoire allowed the ultrasonic audience the best of both worlds. The majestic rhythms of Beethoven, the popular melodies of Tchaikovsky, the complex fugal elaborations of Bach, the abstract images of Schoenberg— all these were raised in frequency above the threshold of conscious audibility. Not only did they become inaudible, but the original works were rescored for the much wider range of the ultrasonic orchestra, became richer in texture, more profound in theme, more sensitive, tender or lyrical as the ultrasonic arranger chose.

The first casualty in this change-over was the human voice. This alone of all instruments could not be rescored, because its sounds were produced by nonmechanical means which the neurophonic engineer could never hope, or bother, to duplicate.

The earliest ultrasonic recordings had met with resistance, even ridicule. Radio programs consisting of nothing but silence interrupted at half-hour intervals by commercial breaks seemed absurd. But gradually the public discovered that the silence was golden, that after leaving the radio switched to an ultrasonic channel for an hour or so a pleasant atmosphere of rhythm and melody seemed to generate itself spontaneously around them. When an announcer suddenly stated that an ultrasonic version of Mozart's *Jupiter Symphony* or Tchaikovsky's *Pathetique* had just been played the listener identified the real source.

A second advantage of ultrasonic music was that its frequencies were so high they left no resonating residues in solid structures, and consequently there was no need to call in the sound-sweep. After an audible performance of most symphonic music, walls and furniture throbbed for days with disintegrating residues that made the air seem leaden and tumid, an entire room virtually uninhabitable.

An immediate result was the swift collapse of all but a few symphony orchestras and opera companies. Concert halls and opera houses closed overnight. In the age of noise the tranquilizing balms of silence began to be rediscovered.

But the final triumph of ultrasonic music had come with

a second development—the short-playing record, spinning at 900 r.p.m., which condensed the 45 minutes of a Beethoven symphony to 20 seconds of playing time, the three hours of a Wagner opera to little more than two minutes. Compact and cheap, SP records sacrificed nothing to brevity. One 30-second SP record delivered as much neurophonic pleasure as a natural length recording, but with deeper penetration, greater total impact.

Ultrasonic SP records swept all others off the market. Sonic LP records became museum pieces—only a crank would choose to listen to an audible full-length version of *Siegfried* or the *Barber of Seville* when he could have both wrapped up inaudibly inside the same five-minute package *and* appreciate their full musical value.

The heyday of Madame Gioconda was over. Unceremoniously left on the shelf, she had managed to survive for a few months vocalizing on radio commercials. Soon these too went ultrasonic. In a despairing act of revenge she bought out the radio station which fired her and made her home on one of the sound stages. Over the years the station became derelict and forgotten, its windows smashed, neon portico collapsing, aerials rusting. The huge eight-lane flyover built across it sealed it conclusively into the past.

Now Madame Gioconda proposed to win her way back at stiletto-point.

Mangon watched her impassively as she ranted on nastily in a cloud of purple cigarette smoke, a large seedy witch. The phenobarbitone was making her drowsy and her threats and ultimatums were becoming disjointed.

". . . memoirs too, don't forget, Hector. Frank exposure, no holes barred. I mean . . . damn, have to get a ghost. Hotel de Paris at Monte, lots of pictures. Oh, yes, I kept the photographs." She grubbed about on the couch, came up with a crumpled soap coupon and a supermarket pay slip. "Wait till those lawyers see them. Hector—" Suddenly she broke off, stared glassily at Mangon and sagged back.

Mangon waited until she was finally asleep, stood up and peered closely at her. She looked forlorn and desperate. He watched her reverently for a moment, then tiptoed to the rheostat mounted on the control panel behind the couch, damped down the lamp at Madame Gioconda's feet and left the stage.

He sealed the auditorium doors behind him, made his way down to the foyer and stepped out, sad but at the same time oddly exhilarated, into the cool midnight air. At last he accepted that he would have to act swiftly if he was to save Madame Gioconda.

2

Driving his sound truck into the city shortly after nine the next morning, Mangon decided to postpone his first call— the weird Neo-Corbusier Episcopalian Oratory sandwiched among the office blocks in the downtown financial sector— and instead turned west on Mainway and across the park toward the white-faced apartment batteries which reared up above the trees and lakes along the north side.

The Oratory was a difficult and laborious job that would take him three hours of concentrated effort. The Dean had recently imported some rare 13th Century pediments from the Church of St. Francis at Assisi, beautiful sonic matrices rich with seven centuries of Gregorian chant, overlaid by the timeless tolling of the Angelus. Mounted into the altar they emanated an atmosphere resonant with litany and devotion, a mellow, deeply textured hymn that silently evoked the most sublime images of prayer and meditation.

But at 50,000 dollars each they also represented a terrifying hazard to the clumsy sound-sweep. Only two years earlier the entire north transept of Rheims Cathedral, rose window intact, purchased for a record 1,000,000 dollars and re-erected in the new Cathedral of St. Joseph at San Diego, had been drained of its priceless heritage of tonal inlays by a squad of illiterate sound-sweeps who had misread their instructions and accidentally swept the wrong wall.

Even the most conscientious sound-sweep was limited by his skill, and Mangon, with his auditory supersensitivity, was greatly in demand for his ability to sweep selectively, draining from the walls of the Oratory all extraneous and discordant noises—coughing, crying, the clatter of coins and mumble of prayer—leaving behind the chorales and liturgical chants which enhanced their devotional overtones. His skill alone would lengthen the life of the Assisi pediments by twenty years; without him they would soon become contaminated by the miscellaneous traffic of the congregation. Consequently he had no fears that the Dean would complain if he failed to appear as usual that morning.

Halfway along the north side of the park he swung off into the forecourt of a huge forty-story apartment block, a glittering white cliff ribbed by jutting balconies. Most of the apartments were Superlux duplexes occupied by show business people. No one was about, but as Mangon entered the hallway, sonovac in one hand, the marble walls and columns buzzed softly with the echoing chatter of guests leaving parties four or five hours earlier.

In the elevator the residues were clearer—confident male tones, the sharp wheedling of querulous wives, soft negatives of amatory blondes, punctuated by countless repetitions of "dahling." Mangon ignored the echoes, which were almost inaudible, a dim insect hum. He grinned to himself as he rode up to the penthouse apartment; if Madame Gioconda had known his destination she would have strangled him on the spot.

Ray Alto, doyen of the ultrasonic composers and the man more than any other responsible for Madame Gioconda's decline, was one of Mangon's regular calls. Usually Mangon swept his apartment once a week, calling at three in the afternoon. Today, however, he wanted to make sure of finding Alto before he left for Video City, where he was a director of program music.

The houseboy let him in. He crossed the hall and made his way down the black glass staircase into the sunken lounge. Wide studio windows revealed an elegant panorama of park and midtown skyscrapers.

A white-slacked young man sitting on one of the long slab sofas—Paul Merrill, Alto's arranger—waved him back.

"Mangon, hold on to your dive breaks. I'm really on reheat this morning." He twirled the ultrasonic trumpet he was playing, a tangle of stops and valves from which half a dozen leads trailed off across the cushions to a cathode tube and tone generator at the other end of the sofa.

Mangon sat down quietly and Merrill clamped the mouthpiece to his lips. Watching the ray tube intently, where he could check the shape of the ultrasonic notes, he launched into a brisk allegretto sequence, then quickened and flicked out a series of brilliant arpeggios, stripping off high P and Q notes that danced across the cathode screen like frantic eels, fantastic glissandos that raced up twenty octaves in as many seconds, each note distinct and symmetrically exact, tripping off the tone generator in turn so that escalators of electronic chords interweaved the original scale, a multichannel melodic stream that crowded the cathode screen with exquisite, flickering patterns. The whole thing was inaudible, but the air around Mangon felt vibrant and accelerated, charged with gaiety and sparkle, and he applauded generously when Merrill threw off a final dashing riff.

"Flight of the Bumble Bee," Merrill told him. He tossed the trumpet aside and switched off the cathode tube. He lay back and savored the glistening air for a moment. "Well, how are things?"

Just then the door from one of the bedrooms opened and Ray Alto appeared, a tall, thoughtful man of about forty, with thinning blond hair, wearing pale blue sunglasses over cool eyes.

"Hello, Mangon," he said, running a hand over Mangon's head. "You're early today. Full program?" Mangon nodded. "Don't let it get you down." Alto picked a dictaphone off one of the end tables, carried it over to an armchair. "Noise, noise, noise—the greatest single disease-vector of civilization. The whole world's rotting with it, yet all they can afford is a few people like Mangon fooling around with sonovacs. It's hard to believe that only a few years ago people completely failed to realize that sound left any residues."

"Are we any better?" Merrill asked. "This month's *Transonics* claims that eventually unswept sonic reson-

ances will build up to a critical point where they'll literally
start shaking buildings apart. The entire city will come
down like Jericho."

"Babel," Alto corrected. "Okay, now, let's shut up. We'll
be gone soon, Mangon. Buy him a drink would you, Paul."

Merrill brought Mangon a Coke from the bar, then wandered off. Alto flipped on the dictaphone, began to speak
steadily into it. "Memo 7: Betty, when does the copyright
on Stravinsky lapse? Memo 8: Betty, file melody for pro-
jected nocturne: L, L sharp, BB, Y flat, Q, VT, L, L
sharp. Memo 9: Paul, the bottom three octaves of the ultra-
tuba are within the audible spectrum of the canine ear—
congrats on that SP of the *Anvil Chorus* last night; about
three million dogs thought the roof had fallen in on them.
Memo 10: Betty—" He broke off, put down the microphone. "Mangon, you look worried."

Mangon, who had been lost in reverie, pulled himself together and shook his head.

"Working too hard?" Alto pressed. He scrutinized Mangon suspiciously. "Are you still sitting up all night with
that Gioconda woman?"

Embarrassed, Mangon lowered his eyes. His relationship
with Alto was, obliquely, almost as close as that with Madame Gioconda. Although Alto was brusque and often irritable with Mangon, he took a sincere interest in his wel-
fare. Possibly Mangon's muteness reminded him of the
misanthropic motives behind his hatred of noise, made him
feel indirectly responsible for the act of violence Mangon's
mother had committed. Also, one artist to another, he respected Mangon's phenomenal auditory sensitivity.

"She'll exhaust you, Mangon, believe me." Alto knew
how much the personal contact meant to Mangon and hesitated to be overcritical. "There's nothing you can do for
her. Offering her sympathy merely fans her hopes for a
comeback. She hasn't a chance."

Mangon frowned, wrote quickly on his wrist-pad: *She
WILL sing again!*

Alto read the note pensively. Then, in a harder voice, he
said, "She's using you for her own purposes, Mangon. At
present you satisfy one whim of hers—the neurotic head-

aches and fantasy applause. God forbid what the next whim might be."

She is a great artist.

"She *was,*" Alto pointed out. "No more, though, sad as it is. I'm afraid that the times change."

Annoyed by this, Mangon gritted his teeth and tore off another sheet: *Entertainment, perhaps. Art, no!*

Alto accepted the rebuke silently; he reproved himself as much as Mangon did for selling out to Video City. In his four years there his output of original ultrasonic music consisted of little more than one nearly finished symphony— aptly titled *Opus Zero*—shortly to receive its first performance, a few nocturnes and one quartet. Most of his energies went into program music, prestige numbers for spectaculars and a mass of straight transcriptions of the classical repertoire. The last he particularly despised, fit work for Paul Merrill, but not for a responsible composer.

He added the sheet to the two in his left hand and asked, "Have you ever heard Madame Gioconda sing?"

Mangon's answer came back scornfully: *No! But you have. Please describe.*

Alto laughed shortly, tore up the sheets and walked across to the window.

"All right, Mangon, you've made your point. You're carrying a torch for art, doing your duty to one of the few perfect things the world has ever produced. I hope you're equal to the responsibility. La Gioconda might be quite a handful. Do you know that at one time the doors of Covent Garden, La Scala *and* the Met were closed to her? They said Callas had temperament, but she was a girl guide compared with Gionconda. Tell me, how is she? Eating enough?"

Mangon held up his Coke bottle.

"Snow? That's tough. But how does she afford it?" He glanced at his watch. "Dammit, I've got to leave. Clean this place out thoroughly, will you? It gives me a headache just listening to myself think."

He started to pick up the dictaphone but Mangon was scribbling rapidly on his pad: *Give Madame Gioconda a job.*

Alto read the note, then gave it back to Mangon, puzzled. "Where? In this apartment?" Mangon shook his head. "Do you mean at V.C.? *Singing?*" When Mangon began to nod vigorously he looked up at the ceiling with a despairing groan. "For heaven's sake, Mangon, the last vocalist sang at Video City over ten years ago. No audience would stand for it. If I even suggested such an idea they'd tear my contract into a thousand pieces." He shuddered, only half-playfully. "I don't know about you, Mangon, but I've got my ulcer to support."

He made his way to the staircase, but Mangon intercepted him, pencil flashing across the wrist-pad: *Please. Madame Gioconda will start blackmail soon. She is desperate. Must sing again. Could arrange make-believe program in research studios. Closed circuit.*

Alto folded the note carefully, left the dictaphone on the staircase and walked slowly back to the window.

"This blackmail. Are you absolutely sure? Who, though, do you know?" Mangon nodded, but looked away. "Okay, I won't press you. LeGrande, probably, eh?" Mangon turned round in surprise, then gave an elaborate parody of a shrug.

"Hector LeGrande. Obvious guess. But there are no secrets there, it's all on open file. I suppose she's just threatening to make enough of an exhibition of herself to block his governorship." Alto pursed his lips. He loathed LeGrande, not merely for having bribed him into a way of life he could never renounce, but also because, once having exploited his weakness, LeGrande never hesitated to remind Alto of it, treating him and his music with contempt. If Madame Gionconda's blackmail had the slightest hope of success he would have been only too happy, but he knew LeGrande would destroy her, probably take Mangon too.

Suddenly he felt a paradoxical sense of loyalty for Madame Gioconda. He looked at Mangon, waiting patiently, big spaniel eyes wide with hope.

"The idea of a closed circuit program is insane. Even if we went to all the trouble of staging it she wouldn't be satisfied. She doesn't want to sing, she wants to be a *star*. It's the trappings of stardom she misses—the cheering galleries, the piles of bouquets, the greenroom parties. I could arrange a half-hour session on closed circuit with some trainee technicians—a few straight selections from *Tosca* and *Butterfly*, say, with even a sonic piano accompaniment, I'd be glad to play it myself—but I can't provide the gossip columns and theater reviews. What would happen when she found out?"

She wants to SING.

Alto reached out and patted Mangon on the shoulder. "Good for you. All right, then, I'll think about it. God knows how we'd arrange it. We'd have to tell her that she'll be making a surprise guest appearance on one of the big shows—that'll explain the absence of any program announcement and we'll be able to keep her in an isolated studio. Stress the importance of surprise, to prevent her from contacting the newspapers . . . Where are you going?"

Mangon reached the staircase, picked up the dictaphone and returned to Alto with it. He grinned happily, his jaw working wildly as he struggled to speak. Strangled sounds quavered in his throat.

Touched, Alto turned away from him and sat down. "Okay, Mangon," he snapped brusquely, "you can get on with your job. Remember, I haven't promised anything." He flicked on the dictaphone, then began: "Memo 11: Ray . . ."

3

It was just after four o'clock when Mangon braked the sound truck in the alley behind the derelict station. Overhead the traffic hammered along the flyover, dinning down onto the cobbled walls. He had been trying to finish his rounds early enough to bring Madame Gioconda the big news before her headaches began. He had swept out the Oratory in an hour, whirled through a couple of movie theaters, the Museum of Abstract Art, and a dozen private calls in half his usual time, driven by his almost overwhelming joy at having won a promise of help from Ray Alto.

He ran through the foyer, already fumbling at his wristpad. For the first time in many years he really regretted his muteness, his inability to tell Madame Gioconda orally of his triumph that morning.

Studio 2 was in darkness, the rows of seats and litter of old programs and ice cream cartons reflected dimly in the single light masked by the tall flats. His feet slipped in some shattered plaster fallen from the ceiling and he was out of breath when he clambered up onto the stage and swung round the nearest flat.

Madame Gioconda had gone!

The stage was deserted, the couch a rumpled mess, a clutter of cold saucepans on the stove. The wardrobe door was open, dresses wrenched outwards off their hangers.

For a moment Mangon panicked, unable to visualize why she should have left, immediately assuming that she had discovered his plot with Alto.

Then he realized that never before had he visited the studio until midnight at the earliest, and that Madame Gioconda had merely gone out to the supermarket. He smiled at his own stupidity and sat down on the couch to wait for her, sighing with relief.

Suddenly the words struck him like the blows of a pole-ax!

As vivid as if they had been daubed in letters ten feet deep, they leapt out from the walls, nearly deafening him with their force.

"You grotesque old witch, you must be insane! You ever threaten me again and I'll have you destroyed! LISTEN, you pathetic—"

Mangon spun round helplessly, trying to screen his ears. The words must have been hurled out in a paroxysm of abuse, they were only an hour old, vicious sonic scars slashed across the immaculately swept walls.

His first thought was to rush out for the sonovac and sweep the walls clear before Madame Gioconda returned. Then it dawned on him that she had already heard the original of the echoes—in the background he could just detect the muffled rhythms and intonations of her voice.

All too exactly, he could identify the man's voice.

He had heard it many times before, raging in the same ruthless tirades, when, deputizing for one of the sound-sweeps, he had swept out the main board room at Video City.

Hector LeGrande! So Madame Gioconda had been more desperate than he thought.

The bottom drawer of the dressing table lay on the floor, it's contents upended. Propped against the mirror was an old silver portrait frame, dull and verdigrised, some cotton wool and a tin of cleansing fluid next to it. The photograph was one of LeGrande, taken twenty years earlier. She must have known LeGrande was coming and had searched out the old portrait, probably regretting the threat of blackmail.

But the sentiment had not been shared.

Mangon walked round the stage, his heart knotting with rage, filling his ears with LeGrande's taunts. He picked up the portrait, pressed it between his palms, and suddenly smashed it across the edge of the dressing table.

"Mangon!"

The cry riveted him to the air. He dropped what was left of the frame, saw Madame Gioconda step quietly from behind one of the flats.

"Mangon, please," she protested gently. "You frighten me." She sidled past him toward the bed, dismantling an enormous purple hat. "And do clean up all that glass, or I shall cut my feet."

She spoke drowsily and moved in a relaxed, sluggish way that Mangon first assumed indicated acute shock. Then she drew from her handbag six white vials and lined them up carefully on the bedside table. These were her favorite confectionery—so LeGrande had sweetened the pill with another check. Mangon began to scoop the glass together with his feet, at the same time trying to collect his wits. The sounds of LeGrande's abuse dinned the air, and he broke away and ran off to fetch the sonovac.

Madame Gioconda was sitting on the edge of the bed when he returned, dreamily dusting a small bottle of bourbon which had followed the cocaine vials out of the handbag. She hummed to herself melodically and stroked one of the feathers in her hat.

"Mangon," she called when he had almost finished. "Come here."

Mangon put down the sonovac and went across to her.

She looked up at him, her eyes suddenly very steady. "Mangon, why did you break Hector's picture?" She held up a piece of the frame. "Tell me."

Mangon hesitated, then scribbled on his pad: *I am sorry. I adore you very much. He said such foul things to you.*

Madame Gioconda glanced at the note, then gazed back thoughtfully at Mangon. "Were you hiding here when Hector came?"

Mangon shook his head categorically. He started to write on his pad but Madame Gioconda restrained him.

"That's all right, dear. I thought not." She looked around the stage for a moment, listening carefully. "Mangon, when you came in could you hear what Mr. LeGrande said?"

Mangon nodded. His eyes flickered to the obscene phrases on the walls and he began to frown. He still felt LeGrande's presence and his attempt to humiliate Madame Gioconda.

Madame Gioconda pointed around them. "And you can actually hear what he said even now? How remarkable. Mangon, you have a wondrous talent."

I am sorry you have to suffer so much.

Madame Gioconda smiled at this. "We all have our crosses to bear. I have a feeling you may be able to lighten mine considerably." She patted the bed beside her. "Do sit down, you must be tired." When he was settled she went on. "I'm very interested, Mangon. Do you mean you can distinguish entire phrases and sentences in the sounds you sweep? You can hear complete conversations hours after they have taken place?"

Something about Madame Gioconda's curiosity made Mangon hesitate. His talent, so far as he knew, was unique, and he was not so naïve as to fail to appreciate its potentialities. It had developed in his late adolescence and so far he had resisted any temptation to abuse it. He had never revealed the talent to anyone, knowing that if he did his days as a sound-sweep would be over.

Madame Gioconda was watching him, an expectant smile on her lips. Her thoughts, of course, were solely of revenge. Mangon listened again to the walls, focused on the abuse screaming out into the air. *Not complete conversations. Long fragments, up to twenty syllables. Depending on resonances and matrix. Tell no one. I will help you have revenge on LeGrande.*

Madame Gioconda squeezed Mangon's hand. She was about to reach for the bourbon bottle when Mangon suddenly remembered the point of his visit. He leapt off the bed and started frantically scribbling on his wrist-pad.

He tore off the first sheet and pressed it into her startled hands, then filled three more, describing his encounter with the musical director at V.C., the latter's interest in Madame Gioconda and the conditional promise to arrange her guest appearance. In view of LeGrande's hostility he stressed the need for absolute secrecy.

He waited happily while Madame Gioconda read quickly through the notes, tracing out Mangon's childlike script with a long scarlet fingernail. When she finished, he nodded his head rapidly and gestured triumphantly in the air.

Bemused, Madame Gioconda gazed uncomprehendingly at the notes. Then she reached out and pulled Mangon to her, taking his big faunlike head in her jeweled hands and pressing it to her lap.

"My dear child, how much I need you. You must never leave me now."

As she stroked Mangon's hair her eyes roved questingly around the walls.

The miracle happened shortly before eleven o'clock the next morning.

After breakfast, sprawled across Madame Gioconda's bed with her scrapbooks, an old gramophone salvaged by Mangon from one of the studios playing operatic selections, they had decided to drive out to the stockades—the sound-sweeps left for the city at nine and they would be able to examine the sonic dumps unmolested. Having spent so much time with Madame Gioconda and immersed himself so deeply in her world, Mangon was eager now to intro-

duce Madame Gioconda to his. The stockades, bleak
though they might be, were all he had to show her.

For Mangon, Madame Gioconda had now become the
entire universe, a source of certainty and wonder as potent
as the sun. Behind him his past life fell away like the discarded chrysalis of a brilliant butterfly, the gray years of
his childhood at the orphanage dissolving into the magical
kaleidoscope that revolved around him. As she talked and
murmured affectionately to him, the drab flats and props
in the studio seemed as brightly colored and meaningful as
the landscape of a mescaline fantasy, the air tingling with
a thousand vivid echoes of her voice.

They set off down F Street at ten, soon left behind the
dingy warehouses and abandoned tenements that had en-
closed Madame Gioconda for so long. Squeezed together in
the driving cab of the sound truck they looked an incon-
gruous pair—the gangling Mangon, in zip-fronted yellow
plastic jacket and yellow peaked cap, at the wheel, dwarfed
by the vast flamboyant Madame Gioconda, wearing a par-
rot-green cartwheel hat and veil, her huge creamy breast
glittering with pearls, gold stars and jeweled crescents, a
small selection of the orders that had showered upon her in
her heyday.

She had breakfasted well, on one of the vials and a tooth
glass of bourbon. As they left the city she gazed out ami-
ably at the fields stretching away from the highway, and
trilled out a light recitative from *Figaro*.

Mangon listened to her happily, glad to see her in such
good form. Determined to spend every possible minute
with Madame Gioconda, he had decided to abandon his
calls for the day, if not for the next week and month. With
her he at last felt completely secure. The pressure of her
hand and the warm swell of her shoulder made him feel
confident and invigorated, all the more proud that he was
able to help her back to fame.

He tapped on the windshield as they swung off the highway onto the narrow dirt track that led toward the stockades. Here and there among the dunes they could see the
low ruined outbuildings of the old explosives plant, the
white galvanized iron roof of one of the sound-sweeps'

cabins. Desolate and unfrequented, the dunes ran on for miles. They passed the remains of a gateway that had collapsed to one side of the road; originally a continuous fence ringed the stockade, but no one had any reason for wanting to penetrate it. A place of strange echoes and festering silences, overhung by a gloomy miasma of a million compacted sounds, it remained remote and haunted, the graveyard of countless private babels.

The first of the sonic dumps appeared two or three hundred yards away on their right. This was reserved for aircraft sounds swept from the city's streets and municipal buildings, and was a tightly packed collection of sound-absorbent baffles covering several acres. The baffles were slightly larger than those in the other stockades; twenty feet high and fifteen wide, each supported by heavy wooden props, they faced each other in a random labyrinth of alleyways, like a store lot of advertisement hoardings. Only the top two or three feet were visible above the dunes, but the changed air hit Mangon like a hammer, a pounding niagara of airliners blaring down the glideway, the piercing whistle of jets jockeying at take-off, the ceaseless mind-sapping roar that hangs like a vast umbrella over any metropolitan complex.

All around, odd sounds shaken loose from the stockades were beginning to reach them. Over the entire area, fed from the dumps below, hung an unbroken phonic high, invisible but nonetheless as tangible and menacing as an enormous black thundercloud. Occasionally, when supersaturation was reached after one of the summer holiday periods, the sonic pressure fields would split and discharge, venting back into the stockades a nightmarish cataract of noise, raining onto the sound-sweeps not only the howling of cats and dogs, but the multilunged tumult of cars, express trains, fairgrounds and aircraft, the cacophonic *musique concrete* of civilization.

To Mangon the sounds reaching them, though scaled higher in the register, were still distinct, but Madame Gioconda could hear nothing and felt only an overpowering sense of depression and irritation. The air seemed to grate and rasp. Mangon noticed her beginning to frown and hold her hand to her forehead. He wound up his window and indicated to her to do the same. He switched on the sonovac mounted under the dashboard and let it drain the discordancies out of the sealed cabin.

Madame Gioconda relaxed in the sudden blissful silence. A little farther on, when they passed another stockade set closer to the road, she turned to Mangon and began to say something to him.

Suddenly she jerked violently in alarm, her hat toppling. Her voice had frozen! Her mouth and lips moved frantically, but no sounds emerged. For a moment she was paralyzed. Clutching her throat desperately, she filled her lungs and screamed.

A faint squeak piped out of her cavernous throat, and Mangon swung round in alarm to see her gibbering apoplectically, pointing helplessly to her throat.

He stared at her bewildered, then doubled over the wheel in a convulsion of silent laughter, slapping his thigh and thumping the dashboard. He pointed to the sonovac, then reached down and turned up the volume.

". . . aaauuuoooh," Madame Gioconda heard herself groan. She grasped her hat and secured it. "Mangon, what a dirty trick, you should have warned me."

Mangon grinned. The discordant sounds coming from the stockades began to fill the cabin again, and he turned down the volume. Gleefully, he scribbled on his wristpad: *Now you know what it is like!*

Madame Gioconda opened her mouth to reply, then stopped in time, hiccupped and took his arm affectionately.

4

Mangon slowed down as they approached a side road. Two hundred yards away on their left a small pink-washed cabin stood on a dune overlooking one of the stockades. They drove up to it, turned into a circular concrete apron below the cabin and backed up against one of the unloading bays, a battery of red-painted hydrants equipped with manifold gauges and release pipes running off into the stockade. This was only twenty feet away at its nearest point, a forest of door-shaped baffles facing each other in winding corridors, like a set from a surrealist film.

As she climbed down from the truck Madame Gioconda expected the same massive wave of depression and overload that she had felt from the stockade of aircraft noises, but instead the air seemed brittle and frenetic, darting with sudden flashes of tension and exhilaration.

As they walked up to the cabin Mangon explained: *Party noises—company for me.*

The twenty or thirty baffles nearest the cabin he reserved for these screened him from the miscellaneous chatter that filled the rest of the stockade. When he woke in the mornings he would listen to the laughter and small talk, enjoy the gossip and wisecracks as much as if he had been at the parties himself.

The cabin was a single room with a large window overlooking the stockade, well insulated from the hubub below. Madame Gioconda showed only a cursory interest in Mangon's meager belongings, and after a few general remarks came to the point and went over to the window. She opened it slightly, listened experimentally to the stream of atmospheric shifts that crowded past her.

She pointed to the cabin on the far side of the stockade. "Mangon, who's is that?"

Gallagher's. My partner. He sweeps City Hall, University, V.C., big mansions on 5th and A. Working now.

Madame Gioconda nodded and surveyed the stockade with interest. "How fascinating. It's like a zoo. All that talk, talk, talk. And *you* can hear it all." She snapped back her bracelets with swift decisive flicks of the wrist.

Mangon sat down on the bed. The cabin seemed small and dingy, and he was saddened by Madame Gioconda's disinterest. Having brought her all the way out to the dumps he wondered how he was going to keep her amused. Fortunately the stockade intrigued her. When she suggested a stroll through it, he was only too glad to oblige.

Down at the unloading bay he demonstrated how he emptied the tanker, clipping the exhaust leads to the hydrant, regulating the pressure through the manifold and then pumping the sound away into the stockade.

Most of the stockade was in a continuous state of uproar, sounding something like a crowd in a football stadium, and as he led her out among the baffles he picked their way carefully through the quieter aisles. Around them voices chattered and whined fretfully, fragments of conversation drifted aimlessly over the air. Somewhere a woman pleaded in thin nervous tones, a man grumbled to himself, another swore angrily, a baby bellowed. Behind it all was the steady background murmur of countless TV programs, the easy patter of announcers, the endless monotones of race-track commentators, the shrieking audiences of quiz shows, all pitched an octave up the scale so that they sounded an eerie parody of themselves.

A shot rang out in the next aisle, followed by screams and shouting. Although she heard nothing, the pressure pulse made Madame Gioconda stop.

"Mangon, wait. Don't be in so much of hurry. Tell me what they're saying."

Mangon selected a baffle and listened carefully. The sounds appeared to come from an apartment over a launderette. A battery of washing machines chuntered to themselves, a cash register slammed interminably, there was a dim almost subthreshold echo of 60-cycle hum from an SP record player.

He shook his head, waved Madame Gioconda on.

"Mangon, what did they *say?*" she pestered him. He stopped again, sharpened his ears and waited. This time he was more lucky, an overemotional female voice was gasping, "... but if he finds you here he'll kill you, he'll kill us both, what shall we do ..." He started to scribble down this outpouring, Madame Gioconda craning breathlessly over his shoulder, then recognized its source and screwed up the note.

"Mangon, for heaven's sake, what was it? Don't throw it away! Tell me!" She tried to climb under the wooden superstructure of the baffle to recover the note, but Mangon restrained her and quickly scribbled another message: *Adam and Eve. Sorry.*

"What, the film? Oh, how ridiculous! Well, come on, try again."

Eager to make amends, Mangon picked the next baffle, one of a group serving the staff married quarters of the University. Always a difficult job to keep clean, he struck paydirt almost at once.

". . . my God, there's Bartok all over the place, that damned Steiner woman, I'll swear she's sleeping with her . . ."

Mangon took it all down, passing the sheets to Madame Gioconda as soon as he covered them. Squinting hard at his crabbed handwriting, she gobbled them eagerly, disappointed when, after half a dozen, he lost the thread and stopped.

"Go on, Mangon, what's the matter?" She let the notes fall to the ground. "Difficult, isn't it? We'll have to teach you shorthand."

They reached the baffles Mangon had just filled from the previous day's rounds. Listening carefully he heard Paul Merrill's voice: ". . . month's *Transonics* claims that . . . the entire city will come down like Jericho."

He wondered if he could persuade Madame Gioconda to wait for fifteen minutes, when he would be able to repeat a few carefully edited fragments from Alto's promise to arrange her guest appearance, but she seemed eager to move deeper into the stockade.

"You said your friend Gallagher sweeps out Video City, Mangon. Where would that be?"

Hector LeGrande. Of course, Mangon realized, why had he been so obtuse. This was the chance to pay the man back.

He pointed to an area a few aisles away. They climbed between the baffles, Mangon helping Madame Gioconda over the beams and props, steering her full skirt and wide hat brim away from splinters and rusted metalwork.

The task of finding LeGrande was simple. Even before the baffles were in sight Mangon could hear the hard unyielding bite of the tycoon's voice, dominating every other sound from the Video City area. Gallagher in fact swept only the senior dozen or so executive suites at V.C., chiefly to relieve their occupants of the distasteful echoes of Le-Grande's voice.

Mangon steered their way among these, searching for LeGrande's master suite, where anything of a really confidential nature took place.

There were about twenty baffles, throwing off an unending chorus of "Yes, H. L.," "Thanks, H. L.," "Brilliant, H. L." Two or three seemed strangely quiet, and he drew Madame Gioconda over to them.

This was LeGrande with his personal secretary and PA. He took out his pencil and focused carefully.

". . . of Third National Bank, transfer two million to private holding and threatened claim for stock depreciation . . . redraft escape clauses, including nonliability purchase benefits . . ."

Madame Gioconda tapped his arm but he gestured her away. Most of the baffle appeared to be taken up by dubious financial dealings, but nothing that would really hurt LeGrande if revealed.

Then he heard—

". . . Bermuda Hilton. Private Island, with anchorage, have the beach cleaned up, last time the water was full of fish. . . . I don't care, poison them, hang some nets out. . . . Imogene will fly in from Idlewild as Mrs. Edna Burgess, warn customs to stay away. . . ."

". . . call Cartier's, something for the Comtessa, 17 carats say, ceiling of ten thousand. No, make it eight thousand. . . ."

". . . hat-check girl at Tropicabana. Usual dossier . . ."

Mangon scribbled furiously, but LeGrande was speaking at rapid dictation speed and he could get down only a few fragments. Madame Gioconda barely deciphered his handwriting, and became more and more frustrated as her appetite was whetted. Finally she flung away the notes in a fury of exasperation.

"This is absurd, you're missing everything!" she cried. She pounded on one of the baffles, then broke down and began to sob angrily. "Oh, God, God, *God,* how ridiculous! Help me, I'm going insane. . . ."

Mangon hurried across to her, put his arms round her shoulders to support her. She pushed him away irritably, railing at herself to discharge her impatience. "It's useless, Mangon, it's stupid of me, I was a fool—"

"STOP!"

The cry split the air like the blade of a guillotine.

They both straightened, stared at each other blankly. Mangon put his fingers slowly to his lips, then reached out tremulously and put his hands in Madame Gioconda's. Somewhere within him a tremendous tension had begun to dissolve.

"Stop," he said again in a rough but quiet voice. "Don't cry. I'll help you."

Madame Gioconda gaped at him with amazement. Then she let out a tremendous whoop of triumph.

"Mangon, you can talk! You've got your voice back! It's absolutely astounding! Say something, quickly, for heaven's sake!"

Mangon felt his mouth again, ran his fingers rapidly over his throat. He began to tremble with excitement, his face brightened, he jumped up and down like a child.

"I can talk," he repeated wonderingly. His voice was gruff, then seesawed into a treble. "I can talk," he said louder, controlling its pitch. "I can talk, I can talk, *I can talk!*" He flung his head back, let out an ear-shattering shout. "I CAN TALK! HEAR ME!" He ripped the wrist-pad off his sleeve, hurled it away over the baffles.

Madame Gioconda backed away, laughing agreeably. "We can hear you, Mangon. Dear me, how sweet." She watched Mangon thoughtfully as he cavorted happily in the narrow interval between the aisles. "Now don't tire yourself out or you'll lose it again."

Mangon danced over to her, seized her shoulders and squeezed them tightly. He suddenly realized that he knew no diminutive or Christian name for her.

"Madame Gioconda," he said earnestly, stumbling over the syllables, the words that were so simple yet so enormously complex to pronounce. "You gave me back my voice. Anything you want—" He broke off, stuttering happily, laughing through his tears. Suddenly he buried his head in her shoulder, exhausted by his discovery, and cried gratefully, "It's a *wonderful* voice."

Madame Gioconda steadied him maternally. "Yes, Mangon," she said, her eyes on the discarded notes lying in the dust. "You've got a wonderful voice, all right." Sotto voce, she added, "But your hearing is even more wonderful."

Paul Merrill switched off the SP player, sat down on the arm of the sofa and watched Mangon quizzically.

"Strange. You know, my guess is that it was psychosomatic."

Mangon grinned. "Psychosemantic," he repeated, garbling the word half-deliberately. "Clever. You can do amazing things with words. They help to crystallize the truth."

Merrill groaned playfully. "God, you sit there, you drink your Coke, you philosophize. Don't you realize you're supposed to stand quietly in a corner, positively dumb with gratitude? Now you're even ramming your puns down my throat. Never mind, tell me again how it happened."

"Once a pun a time—" Mangon ducked the magazine Merrill flung at him, let out a loud "Olee!"

For the last two weeks he had been *en fête*.

Every day he and Madame Gioconda followed the same routine; after breakfast at the studio they drove out to the stockade, spent two or three hours compiling their confidential file on LeGrande, lunched at the cabin and then drove back to the city, Mangon going off on his rounds while Madame Gioconda slept until he returned shortly before midnight. For Mangon their existence was idyllic; not only was he rediscovering himself in terms of the complex spectra and patterns of speech—a completely new category of existence—but at the same time his relationship with Madame Gioconda revealed areas of sympathy, affection and understanding that he had never previously seen. If he sometimes felt that he was too preoccupied with his side of their relationship and the extraordinary benefits it had brought him, at least Madame Gioconda had been equally well served. Her headaches and mysterious phantoms had gone, she had cleaned up the studio and begun to salvage a little dignity and self-confidence, which made her single-minded sense of ambition seem less obsessive. Psychologically, she needed Mangon less now than he needed her, and he was sensible to restrain his high spirits and give her plenty of attention. During the first week Mangon's incessant chatter had been rather wearing, and once, on their way to the stockade, she had switched on the sonovac in the driving cab and left Mangon mouthing silently at the air like a stranded fish. He had taken the hint.

"What about the sound-sweeping?" Merrill asked. "Will you give it up?"

Mangon shrugged. "It's my talent, but living at the stockade, let in at back doors, cleaning up the verbal garbage— it's a degraded job. I want to help Madame Gioconda. She will need a secretary when she starts to go on tour."

Merrill shook his head warily. "You're awfully sure there's going to be a sonic revival, Mangon. Every sign is against it."

"They have not heard Madame Gioconda sing. Believe me, I know the power and wonder of the human voice. Ultrasonic music is great for atmosphere, but it has no content. It can't express ideas, only emotions."

"What happened to that closed circuit program you and Ray were going to put on for her?"

"It—fell through," Mangon lied. The circuits Madame Gioconda would perform on would be open to the world. He had told them nothing of the visits to the stockade, of his power to read the baffles, of the accumulating file on LeGrande. Soon Madame Gioconda would strike.

Above them in the hallway a door slammed, someone stormed through into the apartment in a tempest, kicking a chair against a wall. It was Alto. He raced down the staircase into the lounge, jaw tense, fingers flexing angrily.

"Paul, don't interrupt me until I've finished," he snapped, racing past without looking at them. "You'll be out of a job, but I warn you, if you don't back me up one hundred per cent I'll shoot you. That goes for you too, Mangon, I need you in on this." He whirled over to the window, bolted out the traffic noises below, then swung back and watched them steadily, feet planted firmly in the carpet. For the first time in the three years Mangon had known him he looked aggressive and confident.

"Headline," he announced. "The Gioconda is to sing again! Incredible and terrifying though the prospect may seem, exactly two weeks from now the live uncensored voice of the Gioconda will go out coast-to-coast on all three V.C. radio channels. Surprised, Mangon? It's no secret, they're printing the bills right now. Eight-thirty to nine-thirty, right up on the peak, even if they have to give the time away."

Merrill sat forward. "Bully for her. If LeGrande wants to drive the whole ship into the ground, why worry?"

Alto punched the sofa viciously. "Because you and I are going to be on board! Didn't you hear me? Eight-thirty, a fortnight today! *We* have a program on then. Well, guess who our guest star is?"

Merrill struggled to make sense of this. "Wait a minute, Ray. You mean she's actually going to appear—she's going to *sing*—in the middle of *Opus Zero?*" Alto nodded grimly. Merrill threw up his hands and slumped back. "It's crazy, she can't. Who says she will?"

"Who do you think? The great LeGrande." Alto turned to Mangon. "She must have raked up some real dirt to frighten him into this. I can hardly believe it."

"But why on *Opus Zero?*" Merrill pressed. "Let's switch the première to the week after."

"Paul, you're missing the point. Let me fill you in. Sometime yesterday Madame Gioconda paid a private call on LeGrande. Something she told him persuaded him that it would be absolutely wonderful for her to have a whole hour to herself on one of the feature music programs, singing a few old-fashioned songs from the old-fashioned shows, with a full-scale ultrasonic backing. Eager to give her a completely free hand he even asked her which of the regular programs she'd like. Well, as the last show she appeared on ten years ago was canceled to make way for Ray Alto's *Total Symphony* you can guess which one she picked."

Merrill nodded. "It all fits together. We're broadcasting from the concert studio. A single ultrasonic symphony, no station breaks, not even a commentary. Your first world première in three years. There'll be a big invited audience. White tie, something like the old days. Revenge is sweet." He shook his head sadly. "Hell, all that work."

Alto snapped, "Don't worry, it won't be wasted. Why should we pay the bill for LeGrande? This symphony is the one piece of serious music I've written since I joined V.C. and it isn't going to be ruined." He went over to Mangon, sat down next to him. "This afternoon I went down to the rehearsal studios. They'd found an ancient sonic grand somewhere and one of the old-timers was accompanying her. Mangon, it's ten years since she sang last. If she'd practiced for two or three hours a day she might have preserved her voice, but you sweep her radio station, you know she hasn't sung a note. She's an old woman now. What time alone hasn't done to her, cocaine and self-pity have." He paused, watching Mangon searchingly. "I hate to say it, Mangon, but it sounded like a cat being strangled."

You lie, Mangon thought icily. *You are simply so ignorant, your taste in music is so debased, that you are unable to recognise real genius when you see it.* He looked at Alto with contempt, sorry for the man, with his absurd silent symphonies. He felt like shouting: *I know what silence is! The voice of the Gioconda is a stream of gold, molten and pure, she will find it again as I found mine.* However, something about Alto's manner warned him to wait.

He said, "I understand." Then, "What do you want me to do?"

Alto patted him on the shoulder. "Good boy. Believe me, you'll be helping her in the long run. What I propose will save all of us from looking foolish. We've got to stand up to LeGrande, even if it means a one-way ticket out of V.C. Okay, Paul?" Merrill nodded firmly and he went on, "Orchestra will continue as scheduled. According to the program Madame Gioconda will be singing to an accompaniment by *Opus Zero*, but that means nothing and there'll be no connection at any point. In fact she won't turn up until the night itself. She'll stand well down-stage on a special platform, and the only microphone will be an aerial about twenty feet diagonally above her. It will be live—*but her voice will never reach it*. Because you, Mangon, will be in the cue-box directly in front of her, with the most powerful sonovac we can lay our hands on. As soon as she opens her mouth you'll let her have it. She'll be at least ten feet away from you so she'll hear herself and won't suspect what is happening."

"What about the audience?" Merrill asked.

"They'll be listening to my symphony, enjoying a neurophonic experience of sufficient beauty and power, I hope, to distract them from the sight of a blowzy prima donna gesturing to herself in a cocaine fog. They'll probably think she's conducting. Remember, they may be expecting her to sing but how many people still know what the word really means? Most of them will assume its ultrasonic."

"And LeGrande?"

"He'll be in Bermuda. Business conference."

5

Madame Gioconda was sitting before her dressing table mirror, painting on a face like a Halloween mask. Beside her the gramophone played scratchy sonic selections from *Traviata*. The stage was still a disorganized jumble, but there was now an air of purpose about it.

Making his way through the flats, Mangon walked up to her quietly and kissed her bare shoulder. She stood up with a flourish, an enormous monument of a woman in a magnificent black silk dress sparkling with thousands of sequins.

"Thank you, Mangon," she sang out when he complimented her. She swirled off to a hat-box on the bed, pulled out a huge peacock feather and stabbed it into her hair.

Mangon had come round at six, several hours before usual; over the past two days he had felt increasingly uneasy. He was convinced that Alto was in error, and yet logic was firmly on his side. Could Madame Gioconda's voice have preserved itself? Her spoken voice, unless she was being particularly sweet, was harsh and uneven, recently even more so. He assumed that with only a week to her performance nervousness was making her irritable.

Again she was going out, as she had done almost every night. With whom, she never explained; probably to the theater restaurants, to renew contacts with agents and managers. He would like to have gone with her, but he felt out of place on this plane of Madame Gioconda's existence.

"Mangon, I won't be back until very late," she warned him. "You look rather tired and pasty. You'd better go home and get some sleep."

Mangon noticed he was still wearing his yellow peaked cap. Unconsciously he must already have known he would not be spending the night there.

"Do you want to go to the stockade tomorrow?" he asked.

"Hmmmh . . . I don't think so. It gives me rather a headache. Let's leave it for a day or two."

She turned on him with a tremendous smile, her eyes glittering with sudden affection.

"Good-by, Mangon, it's been wonderful to see you." She bent down and pressed her cheek maternally to his, engulfing him in a heady wave of powder and perfume. In an instant all his doubts and worries evaporated, he looked forward to seeing her the next day, certain that they would spend the future together.

For half an hour after she had gone he wandered around the deserted sound stage, going through his memories. Then he made his way out to the alley and drove back to the stockade.

As the day of Madame Gioconda's performance drew closer Mangon's anxieties mounted. Twice he had been down to the concert studio at Video City, had rehearsed with Alto his entry beneath the stage to the cue-box, a small compartment off the corridor used by the electronics engineers. They had checked the power points, borrowed a sonovac from the services section—a heavy duty model used for shielding VIP's and commentators at airports—and mounted its nozzle in the cue-hood.

Alto stood on the platform erected for Madame Gioconda, shouted at the top of his voice at Merrill sitting in the third row of the stalls.

"Hear anything?" he called afterward.

Merrill shook his head. "Nothing, no vibration at all."

Down below Mangon flicked the release toggle, vented a long drawn-out "Fiivvveeee! ... Foouuurrr! ... Thrreeeee! ... Twooooo! ... Onnneeee... !"

"Good enough," Alto decided. Chicago-style, they hid the sonovac in a triple-bass case, stored it in Alto's office.

"Do you want to hear her sing, Mangon?" Alto asked. "She should be rehearsing now."

Mangon hesitated, then declined.

"It's tragic that she's unable to realize the truth herself," Alto commented. "Her mind must be fixed fifteen or twenty years in the past, when she sang her greatest roles at La Scala. That's the voice she hears, the voice she'll probably always hear."

Mangon pondered this. Once he tried to ask Madame Gioconda how her practice sessions were going, but she was moving into a different zone and answered with some grandiose remark. He was seeing less and less of her, whenever he visited the station she was either about to go out or else tired and eager to be rid of him. Their trips to the stockade had ceased. All this he accepted as inevitable; after the performance, he assured himself, after her triumph, she would come back to him.

He noticed, however, that he was beginning to stutter.

On the final afternoon, a few hours before the performance that evening, Mangon drove down to F Street for what was to be the last time. He had not seen Madame Gioconda the previous day and he wanted to be with her and give her any encouragement she needed.

As he turned into the alley he was surprised to see two large removal vans parked outside the station entrance. Four or five men were carrying out pieces of furniture and the great scenic flats from the sound stage.

Mangon ran over to them. One of the vans was full; he recognized all Madame Gioconda's possessions—the rococo wardrobe and dressing table, the couch, the huge Desdemona bed, up-ended and wrapped in corrugated paper—as he looked at it he felt that a section of himself had been torn from him and rammed away callously. In the bright daylight the peeling threadbare flats had lost all illusion of reality; with them Mangon's whole relationship with Madame Gioconda seemed to have been dismantled.

The last of the workmen came out with a gold cushion under his arm, tossed it into the second van. The foreman sealed the doors and waved on the driver.

"W . . . wh . . . where are you going?" Mangon asked him urgently.

The foreman looked him up and down. "You're the sweeper, are you?" He jerked a thumb toward the station. "The old girl said there was a message for you in there. Couldn't see one myself."

Mangon left him and ran into the foyer and up the stairway toward Studio 2. The removers had torn down the blinds and a gray light was flooding into the dusty auditorium. Without the flats the stage looked exposed and derelict.

He raced down the aisle, wondering why Madame Gioconda had decided to leave without telling him.

The stage had been stripped. The music stands had been kicked over, the stove lay on its side with two or three old pans around it, underfoot there was a miscellaneous litter of paper, ash and empty vials.

Mangon searched around for the message, probably pinned to one of the partitions.

Then he heard it screaming at him from the walls, violent and concise.

"GO AWAY YOU UGLY CHILD! NEVER TRY TO SEE ME AGAIN!"

He shrank back, involuntarily tried to shout as the walls seemed to fall in on him, but his throat had frozen.

As he entered the corridor below the stage shortly before eight-twenty, Mangon could hear the sounds of the audience arriving and making their way to their seats. The studio was almost full, a hubbub of well-heeled chatter. Lights flashed on and off in the corridor, and oblique atmospheric shifts cut through the air as the players on the stage tuned their instruments.

Mangon slid past the technicians manning the neurophonic rigs which supplied the orchestra, trying to make the enormous triple-bass case as inconspicuous as possible. They were all busy checking the relays and circuits, and he reached the cue-box and slipped through the door unnoticed.

The box was almost in darkness, a few rays of colored light filtering through the pink and white petals of the chrysanthemums stacked over the hood. He bolted the door, then opened the case, lifted out the sonovac and clipped the snout into the cannister. Leaning forward, with his hands he pushed a small aperture among the flowers.

Directly in front of him he could see a velvet-lined platform, equipped with a white metal rail to the center of which a large floral ribbon had been tied. Beyond was the orchestra, disposed in a semicircle, each of the twenty members sitting at a small boxlike desk on which rested his instrument, tone generator and cathode tube. They were all present, and the light reflected from the ray screens threw a vivid phosphorescent glow onto the silver wall behind them.

Mangon propped the nozzle of the sonovac into the aperture, bent down, plugged in the lead and switched on.

Just before eight twenty-five someone stepped across the platform and paused in front of the cue-hood. Mangon crouched back, watching the patent leather shoes and black trousers move near the nozzle.

"Mangon!" he heard Alto snap. He craned forward, saw Alto eyeing him. Mangon waved to him and Alto nodded slowly, at the same time smiling to someone in the audience, then turned on his heel and took his place in the orchestra.

At eight-thirty a sequence of red and green lights signaled the start of the program. The audience quietened, waiting while an announcer in an offstage booth introduced the program.

A compere appeared on stage, standing behind the cue-hood, and addressed the audience. Mangon sat quietly on the small wooden seat fastened to the wall, staring blankly at the cannister of the sonovac. There was a round of applause, and a steady green light shone downward through the flowers. The air in the cue-box began to sweeten, a cool motionless breeze eddied vertically around him as a rhythmic ultrasonic pressure wave pulsed past. It relaxed the confined dimensions of the box, and had a strange mesmeric tug that held his attention. Somewhere in his mind he realized that the symphony had started, but he was too distracted to pull himself together and listen to it consciously.

Suddenly, through the gap between the flowers and the sonovac nozzle, he saw a large white mass shifting about on the platform. He slipped off the seat and peered up.

Madame Gioconda had taken her place on the platform. Seen from below she seemed enormous, a towering cataract of glistening white satin that swept down to her feet. Her arms were folded loosely in front of her, fingers flashing with blue and white stones. He could only just glimpse her face, the terrifying witchlike mask turned in profile as she waited for some offstage signal.

Mangon mobilized himself, slid his hand down to the trigger of the sonovac. He waited, feeling the steady subliminal music of Alto's symphony swell massively within him, its tempo accelerating. Presumably Madame Gioconda's arranger was waiting for a climax at which to introduce her first aria.

Abruptly Madame Gioconda looked forward at the audience and took a short step to the rail. Her hands parted and opened palms upward, her head moved back, her bare shoulders swelled.

The wave front pulsing through the cue-box stopped, then soared off into a continuous unbroken crescendo. At the same time Madame Gioconda thrust her head out, her throat muscles contracted powerfully.

As the sound burst from her throat Mangon's finger locked rigidly against the trigger guard. An instant later, before he could think, a shattering blast of sound ripped through his ears, followed by a slightly higher note that appeared to strike a hidden ridge halfway along its path, wavered slightly, then recovered and sped on, like an express train crossing lines.

Mangon listened to her numbly, hands gripping the barrell of the sonovac. The voice exploded in his brain, flooding every nexus of cells with its violence. It was grotesque, an insane parody of a classical soprano. Harmony, purity, cadence had gone. Rough and cracked, it jerked sharply from one high note to a lower, its breath intervals uncontrolled, sudden precipices of gasping silence which plunged through the volcanic torrent, dividing it into a loosely connected sequence of bravura passages.

He barely recognized what she was singing: the Toreador song from *Carmen*. Why she had picked this he could not imagine. Unable to reach its higher notes she fell back on the swinging rhythm of the refrain, hammering out the rolling phrases with tosses of her head. After a dozen bars her pace slackened, she slipped into an extempore humming, then broke out of this into a final climactic assault.

Appalled, Mangon watched as two or three members of the orchestra stood up and disappeared into the wings. The others had stopped playing, were switching off their instruments and conferring with each other. The audience was obviously restive; Mangon could hear individual voices in the intervals when Madame Gioconda refilled her lungs.

Behind him someone hammered on the door. Startled, Mangon nearly tripped across the sonovac. Then he bent down and wrenched the plug out of its socket. Snapping open the two catches beneath the chassis of the sonovac, he pulled off the cannister to reveal the valves, amplifier and generator. He slipped his fingers carefully through the leads and coils, seized them as firmly as he could and ripped them out with a single motion. Tearing his nails, he stripped the printed circuit off the bottom of the chassis and crushed it between his hands.

Satisfied, he dropped the sonovac to the floor, listened for a moment to the caterwauling above, which was now being drowned by the mounting vocal opposition of the audience, then unlatched the door.

Paul Merrill, his bow tie askew, burst in. He gaped blankly at Mangon, at the blood dripping from his fingers and the smashed sonovac on the floor.

He seized Mangon by the shoulders, shook him roughly. "Mangon, are you crazy? What are you trying to do?"

Mangon attempted to say something, but his voice had

died. He pulled himself away from Merrill, pushed past into the corridor.

Merrill shouted after him. "Mangon, help me fix this! Where are you going?" He got down on his knees, started trying to piece the sonovac together.

From the wings Mangon briefly watched the scene on the stage.

Madame Gioconda was still singing, her voice completely inaudible in the uproar from the auditorium. Half the audience were on their feet, shouting toward the stage and apparently remonstrating with the studio officials. All but a few members of the orchestra had left their instruments, these sitting on their desks and watching Madame Gioconda in amazement.

The program director, Alto and one of the comperes stood in front of her, banging on the rail and trying to attract her attention. But Madame Gioconda failed to notice them. Head back, eyes on the brilliant ceiling lights, hands gesturing majestically, she soared along the private causeways of sound that poured unrelentingly from her throat, a great white angel of discord on her homeward flight.

Mangon watched her sadly, then slipped away through the stage hands pressing around him. As he left the theater by the stage door a small crowd was gathering by the main entrance. He flicked away the blood from his fingers, then bound his handkerchief round them.

He walked down the side street to where the sound truck was parked, climbed into the cab and sat still for a few minutes, looking out at the bright evening lights in the bars and shop-fronts.

Opening the dashboard locker, he hunted through it and pulled out an old wrist-pad, clipped it into his sleeve.

In his ears the sound of Madame Gioconda singing echoed like an insane banshee.

He switched on the sonovac under the dashboard, turned it full on, then started the engine and drove off into the night.

PLENITUDE

by Will Worthington

from *Fantasy and Science Fiction*

There seems to be some doubt as to whether this was the first, second, or third story of three bought and published by three different magazines almost simultaneously. It marks, in any case, one-third of the debut of yet another striking new talent in the s-f field. Unlike Mr. Keyes, who has a long background in publishing, or Mr. Langart, who has written—I understand—in other fields, Mr. Worthington has turned to writing after years of experience in government work. There is a freshness of language and vigor of thought in all the stories of his I have seen which are rarely equaled by the more experienced writers in the field.

"Why can't we go home now, Daddy?" asked Mike, the youngest, and the small tanned face I saw there in the skimpy shade of the olive tree was mostly a matter of eyes —all else, hair, cheeks, thumb-sized mouth, jelly-bean body and usually flailing arms and legs, were mere accessories to the round, blue, endlessly wondering *eyes*. (*"The Wells of 'Why'"* . . . It would make a poem, I thought, if a poem were needed, and if I wasn't so damned tired. And I also thought, "Oh, God! It begins. Five years old. No, not quite. Four.")

"Because Daddy has to finish weeding this row of beans," I said. "We'll go back to the house in a little while."

I would go back to the house and then I would follow the path around the rocks to the hot springs, and there I would peel off what was left of my clothes and I would soak myself in the clear but pungent water that came bubbling—perfect—from a cleft in the rocks to form a pool in the hollow of a pothole—also perfect. And while I steeped in the mineral water I could think about the fish which was soon to be broiling on the fire, and I could think of Sue turning it, poking at it and sprinkling herbs over it as though it was the first or perhaps the last fish that would ever be broiled and eaten by human creatures. She would perform that office with the same total and unreserved dedication with which, since sun-up, she had scraped deer-skin, picked worms from new cabbage-leaves, gathered firewood, caulked the walls of the cabin where the old chinking had fallen away or been chewed or knocked away by other hungry or merely curious creatures, and otherwise filled in the numberless gaps in the world—trivial things mostly which would not be noticed and could not become great things in a man's eyes unless she were to go away or cease to be. I don't think of this because, for all immediate purposes—there are no others—she is the first Woman in the world and quite possibly—the last.

"Why don't we live in the Old House in the valley, Daddy?"

It is All-Eyes again. Make no mistake about it; there is a kind of connectedness between the seemingly random questions of very small kids. These are the problems posed by an *Ur*-logic which is much closer to the pulse of reality than are any of the pretentious, involuted systems and the mincing nihilations and category-juggling of adults. It is we who are confused and half-blinded with the varieties of special knowledge. But how explain? What good is my experience to him?

"There are too many old things in the Old House which don't work," I say, even as I know that I merely open the floodgates of further questions.

"Don't the funny men work, Daddy? I want to see the funny men! Daddy, I want . . ."

The boy means the robots. I took him down to see the Old House in the valley once before. He rode on top of my haversack and hung on to my hair with his small fingers. It was all a lark for him. I had gone to fetch some books—gambling that there might be a bagful of worthwhile ones that had not been completely eaten by bugs and mice; and if the jaunt turned out depressing for me, it was my fault, which is to say the fault of memory and the habit of comparing what has been with what is—natural, inevitable, unavoidable, but oh, God, just the same . . . The robots which still stood on their size-thirty metal feet looked like grinning Mexican mummies. They gave me a bad turn even though I knew what they were, and should have known what changes to expect after a long, long absence from that house, but to the kid they were a delight. Never mind transphenomenality of rusted surfaces and uselessly dangling wires; never mind the history of a senile generation. They were the funny men. I wish I could leave it at that, but of course I can't. I hide my hoe in the twigs of the olive tree and pick up Mike. This stops the questions for a while.

"Let's go home to Mummy," I say; and also, hoping to hold back the questions about the Old House long enough to think of some real answers, "Now aren't you glad we live up here where we can see the ocean and eagles and hot springs?"

"Yeth," says Mike firmly by way of making a querulous and ineffectual old man feel better about his decision. What a comfort to me the little one is!

I see smoke coming from the chimney, and when we round the last turn in the path we see the cabin. Sue waves from the door. She has worked like a squaw since dawn, and she smiles and waves. I can remember when women would exhaust themselves talking over the phone and eating bonbons all day and then fear to smile when their beat husbands came home from their respective nothing-foundries lest they crack the layers of phony "youthful glow" on their faces. Not like Sue. Here is Sue with smudges of charcoal on her face and fish-scales on her leather pants. Her scent is of woodsmoke and of sweat. There is no artificial scent like this—none more endearing nor more completely "correct." There was a time when the odor of perspiration would have been more of a social disaster for a woman than the gummata of tertiary pox. Even men were touched by this strange phobia.

Sue sees the question on my face and she knows why my smile is a little perfunctory and strained.

"Chris . . . ?" I start to ask finally.

"No. He took his bow and his sleeping-bag. Muttered something about an eight-point buck."

We do not *need* the venison. If anything has been made exhaustively and exaustingly clear to the boy it is that our blessings consist in large part of what we do not need. But this is not the point, and I know it is not the point.

"Do you think he'll ever talk to me again, Sue?"

"Of course he will." She pulls off my sweaty shirt and hands me a towel. "You know how twelve is. Everything in technicolor and with the throbbiest possible background music. Everything drags or jumps or swings or everything is Endsville or something else which it actually isn't. If it can't be turned into a drama it doesn't exist. He'll get over it."

I can think of no apt comment. Sue starts to busy herself with the fire, then turns back to me.

"You did the best thing. You did what you had to do, that's all. Go take your bath. I'm getting hungry."

I make my way up the path to the hot springs and I am wearing only the towel and the soles of an ancient pair of sneakers held on with thongs. I am thinking that the hot water will somehow dissolve the layers of sickly thought that obscure all the colors of the world from my mind, just as it will rid me of the day's accretion of grime, but at once I know that I am yielding to a vain and superstitious hope. I can take no real pleasure in the anticipation of my bath.

When I emerge from the underbrush and come in sight of the outcroppings of rock where the springs are, I can see Sato, our nearest neighbor and my oldest friend, making his way along the path from his valley on the other side of the mountain. I wave at him, but he does not wave back. I tell myself that he is concentrating on his feet and simply does not see me, but myself answers back in much harsher terms. Sato knows what happened when I took my older son to the City, and he knows why my son has not spoken more than a dozen coherent words since returning. He knows what I have done, and while it is not in the man's nature to rebuke another or set himself above another or mouth moral platitudes, there are limits.

Sato is some kind of a Buddhist. Only vaguely and imperfectly do I understand what this implies; not being unnecessarily explicit about itself is certainly a part of that doctrine. But there is also the injunction against killing. And I am—notwithstanding every meretricious attempt of my own mind to convert that fact into something more comfortable—a killer. And so . . . I may now contemplate what it will mean not merely to have lost my older son, but also the priceless, undemanding and yet immeasurably rewarding friendship of the family in the next valley.

"It was not intentional," I tell myself as I lower my griminess and weariness into the hot water. "It was necessary. How else explain why we chose . . . ?" But it isn't worth a damn. I might as well mumble Tantric formulae. The water feels lukewarm—*used*.

I go on flaying myself in this manner. I return to the house and sit down to supper. The food I had looked forward to so eagerly tastes like raw fungus or my old sneakers. Nothing Sue says helps, and I even find myself wishing she would go to hell with her vitamin-enriched cheerfulness.

On our slope of the mountain the darkness comes as it must come to a lizard which is suddenly immured in a cigar box. Still no sign of Chris and so, of course, the pumas are more vocal than they have been all year. I itemize and savor every disaster that roars, rumbles, creeps, slithers, stings, crushes or bites: everything from rattlers to avalanches, and I am sure that one or all of these dire things will befall Chris before the night is over. I go outside every time I hear a sound—which is often—and I squint at the top of the ridge and into the valley below. No Chris.

Sue, from her bunk, says, "If you don't stop torturing yourself, you'll be in no condition to *do* anything if it *does* become necessary." She is right, of course, which makes me mad as hell on top of everything else. I lie on my bunk and for the ten-millionth time reconstruct the whole experience:

We had been hacking at elder bushes, Chris and I. It had been a wet winter and clearing even enough land for garden truck out of the encroaching vegetation began to seem like trying to hold back the sea with trowels. This problem and the gloomy knowledge that we had about one hatful of beans left in the cabin had conspired to produce a mood in which nothing but hemlock could grow. And I'd about had it with the questions. Chris had started the "Why" routine at about the same age as little Mike, but the questions, instead of leveling off as the boy began to exercise his own powers of observation and deduction, merely became more involved and challenging.

The worst thing about this was that I could not abdicate: other parents in other times could fluff off the questions of their kids with such hopeless and worthless judgments as "Well, that's how things *are*," thereby implying that both the questioner and the questioned are standing passively at the dead end of a chain of historical cause, or are existentially trapped in the eye of a storm of supernal origin, or are at the nexus of a flock of processes arising out of the choices of too many other agencies to pinpoint and blame definitively ... *our* life, on the other hand, was clearly and in every significant particular our own baby. It did not merely proceed out of one particular historical choice, complete with foreseeable contingencies, but was an entire fabric of choices—*ours*. Here was total responsibility, complete with crowding elder bushes, cold rain, chiggers, rattlers, bone-weariness and mud. I had elected to live it—even to impose it upon my progeny—and I was prepared for its hardships, but what galled me was having to justify it.

"The people in the City don't have to do *this*, do they?" ("This" is grubbing out elder bushes, and he is right. The people in the City do not have to do *This*. They do not have to hunt, fish, gather or raise their own food. They do not have to build their own cabins, carry their own water from springs or fashion their own clothes from the skins of beautiful, murdered—by me—animals. They do not have to perspire. One of these days I will have to explain that they do not even have to sleep with their own wives. *That* of itself should be the answer of answers, but twelve is not yet ready; twelve cares about things with wheels, things which spin, roar, roll, fly, explode, exude noise and stench. Would that twelve were fourteen!)

In the meantime it is *dig—hack—heave; dig—hack—heave!* "Come on, Chris! It isn't sundown yet."

"Why couldn't we bring an old tractor up here in pieces and put it together and fix it up and find oil and . . ." (I try to explain for the fifty-millionth time that you do not simply "fix up" something which is the outgrowth of an enormous Organization of interdependent Organizations, the fruit of a dead tree, as it were. The wheel will not be turned back. The kid distrusts abstractions and generalities, and I don't blame him, but God I'm tired!) "Let's just clear off this corner by the olive tree, Chris, and then we'll knock off for the day."

"Are we *better* than the City-People?"

(This one hit a nerve. "Better" is a judgment made by people after the fact of their own decisions. Or there isn't any "Better." As for the Recalcitrants, of which vague class of living creatures we are members, they were and are certainly both more and less *something* than the others were —the City people—the ones who elected to Go Along with the Organization. Of all the original Recalcitrant families, I would guess that not ten per cent are now alive. I would if I had any use for statistics. If these people had something in common, you would have to go light-years away to find a name for it. I think it was a common lack of something—a disease perhaps. Future generations will take credit for it and refer to their origins as Fine Old Stock. I think most of them were crazy. I am glad they were, but most of them were just weird. Southern California. I have told Chris about the Peters family. They were going to make it on nothing but papaya juice and stewed grass augmented by East Indian breathing exercises. Poor squittered-out souls! Their corpses were like balsa wood. Better? What is Better? Grandfather was going to live on stellar emanations and devote his energies to whittling statues out of fallen redwoods. Thank Nature his stomach had other ideas! And God I'm tired and fed up!)

"Dammit, boy! Tomorrow I'll *take* you to the City and let you answer your own questions!"

And I did. Sue protested and old Sato just gave me that look which said, "I'm not saying anything," but I *did*.

The journey to the City is necessarily one which goes from bad to worse. As a deer and a man in the wilderness look for downward paths and lush places if they would find a river, the signs which lead to the centers of human civilization are equally recognizable.

You look for ugliness and senselessness. It is that simple. Look for places which have been overlaid with mortar so that nothing can grow or change at its will. Look for things which have been fashioned at great expense of time and energy and then discarded. Look for tin and peeling paint, for rusted metal, broken neon tubing, drifts and drifts of discarded containers—cans, bottles, papers. Look for flies and let your nose lead you where it would rather not go.

What is the difference between the burrow of a fox and a huge sheet-metal hand which bears the legend, in peeling, garish paint: THIS WAY TO PERPETUAL PARMENIDEAN PALACES . . . ? I do not know why one is better than the other, or *if* it is. I know that present purposes—purposes of intellect—lead one way, and intuition leads the other. So we resist intuition, and the path of greatest resistance leads us from one vast, crumbling, frequently stinking artifact or monument to another.

Chris is alternately nauseated and thrilled. He wants to stay in the palatial abandoned houses in the outskirts, but I say "no." For one thing, the rats look like Doberman Pinschers and for another . . . well, never mind what it is that repels me.

Much of the city looks grand until we come close enough to see where cement and plaster, paint and plastic have sloughed away to reveal ruptured tubes and wires which gleam where their insulation has rotted away, and which are connected to nothing with any life in it. We follow a monorail track which is a silver thread seen from a distance, but which has a continuous ridge of rust and bird droppings along its upper surface as far as the eye can see. We see more of the signs which point to the PERPETUAL PARMENIDEAN PALACES, and we follow them, giving our tormented intuition a rest even while for our eyes and our spirits there is no relief.

When we first encounter life we are not sure that it *is* life.

"They look like huge grapes!" exclaims Chris when we

find them, clustered about a central tower in a huge sunken place like a stadium. The P. P. Palaces are indeed like huge grapes—reddish, semitransparent, about fifteen feet in diameter, or perhaps twenty. I am not used to measuring spaces in such terms any more. The globes are connected to the central tower, or stem, by means of thick cables ... their umbilicals. A high, wire-mesh fence surrounds the area, but here and there the rust has done its work in spite of zinc coating on the wire. With the corn-knife I have brought to defend us from the rats and God knows what, I open a place in the fence. We are trespassing, and we know this, but we have come this far.

"Where are the people?" asks Chris, and I see that he looks pale. He has asked the question reluctantly, as though preferring no answer. I give none. We come close to one of the spheres, feeling that we do the wrong thing and doing it anyway. I see our objective and I point. It is a family of them, dimly visible like floating plants in an un-cleaned aquarium. It is their frightened eyes we first see.

I do not know very much about the spheres except from hearsay and dim memory. The contents, including the oc-cupants, are seen only dimly, I know, because the outer skins of the thing are filled with a self-replenishing liquid nutrient which requires the action of the sun and is aug-mented by the waste-products of the occupants. We look closer, moving so that the sun is directly behind the sphere, revealing its contents in sharper outline.

"Those are not real people," says Chris. Now he looks a little sick. "What are all those tubes and wires for if they're real people? Are they robots or dolls or what?"

I do not know the purpose of all the tubes and wires my-self. I do know that some are connected with veins in their arms and legs, others are nutrient enemata and for collec-tion of body wastes, still others are only mechanical tenta-cles which support and endlessly fondle and caress. I know that the wires leading to the metal caps on their heads are part of an invention more voracious and terrible than the ancient television—direct stimulation of certain areas of the brain, a constant running up and down the diapason of pleasurable sensation, controlled by a sort of electronic kaleidoscope.

My imagination stops about here. It would be the ultimate artificiality, with nothing of reality about it save endless variation. Of senselessness I will not think. I do not know if they see constantly shifting masses or motes of color, or smell exotic perfumes, or hear unending and constantly swelling music. I think not. I doubt that they even experience anything so immediate and yet so amorphous as the surge and recession of orgasm or the gratification of thirst being quenched. It would be stimulation without real stimulus; ultimate removal from reality. I decide not to speak of this to Chris. He has had enough. He has seen the wires and the tubes.

I have never sprung such abstractions as "Dignity" upon the boy. What good are such absolutes on a mountainside? If there is Dignity in grubbing out weeds and planting beans, those pursuits must be more dignified *than* something, because, like all words, it is a meaningless wisp of lint once removed from its relativistic fabric. The word does not exist until he invents it himself. The hoe and the rocky soil or the nutrient enema and the electronic ecstasy: He must judge for himself. That is why I have brought him here.

"Let's get away from here," he says. "Let's go home!"

"Good," I say, but even as I say it I can see that the largest of the pallid creatures inside the "grape" is doing something—I cannot tell what—and to my surprise it seems capable of enough awareness of us to become alarmed. What frightening creatures we must be—dirty, leather clothes with patches of dried animal blood on them, my beard and the small-boy grime of Chris! Removed as I am from these helpless aquarium creatures, I cannot blame them. But my compassion was a short-lived thing. Chris screamed.

I turned in time to see what can only be described as a huge metal scorpion rushing at Chris with its tail lashing, its fore-claws snapping like pruning shears and red lights flashing angrily where its eyes should have been. A guard robot, of course. Why I had not foreseen such a thing I will never know. I supposed at the time that the creature inside the sphere had alerted it.

The tin scorpion may have been a match for the reactions and the muscles of less primitive, more "civilized" men than ourselves, or the creators of the Perpetual Parmenidean Palaces had simply not foreseen barbarians with heavy corn-knives. I knocked Chris out of the way and dispatched the tin bug, snipping off its tail-stinger with a lucky slash of the corn-knife and jumping up and down on its thorax until all its appendages were still.

When the reaction set in, I had to attack something else. I offer no other justification for what I did. We were the intruders—the invading barbarians. All the creatures in the spheres wanted was their security. The man in the sphere set the scorpion on us, but he was protecting his family. I can see it that way now. I wish I couldn't. I wish I was one of those people who can always contrive to have been Right.

I saw the frightened eyes of the things inside the sphere, and I reacted to it as a predatory animal reacts to the scent of urea in the sweat of a lesser animal. And they had menaced my son with a hideous machine in order to be absolutely *secure!* If I reasoned at all, it was along this line.

The corn-knife was not very sharp, but the skin of the sphere parted with disgusting ease. I heard Chris scream, "No! Dad! No!"... but I kept hacking. We were nearly engulfed in the pinkish, albuminous nutritive which gushed from the ruptured sac. I can still smell it.

The creatures inside were more terrible to see in the open air than they had been behind their protective layers of plastic material. They were dead white and they looked to be soft, although they must have had normal human skeletons. Their struggles were blind, pointless and feeble, like those of some kind of larvae found under dead wood, and the largest made a barely audible mewing sound as it groped about in search of what I cannot imagine.

I heard Chris retching violently, but could not tear my attention away from the spectacle. The sphere now looked like some huge coelenterate which had been halved for study in the laboratory, and the hoselike tentacles still moved like groping cilia.

The agony of the creatures in the "grape" (I cannot

think of them as People) when they were first exposed to unfiltered, unprocessed air and sunlight, when the wires and tubes were torn from them, and especially when the metal caps on their heads fell off in their panicky struggles and the whole universe of chilly external reality rushed in upon them at once, is beyond my imagining; and perhaps this is merciful. This and the fact that they lay in the stillness of death after only a very few minutes in the open air.

Memory is merciful too in its imperfection. All I remember of our homeward journey is the silence of it.

"Wake up! We have company, old man!"

It is Sue shaking me. Somehow I did sleep—in spite of Chris and in spite of the persistent memory. It must be midmorning. I swing my feet down and scrub at my gritty eyes. Voices outside. Cheerful. How cheerful?

It is Sato and he has his old horse hitched to a crude travois of willow poles. It is Sato and his wife and three kids and my son Chris. There trussed up on the travois is the biggest buck I have seen in ten years, its neck transfixed with an arrow. A perfect shot and one that could not have been scored without the most careful and skillful stalking. I remember teaching him that only a bad hunter . . . a heedless and cruel one . . . would risk a distant shot with a bow.

Chris is grinning and looking sheepish. Sato's daughter is there, which accounts for the look of benign idiocy. I was wondering when he would notice. Then he sees me standing in the door of the cabin and his face takes on about ten years of gravity and thought, but this is not for the benefit of the teen-age female. Little Mike is clawing at Chris and asking *why* he went away like that and *why* he went hunting without Daddy, and several other *whys* which Chris ignores. His answer is for his old man:

"I'm sorry, Dad. I wasn't mad at you . . . just sort of crazy. Had to do . . . this. . . ." He points at the deer. "Anyhow, I'm back."

"And I'm glad," I managed.

"Dad, those elder bushes . . ."

"To hell with them," say I. "Wednesday is soon enough."

Sato moves in grinning, and just in time to relieve the awkwardness. "Dressed out this buck and carried it down the mountain by himself." I think of mountain lions. "He was about pooped when I found him in a pasture."

Sue holds open the cabin door and the Satos file in. Himself first, carrying a jug of wine, then Mrs. Sato, grinning greetings. She has never mastered English. It has not been necessary.

I drag up what pass for chairs. Made them myself. We begin talking about weeds and beans, and weather, bugs and the condition of fruit trees. It is Sato who has steered the conversation into these familiar ways, bless his knowing heart. He uncorks the wine. Sue and Mrs. Sato, meanwhile, are carrying on one of their lively conversations. Someday I will listen to them, but I doubt that I will ever learn how they communicate . . . or what. Women.

I can hear Chris outside talking to Yuki, Sato's daughter. He is not boasting about the deer; he is telling her about the fight with the tin scorpion and the grape-people.

"Are they blind . . . the grape-people?" the girl asks.

"Heck no," says Chris. "At least one of them wasn't. One of them sicced the robot bug on us. They were going to kill us. And so, Dad did what he had to do. . . ."

I don't hear the details over the interjections of Yuki and little Mike, but I can imagine they are as pungent as the teen-age powers of physiological description allow. I hear Yuki exclaim, "Oh how utterly *germy!*" and another language problem occurs to me. How can kids who have never hung around a drugstore still manage to evolve languages of their own . . . characteristically adolescent dialects? It is one more mystery which I shall never solve. I hear little Mike asking for reasons and causes with his favorite word. "*Why*, Chris?"

"I'll explain it when you get older," says Chris, and oddly it doesn't sound ridiculous.

Sato pours a giant-size dollop of wine in each tumbler.

"What's the occasion?" I ask.

Sato studies the wine critically, holding the glass so the light from the door shines through.

"It's Tuesday," he says.

THE MAN WHO LOST THE SEA

by Theodore Sturgeon

from "The Best from Fantasy and Science Fiction: Series Nine" (Doubleday, 1960)

". . . But science," they're still telling us, "has caught up with science fiction. . . ." Or: "What are you guys gonna write about now you *got* space flight?"

Obviously, not about space flight. Not one of the eighteen selections preceding this has been concerned with rocketry or astrogation or planet-hopping, except as an occasional incidental background touch.

Science—at least nuclear physics and space-flight technology—have caught up with us enough so that the speculative gleanings in these fields are sparse indeed. We are migrating to the less well-harvested neo-scientific fertile acreage of the "humanic studies."

I say, "migrate," and I do mean like a flock of birds. Thing now is to figure out whether Solo Sturgeon stayed behind on this one—or went way out, reconnoitering the next flight.

Say you're a kid, and one dark night you're running along the cold sand with this helicopter in your hand, saying very fast *witchy-witchy-witchy.* You pass the sick man and he wants you to shove off with that thing. Maybe he thinks you're too old to play with toys. So you squat next to him in the sand and tell him it isn't a toy, it's a model. You tell him look here, here's something most people don't know about helicopters. You take a blade of the rotor in your fingers and show him how it can move in the hub, up and down a little, back and forth a little, and twist a little, to change pitch. You start to tell him how this flexibility does away with the gyroscopic effect, but he won't listen. He doesn't want to think about flying, about helicopters, or about you, and he most especially does not want explanations about anything by anybody. Not now. Now, he wants to think about the sea. So you go away.

The sick man is buried in the cold sand with only his head and his left arm showing. He is dressed in a pressure suit and looks like a man from Mars. Built into his left sleeve is a combination time-piece and pressure gauge, the gauge with a luminous blue indicator which makes no sense, the clock hands luminous red. He can hear the pounding of surf and the soft swift pulse of his pumps. One time long ago when he was swimming he went too deep and stayed down too long and came up too fast, and when he came to it was like this: they said, "Don't move, boy. You've got the bends. Don't even *try* to move." He had tried anyway. It hurt. So now, this time, he lies in the sand without moving, without trying.

His head isn't working right. But he knows clearly that it isn't working right, which is a strange thing that happens to people in shock sometimes. Say you were that kid, you could say how it was, because once you woke up lying in the gym office in high school and asked what had happened. They explained how you tried something on the parallel bars and fell on your head. You understood exactly, though you couldn't remember falling. Then a minute later you asked again what had happened and they told you. You understood it. And a minute later ... forty-one times they told you, and you understood. It was just that no matter how many times they pushed it into your head, it wouldn't stick there; but all the while you *knew* that your head would start working again in time. And in time it did. . . . Of course, if you were that kid, always explaining things to people and to yourself, you wouldn't want to bother the sick man with it now.

Look what you've done already, making him send you away with that angry shrug of the mind (which, with the eyes, are the only things which will move just now). The motionless effort costs him a wave of nausea. He has felt seasick before but he has never *been* seasick, and the formula for that is to keep your eyes on the horizon and stay busy. Now! Then he'd better get busy—now; for there's one place especially not to be seasick in, and that's locked up in a pressure suit. Now!

So he busies himself as best he can, with the seascape, landscape, sky. He lies on high ground, his head propped on a vertical wall of black rock. There is another such outcrop before him, whip-topped with white sand and with smooth flat sand. Beyond and down is valley, salt-flat, estuary; he cannot yet be sure. He is sure of the line of footprints, which begin behind him, pass to his left, disappear in the outcrop shadows, and reappear beyond to vanish at last into the shadows of the valley.

Stretched across the sky is old mourning-cloth, with starlight burning holes in it, and between the holes the black is absolute—wintertime, mountaintop sky-black.

(Far off on the horizon within himself, he sees the swell and crest of approaching nausea; he counters with an undertow of weakness, which meets and rounds and settles the wave before it can break. Get busier. *Now*.)

Burst in on him, then, with the X-15 model. That'll get him. Hey, how about this for a gimmick? Get too high for the thin air to give you any control, you have these little jets in the wingtips, see? and on the sides of the empennage: bank, roll; yaw, whatever, with squirts of compressed air.

But the sick man curls his sick lip: oh, git, kid, git, will you?—that has nothing to do with the sea. So you git.

Out and out the sick man forces his view, etching all he sees with a meticulous intensity, as if it might be his charge, one day, to duplicate all this. To his left is only starlit sea, windless. In front of him across the valley, rounded hills with dim white epaulettes of light. To his right, the jutting corner of the black wall against which his helmet rests. (He thinks the distant moundings of nausea becalmed, but he will not look yet.) So he scans the sky, black and bright, calling Sirius, calling Pleiades, Polaris, Ursa Minor, calling that . . . that . . . Why, it *moves*. Watch it: yes, it moves! It is a fleck of light, seeming to be wrinkled, fissured, rather like a chip of boiled cauliflower in the sky. (Of course, he knows better than to trust his own eyes just now.) But that movement . . .

As a child he had stood on cold sand in a frosty Cape Cod

evening, watching Sputnik's steady spark rise out of the haze (madly, dawning a little north of west); and after that he had sleeplessly wound special coils for his receiver, risked his life restringing high antennas, all for the brief capture of an unreadable *tweetle-eep-tweetle* in his earphones from Vanguard, Explorer, Lunik, Discoverer, Mercury. He knew them all (well, some people collect match-covers, stamps) and he knew especially that unmistakable steady sliding in the sky.

This moving fleck was a satellite, and in a moment, motionless, uninstrumented but for his chronometer and his part-brain, he will know which one. (He is grateful beyond expression—without that sliding chip of light, there were only those footprints, those wandering footprints, to tell a man he was not alone in the world.)

Say you were a kid, eager and challengeable and more than a little bright, you might in a day or so work out a way to measure the period of a satellite with nothing but a timepiece and a brain; you might eventually see that the shadow in the rocks ahead had been there from the first only because of the light from the rising satellite. Now if you check the time exactly at the moment when the shadow on the sand is equal to the height of the outcrop, and time it again when the light is at the zenith and the shadow gone, you will multiply this number of minutes by 8—think why, now: horizon to zenith is one-fourth of the orbit, give or take a little, and halfway up the sky is half that quarter—and you will then know this satellite's period. You know all the periods—ninety minutes, two, two-and-a-half hours; with that and the appearance of this bird, you'll find out which one it is.

But if you were that kid, eager or resourceful or whatever, you wouldn't jabber about it to the sick man, for not only does he not want to be bothered with you, he's thought of all that long since and is even now watching the shadows for that triangular split second of measurement. *Now!* His eyes drop to the face of his chronometer: 0400, near as makes no never mind.

He has minutes to wait now—ten? . . . thirty? . . . twenty-three?—while this baby moon eats up its slice of shadowpie;

and that's too bad, the waiting, for though the inner sea is calm there are currents below, shadows that shift and swim. Be busy. Be busy. He must not swim near that great invisible ameba, whatever happens: its first cold pseudopod is even now reaching for the vitals.

Being a knowledgeable young fellow, not quite a kid any more, wanting to help the sick man too, you want to tell him everything you know about that cold-in-the-gut, that reaching invisible surrounding implacable ameba. You know all about it—listen, you want to yell at him, don't let that touch of cold bother you. Just know what it is, that's all. Know what it is that is touching your gut. You want to tell him, listen:

Listen, this is how you met the monster and dissected it. Listen, you were skin-diving in the Grenadines, a hundred tropical shoal-water islands; you had a new blue snorkel mask, the kind with face-plate and breathing-tube all in one, and new blue flippers on your feet, and a new blue spear-gun—all this new because you'd only begun, you see; you were a beginner, aghast with pleasure at your easy intrusion into this underwater otherworld. You'd been out in a boat, you were coming back, you'd just reached the mouth of the little bay, you'd taken the notion to swim the rest of the way. You'd said as much to the boys and slipped into the warm silky water. You brought your gun.

Not far to go at all, but then beginners find wet distances deceiving. For the first five minutes or so it was only delightful, the sun hot on your back and the water so warm it seemed not to have any temperature at all and you were flying. With your face under the water, your mask was not so much attached as part of you, your wide blue flippers trod away yards, your gun rode all but weightless in your hand, the taut rubber sling making an occasional hum as your passage plucked it in the sunlit green. In your ears crooned the breathy monotone of the snorkel tube, and through the invisible disk of plate glass you saw wonders. The bay was shallow—ten, twelve feet or so—and sandy, with great growths of brain-, bone-, and fire-coral, intricate waving sea-fans, and fish—such fish! Scarlet and green and aching azure, gold and rose and slate-color studded with sparks of enamel-blue, pink and peach and silver. And that *thing* got into you, that . . . monster.

There were enemies in this otherworld: the sand-colored spotted sea-snake with his big ugly head and turned-down mouth, who would not retreat but lay watching the intruder pass; and the mottled moray with jaws like bolt-cutters; and somewhere around, certainly, the barracuda with his undershot face and teeth turned inward so that he must take away whatever he might strike. There were urchins—the plump white sea-egg with its thick fur of sharp quills and the black ones with the long slender spines that would break off in unwary flesh and fester there for weeks; and file-fish and stone-fish with their poisoned barbs and lethal meat; and the stingaree who could drive his spike through a leg bone. Yet these were not *monsters*, and could not matter to you, the invader churning along above them all. For you were above them in so many ways—armed, rational, comforted by the close shore (ahead the beach, the rocks on each side) and by the presence of the boat not too far behind. Yet you were . . . attacked.

At first it was uneasiness, not pressing, but pervasive, a contact quite as intimate as that of the sea; you were sheathed in it. And also there was the touch—the cold inward contact. Aware of it at last, you laughed: for Pete's sake, what's there to be scared of?

The monster, the ameba.

You raised your head and looked back in air. The boat had edged in to the cliff at the right; someone was giving a last poke around for lobster. You waved at the boat; it was your gun you waved, and emerging from the water it gained its latent ounces so that you sank a bit, and as if you had no snorkle on, you tipped your head back to get a breath. But tipping your head back plunged the end of the tube under water; the valve closed; you drew in a hard lungful of nothing at all. You dropped your face under; up came the tube; you got your air, and along with it a bullet of sea-water which struck you somewhere inside the throat. You coughed it out and floundered, sobbing as you sucked in air, inflating your chest until it hurt, and the air you got seemed no good, no good at all, a worthless devitalized inert gas.

You clenched your teeth and headed for the beach, kicking strongly and knowing it was the right thing to do; and then below and to the right you saw a great bulk mounding up out of the sand floor of the sea. You knew it was only the reef, rocks and coral and weed, but the sight of it made you scream; you didn't care what you knew. You turned hard left to avoid it, fought by as if it would reach for you, and you couldn't get air, couldn't get air, for all the unobstructed hooting of your snorkel tube. You couldn't bear the mask, suddenly, not for another second, so you shoved it upward clear of your mouth and rolled over, floating on your back and opening your mouth to the sky and breathing with a quacking noise.

It was then and there that the monster well and truly engulfed you, mantling you round and about within itself—formless, borderless, the illimitible ameba. The beach, mere yards away, and the rocky arms of the bay, and the not-too-distant boat—these you could identify but no longer distinguish, for they were all one and the same thing . . . the thing called unreachable.

You fought that way for a time, on your back, dangling the gun under and behind you and straining to get enough warm sun-stained air into your chest. And in time some particles of sanity began to swirl in the roil of your mind, and to dissolve and tint it. The air pumping in and out of your square-grinned frightened mouth began to be meaningful at last, and the monster relaxed away from you.

You took stock, saw surf, beach, a leaning tree. You felt the new scend of your body as the rollers humped to become breakers. Only a dozen firm kicks brought you to where you could roll over and double up; your shin struck coral with a lovely agony and you stood in foam and waded ashore. You gained the wet sand, hard sand, and ultimately with two more paces powered by bravado, you crossed high-water mark and lay in the dry sand, unable to move.

You lay in the sand, and before you were able to move or to think, you were able to feel a triumph—a triumph because you were alive and knew that much without thinking at all.

When you *were* able to think, your first thought was of the gun, and the first move you were able to make was to let go at last of the thing. You had nearly died because you had not let it go before; without it you would not have been burdened and you would not have panicked. You had (you began to understand) kept it because someone else would have had to retrieve it—easily enough—and you could not have stood the laughter. You had almost died because They might laugh at you.

This was the beginning of the dissection, analysis, study of the monster. It began then; it had never finished. Some of what you had learned from it was merely important; some of the rest—vital.

You had learned, for example, never to swim farther with a snorkel than you could swim back without one. You learned never to burden yourself with the unnecessary in an emergency: even a hand or a foot might be as expendable as a gun; pride was expendable, dignity was. You learned never to dive alone, even if They laugh at you, even if you have to shoot a fish yourself and say afterward "we" shot it. Most of all, you learned that fear has many fingers, and one of them—a simple one, made of too great a concentration of carbon dioxide in your blood, as from too-rapid breathing in and out of the same tube—is not really fear at all but feels like fear, and can turn into panic and kill you.

Listen, you want to say, listen, there isn't anything wrong with such an experience or with all the study it leads to, because a man who can learn enough from it could become fit enough, cautious enough, foresighted, unafraid, modest, teachable enough to be chosen, to be qualified for—

You lose the thought, or turn it away, because the sick man feels that cold touch deep inside, feels it right now, feels it beyond ignoring, above and beyond anything that you, with all your experience and certainty, could explain to him even if he would listen, which he won't. Make him, then; tell him the cold touch is some simple explainable thing like anoxia, like gladness even: some triumph that he will be able to appreciate when his head is working right again.

Triumph? Here he's alive after . . . whatever it is, and that doesn't seem to be triumph enough, though it was in the Grenadines, and that other time, when he got the bends, saved his own life, saved two other lives. Now, somehow, it's not the same: there seems to be a reason why just being alive afterward isn't a triumph.

Why not triumph? Because not twelve, not twenty, not even thirty minutes is it taking the satellite to complete its eighth-of-an-orbit: fifty minutes are gone, and still there's a slice of shadow yonder. It is this, *this* which is placing the cold finger upon his heart, and he doesn't know why, he doesn't know why, he *will* not know why; he is afraid he shall when his head is working again. . . .

Oh, where's the kid? Where is any way to busy the mind, apply it to something, anything else but the watchhand which outruns the moon? Here, kid: come over here—what you got there?

If you were the kid, then you'd forgive everything and hunker down with your new model, not a toy, not a helicopter or a rocket-plane, but the big one, the one that looks like an overgrown cartridge. It's so big, even as a model, that even an angry sick man wouldn't call it a toy. A giant cartridge, but watch: the lower four-fifths is Alpha—all muscle—over a million pounds thrust. (Snap it off, throw it away.) Half the rest is Beta—all brains—it puts you on your way. (Snap it off, throw it away.) And now look at the polished fraction which is left. Touch a control somewhere and see—see? it has wings—wide triangular wings. This is Gamma, the one with wings, and on its back is a small sausage; it is a moth with a sausage on its back. The sausage (click! it comes free) is Delta. Delta is the last, the smallest: Delta is the way home.

What will they think of next? Quite a toy. Quite a toy. Beat it, kid. The satellite is almost overhead, the sliver of shadow going—going—almost gone and . . . gone.

Check: 0459. Fifty-nine minutes? give or take a few. Times eight . . . 472 . . . is, uh, 7 hours 52 minutes.

Seven hours fifty-two minutes? Why, there isn't a satellite round earth with a period like that. In all the solar system there's only . . .

The cold finger turns fierce, implacable.

The east is paling and the sick man turns to it, wanting the light, the sun, an end to questions whose answers couldn't be looked upon. The sea stretches endlessly out to the growing light, and endlessly, somewhere out of sight, the surf roars. The paling east bleaches the sandy hilltops and throws the line of footprints into aching relief. That would be the buddy, the sick man knows, gone for help. He cannot at the moment recall who the buddy is, but in time he will, and meanwhile the footprints make him less alone.

The sun's upper rim thrusts itself above the horizon with a flash of green, instantly gone. There is no dawn, just the green flash and then a clear white blast of unequivocal sun-up. The sea could not be whiter, more still, if it were frozen and snow-blanketed. In the west, stars still blaze, and overhead the crinkled satellite is scarcely abashed by the growing light. A formless jumble in the valley below begins to resolve itself into a sort of tent-city, or installation of some kind, with tubelike and saillike buildings. This would have meaning for the sick man if his head were working right. Soon, it would. Will. (Oh . . .)

The sea, out on the horizon just under the rising sun, is behaving strangely, for in that place where properly belongs a pool of unbearable brightness, there is instead a notch of brown. It is as if the white fire of the sun is drinking dry the sea—for look, look! the notch becomes a bow and the bow a crescent, racing ahead of the sunlight, white sea ahead of it and behind it a cocoa-dry stain spreading across and down toward where he watches.

Beside the finger of fear which lies on him, another finger places itself, and another, making ready for that clutch, that grip, that ultimate insane squeeze of panic. Yet beyond that again, past that squeeze when it comes, to be savored if the squeeze is only fear and not panic, lies triumph—triumph, and a glory. It is perhaps this which constitutes his whole battle: to fit himself, prepare himself to bear the utmost that fear could do, for if he can do that, there is a triumph on the other side. But . . . not yet. Please, not yet awhile.

Something flies (or flew, or will fly—he is a little confused on this point) toward him, from the far right where the stars still shine. It is not a bird and it is unlike any aircraft on earth, for the aerodynamics are wrong. Wings so wide and so fragile would be useless, would melt and tear away in any of earth's atmosphere but the outer fringes. He sees then (because he prefers to see it so) that it is the kid's model, or part of it, and for a toy, it does very well indeed.

It is the part called Gamma, and it glides in, balancing, parallels the sand and holds away, holds away slowing, then settles, all in slow motion, throwing up graceful sheet-fountains of fine sand from its skids. And it runs along the ground for an impossible distance, letting down its weight by the ounce and stingily the ounce, until *look out* until a skid *look out* fits itself into a bridged crevasse *look out, look out!* and still moving on, it settles down to the struts. Gamma then, tired, digs her wide left wingtip carefully into the racing sand, digs it in hard; and as the wing breaks off, Gamma slews, sidles, slides slowly, pointing her other triangular tentlike wing at the sky, and broadside crushes into the rocks at the valley's end.

As she rolls smashing over, there breaks from her broad back the sausage, the little Delta, which somersaults away to break its back upon the rocks, and through the broken hull, spill smashed shards of graphite from the moderator of her power-pile. *Look out! Look out!* and at the same instant from the finally checked mass of Gamma there explodes a doll, which slides and tumbles into the sand, into the rocks and smashed hot graphite from the wreck of Delta.

The sick man numbly watches this toy destroy itself: what will they think of next?—and with a gelid horror prays at the doll lying in the raging rubble of the atomic pile: *don't stay there, man—get away! get away! that's hot, you know?* But it seems like a night and a day and half another night before the doll staggers to its feet and, clumsy in its pressure-suit, runs away up the valleyside, climbs a sand-topped outcrop, slips, falls, lies under a slow cascade of cold ancient sand until, but for an arm and the helmet, it is buried.

The sun is high now, high enough to show the sea is not a sea, but brown plain with the frost burned off it, as now it burns away from the hills, diffusing in air and blurring the edges of the sun's disk, so that in a very few minutes there is no sun at all, but only a glare in the east. Then the valley below loses its shadows, and like an arrangement in a diorama, reveals the form and nature of the wreckage below: no tent-city this, no installation, but the true real ruin of Gamma and the eviscerated hulk of Delta. (Alpha was the muscle, Beta the brain; Gamma was a bird, but Delta, Delta was the way home.)

And from it stretches the line of footprints, to and by the sick man, above to the bluff, and gone with the sand-slide which had buried him there. Whose footprints?

He knows whose, whether or not he knows that he knows, or wants to or not. He knows what satellite has (give or take a bit) a period like that (want it exactly?—it's 7.66 hours). He knows what world has such a night, and such a frosty glare by day. He knows these things as he knows how spilled radioactives will pour the crash and mutter of surf into a man's earphones.

Say you were that kid: say, instead, at last, that you are the sick man, for they are the same; surely then you can understand why of all things, even while shattered, shocked, sick with radiation calculated (leaving) radiation computed (arriving) and radiation past all bearing (lying in the wreckage of Delta) you would want to think of the sea. For no farmer who fingers the soil with love and knowledge, no poet who sings of it, artist, contractor, engineer, even child bursting into tears at the inexpressible beauty of a field of daffodils—none of these is as intimate with Earth as those who live on, live with, breathe and drift in its seas. So of these things you must think; with these you must dwell until you are less sick and more ready to face the truth.

The truth, then, is that the satellite fading here is Phobos, that those footprints are your own, that there is no sea here, that you have crashed and are killed and will in a moment be dead. The cold hand ready to squeeze and still your heart is not anoxia or even fear, it is death. Now, if there is something more important than this, now is the time for it to show itself.

The sick man looks at the line of his own footprints, which testify that he is alone, and at the wreckage below, which states that there is no way back, and at the white east and the mottled west and the paling flecklike satellite above. Surf sounds in his ears. He hears his pumps. He hears what is left of his breathing. The cold clamps down and folds him round past measuring, past all limit.

Then he speaks, cries out: then with joy he takes his triumph at the other side of death, as one takes a great fish, as one completes a skilled and mighty task, rebalances at the end of some great daring leap; and as he used to say "we shot a fish" he uses no "I":

"God," he cries, dying on Mars, "God, we made it!"

MAKE A PRISON

by Lawrence Block

from *Original Science Fiction Stories*

A special feature of your enterprising annual anthologist:
the self-help do-it-yourself diagnostic puzzle, as provided in
all the best general magazines.

Your problem is to make your mind up, sometime before
you hit the final paragraph, about which human is the
human here?

The first Althean said, "Well, the tower is completed."

The second Althean smiled. "Good. It is all ready for the
prisoner, then?"

"Yes."

"Are you sure he'll be quite comfortable? He won't lan-
guish and die in such a state?"

"No," said the first Althean. "He'll be all right. It's taken
a long time to build the tower, and I've had ample opportunity to study the creature. We've made his habitat as
ideal for him as possible."

"I suppose so." The second Althean shuddered slightly.
"I don't know," he said. "I suppose it's nothing more than
projection on my part, but the mere thought of a *prison*..."
He broke off and shuddered again.

"I know," said the other, sympathetically. "It's something
none of us have ever had to conceive of before. The whole
notion of locking up a fellow-being is an abominable one,
I'll admit. But for that matter, consider the creature itself!"

"It wouldn't do for him to be loose."

"Wouldn't do! Why, it would be quite impossible. He
actually *murders*. He killed three of our fellow-beings before we were able to subdue him."

The second Althean shuddered more violently than before, and it appeared for a moment as though he was about to become physically ill. "But *why?* What type of being is he, for goodness sake? Where does he come from? What's he doing here?"

"Ah," said the first, "now you've hit upon it. You see, there's no way of knowing any of those answers. One morning he was discovered by a party of ten. They attempted to speak to him, and what do you think his rejoinder was?"

"He struck out at them, the way I heard it."

"Precisely! Utterly unprovoked assault, with three of their number dead as a result. The first case of murder on record here in thirty generations. Incredible!"

"And since then . . ."

"He's been a prisoner. No communication, no new insights, nothing. He eats whatever we feed him—he sleeps when the darkness comes and wakes when it goes. We have learned nothing about him, but I can tell you this for a fact. He is dangerous."

"Yes," said the second Althean.

"Very dangerous. He must be kept locked up. Of course, we wish him no harm—so we've made his prison as secure as possible, while keeping it as comfortable as possible. I daresay we've done a good job."

"Look," said the second, "perhaps I'm squeamish. I don't know. But are you sure he can never escape?"

"Positive."

"How can you be sure?"

The first Althean sighed. "The tower is one hundred thirty feet high. A drop from that distance is obviously fatal. Right?"

"Right."

"The prisoner's quarters are at the top of the tower, and the top is wider than the base—that is, the sides slope inward. And the sides are very, very smooth—so climbing down is quite impossible."

"Couldn't he come down the same way he'll go up? It only stands to reason."

"Again, quite impossible. He'll be placed in his quarters by means of a pneumatic tube, and the same tube will be used to send him his food. The entire tower is so designed that it can be entered via the tube, and can only be left by leaping from the top. The food that he doesn't eat, as well as any articles which he tires of, may be thrown over the side."

The second Althean hesitated. "It *seems* safe."

"It should. It *is* safe."

"I suppose so. I suppose it's safe, and I suppose it's not cruel, but somehow... Well, when will the prisoner be placed in the tower? Is it all ready for his occupancy?"

"It's ready, all right. And, as a matter of fact, we're taking him there in just a few minutes. Would you care to come along?"

"It might be interesting, at that."

"Then come along."

The two walked in silence to the first Althean's motor car and drove in silence to the tower. The tower was, indeed, a striking structure, both in terms of size and of design. They stepped out of the motor car and waited, and a large motor truck drew up shortly, pulling to a stop at the base of the tower. Three Althean guards stepped out of the truck, followed by the prisoner. His limbs were securely shackled.

"See?" demanded the first Althean. "He'll be placed in the tube like that, and he'll discover the key to his shackles in his quarters."

"Clever."

"We've worked it out carefully," the first explained. "I don't mean to sound boastful, but we've figured out all the angles."

The prisoner was placed in the tube, the aperture of which was located at the very base of the tower. Once inside, it was closed securely and bolted shut. The three Althean guards hesitated for several moments until a red light at the base indicated that the prisoner had entered his quarters. Then they returned to the motor truck and drove off down the road.

"We could go now," said the first. "I'd like to wait and see if he'll throw down the shackles, though. If you don't mind."

"Not at all. I'm rather interested now, you know. It's not something you see every day."

They waited. After several minutes, a pair of shackles plummeted through the air and dropped to the ground about twenty yards from the two Altheans.

"Ah," said the first. "He's found the key."

Moments later, the second pair of shackles followed the first, and the key followed soon thereafter. Then the prisoner walked to the edge of the tower and leaned over the railing, gazing down at them.

"Awesome," said the second Althean. "I'm glad he can't escape."

The prisoner regarded them thoughtfully for several seconds. Then he mounted the railing, flapped his wings, and soared off into the sky.

WHAT NOW, LITTLE MAN?

by Mark Clifton
from Fantasy and Science Fiction

It is just about ten years now, since Mark Clifton hit the
science fiction world like a cloudburst, pouring out a seemingly inexhaustible flood of provocative, exciting, irritating,
and informative thinking. I know of no contemporary author, with the possible exception of Robert Heinlein ten
years earlier, who has exercised so much developmental influence, not just on the readers, but in the basic thinking of
other *writers* in the field. There was a short spell, I recall,
when some disgruntled souls referred to *Astounding* (now,
Analog) as *The Clifton House Organ*.

For the past almost five years, other work has kept him
too busy to leave much time for s-f. Now it would seem the
spring floods are back, or so one hopes, on the basis of
this story and the new Doubleday novel, *Eight Keys to Eden*.

The mystery of what made the goonie tick tormented me
for twenty years.

Why, when that first party of big game hunters came to
Libo, why didn't the goonies run away and hide, or fight
back? Why did they instantly, immediately, almost seem to
say, "You want us to die, Man? For you we will do it
gladly!" Didn't they have any sense of survival at all? How
could a species survive if it lacked that sense?

"Even when one of the hunters, furious at being denied
the thrill of the chase, turned a machine gun on the drove
of them," I said to Paul Tyler, "they just stood there and
let him mow them down."

Paul started to say something in quick protest, then
simply looked sick.

"Oh, yes," I assured him. "One of them did just that.
There was a hassle over it. Somebody reminded him that

the machine gun was designed just to kill human beings, that it wasn't sporting to turn it on game. The hassle sort of took the edge off their fun, so they piled into their space yacht and took off for some other place where they could count on a chase before the kill."

I felt his sharp stare, but I pretended to be engrossed in measuring the height of Libo's second sun above the mountain range in the west. Down below us, from where we sat and smoked on Sentinel Rock, down in my valley and along the sides of the river, we could see the goonie herds gathering under their groves of pal trees before night fell.

Paul didn't take issue, or feed me that line about harvesting the game like crops, or this time even kid me about my contempt for Earthers. He was beginning to realize that all the old-timer Liboans felt as I did, and that there was reasonable justification for doing so. In fact, Paul was fast becoming Liboan himself. I probably wouldn't have told him the yarn about that first hunting party if I hadn't sensed it, seen the way he handled his own goonies, the affection he felt for them.

"Why were our animals ever called goonies, Jim?" he asked. "They're . . . Well, you know the goonie."

I smiled to myself at his use of the possessive pronoun, but I didn't comment on it.

"That too," I said, and knocked the dottle out of my pipe. "That came out of the first hunting party." I stood up and stretched to get a kink out of my left leg, and looked back toward the house to see if my wife had sent a goonie to call us in to dinner. It was a little early, but I stood a moment to watch Paul's team of goonies up in the yard, still folding their harness beside his rickshaw. I'd sold them to him, as yearlings, a couple of years before, as soon as their second pelt showed they'd be a matched pair. Now they were mature young males, and as handsome a team as could be found anywhere on Libo.

I shook my head and marveled, oh, for maybe the thousandth time, at the impossibility of communicating the goonie to anyone who hadn't seen them. The ancient Greek sculptors didn't mind combining human and animal form, and somebody once said the goonie began where those sculptors left off. No human muscle cultist ever managed quite the perfect symmetry natural to the goonie—grace without calculation, beauty without artifice. Their pelts varied in color from the silver blond of this pair to a coal black, and their huge eyes from the palest topaz to an emerald green, and from emerald green to deep-hued amethyst. The tightly curled mane spread down the nape and flared out over the shoulders like a cape to blend with the short, fine pelt covering the body. Their faces were like Greek sculpture, too, yet not human. No, not human. Not even humanoid, because—well, because, that was a comparison never made on Libo. That comparison was one thing we couldn't tolerate. Definitely, then, neither human nor humanoid.

I turned from watching the team which, by now, had finished folding their harness into neat little piles and had stretched out on the ground to rest beside the rickshaw. I sat back down and packed my pipe again with a Libo weed we called tobacco.

"Why do we call them goonies?" I repeated Paul's question. "There's a big bird on Earth. Inhabits some of the South Sea islands, millions of them crowd together to nest. Most stupid creature on Earth, seems like, the way they behave on their nesting grounds. A man can hardly walk among them; they don't seem to know enough to move out of the way, and don't try to protect themselves or their nests. Some reason I don't know, it's called the Goonie Bird. Guess the way these animals on Libo behaved when that hunting party came and shot them down, didn't run away, hide, or fight, reminded somebody of that bird. The name stuck."

Paul didn't say anything for a while. Then he surprised me.

"It's called the Goonie Bird when it's on the ground," he said slowly. "But in the air it's the most magnificent flying creature known to man. In the air, it's called the albatross."

I felt a chill. I knew the legend, of course, the old-time sailor superstition. Kill an albatross and bad luck will haunt you, dog you all the rest of your days. But either Paul didn't know *The Rime of the Ancient Mariner* or was too tactful a young man to make it plainer. I supplied the Libo colony with its fresh meat. The only edible animal on the planet was the goonie.

Carson's Hill comes into the yarn I have to tell—in a way is responsible. Sooner or later almost every young tenderfoot finds it, and in his mind it is linked with anguish, bitterness, emotional violence, suppressed fury.

It is a knoll, the highest point in the low range of hills that separates my valley from the smaller cup which shelters Libo City. Hal Carson, a buddy of mine in the charter colony, discovered it. Flat on top, it is a kind of granite table surrounded by giant trees, which make of it a natural amphitheater, almost like a cathedral in feeling. A young man can climb up there and be alone to have it out with his soul.

At one time or another, most do. *"Go out to the stars, young man, and grow up with the universe!"* the posters say all over Earth. It has its appeal for the strongest, the brightest, the best. Only the dull-eyed breeders are content to stay at home.

In the Company recruiting offices they didn't take just anybody, no matter what his attitude was—no indeed. Anybody, for example, who started asking questions about how and when he might get back home—with the fortune he would make—was coldly told that if he was already worrying about getting back he shouldn't be going.

Somehow, the young man was never quite sure how, it became a challenge to his bravery, his daring, his resourcefulness. It was a bait which a young fellow, anxious to prove his masculinity, the most important issue of his life, couldn't resist. The burden of proof shifted from the Company to the applicant, so that where he had started out cautiously inquiring to see if this offer might suit him, he wound up anxiously trying to prove he was the one they wanted.

Some wag in the barracks scuttlebutt once said, "They make you so afraid they won't take you, it never occurs to you that you'd be better off if they didn't."

"A fine mess," somebody else exclaimed, and let it a little

of his secret despair show through. "To prove you are a man, you lose the reason for being one."

That was the rub, of course.

Back when man was first learning how to misuse atomic power, everybody got all excited about the effects of radiation on germ plasm. Yet nobody seemed much concerned over the effects of unshielded radiation in space on that germ plasm—out from under the protecting blanket of Earth's atmosphere, away from the natural conditions where man had evolved.

There could be no normal colony of man here on Libo—no children. Yet the goonies, so unspeakably resembling man, could breed and bear. It gave the tenderfoot a smoldering resentment against the goonie which a psychologist could have explained; that wild, unreasoning fury man must feel when frustration is tied in with prime sex—submerged and festering because simple reason told the tenderfoot that the goonie was not to blame.

The tide of bitterness would swell up to choke the young tenderfoot there alone on Carson's Hill. No point to thinking of home, now. No point to dreaming of his triumphant return—space-burnt, strong, virile, remote with the vastness of space in his eyes—ever.

Unfair to the girl he had left behind that he should hold her with promises of loyalty, the girl, with ignorance equal to his own, who had urged him on. Better to let her think he had changed, grown cold, lost his love of her—so that she could fulfill her function, turn to someone else, some damned Company reject—but a reject who could still father children.

Let them. Let them strain themselves to populate the universe!

At this point the angry bitterness would often spill over into unmanly tears (somebody in the barracks had once said that Carson's Hill should be renamed Crying Hill, or Tenderfoot's Lament). And the tortured boy, despising himself, would gaze out over my valley and long for home, long for the impossible undoing of what had been done to him.

Yes, if there hadn't been a Carson's Hill there wouldn't

be a yarn to tell. But then, almost every place has a Carson's Hill, in one form or another, and Earthers remain Earthers for quite a while. They can go out to the stars in a few days or weeks, but it takes a little longer before they begin to grow up with the universe.

Quite a little longer, I was to find. Still ahead of me, I was to have my own bitter session there again, alone—an irony because I'd thought I'd come to terms with myself up there some twenty years ago.

It is the young man who is assumed to be in conflict with his society, who questions its moral and ethical structures, and yet I wonder. Or did I come of age late, very late? Still, when I look back, it was the normal thing to accept things as we found them, to be so concerned with things in their relationship to us that we had no time for wonder about relationships not connected with us. Only later, as man matures, has time to reflect—has something left over from the effort to survive . . .

When I first came to Libo, I accepted the goonie as an animal, a mere source of food. It was Company policy not to attempt a colony where there was no chance for self-support. Space shipping-rates made it impossible to supply a colony with food for more than a short time while it was being established. Those same shipping-rates make it uneconomical to ship much in the way of machinery, to say nothing of luxuries. A colony has to have an indigenous source of food and materials, and if any of that can also be turned into labor, all the better. I knew that. I accepted it as a matter of course.

And even as I learned about my own dead seed, I learned that the same genetic principles applied to other Earth life, that neither animal nor plant could be expected to propagate away from Earth. No, the local ecology had to be favorable to man's survival, else no colony. I accepted that, it was reasonable.

The colony of Libo was completely dependent on the goonie as the main source of its food. The goonie was an animal to be used for food, as is the chicken, the cow, the rabbit, on Earth. The goonie is beautiful, but so is the gazelle, which is delicious. The goonie is vaguely shaped like a human, but so is the monkey which was once the prime source of protein food for a big part of Earth's population. I accepted all that, without question.

Perhaps it was easy for me. I was raised on a farm, where slaughtering of animals for food was commonplace. I had the average farm boy's contempt for the dainty young lady in the fashionable city restaurant who, without thought, lifts a bite of rare steak, dripping with blood, to her pearly teeth; but who would turn pale and retch at the very thought of killing an animal. Where did she think that steak came from?

At first we killed the goonies around our encampment which was to become Libo City; went out and shot them as we needed them, precisely as hunters do on Earth. In time we had to go farther and farther in our search for them, so I began to study them, in hope I could domesticate them. I learned one of their peculiarities—they were completely dependent upon the fruit of the pal tree, an ever-bearing tree. Each goonie had its own pal tree, and we learned by experiment that they would starve before they would eat the fruit from any other pal tree.

There was another peculiarity which we don't yet understand, and yet we see it in rudimentary form on Earth where game breeds heartily during seasons of plentiful food, and sparsely in bad years. Here, the goonie did not bear young unless there were unclaimed pal trees available, and did bear young up to a limit of such trees.

My future was clear, then. Obtain the land and plant the pal trees to insure a constant supply of meat for the colony. It was the farm boy coming out in me, no doubt, but no different from any farm boy who grows up and wants to own his own farm, his own cattle ranch.

I was a young man trying to build a secure future for himself. There was no thought of the goonie except as a meat supply. I accepted that as a matter of course. And as Libo City grew, I continued to increase my planting of pal trees in my valley, and my herds of goonies.

It was only later, much later, that I found the goonie could also be trained for work of various kinds. I accepted this, too, in the same spirit we trained colts on the farm to ride, to pull the plow, to work.

Perhaps it was this training, only for the crudest tasks at first, then later, calling for more and more skill, that proved my undoing. On the farm we separated our pet animals from the rest; we gave our pets names, but we never gave names to those destined for slaughter, nor formed any affection for them. This was taboo. I found myself carrying out the same procedures here. I separated those goonies I trained from the meat herds. Then I separated the common labor goonies from the skilled labor.

I should have stopped there—at least there. But when man's curiosity is aroused . . . Can we say to the research scientist, "You may ask this question, but you are forbidden to ask that one. You may take this step, but you must not take a second, to see what lies beyond." Can we say that to the human mind? I did not say it to myself.

I taught certain goonies to speak, to read, to write.

The goonies accepted this training in the same joyful exuberance they accepted everything else from man. I never understood it, not until now. Their whole behavior, their whole being seemed the same as greeted the first hunting party. "You want us to die, man? For you, we will do it gladly."

Whatever man wanted, the goonie gave, to the limit of his capacity. And I had not found that limit.

I took one step too many. I know that now.

And yet, should I not have taken that last step—teaching them to speak, to read, to write? The capacity was in them for learning it all the time. Was it finding it out that made the difference? But what kind of moral and ethic structure is it that depends on ignorance for its support?

Miriam Wellman comes into the yarn, too. She was the catalyst. My destruction was not her fault. It would have come about anyway. She merely hastened it. She had a job to do, she did it well. It worked out as she planned, a cauterizing kind of thing, burning out a sore that was beginning to fester on Libo—to leave us hurting a little, but clean.

Important though she was, she still remains a little hazy to me, a little unreal. Perhaps I was already so deep into my quandary, without knowing it, that both people and things were a little hazy, and the problem deep within me my only reality.

I was in Libo City the day she landed from the tender that serviced the planets from the mother ship orbiting out in space. I saw her briefly from the barbershop across the street when she came out of the warehouse and walked down our short main street to the Company Administration Building. She was a dark-haired little thing, sharp-eyed, neither young nor old—a crisp, efficient career gal, she seemed to me. I didn't see any of the men on the street make a pass at her. She had the looks, all right, but not the look.

There weren't more than a dozen women on the whole planet, childless women who had forgone having children, who had raked up the exorbitant space fare and come on out to join their man anyhow; and the men should have been falling all over Miriam Wellman—but they weren't. They just looked, and then looked at each other. Nobody whistled.

I got a little more of what had happened from the head warehouseman, who was a friend of mine. He smelled something wrong, he said, the minute the tender cut its blasts and settled down. Usually there's joshing, not always friendly, between the tender crew and the warehouse crew —the contempt of the spaceman for the landbound; the scorn of the landbound for the glamor-boy spacemen who think their sweat is wine.

Not today. The pilot didn't come out of his cabin at all to stretch his legs; he sat there looking straight ahead, and the ship's crew started hustling the dock loaders almost before the hatches opened for unloading a few supplies and loading our packages of libolines—the jewel stone which is our excuse for being.

She came down the gangplank, he said, gave a crisp, careless flick of her hand toward the pilot, who must have caught it out of the corner of his eye for he nodded briefly, formally, and froze. Later we learned he was not supposed to tell us who she really was, but he did his best. Only we didn't catch it.

She came across the yard with all the human warehousemen staring, but not stepping toward her. Only the goonies seemed unaware. In their fashion, laughing and playing, and still turning out more work than humans could, they were already cleaning out the holds and trucking the supplies over to the loading dock.

She came up the little flight of stairs at the end of the dock and approached Hal, the head warehouseman, who, he said, was by that time bug-eyed.

"Do you always let those creatures go around stark naked?" she asked in a low, curious voice. She waved toward the gangs of goonies.

He managed to get his jaw unhinged enough to stammer. "Why, ma'am," he says he said, "they're only animals."

Nowadays, when he tells it, he claims he saw a twinkle of laughter in her eyes. I don't believe it. She was too skilled in the part she was playing.

She looked at him, she looked back at the goonies, and she looked at him again. By then he said he was blushing all over, and sweating as if the dry air of Libo was a steam room. It wasn't any trick to see how she was comparing, what she was thinking. And every stranger was warned, before he landed, that the one thing the easy-going Liboan wouldn't tolerate was comparison of goonie with man. Beside them we looked raw, unfinished, poorly done by an amateur. There was only one way we could bear it—there could be no comparison.

He says he knows he turned purple, but before he could think of anything else to say, she swept on past him, through the main aisle of the warehouse, and out the front door. All he could do was stand there and try to think of some excuse for living, he said.

She had that effect on people—she cut them down to bedrock with a word, a glance. She did it deliberately. Yes, she came as a Mass Psychology Therapist, a branch of pseudo-science currently epidemic on Earth which believed in the value of emotional purges whipped up into frenzies.

She came as a prime trouble-maker, as far as we could see at the time. She came to see that the dear, fresh boys who were swarming out to conquer the universe didn't fall into the evil temptations of space.

She came at the critical time. Libo City had always been a small frontier spaceport, a lot like the old frontier towns of primitive Earth—a street of warehouses, commissaries, an Administration building, couple of saloons, a meeting hall, the barracks, a handful of cottages for the men with wives, a few more cottages built by pairs of young men who wanted to shake free of barracks life for a while, but usually went back to it. Maybe there should have been another kind of House, also, but Earth was having another of its periodic moral spasms, and the old women of the male sex who comprised the Company's Board of Directors threw up their hands in hypocritical horror at the idea of sex where there was no profit to be made from the sale of diapers and cribs and pap.

Now it was all changing. Libo City was mushrooming. The Company had made it into a shipping terminal to serve the network of planets still out beyond as the Company extended its areas of exploitation. More barracks and more executive cottages were going up as fast as goonie labor could build them. Hundreds of tenderfoot Earthers were being shipped in to handle the clerical work of the terminal. Hundreds of Earthers, all at once, to bring with them their tensions, their callousness, swaggering, boasting, cruelties and sadisms which were natural products of life on Earth—and all out of place here where we'd been able to assimilate a couple or so at a time, when there hadn't been enough to clique up among themselves; they'd had to learn a life of calmness and reason if they wanted to stay.

Perhaps Miriam Wellman was a necessity. The dear, fresh boys filled the meeting hall, overflowed it, moved the nightly meetings to the open ground of the landing field. She used every emotional trick of the rabble-rouser to whip them up into frenzies, made them drunk on emotion, created a scene of back-pounding, shouting, jittering maniacs. It was a good lesson for anybody who might believe in the progress of the human race toward reason, intelligence.

I had my doubts about the value of what she was doing, but for what it was, she was good. She knew her business.

Paul Tyler put the next part of the pattern into motion. I hadn't seen him since our talk about the first hunting party, but when we settled down in our living-room chairs with our pipes and our tall cool glasses, it was apparent he'd been doing some thinking. He started off obliquely.

"About three years ago," he said, as he set his glass back down on the table, "just before I came out here from Earth, I read a book by an Australian hunter of kangaroos."

The tone of his voice made it more than idle comment. I waited.

"This fellow *told* the reader, every page or so, how stupid the kangaroo is. But everything he said *showed* how intelligent it is, how perfectly it adapts to its natural environment, takes every advantage. Even a kind of rough tribal organization in the herds, a recognized tribal ownership of lands, battles between tribes or individuals that try to poach, an organized initiation of a stray before it can be adopted into a tribe."

"Then how did he justify calling it stupid?" I asked.

"Maybe the real question is 'Why?' "

"You answer it," I said.

"The economy of Australia is based on sheep," he said. "And sheep, unaided, can't compete with kangaroos. The kangaroo's teeth are wedge-shaped to bite clumps, and they can grow fat on new growth while sheep are still down into the heart of grass unable to get anything to eat. The kangaroo's jump takes him from clump to sparse clump where the sheep will walk himself to death trying to stave off starvation. So the kangaroo has to go, because it interferes with man's desires."

"Does that answer 'Why?' " I asked.

"Doesn't it?" he countered. "They have to keep it killed off, if man is to prosper. So they have to deprecate it, to keep their conscience clear. If we granted the goonie equal intelligence with man, could we use it for food? Enslave it for labor?"

I was quick with a denial.

"The goonie was tested for intelligence," I said sharply. "Only a few months after the colony was founded. The Department of Extraterrestrial Psychology sent out a team of testers. Their work was exhaustive, and their findings unequivocal."

"This was before you trained goonies for work?" he asked.

"Well, yes," I conceded. "But as I understood it, their findings ran deeper than just breaking an animal to do some work patterns. It had to do with super-ego, conscience. You know, we've never seen any evidence of tribal organization, any of the customs of the primitive man, no sense of awe, fear, worship. Even their mating seems to be casual, without sense of pairing, permanence. Hardly even herd instinct, except that they grouped where pal trees clustered. But on their own, undirected, nobody ever saw them plant the pal tree. The psychologists were thorough. They just didn't find evidence to justify calling the goonie intelligent."

"That was twenty years ago," he said. "Now they understand our language, complicated instruction. You've taught them to speak, read, and write."

I raised my brows. I didn't think anyone knew about that except Ruth, my wife.

"Ruth let the cat out of the bag," he said with a smile. "But I already knew about the speaking. As you say, the goonie has no fear, no conscience, no sense of concealment. They speak around anybody. You can't keep it concealed, Jim."

"I suppose not," I said.

"Which brings me to the point. Have you gone a step farther? Have you trained any to do clerical work?"

"Matter of fact," I admitted, "I have. The Company has sharp pencils. If I didn't keep up my records, they'd take the fillings out of my teeth before I knew what was happening. I didn't have humans, so I trained goonies to do the job. Under detailed instruction, of course," I added.

"I need such a clerk, myself," he said. "There's a new office manager, fellow by the name of Carl Hest. A—well, maybe you know the kind. He's taken a particular dislike to me for some reason—well, all right, I know the reason. I caught him abusing his rickshaw goonie, and told him off before I knew who he was. Now he's getting back at me through my reports. I spend more time making corrected reports, trying to please him, than I do in mining libolines. It's rough. I've got to do something, or he'll accumulate enough evidence to get me shipped back to Earth. My reports didn't matter before, so long as I brought in my quota of libolines—the clerks in Libo City fixed up my reports for me. But now I've got to do both, with every T crossed and I dotted. It's driving me nuts."

"I had a super like that when I was a Company man," I said, with sympathy. "It's part of the nature of the breed."

"You train goonies and sell them for all other kinds of work," he said, at last. "I couldn't afford to buy an animal trained that far, but could you rent me one? At least while I get over this hump?"

I was reluctant, but then, why not? As Paul said, I trained goonies for all other kinds of work, why not make a profit on my clerks? What was the difference? And, it wouldn't be too hard to replace a clerk. They may have no intelligence, as the psychologists defined it, but they learned fast, needed to be shown only once.

"About those kangaroos," I said curiously. "How did that author justify calling them stupid?"

Paul looked at me with a little frown.

"Oh," he said, "various ways. For example, a rancher puts up a fence, and a chased kangaroo will beat himself to death trying to jump over it or go through it. Doesn't seem to get the idea of going around it. Things like that."

"Does seem pretty stupid," I commented.

"An artificial, man-made barrier," he said. "Not a part of its natural environment, so it can't cope with it."

"Isn't that the essence of intelligence?" I asked. "To analyze new situations, and master them?"

"Looking at it from man's definition of intelligence, I guess," he admitted.

"What other definition do we have?" I asked. . . .

I went back to the rental of the goonie, then, and we

came to a mutually satisfactory figure. I was still a little reluctant, but I couldn't have explained why. There was something about the speaking, reading, writing, clerical work—I was reluctant to let it get out of my own hands, but reason kept asking me why. Pulling a rickshaw, or cooking, or serving the table, or building a house, or writing figures into a ledger and adding them up—what difference?

In the days that followed, I couldn't seem to get Paul's conversation out of my mind. It wasn't only that I'd rented him a clerk against my feelings of reluctance. It was something he'd said, something about the kangaroos. I went back over the conversation, reconstructed it sentence by sentence, until I pinned it down.

"Looking at it from man's definition of intelligence," he had said.

"What other definition do we have?" I had asked.

What about the goonie's definition? That was a silly question. As far as I knew, goonies never defined anything. They seemed to live only for the moment. Perhaps the unfailing supply of fruit from their pal tree, the lack of any natural enemy, had never taught them a sense of want, or fear. And therefore, of conscience? There was no violence in their nature, no resistance to anything. How, then, could man ever hope to understand the goonie? All right, perhaps a resemblance in physical shape, but a mental life so totally alien . . .

Part of the answer came to me then.

Animal psychology tests, I reasoned, to some degree *must* be based on how man, himself, would react in a given situation. The animal's intelligence is measured largely in terms of how close it comes to the behavior of man. A man would discover, after a few tries, that he must go around the fence; but the kangaroo couldn't figure that out—it was too far removed from anything in a past experience which included no fences, no barriers.

Alien beings are not man, and do not, cannot, react in the same way as man. Man's tests, therefore, based solely on his own standards, will never prove any other intelligence in the universe equal to man's own!

The tests were as rigged as a crooked slot machine.

But the goonie did learn to go around the fence. On his own? No, I couldn't say that. He had the capacity for doing what was shown him, and repeating it when told. But he never did anything on his own, never initiated anything, never created anything. He followed complicated instructions by rote, but only by rote. Never as if he understood the meanings, the abstract meanings. He made sense when he did speak, did not just jabber like a parrot, but he spoke only in direct monosyllables—the words, themselves, a part of the mechanical pattern. I gave it up. Perhaps the psychologists were right, after all.

A couple of weeks went by before the next part of the pattern fell into place. Paul brought back the goonie clerk.

"What happened?" I asked, when we were settled in the living room with drinks and pipes. "Couldn't he do the work?"

"Nothing wrong with the goonie," he said, a little sullenly. "I don't deserve a smart goonie. I don't deserve to associate with grown men. I'm still a kid with no sense."

"Well, now," I said with a grin. "Far be it from me to disagree with a man's own opinion of himself. What happened?"

"I told you about this Carl Hest? The office manager?"

I nodded.

"This morning my monthly reports were due. I took them into Libo City with my libolines. I wasn't content just to leave them with the receiving clerk, as usual. Oh, no! I took them right on in to Mr. High-and-mighty Hest, himself. I slapped them down on his desk and I said, 'All right, bud, see what you can find wrong with them this time.'"

Paul began scraping the dottle out of his pipe and looked at me out of the corner of his eyes.

I grinned more broadly.

"I can understand," I said. "I was a Company man once, myself."

"This guy Hest," Paul continued, "raised his eyebrows, picked up the reports as if they'd dirty his hands, flicked through them to find my dozens of mistakes at a glance. Then he went back over them—slowly. Finally, after about ten minutes, he laid them down on his desk. 'Well, Mr. Tyler,' he said in that nasty voice of his. 'What happened to you? Come down with an attack of intelligence?'

"I should have quit when my cup was full," Paul said, after I'd had my laugh. "But oh, no. I had to keep pouring and mess up the works—I wasn't thinking about anything but wiping that sneer off his face. 'Those reports you think are so intelligent,' I said, 'were done by a goonie.' Then I said, real loud because the whole office was dead silent, 'How does it feel to know that a goonie can do this work as well as your own suck-up goons—as well as you could, probably, and maybe better?'

"I walked out while his mouth was still hanging open. You know how the tenderfeet are. They pick up the attitude that the goonie is an inferior animal, and they ride it for all it's worth; they take easily to having something they can push around. You know, Jim, you can call a man a dirty name with a smile, and he'll sort of take it; maybe not quite happy about it but he'll take it because you said it right. But here on Libo you don't compare a man with a goonie—not anytime, no how, no matter how you say it."

"So then what happened?" I'd lost my grin suddenly.

"It all happened in front of his office staff. He's got a lot of those suck-ups that enjoy his humor when he tongue-skins us stupid bastards from out in the field. Their ears were all flapping. They heard the works. I went on about my business around town, and it wasn't more than an hour before I knew I was an untouchable. The word had spread. It grew with the telling. Maybe an outsider wouldn't get the full force of it, but here in Libo, well, you know what it would mean to tell a man he could be replaced by a goonie."

"I know," I said around the stem of my pipe, while I watched his face. Something had grabbed my tailbone and was twisting it with that tingling feeling we get in the face of danger. I wondered if Paul even yet, had fully realized what he'd done.

"Hell! All right, Jim, goddamn it!" he exploded. "Suppose a goonie could do their work better? That's not going to throw them out of a job. There's plenty of work, plenty of planets besides this one—even if the Company heard about it and put in goonies at the desks."

"It's not just that," I said slowly. "No matter how low down a man is, he's got to have something he thinks is still lower before he can be happy. The more inferior he is, the more he needs it. Take it away from him and you've started something."

"I guess," Paul agreed, but I could see he had his reserve of doubt. Well, he was young, and he'd been fed that scout-master line about how noble mankind is. He'd learn.

"Anyhow," he said. "Friend of mine, better friend than most, I've found out, tipped me off. Said I'd better get rid of that goonie clerk, and quick, if I knew which side was up. I'm still a Company man, Jim. I'm like the rest of these poor bastards out here, still indentured for my space fare, and wouldn't know how to keep alive if the Company kicked me out and left me stranded. That's what could happen. Those guys can cut my feet out from under me every step I take. You know it. What can I do but knuckle under? So—I brought the goonie back."

I nodded.

"Too bad you didn't keep it under your hat, the way I have," I said. "But it's done now."

I sat and thought about it. I wasn't worried about my part in it—I had a part because everybody would know I'd trained the goonie, that Paul had got him from me. It wasn't likely a little two-bit office manager could hurt me with the Company. They needed me too much. I could raise and train, or butcher, goonies and deliver them cheaper than they could do it themselves. As long as you don't step on their personal egos, the big boys in business don't mind slapping down their underlings and telling them to behave themselves, if there's a buck to be made out of it.

Besides, I was damn good advertising, a real shill for their recruiting offices. "See?" they'd say. "Look at Jim Mac-Pherson. Just twenty years ago he signed up with the Company to go out to the stars. Today he's a rich man, independent, free enterprise. What he did, you can do." Or they'd make it seem that way. And they were right. I could go on being an independent operator so long as I kept off the toes of the big boys.

But Paul was a different matter.

"Look," I said. "You go back to Libo City and tell it around that it was just a training experiment I was trying. That it was a failure. That you exaggerated, even lied, to jolt Hest. Maybe that'll get you out from under. Maybe we won't hear any more about it."

He looked at me, his face stricken. But he could still try to joke about it, after a fashion.

"You said everybody finds something inferior to himself," he said. "I can't think of anything lower than I am. I just can't."

I laughed.

"Fine," I said with more heartiness than I really felt. "At one time or another most of us have to get clear down to rock bottom before we can begin to grow up."

I didn't know then that there was a depth beyond rock bottom, a hole one could get into, with no way out. But I was to learn.

I was wrong in telling Paul we wouldn't hear anything more about it. I heard, the very next day. I was down in the south valley, taking care of the last planting in the new orchard, when I saw a caller coming down the dirt lane between the groves of pal trees. His rickshaw was being pulled by a single goonie, and even at a distance I could see the animal was abused with overwork, if not worse.

Yes, worse, because as they came nearer I could see whip welts across the pelt covering the goonie's back and shoulders. I began a slow boil inside at the needless cruelty, needless because anybody knows the goonie will kill himself with overwork if the master simply asks for it. So my caller was one of the new Earthers, one of the petty little squirts who had to demonstrate his power over the inferior animal.

Apparently Ruth had had the same opinion for instead of treating the caller as an honored guest and sending a goonie to fetch me, as was Libo custom, she'd sent him on down to the orchard. I wondered if he had enough sense to know he'd been insulted. I hoped he did.

Even if I hadn't been scorched to a simmering rage by the time the goonie halted at the edge of the orchard—and sank down on the ground without even unbuckling his harness—I wouldn't have liked the caller. The important way he climbed down out of the rickshaw, the pompous stride he affected as he strode toward me, marked him as some petty Company official.

I wondered how he had managed to get past Personnel. Usually they picked the fine, upstanding, cleancut hero type—a little short on brains, maybe, but full of noble derring-do, and so anxious to be admired they never made any trouble. It must have been Personnel's off day when this one got through—or maybe he had an uncle.

"Afternoon," I greeted him, without friendliness, as he came up.

"I see you're busy," he said briskly. "I am, too. My time is valuable, so I'll come right to the point. My name is Mr. Hest. I'm an executive. You're MacPherson?"

"Mister MacPherson," I answered dryly.

He ignored it.

"I hear you've got a goonie trained to bookkeeping. You leased it to Tyler on a thousand-dollar evaluation. An outrageous price, but I'll buy it. I hear Tyler turned it back."

I didn't like what I saw in his eyes, or his loose, fat-lipped mouth. Not at all.

"The goonie is unsatisfactory," I said. "The experiment didn't work, and he's not for sale."

"You can't kid me, MacPherson," he said. "Tyler never made up those reports. He hasn't the capacity. I'm an accountant. If you can train a goonie that far, I can train him on into real accounting. The Company could save millions if goonies could take the place of humans in office work."

I knew there were guys who'd sell their own mothers into a two-bit dive if they thought it would impress the boss, but I didn't believe this one had that motive. There was something else, something in the way his avid little eyes looked me over, the way he licked his lips, the way he came out with an explanation that a smart man would have kept to himself.

"Maybe you're a pretty smart accountant," I said in my best hayseed drawl, "but you don't know anything at all about training goonies." I gestured with my head. "How come you're overworking your animal that way, beating him to make him run up those steep hills on those rough roads? Can't you afford a team?"

"He's my property," he said.

"You're not fit to own him," I said, as abruptly. "I wouldn't sell you a goonie of any kind, for any price."

Either the man had the hide of a rhinoceros, or he was driven by a passion I couldn't understand.

"Fifteen hundred," he bid. "Not a penny more."

"Not at any price. Good day, Mr. Hest."

He looked at me sharply, as if he couldn't believe I'd refuse such a profit, as if it were a new experience for him to find a man without a price. He started to say something, then shut his mouth with a snap. He turned abruptly and strode back to his rickshaw. Before he reached it, he was shouting angrily to his goonie to get up out of that dirt and look alive.

I took an angry step toward them and changed my mind. Whatever I did, Hest would later take it out on the goonie. He was that kind of man. I was stopped, too, by the old Liboan custom of never meddling in another man's affairs. There weren't any laws about handling goonies. We hadn't needed them. Disapproval had been enough to bring tenderfeet into line, before. And I hated to see laws like that come to Libo, morals-meddling laws—because it was men like Hest who had the compulsion to get in control of making and enforcing them, who hid behind the badge so they could get their kicks without fear of reprisal.

I didn't know what to do. I went back to planting the orchard and worked until the first sun had set and the second was close behind. Then I knocked off, sent the goonies to their pal groves, and went on up to the house.

Ruth's first question, when I came through the kitchen door, flared my rage up again.

"Jim," she said curiously, and a little angry, "why did you sell that clerk to a man like Hest?"

"But I didn't," I said.

"Here's the thousand, cash, he left with me," she said and pointed to the corner of the kitchen table. "He said it was the price you agreed on. He had me make out a bill of sale. I thought it peculiar because you always take care of business, but he said you wanted to go on working."

"He pulled a fast one, Ruth," I said, my anger rising.

"What are you going to do?" she asked.

"Right after supper I'm going into Libo City. Bill of sale, or not, I'm going to get that goonie back."

"Jim," she said, "be careful." There was worry in her eyes. "You're not a violent man—and you're not as young as you used to be."

That was something a man would rather not be reminded of, not even by his wife—especially not by his wife.

Inquiry in Libo City led me to Hest's private cottage, but it was dark. I couldn't arouse any response, not even a goonie. I tried the men's dormitories to get a line on him. Most of the young Earthers seemed to think it was a lark, and their idea of good sportsmanship kept them from telling me where to find him. From some of them I sensed a deeper, more turgid undercurrent where good, clean fun might not be either so good or so clean.

In one of the crowded saloons there was a booth of older men, men who'd been here longer, and kept a disdainful distance away from the new Earthers.

"There's something going on, Jim," one of them said. "I don't know just what. Try that hell-raisin', snortin' female. Hest's always hanging around her."

I looked around the booth. They were all grinning a little. So the story of how Hest had outfoxed me had spread, and they could enjoy that part of it. I didn't blame them. But I could tell they didn't sense there was anything more to it than that. They told me where to locate Miriam Wellman's cottage, and added as I started to leave, "You need any

help, Jim, you know where to look." Part of it was to say
that in a showdown against the Earthers they were on my
side, but most of it was a bid to get in on a little fun, break
the monotony.

I found the woman's cottage without trouble, and she
answered the door in person. I told her who I was, and she
invited me in without any coy implications about what the
neighbors might think. The cottage was standard, furnished
with goonie-made furniture of native materials.

"I'll come right to the point, Miss Wellman," I said.

"Good," she answered crisply. "The boys will be gathering for their meeting, and I like to be prompt."

I started to tell her what I thought of her meetings, how
much damage she was doing, how far she was setting Libo
back. I decided there wouldn't be any use. People who do
that kind of thing, her kind of thing, get their kicks out of
the ego-bloating effect of their power over audiences and
don't give a good goddamn about how much damage they
do.

"I'm looking for Carl Hest," I said. "I understand he's
one of your apple-polishers."

She was wearing standard coverall fatigues, but she made
a gesture as if she were gathering up folds of a voluminous
skirt to show me there was nothing behind them. "I am not
hiding Carl Hest," she said scornfully.

"Then you know he is hiding." I paused, and added,
"And you probably know he conned my wife out of a valuable goonie. You probably know what he's got in mind to
do."

"I do, Mr. MacPherson," she said crisply. "I know very
well."

I looked at her, and felt a deep discouragement. I
couldn't see any way to get past that shell of hers, that armor of self-righteousness— No, that wasn't it. She wasn't
quoting fanatic, meaningless phrases at me, clouding the
issue with junk. She was a crisp business woman who had
a situation well in hand.

"Then you know more than I do," I said. "But I can
guess some things. I don't like what I can guess. I trained
that goonie, I'm responsible. I'm not going to have it—

well, whatever they plan to do with it—just because I trained it to a work that Hest and his toadies don't approve."

"Very commendable sentiments, Mr. MacPherson," she said dryly. "But suppose you keep out of an affair that's none of your business. I understood that was Liboan custom, not to meddle in other people's doings."

"That *was* the custom," I said.

She stood up suddenly and walked with quick, short strides across the room to a closet door. She turned around and looked at me, as if she had made up her mind to something.

"It's still a good custom," she said. "Believe it or not, I'm trying to preserve it."

I looked at her dumfounded.

"By letting things happen, whatever's going to happen to that goonie?" I asked incredulously. "By coming out here and whipping up the emotions of these boys, stirring up who knows what in them?"

She opened the door of the closet and I could see she was taking out a robe, an iridescent, shimmering thing.

"I know precisely what I'm stirring up," she said. "That's my business. That's what I'm here for."

I couldn't believe it. To whip up the emotions of a mob just for the kicks of being able to do it was one thing. But to do it deliberately, knowing the effect of arousing primitive savagery . . .

She turned around and began slipping into the garment. She zipped up the front of it with a crisp motion, and it transformed her. In darkness, under the proper spotlights, the ethereal softness completely masked her calculating efficiency.

"Why?" I demanded. "If you know, if you really do know, why?"

"My work here is about finished," she said, as she came over to her chair and sat down again. "It will do no harm to tell you why. You're not a Company man, and your reputation is one of discretion. . . . The point is, in mass hiring for jobs in such places as Libo, we make mistakes in Personnel. Our tests are not perfect."

"We?" I asked.

"I'm a trouble-shooter for Company Personnel," she said.

"All this mumbo-jumbo," I said. "Getting out there and whipping these boys up into frenzies . . ."

"You know about medical inoculation, vaccination," she said. "Under proper controls, it can be psychologically applied. A little virus, a little fever, and from there on, most people are immune. Some aren't. With some, it goes into a full-stage disease. We don't know which is which without test. We have to test. Those who can't pass the test, Mr. MacPherson, are shipped back to Earth. This way we find out quickly, instead of letting some Typhoid Marys gradually infect a whole colony."

"Hest," I said.

"Hest is valuable," she said. "He thinks he is transferred often because we need him to set up procedures and routines. Actually it's because he is a natural focal point for the wrong ones to gather round. Birds of a feather. Sending him out a couple months in advance of a trouble-shooter saves us a lot of time. We already know where to look when we get there."

"He doesn't catch on?" I asked.

"People get blinded by their own self-importance," she said. "He can't see beyond himself. And," she added, "we vary our techniques."

I sat there and thought about it for a few minutes. I could see the sense in it, and I could see, in the long run, how Libo would be a better, saner place for the inoculation that would make the better-balanced Earthers so sick of this kind of thing they'd never want any more of it. But it was damned cold-blooded. These scientists! And it was aside from the issue of my goonie clerk.

"All right," I said. "I guess you know what you're doing. But it happens I'm more interested in that goonie clerk."

"That goonie clerk is another focal point," she said. "I've been waiting for some such incident."

"You might have waited a long time," I said.

"Oh, no," she answered. "There's always an incident. We wait for a particularly effective one."

I stood up.

"You'd sacrifice the goonie to the job you're doing," I said.

"Yes," she said shortly. "If it were necessary," she added.

"You can find some other incident, then," I said. "I don't intend to see that goonie mistreated, maybe worse, just to get a result for you."

She stood up quickly, a flash of shimmering light.

"You will keep your hands entirely off it, Mr. MacPherson," she said crisply. "I do not intend to have my work spoiled by amateur meddling. I'm a professional. This kind of thing is my business. I know how to handle it. Keep off, Mr. MacPherson. You don't realize how much damage you could do at this point."

"I'm not a Company man, Miss Wellman," I said hotly. "You can't order me."

I turned around and stalked out of her door and went back to the main street of town. It was nearly deserted now. Only a few of the older hands were sitting around in the saloons, a few so disgusted with the frenetic meetings they wouldn't go even to break the monotony.

I went over to the main warehouse and through the gate to the landing field. The crowd was there, sitting around, standing around, moving around, waiting for the show to start. At the far end there was a platform, all lighted up with floods. It was bare except for a simple lectern at the center. Very effective. Miss Wellman hadn't arrived.

Maybe I could spot Hest somewhere up near the platform.

I threaded my way through the crowd, through knots of young Earthers who were shooting the breeze about happenings of the day, the usual endless gossip over trivialities. For a while I couldn't pin it down, the something that was lacking. Then I realized that the rapt, trancelike hypnotism I expected to see just wasn't there. The magic was wearing off. It was at this stage of the game that a smart rabble-rouser would move on, would sense the satiation and leave while he was still ahead, before everybody began to realize how temporary, pointless and empty the whole emotional binge had been. As Miss Wellman had said, her work here was about finished.

But I didn't spot Hest anywhere. I moved on up near the platform. There was a group of five at one corner of the platform.

"Where could I find Mr. Hest?" I asked them casually.

They gave me the big eye, the innocent face, the don't-know shake of the head. They didn't know. I turned away and heard a snicker. I whirled back around and saw only wooden faces, the sudden poker face an amateur puts on when he gets a good hand—later he wonders why everybody dropped out of the pot.

I wandered around some more. I stood on the outside of little knots of men and eavesdropped. I didn't hear anything of value for a while.

It wasn't until there was a buzz in the crowd, and a spotlight swept over to the gate to highlight Miss Wellman's entrance that I heard a snatch of phrase. Maybe it was the excitement that raised that voice just enough for me to hear.

". . . Carson's Hill tonight . . ."

"Shut up, you fool!"

There was a deep silence as the crowd watched Miss Wellman in her shimmering robe; she swept down the path that opened in front of her as if she were floating. But I had the feeling it was an appreciation of good showmanship they felt. I wondered what it had been like a couple of weeks back.

But I wasn't waiting here for anything more. I'd got my answer. Carson's Hill, of course! If Hest and his gang were staging another kind of show, a private one for their own enjoyment, Carson's Hill would be the place. It fitted—the gang of juvenile delinquents who are compelled to burn down the school, desecrate the chapel, stab to death the mother image in some innocent old woman who just happened to walk by at the wrong moment—wild destruction of a place or symbol that represented inner travail.

I was moving quickly through the crowd, the silent crowd. There was only a low grumble as I pushed somebody aside so I could get through. Near the edge I heard her voice come through the speakers, low and thrilling, dulcet sweet.

"My children," she began, "tonight's meeting must be

brief. This is farewell, and I must not burden you with my grief at leaving you . . ."

I made the yard gate and ran down the street to where my goonie team still waited beside the rickshaw.

"Let's get out to Carson's Hill as fast as we can," I said to the team. In the darkness I caught the answering flash of their eyes, and heard the soft sound of harness being slipped over pelt. By the time I was seated, they were away in a smart mile-covering trot.

Miriam Wellman had been damned sure of herself, burning her bridges behind her while Hest and his rowdies were still on the loose, probably up there on Carson's Hill, torturing that goonie for their own amusement. I wondered how in hell she thought that was taking care of anything.

The road that led toward home was smooth enough for a while, but it got rough as soon as the goonies took the trail that branched off toward Carson's Hill. It was a balmy night, warm and sweet with the fragrance of pal-tree blossoms. The sky was full of stars, still close, not yet faded in the light of the first moon that was now rising in the East. It was a world of beauty, and the only flaw in it was Man.

In the starlight, and now the increasing moonlight, Carson's Hill began to stand forth, blocking off the stars to the west. In the blackness of that silhouette, near its crest, I seemed to catch a hint of reddish glow—a fire had been built in the amphitheater.

Farther along, where the steep climb began, I spoke softly to the team, had them pull off the path into a small grove of pal trees. From here on the path wound around and took forever to get to the top. I could make better time with a stiff climb on foot. Avoid sentries, too—assuming they'd had enough sense to post any.

The team seemed uneasy, as if they sensed my tenseness, or knew what was happening up there on top. We understood them so little, how could we know what the goonie sensed? But as always they were obedient, anxious to please man, only to please him, whatever he wanted. I told them to conceal themselves and wait for me. They would.

I left the path and struck off in a straight line toward the top. The going wasn't too bad at first. Wide patches of no trees, no undergrowth, open to the moonlight. I worried about it a little. To anyone watching from above I would be a dark spot moving against the light-colored grass. But I gambled they would be too intent with their pleasures, or would be watching only the path, which entered the grove from the other side of the hill.

Now I was high enough to look off to the southeast where Libo City lay. I saw the lights of the main street, tiny as a relief map. I did not see the bright spot of the platform on the landing field. Too far away to distinguish, something blocking my view at that point . . . or was the meeting already over and the landing field dark?

I plunged into a thicket of vines and brush. The advantage of concealment was offset by slower climbing. But I had no fear of losing my way so long as I climbed. The glow of light was my beacon, but not a friendly one. It grew stronger as I climbed, and once there was a shower of sparks wafting upward as though somebody had disturbed the fire. Disturbed it, in what way?

I realized I was almost running up the hill and gasping for breath. The sound of my feet was a loud rustle of leaves, and I tried to go more slowly, more quietly as I neared the top.

At my first sight of flickering raw flame through the trunks of trees, I stopped.

I had no plan in mind. I wasn't fool enough to think I could plow in there and fight a whole gang of crazed sadists. A fictional hero would do it, of course—and win without mussing his pretty hair. I was no such hero, and nobody knew it better than I.

What would I do then? Try it anyway? At my age? Already panting for breath from my climb, from excitement? Maybe from a fear that I wouldn't admit? Or would I simply watch, horror-stricken, as witnesses on Earth had watched crazed mobs from time immemorial? Surely man could have found some way to leave his barbarisms back on Earth, where they were normal.

I didn't know. I felt compelled to steal closer, to see what was happening. Was this, too, a part of the human pattern? The horror-stricken witness, powerless to turn away, powerless to intervene, appalled at seeing the human being in the raw? To carry the scar of it in his mind all the rest of his days?

Was this, too, a form of participation? And from it a kind of inverse satisfaction of superiority to the mob?

What the hell. I pushed my way on through the last thickets, on toward the flames. I didn't know I was sobbing deep, wracking coughs, until I choked on a hiccup. Careful MacPherson! You're just asking for it. How would you like to join the goonie?

As it was, I almost missed the climax. Five minutes more and I would have found only an empty glade, a fire starting to burn lower for lack of wood, trampled grass between the crevices of flat granite stones.

Now from where I hid I saw human silhouettes limned against the flames, moving in random patterns. I drew closer and closer, dodging from tree to tree. Softly and carefully I crept closer, until the blackness of silhouette gave way to the color-tones of firelight on flesh. I could hear the hoarseness of their passion-drunk voices, and crept still closer until I could distinguish words.

Yet in this, as in the equally barbaric meeting I'd left, something was missing. There wasn't an experienced lyncher among them. At least Personnel had had the foresight to refuse the applications from areas where lynching was an endemic pleasure. The right words, at the right time, would have jelled thought and action into ultimate sadism, but as it was, the men here milled about uncertainly—driven by the desire, the urge, but not knowing quite how to go about it . . . . the adolescent in his first sex attempt.

"Well, let's do something," one voice came clearly. "If hanging's too good for a goonie that tries to be a man, how about burning?"

"Let's skin him alive and auction off the pelt. Teach these goonies a lesson."

I saw the goonie then, spreadeagled on the ground. He did not struggle. He had not fought, nor tried to run away. Naturally; he was a goonie. I felt a wave of relief, so strong it was a sickness. That, too. If he had fought or tried to run away, they wouldn't have needed an experienced lyncher to tell them what to do. The opposition would have been enough to turn them into a raving mob, all acting in one accord.

And then I knew. I knew the answer to the puzzle that had tortured me for twenty years.

But I was not to think about it further then, for the incredible happened. She must have left only moments after I did, and I must have been hesitating there, hiding longer than I'd realized. In any event, Miriam Wellman, in her shimmering robe, walking as calmly as if she were out for an evening stroll, now came into the circle of firelight.

"Boys! Boys!" she said commandingly, chiding, sorrowfully, and without the slightest tremor of uncertainty in her voice. "Aren't you ashamed of yourselves? Teasing that poor animal that way? Cutting up the minute my back is turned? And I trusted you, too!"

I gasped at the complete inadequacy, the unbelievable stupidity of the woman, unprotected, walking into the middle of it and speaking as if to a roomful of kindergarten kids. But these were not kids! They were grown human males in a frenzy of lust for killing. Neither fire hoses, nor tear gas, nor machine-gun bullets had stopped such mobs on Earth.

But she had stopped them. I realized they were standing there, shock still, agape with consternation. For a tense ten seconds they stood there frozen in tableau, while Miss Wellman clucked her tongue and looked about with exasperation. Slowly the tableau began to melt, almost imperceptibly at first—the droop of a shoulder, the eyes that stared at the ground, one sheepish, foolish grin, a toe that made little circles on the rock. One, on the outskirts, tried to melt back into the darkness.

"Oh, no, you don't, Peter Blackburn!" Miss Wellman snapped at him, as if he were four years old. "You come right back here and untie this poor goonie. Shame on you. You, too, Carl Hest. The very idea!"

One by one she called them by name, whipped them with phrases used on small children—but never on grown men.

She was a professional, she knew what she was doing. And she had been right in what she had told me—if I'd butted in, there might have been incalculable damage done.

Force would not have stopped them. It would have egged them on, increased the passion. They would have gloried in resisting it. It would have given meaning to a meaningless thing. The resistance would have been a part, a needed part, and given them the triumph of rape instead of the frustration of encountering motionless, indifferent acceptance.

But she had shocked them out of it, by not recognizing their grown maleness, their lustful dangerousness. She saw them as no more than naughty children—and they became that, in their own eyes.

I watched them in a kind of daze, while, in their own daze, they untied the goonie, lifted him carefully as if to be sure they didn't hurt him. The goonie looked at them from his great glowing green eyes without fear, without wonder. He seemed only to say that whatever man needed of him, man could have.

With complete casualness, Miss Wellman stepped forward and took the goonie's hand. She led it to her own rickshaw at the edge of the grove. She spoke to her team, and without a backward look she drove away.

Even in this she had shown her complete mastery of technique. With no show of hurry, she had driven away before they had time to remember they were determined, angry men.

They stared after her into the darkness. Then meekly, tamely, without looking at one another, gradually even as if repelled by the presence of one another, they moved out of the grove toward their own rickshaws on the other side of the grove near the path.

The party was over.

For those who find violent action a sufficient end in itself, the yarn is over. The goonie was rescued and would be returned to me. The emotional Typhoid Marys had been isolated and would be shipped back to Earth where the disease was endemic and would not be noticed. Paul Tyler would be acceptable again in the company of men. Miriam Wellman would soon be on her way to her next assignment of trouble-shooting, a different situation calling for techniques which would be different but equally effective. The Company was saved some trouble that could have become unprofitable. Libo would return to sanity and reason, the tenderfeet would gradually become Liboans, insured against the spread of disease by their inoculation. . . . The mob unrest and disorders were finished.

But the yarn was not over for me. What purpose to action if, beyond giving some release to the manic-depressive, it has no meaning? In the middle of it all, the answer to the goonie puzzle had hit me. But the answer solved nothing; it served only to raise much larger questions.

At home that night I slept badly, so fitfully that Ruth grew worried and asked if there was anything she could do.

"The goonie," I blurted out as I lay and stared into the darkness. "That first hunting party. If the goonie had run away, they would have given those hunters, man, the chase he needed for sport. After a satisfactory chase, man would have caught and killed the goonie down to the last one. If it had hid, it would have furnished another kind of chase, the challenge of finding it, until one by one all would have been found out, and killed. If it had fought, it would have given man his thrill of battle, and the end would have been the goonie's death."

Ruth lay there beside me, saying nothing, but I knew she was not asleep.

"I've always thought the goonie had no sense of survival," I said. "But it took the only possible means of surviving. Only by the most complete compliance with man's wishes could it survive. Only by giving no resistance in any form. How did it know, Ruth? How did it know? First contact, no experience with man. Yet it knew. Not just some old wise ones knew, but all knew instantly, down to the tiniest cub. What kind of intelligence—?"

"Try to sleep, dear," Ruth said tenderly. "Try to sleep now. We'll talk about it tomorrow. You need your rest. . . ."

We did not talk about it the next day. The bigger questions it opened up for me had begun to take form. I couldn't talk about them. I went about my work in a daze, and in the later afternoon, compelled, drawn irresistibly, I asked the goonie team to take me again to Carson's Hill. I knew that there I would be alone.

The glade was empty, the grasses were already lifting themselves upright again. The fire had left a patch of ashes and blackened rock. It would be a long time before that scar was gone, but it would go eventually. The afternoon suns sent shafts of light down through the trees, and I found the spot that had been my favorite twenty years ago when I had looked out over a valley and resolved somehow to own it.

I sat down and looked out over my valley and should have felt a sense of achievement, of satisfaction that I had managed to do well. But my valley was like the ashes of the burned-out fire. For what had I really achieved?

Survival? What had I proved, except that I could do it? In going out to the stars, in conquering the universe, what was man proving, except that he could do it? What was he proving that the primitive tribesman on Earth hadn't already proved when he conquered the jungle enough to eat without being eaten?

Was survival the end, and all? What about all these noble aspirations of man? How quickly he discarded them when his survival was threatened. What were they then but luxuries of a self-adulation which he practiced only when he could safely afford it?

How was man superior to the goonie? Because he conquered it? Had he conquered it? Through my ranching, there were many more goonies on Libo now than when man had first arrived. The goonie did our work, we slaughtered it for our meat. But it multiplied and throve.

The satisfactions of pushing other life-forms around? We could do it. But wasn't it a pretty childish sort of satisfaction? Nobody knew where the goonie came from, there was no evolutionary chain to account for him here on Libo; and the pal tree on which he depended was unlike any other kind of tree on Libo. Those were important reasons for thinking I was right. Had the goonie once conquered the universe, too? Had it, too, found it good to push other life-forms around? Had it grown up with the universe, out of its childish satisfactions, and run up against the basic question: Is there really anything beyond survival, itself, and if so, what? Had it found an answer, an answer so magnificent that it simply didn't matter that man worked it, slaughtered it, as long as he multiplied it?

And would man, someday, too, submit willingly to a new, arrogant, brash young life-form—in the knowledge that it really didn't matter? But what was the end result of knowing nothing mattered except static survival?

To hell with the problems of man, let him solve them. What about yourself, MacPherson? What are you trying to avoid? What won't you face?

To the rest of man the goonie is an unintelligent animal, fit only for labor and food. But not to me. If I am right, the rest of man is wrong—and I must believe I am right. I *know.*

And tomorrow is slaughtering day.

I can forgive the psychologist his estimation of the goonie. He's trapped in his own rigged slot machine. I can forgive the Institute, for it is, must be, dedicated to the survival, the superiority, of man. I can forgive the Company—it must show a profit to its stockholders or go out of business. All survival, all survival. I can forgive man, because there's nothing wrong with wanting to survive, to prove that you can do it.

And it would be a long time before man had solved enough of his whole survival problem to look beyond it.

But I had looked beyond it. Had the goonie, the alien goonie, looked beyond it? And seen what? What had it seen that made anything we did to it not matter?

We could, in clear conscience, continue to use it for food only so long as we judged it by man's own definitions, and thereby found it unintelligent. But I knew now that there was something beyond man's definition.

All right. I've made my little pile. I can retire, go away. Would that solve anything? Someone else would simply take my place. Would I become anything more than the dainty young thing who lifts a bloody dripping bite of steak to her lips, but shudders at the thought of killing anything?

Suppose I started all over, on some other planet, forgot the goonie, wiped it out of my mind, as humans do when they find reality unpleasant. Would that solve anything? If there are definitions of intelligence beyond man's own, would I not merely be starting all over with new scenes, new creatures, to reach the same end?

Suppose I deadened my thought to reality, as man is wont to do? Could that be done? Could the question once asked, and never answered, be forgotten? Surely other men have asked the question: What is the purpose of survival if there is no purpose beyond survival?

Have any of the philosophies ever answered it? Yes, we've speculated on the survival of the ego after the flesh, that ego so overpoweringly precious to us that we cannot contemplate its end—but survival of ego to what purpose?

Was this the fence across our path? The fence so alien that we tore ourselves to pieces trying to get over it, go through it?

Had the goonies found a way around it, an answer so alien to our kind of mind that what we did to them, how we used them, didn't matter—so long as we did not destroy them all? I had said they did not initiate, did not create, had no conscience—not by *man's* standards. But by their own? How could I know? How could I know?

Go out to the stars, young man, and grow up with the universe!

All right! We're out there!

What now, little man?

ME

by Hilbert Schenck, Jr.
from *Fantasy and Science Fiction*

ME

I think that I shall never see
A calculator made like me.
A me that likes Martinis dry
And on the rocks, a little rye.
A me that looks at girls and such,
But mostly girls, and very much.
A me that wears an overcoat
And likes a risky anecdote.
A me that taps a foot and grins
Whenever Dixieland begins.
They make computers for a fee,
But only moms can make a me.

THE YEAR'S S-F

A Summary

I should not like to have it thought, from my earlier comments, that I take exception to *every*thing Kingsley Amis says. On one point at least I am very much in agreement with him, and that is the urgent need for a new name for this field.

Not to carry the sweetness and light too far—his feeling that " '*Science* fiction' is every day losing some of its appropriateness as a name for science fiction," seems to me typical of his failure to understand what science fiction *is*—but for quite different reasons, I do share his conclusions.

The Sunday *Herald Tribune*, a few weeks ago, published a longish and most favorable review which began:

"This is a curious and original and very serious book, and it will be so satisfactory to the right reader that I think a warning is in order: though the action takes place in the future, and though a space ship takes off on the final page, this should not be confused with what is usually called science fiction. . . . What he has really written is a highly imaginative, and basically joyous, celebration of humankind's instinct to keep going."

The book under discussion was Walter M. Miller, Jr.'s *A Canticle for Liebowitz* (Lippincott, 1959), the work of a skilled, experienced, popular s-f author, first published as a series of long novelettes in *Fantasy and Science Fiction*.

Now "science-fiction" books *by science-fiction authors* are simply not reviewed seriously in the major critical outlets. (These days, they are rarely reviewed at all.) But the canny jacketeers at Lippincott have gotten around this taboo several times now by the simple expedient of not *labeling* their books as s-f. In this case they went a step further: the jacket

flap biography explains that Mr. Miller "compromised between art and engineering by writing science-fiction, *until
this, his first novel.*" (My italics—J.M.)

Then they took care to plaster the jacket with quotes from
"respectable literary" names—all clearly "non-science-fic-
tion" people, except the acceptable exception, Bradbury—
saying, "It falls into no genre, certainly not science fiction,"
and "It is not, really, a 'futuristic' novel." (Plus one from
old friend Amis, who says, ". . . a serious and imaginative
novel. . . .")

Thus freed of the Curse of the Tag, an excellent novel became eligible for consideration on the level on which it was
written—instead of the usual fast paragraph at the space-
opera stand.

Well, if this is what it takes to persuade "literary" folk to
read a good book and enjoy it—down with "science fiction,"
sez I. Let's have a new label. Or none at all. Who knows?
That way, Sturgeon might outsell Pat Frank.

I should confess here, also, that I owe a debt of gratitude
to Mr. Amis. The wildly improbable circulation figures he
quotes in his book led me to get down to a long-postponed
job of research on the cross-the-counter condition of health
of what we still *do* call science fiction—and I emerged un-
expectedly reassured.

Last year I reported here that the number of magazine
titles in the combined fantasy and s-f fields had dropped
from twenty-one to ten. As of the start of 1960, we are down
two more, to eight titles—less than at any time since before
the big boom of the early fifties—since 1946, to be exact.
But—

Of these eight titles, six are monthlies, and two bi-
monthly. In 1945-46, with eight titles, there was an average
of four magazines a month issued; now there are seven. In
1949, when there were also seven magazines a month on the
stands, they comprised *17* titles. In the peak year for s-f
magazine publishing, 1953, there were four times as many
titles as now—but only *twice* as many magazines.

It would be easy—and gratifying—to adduce from this
that the publications surviving today are the solid, sound,

worthy ones: to some degree it must even be true. But to generalize from that to the notion that "science fiction is maturing" (which I keep hearing, hopefully) would be inaccurate. The reason for all these healthy-looking regular monthly magazines has virtually nothing to do with either publishers or buyers; it is the work of the distributors, who last year began putting pressure on the publishers to go monthly or quit. Two who tried to make twelve books a year pay off, failed; two others "suspended" indefinitely without trying.

There is then less cause for alarm than one might think, but small cause for joy either, in the condition of the specialty magazines. In two other fields, however, s-f is thriving: paperback books, and general fiction magazines.

For the past five years the number of paperback books in the combined fantasy and science-fiction fields has held to a remarkably steady all-time high of 70 to 80 per year. From the looks of things, it will rise sharply this year. In short, we may expect more individual paperback books than issues of magazines this year—but the fact is that for the past two or three years, p-bs *have been* outselling magazines in total quantity. 60,000 copies is an exceptionally good circulation for an s-f magazine these days, I understand; but very few book publishers will issue a p-b without being able to sell at *least* that many. The average paperback sale is probably somewhere between 90 and 100 thousand.

In the first volume of *S-F*, reporting on 1955, I pointed out with some pride that as many as 50 or 60 s-f stories had appeared in "slick," quality, and other non-s-f magazines. Last year more than that number was accounted for in the *"Playboy*-type" magazines alone. With what appeared in the slick and quality magazines, there were, I should estimate, upward of 200 stories (fantasy and s-f) published in non-s-f periodicals in 1959—equal to the contents of at least three more full digest-size magazines, but with circulations (in many cases) in the hundreds, instead of tens, of thousands.

Granted that most of this non-specialty material is of low quality—so far. So was most of the stuff in *Amazing* and *Wonder* in the early 'thirties. It's being bought by editors who don't know the field, and often as not from writers not much better informed. (As witness: Jack Kerouac's pretentious "City," in *Nugget*.)

But it is being bought and printed. S-f—or whatever we *don't* call it—is being read and enjoyed more widely than ever before.

The new popular interest in what is still best described as "science-fiction thinking" is evidenced, again, in the really enormous quantity of speculative *non*-fiction appearing on all sides. As with the fiction in the unfamiliar media, much of this wordage is only by courtesy of subject matter "speculative," and when a generally thoughtful or imaginative piece does appear, it is immediately rehashed in a dozen other publications till the last drop of new-think has been squeezed out of it. But the titles alone indicate the latent interest on the part of the mass readership:

"This Is Living in 2000," appeared in *Newsweek* a few months ago. The title approximates Gernsback's old series in the *Air Wonder* of the 'twenties, and the subject matter (subheadings—"Ersatz Coffee," "Climate Control," and "Mining the Ocean Floor") was not much fresher to hardened old readers of s-f. To *Newsweek* readers it was *ahead* of the news. About the same time (the turn of the decade) *The New York Times Magazine* published "Brave World of the Year 2000," and *This Week* produced a pushbutton-happy two pages called "Get Set for the Happy New Decade." And *Esquire*, in its fat gold Christmas issue for 1959, included an article by David Schoenbrun called "1960: Birth of a Century," which was as thoughtful and comprehensive a piece of extrapolative writing as one would wish to see these days.

Then there were the "Adventures of the Mind" series in *The Saturday Evening Post;* the series of articles on ESP, space travel, and chemical warfare, in *Harper's;* and the increasingly fruitful "SR/Research—Science and Humanity" monthly section in the *Saturday Review*.

People—the general public—are getting *used* to the idea that hurt so hard when the first Sputnik blew the roof off: that there is precious little we know, and precious much to be learned; and that science is a method—not an authority.

Because the academicians, politicians, and spokesmen in general always learn more slowly (being already so stuffed with knowledge), it may seem that this kind of "s-f thinking" is making slow headway; but watch the cartoons in your newspaper or weekly magazine—listen to the new gags—check the number of fantasy or s-f themes in TV shows—in pop songs—

That mass readership is going to be ready for *good* (but don't call it) science fiction sooner than most of us have believed.

The changes in this year's *S-F* are obvious—or some of them are. The title, date of publication, size, and price, you'll have noticed by now; also the dropping of the controversial special non-fiction section. There will be more changes next year, I hope; this year, the change in publishing arrangements came too late to do much about adding some of the material I hope to use hereafter.

Special mentions for 1959, besides those regularly included in the short-story honor roll, should be given:

For verse and poetry: to *F&SF*, especially the contributions by Hilbert Schenck, Jr., and Gordon Dickson; and to Prof. Theodore R. Cogswell and his *confrères* in the *Publications of the Institute of Twenty-First Century Studies*.

For novels in the magazines: to Gordon Dickson's explosive "Dorsai!" *(Ast,* May-July), Everett E. Cole's "The Best Made Plans," *(Ast,* Nov.-Dec.); and the magazine version of Pat Frank's "Alas, Babylon" *(Good Housekeeping,* March).

For novels in book form: to Kurt Vonnegut's *The Sirens of Titan* (Dell); John Brunner's *Echo In the Skull* (Ace); and Theodore Sturgeon's *Cosmic Rape* (Dell).

For the short story reprints in the Kornbluth *Marching Morons* (Ballantine); Sturgeon's *Aliens 4* (Avon); and Anthony Boucher's giant two-volume anthology, *A Treasury of Great Science Fiction* (Doubleday).

And above all, for well-worded clear thinking about the troubles, needs, and satisfactions of the (science fiction?) field, the volume, *The Science Fiction Novel* (Advent),

edited by Basil Davenport, and with papers by Robert A.
Heinlein, C. M. Kornbluth, Alfred Bester, and Robert Bloch.
—J. M.

HONORABLE MENTIONS

Abbreviations

Amz   *Amazing Science Fiction Stories*
Ast   *Astounding Science Fiction*
Cos   *Cosmopolitan*
F&SF   *Fantasy and Science Fiction*
"F&SF:9"   "The Best from Fantasy and Science Fiction:
            Series 9," ed. Robert P. Mills (Doubleday,
            1959)
Fant   *Fantastic Science Fiction Stories*
FU   *Fantastic Universe*
Gal   *Galaxy Science Fiction*
Gent   *Gent*
If   *If Science Fiction*
LHJ   *Ladies' Home Journal*
Mr   *Mister*
Neb   *Nebula Science Fiction* (British)
NW   *New Worlds* (British)
Nug   *Nugget*
OSFS   *Original Science Fiction Stories*
Plby   *Playboy*
Rog   *Rogue*
Satl   *Satellite Science Fiction*
SEP   *Saturday Evening Post*
SFR   *San Francisco Review*
"Star" (#5&#6)   "Star Science Fiction Stories," #5 and
                  #6, ed. Frederik Pohl (Ballantine,
                  1959)

BRIAN W. ALDISS   "The Lieutenant," *Neb*, Feb.

POUL ANDERSON   "Brave to Be a King," *F&SF*, Aug.

CHRISTOPHER ANVIL   "The Lawbreakers," *Ast*, Oct.

ISAAC ASIMOV   "Obituary," *F&SF*, Aug.

ALAN BARCLAY   "Nearly Extinct," *NW*, Dec.

CHARLES BEAUMONT   "Sorcerer's Moon," *Plby*, July.

MYRLE BENEDICT   "The Dancing That We Did," *FU*, Sept. "The Comanleigh," *FU*, Nov.

ALFRED BESTER   "The Pi Man," "F&SF:9."

MARION Z. BRADLEY   "The Wind People," *If*, Feb.

RAYMOND BROSSARD   "The Merman," *FU*, July.

FREDRIC BROWN   "Three," *Gent*, Oct.

ROSEL G. BROWN   "Lost in Translation," *F&SF*, May.

ALGIS BUDRYS   "The Man Who Tasted Ashes," *If*, Feb. "The Stoker and the Stars" (Pseud.: John A. Sentry), *Ast*, Feb.

WILLIAM CHAMBERLAIN   "The Flying Jeep," *SEP*, Dec. 5.

A. BERTRAM CHANDLER   "The Man Who Could not Stop," *F&SF*, May. "Familiar Pattern" (Pseud. George Whitley), *Ast*, Aug.

LES COLLINS   "Question of Comfort," *Amz*, Mar.

LUCY CORES   "Deborah and the Djinn," *FU*, Sept.

LEE CORREY   "Letter from Tomorrow," *FU*, May.

C. L. COTTRELL   "Danger! Child at Large," "Star" #6.

AVRAM DAVIDSON   "The Woman Who Thought She Could Read," *F&SF*, Jan.

CHAN DAVIS   "Adrift on the Policy Level," "Star" #5.

CHARLES V. DE VET   "Seedling," *Ast*, Jan.

PHILIP K. DICK   "Recall Mechanism," *If*, July.

GORDON DICKSON   "The Amulet," *F&SF*, April.

G. C. EDMONDSON   "From Caribou to Carrie Nation," *F&SF*, Nov.

GEORGE P. ELLIOTT   "Invasion of the Planet of Love," "F&SF: 9."

HARLAN ELLISON   "The Abnormals," *Fant*, April.

PHILIP JOSE FARMER   "The Alley Man," *F&SF*, June.

HOWARD FAST   "The Cold, Cold Box," *F&SF*, July.

CHARLES G. FINNEY   "The Gilashrikes," *F&SF*, Oct.

CHARLES L. FONTENAY   "Wind," *Amz*, April.

DANIEL F. GALOUYE   "The City of Force," *Gal*, April.

TOM GODWIN "Empathy," *Fant,* Oct.

DAVID GORDON "Despoilers of the Golden Empire," *Ast,* Mar.

". . . or Your Money Back," *Ast,* Sept.

RON GOULART "Parlor Game," *FU,* May.

WILLIAM GRESHAM "Forsaken Earthman," *Satl,* Feb.

W. T. HAGGERT "Lex," *Gal,* Aug.

JIM HARMON "Measure for a Loner," *Amz,* Mar.

LARRY M. HARRIS "Hex," *Ast,* May.

HARRY HARRISON "I See You," *NW,* May.

FRANK HARVEY "The Death Dust," *SEP,* Aug. 8.

ROBERT HEINLEIN "All You Zombies—" *F&SF,* Mar.

ZENNA HENDERSON "And a Little Child . . ." *F&SF,* Oct.

PHILIP E. HIGH "Pseudopath," *NW,* Aug.-Sept.

SHIRLEY JACKSON "Strangers in Town," *SEP,* May 30.

COLIN KAPP "Breaking Point," *NW,* Dec.

GERALD KERSH "The Oracle of the Fish," *Nug,* June.

DAMON KNIGHT "What Rough Beast?" "F&SF:9."

PHILIP LATHAM "Disturbing Sun," *Ast,* May.

JOY LEACHE "Miss Millie's Rose," *FU,* May.

FRITZ LEIBER "The Silver Eggheads," *F&SF,* Jan.

"Fantastic Science Fiction Stories, Nov. (Complete Issue).

C. S. LEWIS "Screwtape Proposes a Toast," *SEP,* Dec. 19.

ANNE MCCAFFREY "The Lady in the Tower," *F&SF,* April.

HAROLD MEAD "The Hunter and the Huntress," *SEP,* Oct. 10.

ROBERT NATHAN "The Snowflake and the Starfish," *SEP,* Aug. 29.

FINN O'DONNEVAN "The Sweeper of Loray," *Gal,* April.

CHAD OLIVER "Transfusion," *Ast,* June.

STUART PALMER "Three-Dimensional Valentine," *F&SF,* Mar.

TOM PEASE "Mount Bettsville," *Mr,* Oct.

ROG PHILLIPS "Camouflage," *Amz,* June.

"Keepers in Space," *Fant,* April.

FREDERICK PILLSBURY "The Marvelous Black Magic Washing Machine," *LHJ,* Aug.

H. BEAM PIPER & JOHN MCGUIRE "Hunter Patrol," *Amz,* May.

FREDERIK POHL "To See Another Mountain," *F&SF,* April.

ROBERT PRESSLIE "Suicide Squad," *Neb,* Feb.

ROGER PRICE "The Tree," *Plby,* Sept.

KEN PURDY "The Noise," *Plby,* March.

KIT REED "Empty Nest," *F&SF*, Aug.

JANE RICE "The Rainbow Gold," *F&SF*, Dec.

E. F. RUSSELL "Now Inhale," *Ast*, April.

WILLIAM SAMBROT "Football Majors at Pacific U.," *Cos*, Oct.

IDRIS SEABRIGHT "Graveyard Shift," *F&SF*, Feb.

ARTHUR SELLINGS "The Scene Shifter," "Star" #5.

MICHAEL SHAARA "Citizen Jell," *Gal*, Aug.

ROBERT SHECKLEY "The World of Heart's Desire," *Plby*, Sept.

JOHN SHEPLEY "The Abyss," *SFR*

ROBERT SILVERBERG "Heap Big Medicine," *OSFS*, July.

CLIFFORD SIMAK "Installment Plan," *Gal*, Feb.

HENRY SLESAR "The Trigger," *Amz*, June.

CORDWAINER SMITH "Angerhelm," "Star" #6.

EVELYN E. SMITH "The People Upstairs," *FU*, March.

GEORGE O. SMITH "The Big Fix," *Ast*, Dec.
"Instinct," *Ast*, March.

JERRY SOHL "Counterweight," *If*, Nov.

WILL STANTON "Who Is Going to Cut the Barber's Hair?"
F&SF, Sept.

LEE SUTTON "Soul Mate," *F&SF*, June.

WILLIAM TENN "The Malted Milk Monster," *Gal*, Aug.

THEODORE L. THOMAS "Broken Tool," *Ast*, July.

ROGER THORNE "The Cage," *Rog*, Nov.

E. C. TUBB "Orange," *If*, Nov.

ANNE WALKER "A Matter of Proportion," *Ast*, Aug.

EDWARD WELLEN "Hear a Pin Drop," *Fant*, April.

KATE WILHELM "One for the Road," *FU*, July.

JAY WILLIAMS "Operation Ladybird," *F&SF*, Aug.

RALPH WILLIAMS "Cat and Mouse," *Ast*, June.

ROBERT F. YOUNG "To Fell a Tree," *F&SF*, July.